MAGE FALL

"Did   find them?"

"I   hed everywhere and found nothing." Balfruss felt his heart lift a   words until he saw the misery etched into her features. "I sp   everal nights listening to drunks tell stories in taverns. In dark   ers, in whispered voices, several spoke of chasing a man and a boy   horseback down to the river, only for a monster to rise from the w   and scare them away." Balfruss tried to speak. To offer her a gli   of hope. A sliver of denial that, perhaps, all was not as it appe   But she wasn't finished. "I went down to the river, to his cabin.   d there, soaked into the boards of the pier, I found blood. There   so much."

Bal   ss saw something dangerous flicker behind her eyes. "I want a nam   said Munroe.

"H   el was being played the whole time. His group of followers were   one branch of a much larger group."

"W   killed my family?" she asked again.

"G   me some more time," he said. For a brief moment he thought she m   t concede but then the steel crept back into her gaze. Her postu   ted, shoulders hunching and hands curling up into tight fists   s out of patience and he was out of time.

      a name," said Munroe.

"A   Her name is Akosh."

MAGE FALL

STEPHEN ARYAN

www.orbitbooks.net

ORBIT

First published in Great Britain in 2018 by Orbit

1 3 5 7 9 10 8 6 4 2

A CIP catalogue record for this book
is available from the British Library.

ISBN 978-0-356-50849-8

Typeset in Garamond by M Rules
Printed and bound by CPI Group (UK) Ltd, Croydon, CR0 4YY

Papers used by Orbit are from well-managed forests
and other responsible sources.

MIX
Paper from
responsible sources
FSC® C104740

Orbit
An imprint of
Little, Brown Book Group
Carmelite House
50 Victoria Embankment
London EC4Y 0DZ

An Hachette UK Company
www.hachette.co.uk

www.orbitbooks.net

For Nic

CHAPTER 1

The piercing scream was so loud that it rattled the windows of the tavern. Garvey ignored it but Phelon flinched and would've run if he hadn't been tied to his chair.

Garvey tore the heel of bread in two and dragged half of it through the thick beef gravy on his plate. The stories about the chef at the Bronze Tiger had not been exaggerations. The food was delicious.

"It was definitely worth the trip," said Garvey, gesturing towards Phelon sitting opposite. He watched as the Mayor tested his bonds again but the knots were tight. His wrists were already red and chafed from his useless struggles. He'd been frantic when the screaming had started but had calmed down now. "The spices are making my tongue tingle."

"You won't get away with this," said Phelon.

Garvey chuckled and gestured at the room around them. "Really? And who is going to stop me? You?"

The Mayor stayed silent as Garvey finished the rest of his food, savouring each mouthful. Even the ale was good. Dark and rich with a hint of smoke, making it a perfect match for the meat. It was made in the small brewery at the far end of the village beside the river.

If not for the famous chef no one would ever visit Garrion's Folly. It was just too small and remote. Not even the bizarre half-finished bridge that led nowhere was interesting enough to attract many visitors. A handful of academics came by every few years but it didn't change life in the village. Over the years trees had grown up around the ruin, hiding it beneath their canopy, but for some unknown reason no lichen grew on the black stones. Despite their age they were still as hard as granite. Yesterday he'd quizzed a few of the locals about it, but not even the oldest crone had any real insight into who had built it or why. But everyone had a favourite story.

"What's your theory about the bridge?" asked Garvey, swirling the last of the ale around the bottom of his mug. He was tempted to get a refill before leaving. After all, he wouldn't be coming back this way again. It was unlikely that he'd be a welcome return visitor to Garrion's Folly.

At first he thought the Mayor wouldn't answer but with little else to do except sulk in silence he finally relented. "I think it was done as part of a wager that someone lost. There are other romantic stories about it being done for love, but I think they're nonsense. My grandpa told me a story once, but it sounded like fantasy to me."

Garvey shrugged. "I'd still like to hear it," he said, moving towards the bar to get himself another drink. Phelon watched Garvey with a sour twist to his mouth as he navigated across the room, stepping over obstacles. Phelon waited until he'd refilled his mug and sat down again before speaking.

"The bridge was part of an ancient doorway."

Garvey raised an eyebrow. "A door to where?"

Phelon shrugged. "My grandpa didn't know that part. He just said it led elsewhere. He believed a Sorcerer built it and that the other half of the bridge is on the other side of the doorway, in some other place. I told you it was ridiculous."

Garvey grunted noncommittally. He ran a hand through his beard as he pondered the Mayor's words. He'd studied the bridge yesterday, noting the lack of decay and the way animals avoided getting too close. In other parts of the forest he could hear birdsong, but here they'd watched him in silence from the branches of surrounding trees as he'd paced around the ruin. It had more than a few things in common with the Red Tower. Phelon thought his grandfather's story was just idle fantasy but to Garvey it seemed the most likely explanation. The two questions he kept coming back to were, who had built it and where did it lead?

For all of the Red Tower's accomplishments with magic in the last two centuries Garvey sometimes felt as if he was a child trying to learn how to read and write. The Grey Councils of old, those who had built the tower itself, had known so much more. Some of their secrets had been written down and were locked up inside the tower library, but unravelling even one ancient and forgotten Talent could take a lifetime of study. There simply weren't enough mages with sufficient skill. Today there were only a handful of magic users alive who could call themselves Sorcerers and he knew they were poor imitations of the originals.

The bridge was yet another reminder of how much they still had to unravel and yet events conspired to prevent them from gaining more knowledge. In other circumstances a mage could spend their entire life in Garrion's Folly, studying the bridge and trying to unlock its ancient secrets. There were times when such a quiet life was enormously appealing to him. But it was far too late for that.

"If only you'd been more welcoming," muttered Garvey, gulping down his ale and savouring the rich smoky taste. "All of this unpleasantness could've been avoided."

"You're a wanted murderer. I could not stand idly by."

"Yes, you could. You could have said nothing. All I wanted to do was eat a meal in peace and then I would've left. Was it worth it?" asked Garvey, gesturing at the room around him. "Did you think you were being brave? Or perhaps it was pride?"

"You will be punished for your wicked deeds," said Phelon with the confidence of a true believer.

"By whom?" asked Garvey, folding his arms and sitting back on his chair.

"The gods. The Maker or the Holy Mother will strike you down."

Garvey held his arms towards the ceiling. "I'm here," he shouted. "I'm ready for my divine punishment."

Phelon was appalled. "You dare mock the gods?"

"Strike me down!" shouted Garvey, rattling the rafters.

Silence greeted him. He waited for divine retribution but nothing happened. No bolt of lightning. No clutching pain in his chest. No everlasting fire hot enough to melt his bones like candle wax. After a while he lowered his arms.

"I'm not worried about your gods. If they even exist, they just don't care about us any more."

The front door of the Bronze Tiger banged open and a man stumbled in. He was bleeding from his scalp, painting half his face bright red. There was more blood on his shirt and he had a distinct limp on the right side. His left arm was bent at a peculiar angle but the right held a dagger.

With a sigh Garvey raised one hand towards the intruder, embraced the Source and made a twisting motion. The man's neck snapped, his head turning to look behind him into the street. With a strangled choke he dropped to his knees and collapsed onto the floor. A final breath wheezed out between his swollen lips and a deafening silence filled the tavern.

Outside smoke and ash drifted past the open doorway,

bringing with it the smell of burning wood and charred meat. More bodies littered the street, bruised, bloody and silent. There were men, women and children. A stray dog trotted past, doing its best to escape the chaos before it too was struck down.

There were no more screams. That meant it was nearly time to be moving on.

Tahira came into the tavern, her grinning face smeared with ash.

"It's almost done. Most of the buildings have been torn down," she reported, pleased with herself. She had quite the temper but he'd learned it could be controlled if she was occasionally given free rein, like today.

"Good. And the people?" he asked.

"A few fought back but they're dead. We're finishing off the last ones."

"And our people?"

Tahira grimaced. "Nillim didn't listen to your orders and rushed in. He caught an arrow in the neck. Everyone else is unharmed."

Garvey waved it away. "No great loss. He was an idiot. Did any of the villagers try to run?"

"A few, but we brought them down. No one escaped."

"Horses?"

"We have enough for everyone now. The stables here were surprisingly well stocked."

"Well, at least something good came out of our visit," said Garvey. "Tell the others to take as much food as they can carry from the storeroom."

Phelon looked as if he wanted to curse them, or perhaps weep for his fallen friends and neighbours. Instead he remained silent and stony-faced. He watched Garvey's students troop into the back of the tavern and carry out sacks of food taken from the kitchen. It might be a few days before they stopped off at another village and it would make a nice change if they didn't have to forage for their meals.

"It seems as if our time is up," said Garvey, getting to his feet.

"You will pay."

"Think on this, Phelon. You're the Mayor of this village. The others listen to you. They would've followed your lead if you'd told them not to fight. So their deaths are on your hands. You did this, not me."

Garvey glanced around the tavern one last time, staring at the dead faces of the other patrons in the room. Most of them had died at their tables, although one or two had tumbled to the floor. The owner was dead, his body slumped forward over the bar, and in the kitchen the chef lay dead beside his famous creations. The owner's wife had fallen against a wall and seemed to be asleep, her head resting on her chest. The only sign of her death was a small trickle of dried blood from one nostril. None of the others bore any visible wounds. Their deaths had been quick if not entirely painless.

While the Mayor shouted curses at his back Garvey stepped over villagers' dead bodies and joined his followers waiting for him in the street. A month ago they had been children idly daydreaming in classrooms. They had been students seeking knowledge and the ability to control their burgeoning magic. Now they were refugees from the Red Tower and day by day were transforming into something else. A month of constantly being on the move, pursued by enemies, had stripped away most of the fat. Those who remained were lean, scarred from their experience and willing to do whatever was necessary to survive. Each of them carried a weapon on their hip and they all understood the importance of steel, even for those with magic. A few had tried to give the group a name, but he'd stopped that straightaway. This was not a game for children and they were not folk heroes. It was a fight for their lives and their existence as mages.

"Step back," warned Garvey, gesturing at Tahira. She and the others dismounted and led their horses further down what remained of the main street. On either side of the tavern the buildings had been smashed to pieces until nothing remained except a few broken stones. Every beam of wood had been shattered. Every window ripped apart. Every door and floorboard crushed into kindling. Blood was liberally splashed among the ruins from those too slow to escape the buildings when they collapsed. It wouldn't have mattered. Anyone who made it outside had been killed in the street. Garvey could see dozens of bodies with various wounds from where he was standing. Over a hundred people had lived in Garrion's Folly when they'd first arrived.

The rest of the village was the same. The houses, the mill, the temple and the village hall were all gone. Even the brewery beside the river was nothing more than a pile of tumbled stone. Only the Bronze Tiger remained, although without its famous chef it too would quickly be forgotten. As Garvey drew power from the Source he heard Mayor Phelon screaming from inside, cursing him to damnation for all time.

Reaching deep into the ground beneath the tavern he drove tendrils of his will, shattering buried stone and gouging at the earth. At the same time he focused on all of the tiny fissures in the stone walls, pulling them wider until they ran wild like cracks on a broken pane of glass. With a rumble that shook the earth beneath his feet, the walls of the tavern collapsed inwards while the building sank into the fissure. A huge cloud of dust rose up in the sky as the stones fell and the roof broke apart. The sound was deafening, startling birds from the trees, which swayed in the sudden wind from the building's collapse. Slowly the dust cleared and all that remained of the tavern was a few rocks and roof tiles poking out of the ground.

A profound and deep silence returned, enveloping the area. Somewhere nearby a small bird chirped. In time the forest would reclaim the village until it became nothing more than a few piles of mossy rubble. But for now it would serve as another stark reminder for those who thought mages could be eradicated like a disease.

Garvey mounted up and looked around at what had once been Garrion's Folly.

"Let's hope the next place we visit is more hospitable," he said to the others.

"There's a farm a few hours' ride to the west. We could be there before dark," suggested Tahira.

He considered it but shook his head. "We're not going to run and cower in the countryside like common bandits. All we did was defend ourselves."

"There's another village a couple of days' ride to the east," said Tahira.

"I think we should head north," said Garvey. "I could do with a bath, clean sheets and somewhere a bit less rustic."

They all knew what he was suggesting. The border wasn't too far away. If they carried on north the villages would soon give way to towns and then a city in Zecorria. It was more than a little reckless. It was also the last thing they would expect him to do.

"Let's see if they're kinder to strangers in the north," said Garvey, nudging his horse forward.

The others followed in his wake, leaving behind a village full of dead bodies.

CHAPTER 2

Tammy stalked through the halls of the palace, barely noticing the rich decorations all around her. Despite seeing them regularly over the last few weeks she still thought they were gaudy and mismatched. The palace decor reflected none of the character of Perizzi, the capital city, or its people. As the trading heart of the west, Yerskania was a melting pot of cultures, with thousands of visitors passing through every day.

It was perhaps the only place in the world where you could see pale-skinned Zecorrans, horned Morrin, shrewd Drassi, burly Seves and even a few Vorga trading peacefully with one another. Golden-skinned merchants from Shael were dotted throughout the crowd and sometimes a dark-skinned easterner from the desert kingdoms could be seen haggling with the stout locals. With goods from all of those nations it made the port in Perizzi arguably the busiest in the world and yet the city had a unique flavour not found anywhere else.

Perizzi had once been her home, but for the last decade Tammy had been working abroad as a Guardian of the Peace. The Guardians investigated all serious crimes in Yerskania, but they were also unique as other nations sometimes called on their expertise to solve difficult or unusual crimes. Travelling through other countries had given her a deeper understanding of several cultures and, despite their many differences, it allowed her to recognise the commonalities between vastly different human races. She'd spent very little time among the Morrin and no Guardian had ever been invited to the Vorga homeland. Aspects of both races and their cultures remained shrouded in mystery, particularly the savage Vorga, as no outsiders were allowed in their country. Thankfully they tended to keep to themselves and spent as little time in the city as possible, preferring open spaces to the crowded streets.

As the Khevassar, leader of the Guardians, her days of travelling abroad were over and she was slowly becoming reacquainted with the rhythms of the city. As a child she'd run through its streets totally unafraid of the dangers she now realised were lurking in dark corners. That innocence was gone, but her underlying intuition was slowly coming back. It seemed as if it had never really left, merely been buried, gathering dust for many years. For all its flaws she liked her city and in time Tammy hoped it would begin to feel like home again.

Now she was neck deep in the city's streets, soaking up the crime and chaos, wading through the rivers of information swirling all around her.

Every day she heard fresh rumours about a turf war erupting between the crime Families who controlled the city's underworld. The stories were vague but nevertheless she listened keenly. Ordinary people were often caught up, on the fringes, of such a violent conflict and she wanted to avoid the death of innocents.

Recently there'd been a lot of talk about groups of people roaming the streets, searching for mages hiding in their midst. There had been a few beatings and one murder of an innocent woman thought to be a Seeker. A few angry groups had even broken into homes, ransacking them in a desperate search for a golden mask. Her Guardians had made several arrests, coming down hard on the ringleaders, and for the time being the problem seemed to have gone away. But she knew people's resentment of mages ran deep and suspected it had merely gone underground. No one spoke about magic any more but she knew it was still on everyone's mind. It lay at the heart of many problems that cropped up in her city.

The threat of widescale violence and fear of the unknown. Everything was tied together like a giant invisible web hanging over the city. Pull on one thread and the effects of that decision would be felt in another district. There was a complex pattern behind it and she was trying to become as adept as the Old Man had been at interpreting and even predicting what was about to happen. She had no doubt it would come with time, but even so that didn't make it any less frustrating. At the moment all she could see were disparate threads in the chaos.

The Khevassar was the hub through which all Guardians communicated. She didn't see every single report, but received daily summaries of minor cases from which she could still discern relationships. While dealing with all of the local issues, there were ongoing problems abroad, some of which were more pressing than others. Such as the continuing issue with Seekers, the recent destruction of the Red Tower, and the ever-scheming Regent of Zecorria.

It was late at night for a meeting with Queen Morganse but she had asked Tammy to visit her to discuss the mage situation. Dorn, the Queen's chubby secretary, was yawning as she entered the outer office. His eyes were heavy with sleep and he waved her towards the Queen's office, not bothering to get up and announce her. His lax attitude irked her but she let it pass, knocked loudly and went inside.

Queen Morganse of Yerskania was sitting behind her desk but for once she wasn't reading one of the many papers scattered across it. Much to Tammy's surprise the Queen was knitting. For other grandmothers of her age it was probably a common pastime, but this was the first time she'd seen Morganse aping them. It was more than a little disconcerting to see the Queen doing something so ordinary.

"Please, take a seat," said the Queen, setting her needles aside. She caught Tammy's glance at the knitting and offered a wry smile. "Some people pray, some exercise or meditate. I find knitting allows my mind to wander while it keeps my hands busy."

Unsure of how to respond to that she said nothing. Despite her increasingly long hours Tammy made sure that her exercise regime had not changed. She ran for an hour every morning before breakfast and sparred twice a week with a Drassi Swordsmaster. She knew almost nothing about him and they barely spoke, making him the perfect opponent. They had no emotional attachment to one another which meant she didn't hold back because of some anecdote he'd told about his family. After a lifetime of carrying a sword he was far more skilled than she, but he helped her stay sharp and in shape. She would never be able to beat him – he was a master of his craft with decades of experience – but that didn't stop her from trying.

The Queen was looking at Tammy expectantly, waiting for her to say something. Perhaps to reply with a personal anecdote about her hobbies. "I don't think knitting would suit me" was all she said.

"To business then," said Morganse, clearly disappointed by her response. It didn't matter. It wasn't necessary for them to be friends in order to work together. "Although it does make things easier if we have a rapport," added the Queen.

"I disagree," said Tammy, earning another frown.

"Do you have something you want to say?"

"No, your Majesty. You asked me to come to the palace for this meeting. I'm here to talk about magic."

"Don't stop there," said Morganse, sitting back in her chair. "Tell me why you disagree."

Perhaps it was because she hadn't slept properly since taking on her new role a few weeks ago. Or that she was afraid of not living up to the Old Man's reputation. Perhaps it was because there was so much to do each day and not enough hours. Or perhaps it was simply because she disagreed with banning all Seekers in Yerskania. So, for once, Tammy decided to be totally honest and open with the Queen.

"My predecessor has great affection for you. So much so, that I think he was too lenient and it clouded his judgement when it came to his dealings with you."

"Is that so?" asked the Queen.

"Did you speak to him before signing the national ban on Seekers?"

"I did, and he strongly advised me against it."

Tammy was appalled. "And yet you still signed it?"

"I weighed his opinion against all of the facts and my other advisers. It was not a decision I made lightly," admitted Morganse.

"It was a mistake. You panicked and rushed the decision because you were afraid."

"Careful," warned the Queen. "There's a difference between offering your opinion and insubordination."

Tammy would not be intimidated. "If you expect me to agree every time you ask for my opinion, you're going to be sorely disappointed."

"The Khevassar's opinion is one among many I consider. Talk to me again about this when you've my experience with politics."

"I'd say the same thing when you've my experience with mages," replied Tammy. She knew the Old Man would have spoken to Morganse about who would replace him one day. Which also meant the Queen would have studied her history in depth. She knew where Tammy had been and what she'd experienced in the last ten years. "Banning all Seekers in Yerskania was the wrong decision."

An awkward silence settled on the room. Neither was willing to admit that they were wrong. She knew the Queen had rushed into it to give the people the impression of taking affirmative action.

There was a loud knock on the door and a moment later Dorn sidled into the room carrying a stack of papers.

"My apologies, your Majesty, but I have an urgent—" the secretary trailed off as he noticed the frosty atmosphere.

"What is it, Dorn?" asked Morganse, breaking eye contact.

"An urgent report, Majesty. There's been another attack by the rogue mage, Garvey, and his followers."

He passed across a small rolled-up note that must have come from the aviary. The Queen scanned the contents and her frown deepened.

"Thank you, Dorn. That will be all."

He bobbed his head and scuttled out of the room as fast as possible, not wanting to get caught in the middle of their disagreement.

"Garvey has destroyed a small village in the north. He was last seen by a patrol heading towards the border and Zecorria."

"How many are dead?"

"All of them," said Morganse, rubbing her temples. "He wiped the whole village off the map. Flattened every building. Killed every man, woman and child. About a hundred people lived in Garrion's Folly."

Tammy took a moment to think about the dead and the repercussions of what had happened. It seemed hard to believe that only a few weeks ago he'd been a member of the Grey Council. A trusted figure that leaders would call upon for aid in the most dire of circumstances.

"I'm considering sending soldiers after Garvey and his followers," declared Morganse.

"I would advise against that, in the strongest possible terms," said Tammy, trying to keep her voice calm. "It wouldn't help, it could provoke him and even make things worse. We both know what one competent Battlemage can do against an army. He's a Sorcerer. Garvey is also said to have a dozen or more followers with him. It would just be another bloodbath."

The Queen took a deep breath and their staring match resumed before she replied. "Then what would you suggest?"

"Reach out to Balfruss and ask him to help."

Morganse snorted. "Did you see the report about what happened at the Red Tower?"

"I did, but you weren't responsible and he knows that, too. Without help from other mages, I'm not sure what could stop Garvey and the others."

"Do you really think Balfruss would turn on his friend?"

Tammy shook her head. "I don't know, but Garvey is killing innocent people. Balfruss won't stand idly by and let that continue. It goes against everything he is."

"I hope you're right, because I agree with you. Without some kind of magical intervention, the bloodshed will continue."

This was a situation neither of them could have predicted and had never dealt with before. Normally at a time like this they would have reached out to the Red Tower who would dispatch someone to deal with the magical threat, but that door was closed. Even if it weren't, Tammy wasn't sure they would send someone to help. After all Morganse had brought in a nation-wide ban on Seekers. But something needed to be done and Balfruss was their best chance of stopping Garvey.

The situation also made her wonder how something like this had never happened before. With the exception of the Warlock, she couldn't remember any major incidents where a mage had gone rogue, working against the wishes of the Red Tower. Not every mage went to the school for training and yet there'd never been such a killing spree before. She made a mental note to look into it later. There might be something in the Guardian archives about it.

"In the meantime," Morganse was saying, "I must be seen to be doing something. I'm going to increase the number of soldiers in the north. It will reassure the local people, if nothing else, unless you object?"

"No, your Majesty."

"Good. How is the investigation into Habreel's network?"

Now it was Tammy's turn to rub her temples. "We're making progress and have removed several key people. Unfortunately the real target, Akosh, remains hidden and information about her is sketchy. I have some of my people following up on leads." It felt strange to say that, her people, and it had been even harder to send others out to do the work on her behalf. Normally she would have been one of those riding out of the city to gather information. It was going to take a while for her to get used to delegating as well as who was reliable and who wasn't trustworthy. "Do you want a full update?"

Morganse waved it away. "No. I just hope that the next time Balfruss makes contact with one of us, we have some good news to share with him about Habreel. It might make him more amenable to your request."

"I hope so too, Majesty."

"I have some news from my agents, although I'm not sure if it's good." Morganse fished around on her desk until she found a particular letter. They had spoken little about the Queen's network of spies, but every now and then she would share news from one of them. "The number of attacks on Seekers has fallen across the west, although that's to be expected given the widescale ban. There have also been no reports of children in Yerskania dying in accidents because of their magic."

As Tammy's experience with angry mobs in the city had shown, the decrease in attacks on Seekers meant very little. Any real Seeker with even a drop of common sense would have buried or melted down their golden mask by now.

As for the children many communities liked to deal with their own problems and in the past children were drowned, stoned or hanged if they showed any signs of magic. Without the Seekers there was no way to know how many children were being born with the ability. Out of a sense of shame whole communities swallowed the guilt and buried the truth. It was a dangerous time to be associated with magic in any way.

"I've also heard a rumour," admitted Tammy, deciding to share something although the Queen had not asked. "The Regent of Zecorria is considering a national ban on all mages."

"There's truth to that rumour," said Morganse. "And there's a note on my desk from him encouraging me, and other leaders in the west, to do the same. 'To unite against a common and vicious enemy', as he puts it."

"Do I need to tell you what my opinion is of that idea?"

Morganse smiled wryly. "I think I know what you're going to say. Besides, on that at least we agree. The problem with Garvey needs to be addressed, and soon. However, the ban on Seekers was a temporary measure at best. Banning all magic is a ludicrous idea. It won't stop children being born with magic."

"I agree, your Majesty."

The silence that settled on the room was less painful than before. They might not be friends but perhaps there could be common ground between them.

"It's late and I think we both need some sleep," said Morganse. "Keep me updated on any pertinent developments."

Tammy took the hint and moved to the door, but she paused on the threshold and turned back. "I hope you will also do the same, Majesty."

The Queen took a deep breath and Tammy expected another reminder from her of who was in charge or that she was over-stepping her boundaries. Instead Morganse swallowed whatever she'd been about to say and graciously inclined her head.

"I will do that," said Morganse. "By the way, I know they always called him the Old Man. Have they come up with a nickname for you?"

"If they have, it can't be good."

"Why do you say that?"

"Because no one has dared say it to my face," replied Tammy. She shared a brief smile with the Queen then let herself out. Riona met her at the first gate and the friendly Royal Guard escorted her through the palace.

"Quite the change," said Riona, gesturing at Tammy's new Guardian jacket. It was still red and black like the others, but hers was edged in silver instead of black.

"It's not that different."

"It does look good on you, but I didn't mean the jacket," said Riona, returning Tammy's sword to her. "I was talking about you."

It was customary for the Khevassar to go unarmed, but she knew the city had changed a lot since the Old Man had taken on the title and she wasn't taking any chances. Tammy briefly inspected the plain blade before sheathing it. Its unfamiliar weight was a distraction, but her other sword was special and would draw unwanted attention. There had to be no clues for anyone to tie back to her old life. It was the only way to protect her loved ones.

She waited for Riona to clarify what she meant but then noticed her look. Before Tammy's promotion they had been contemporaries of a sort, but now Riona's stare was more formal and less familiar. Thinking back over the last few weeks she realised Riona hadn't shared any new stories about her family on their frequent walks through the palace. She'd always known taking on the office and title of Khevassar would change how people treated her, but perhaps it had already changed her more than she realised.

The most direct route back to Unity Hall took her along a busy street that was full of noise and bright lights. Taverns at opposite ends of the road were competing for customers with live music and a wide variety of locally brewed beers. Crowds of people drifted from one place to the other in search of the best night out while a squad of the Watch made sure everyone was amicable. All of the soldiers stood to attention as she walked past. Tammy acknowledged the leader but didn't stop to chat. She heard the beginning of a whispered conversation before leaving the street and knew she was the main topic of conversation. It made her wonder again about the nickname they'd given her.

Despite the late hour the corridors of Unity Hall weren't silent and were never empty. Guardians drifted in and out at all hours of the night, checking information on old cases, writing up reports and questioning suspects in the cells below. In her outer office Tammy found her assistant, Rummpoe, asleep at her desk amid a stack of papers. A pen was still clutched in one hand and a blot of ink had spread across the top letter.

Tammy gently shook her awake and sent her home to get some sleep. She was more embarrassed at having ruined the report than being found snoring at her desk.

"I'll make sure it's written out again, in full, first thing in the morning," promised Rummpoe.

"That's fine. Get some rest," said Tammy, waving her off before unlocking her office. She closed the door behind her, hung her jacket on the back and sat down behind her desk. Tammy closed her eyes for a moment but only to gather her thoughts. She wouldn't be going to bed for a few hours yet.

"Hello, old friend," said a familiar voice.

Tammy opened her eyes and saw Balfruss sitting across the desk.

CHAPTER 3

As the riders came into view Wren sighed with relief and a huge weight seemed to ease from her shoulders. She didn't realise how anxious she'd been until now.

"You've been hunching your shoulders all day," said Danoph, coming to stand beside her. Since leaving the Red Tower a few weeks ago he remained quite taciturn with others, but was starting to open up more to her and Tianne. The three of them were closer than ever, for which Wren was extremely grateful, as she relied on their support for so many things.

"I'm just glad they're all safe."

"And there's a new face with them," he said, gesturing at the tall girl from Shael.

Tianne was one among the group of five riders who slowly made their way towards their settlement from the mouth of the valley. Wren had a long list of jobs awaiting her attention, but greeting all newcomers and giving them the tour was also part of her role. It was a task that Wren cherished as it gave her an excuse to show how much they had accomplished since leaving the school. However, it also served as a reminder that there was still a lot of work ahead. But with each new arrival the challenge was made just a little easier.

"I'll see you at dinner," said Danoph, moving away towards the woods clutching his basket. He liked to spend a portion of each day combing the woodland for mushrooms and cultivating the herbs he'd planted. Wren watched him for a little while, biting her lip, trying to push away the guilt. She was out of excuses. She would have to talk to him soon about his nightmares and explain what they really meant. The Grey Council had kept the truth from him for over a year. After only a few weeks of carrying around the same secret, it felt as if there was a lead weight strapped to her back. Now she understood one of her grandfather's most popular sayings "the only thing heavier than keeping a secret was guilt".

Her attention was drawn back to the riders as they dismounted and approached on foot, Tianne at the front. Much to her friend's surprise Wren embraced her, giving herself a moment to hide her relief.

"Are you all right?" asked Tianne when Wren released her.

"I'm just glad that you're all safe," she lied. She'd also avoided telling Tianne the whole truth. That would have to change as well. "What happened?"

"It was just as you said. We found the village about three days to the south. Laila was hiding her abilities, but people were starting to get suspicious. She was relieved and happy to leave with us before the inevitable happened."

"You've done well," said Wren, giving her friend a squeeze on the arm. "I'll see you in a while."

Tianne gave her a puzzled look, no doubt trying to work out why she was being so affectionate, but didn't ask. Wren thanked the other former students who led the horses away to the stables until she was standing face-to-face with Laila, the new arrival. She was older than Wren by at least a couple of years but her wide-eyed fear made her seem younger. This was probably the first time she'd ever been away from her village by herself.

Tall, with golden skin and blonde hair, Wren knew of several boys who would find her attractive. She just hoped Laila's experiences in her village had prepared her for how to deal amicably with their attention.

Their community was so new and everyone busy that so far there hadn't been any need to introduce forms of punishment. But if their numbers continued to grow it would become necessary. It was a problem for another day which she pushed to the back of her mind.

"I'm Wren," she said, remembering to hold out her hand towards Laila. It still felt like an odd form of greeting because of her Drassi heritage, but she was doing her best to adopt it. The familiarity of the ritual seemed to make strangers feel comfortable and connected to one another. Every day she was reminded that there was much she could learn from other people, even when they weren't intentionally teaching her.

"Tianne said you're in charge," replied Laila, shaking her hand. There was no surprise at her age or hint of scepticism in her voice which Wren took as a good sign. But as she'd found out in the last year at the Red Tower, first impressions could be deceiving.

"In a way. Let me show you around," said Wren. From their vantage point they had a good view of the entire valley. On the left-hand side was an old forest that had been left untouched by anyone for centuries. It was thick and wild, overgrown in places with trees fighting for space. Beneath the dense canopy they'd found more than a dozen rotting trunks overgrown with moss and swarming with ivy. In the heat and darkness the damp forest floor had become a haven for mushrooms. They'd started thinning out the forest a little, clearing away the dead wood and cutting down some of the largest trees for raw materials.

Opening up sections of the ground to sunlight for·the first time in years was encouraging new growth. The wild flowers and plants brought in a host of insects and with them came birds in search of a feast, filling the trees with their song. Other animals were starting to return as well and only last week someone had spotted a rabbit. And where there was one rabbit there was often ten. With so many mouths to feed she expected they would soon be setting traps in the forest.

On the right of the valley was what had been dry and dusty scrubland covered with scattered lumps of rock from the surrounding cliffs. It too had been transformed in the last few weeks.

"When we arrived in the valley there was nothing here. It was completely abandoned," said Wren. "No one had lived here for a long time. There are some ancient caves at the back and an old well, but it was bone dry."

"Where did the water come from?" asked Laila, gesturing at the two wells in the valley where people were drawing up water.

"We dug new ones," said Wren, allowing a spark of energy to dance between her fingers. "One of our community has a Talent for finding things. She's a natural dowser, so we dug down and tapped into an underground source. It comes down from the mountains into an underground lake."

Digging the wells was the first thing they'd done as a group when they'd accidentally stumbled across the valley. It was remote, difficult to find and no one would normally come to the area as there was no water. It was also the first time that all of them had worked together using their magic. At the Red Tower the students had sparred and worked alongside each other, but had never combined their strength towards a common goal. Being surrounded by so many people embracing the Source was still a special moment that Wren cherished. It connected her to those around her in a way that went beyond imitating customs and rituals.

This far west in Shael the law was not readily enforced as it was in the capital and other districts. The war had decimated the country's population and Queen Olivia didn't have the bodies to protect the entire nation. Whole areas had been abandoned, with every town and village becoming a home only for ghosts, as the population fled to more central areas for protection. In their wake bandits moved in and the number of attacks on travellers in the western region of Shael increased. Any merchant transporting goods into Shael was now protected by a large number of guards or Drassi warriors.

The fringes of the country were the worst and out here in the Rooke district, so close to the western border, they were completely alone. There were no communities for almost a day's ride in every direction, but plenty of abandoned villages that were often frequented by bandits who used them as temporary bases.

"After the wells we dug the fields," said Wren, gesturing at the right side of the valley. Several acres of freshly turned soil were under the keen gaze of two farmers who used to work on the staff at the Red Tower. "Not everyone who lives here has magic, but we all work together. The farmers direct us and we use our magic to help them." A light shower of rain was falling over one of the fields as two students worked together to cool the air directly above it. The work was delicate and tiring but vitally important to their survival. Every mage in their community was growing accustomed to using their magic every day to help with a variety of tasks.

"And the houses?"

Wren gestured for Laila to follow her towards the centre of the village where four large log cabins and several other structures had been built. "Those came next."

Each house was nothing more than a large single room with no windows and one door. The walls of each building were fashioned from logs that had been lashed together and the roof made from clay tiles that made the interior waterproof. At the back of each cabin was a chimney that they fed with firewood to keep the chill at bay during the night. They were crude but provided shelter and were better than sleeping in the caves, which they'd had to endure when they'd first arrived.

They were currently building real homes and were carefully planning the layout of the village, but the work was slow and it took a lot of patience and skill. Despite using her magic in many ways she would never have anticipated, Wren was slowly learning that magic could only do so much. Stone for the foundations was being scavenged from abandoned villages and carried here, while wooden planks and beams were being fashioned for the roofs in the workshop. She was desperate for a glassblower, but so far they'd not found anyone with the skill. The few windows they'd taken from other buildings were not perfect, but they would have to do for the time being.

"Every day we use our magic in all sorts of practical ways," said Wren, gesturing towards where three students were slowly lowering a block of stone into place for the foundation of another house. "The more you get used to using it, the easier it becomes."

"I can't control it and I'm not very strong," apologised Laila.

"You'll get there and we all have different strengths," said Wren, leading her towards a rhythmic clanging sound coming from a rare stone building with a sloping wooden roof. The forge had several large shuttered windows without glass and a broad door, all of which were wide open to let out the heat. Inside the smith, Leonie, was fashioning tools and equipment. They had one plough but she was busy making another while several students took turns maintaining the heat. It was hard physical labour and currently one of several substitutes for weapons training with Master Choss. Survivors who'd stayed behind to defend the school had brought no news about him, forcing Wren to accept that the worst had happened. They still practised with wooden swords and their fists every day, but it wasn't the same without him.

"This place is very different from the Red Tower," said Wren, still having mixed feelings about criticising the school and its methods. "Our goal is to teach you control and, after that, you'll learn some of the basics. How to create light, fire and hopefully how to heal."

Laila was stunned. "You know how to heal people?"

"It's difficult," admitted Wren, knowing that she still had a long way to go. She had daily lessons with Master Yettle, alongside every other student, but so far she had yet to master the basics. The Healer had not been with them during the evacuation, but one day he'd just appeared at the mouth of the valley as if summoned. "We believe in pairing everything with practical skills. So you'll learn how to defend yourself with magic, but also how to fight with a sword or your fists. You'll also learn herb-lore, from Morag, in partnership with healing from Master Yettle. Combining the two is more effective and it gives us all a greater understanding of the body. Thankfully we have some very patient teachers."

"I thought I'd be spending my days reading in a classroom."

"Sometimes that's necessary, but we're trying to adopt techniques from all over the world." Wren knew that the First People also used magic every day for practical purposes, such as hunting and fishing. Part of her wished she'd gone with Eloise, if only to see how the Jhanidi used their abilities in the desert kingdoms. She suspected there was much she could have learned that would be beneficial to their community in the coming months.

"Where do I start?" asked Laila. Wren took it as a good sign that she was keen to be doing something. There were a few students who had thought the new community would be run in the same way as the school. Where meals were prepared for them and many of their daily needs were dealt with by a staff of helpers. Their only real responsibility at the Red Tower had been to their studies. It had come as quite a rude awakening for some to realise they were now mostly responsible for looking after themselves. Help was given and guidance offered, but everyone had to contribute to the chores. It was proving a difficult adjustment for some, but no one here was about to do it for them. Many a soft hand was now developing calluses and getting soil under its fingernails for the first time.

"Control. Once you've mastered that we'll put you to work," said Wren, offering Laila a smile. "After that it's up to you. Some people here have a greater affinity for certain areas. Some are generalists and others have Talents, like our dowser. Our goal is to teach you how to protect yourself and be ready for any situation."

"Are we building an army?" asked Laila with a smile.

Wren's expression turned stony. "No." That one word hung in the air between them and slowly Laila's mirth drained away. Wren waited in silence until the seriousness of the situation became apparent to Laila. "I assume you know about Garvey and what he's done?" she asked quietly.

"I've heard the stories."

"He's creating living weapons and he enjoys hurting people." Wren wasn't sure what to believe about the man who had once been her teacher, but stories of his atrocious crimes were commonplace and there were too many for them all to be fiction.

"Magic is a powerful force and in the wrong hands it is dangerous and destructive. Here, we will teach you how to control your power, but also how to blend in with those without magic. What you do after that is up to you. Some people at the Red Tower learned control so that they could move abroad and start new lives without their magic. What we're offering here is a little different, but if you choose that path no one will stop you. I want to be very honest with you, Laila. You're not a prisoner here. You can leave any time you want, but the longer you stay the more we'll teach you."

"I don't really know what I want to do," admitted Laila. "I've just been so scared that someone would find out. I've come so close to hurting people by accident. I don't want to be afraid any more."

Wren's frown eased and she gave Laila a moment to regain her composure, waiting until she'd wiped away her tears. It seemed that crying in public, no matter where you came from, was uncomfortable and awkward.

"There's still a lot to be done here," said Wren, pretending that nothing had happened.

"I'd like to help in any way I can."

"That's good. How about we get you settled in and tomorrow you can start with your lessons?" suggested Wren. "Maybe once your magic is under control, then you can start to think about what you want to do with it."

They passed the stables and the workshop that were always busy with people. Every day a group of riders scoured the surrounding area and they always returned with something useful from one of the abandoned villages. The best day was when they'd returned with half a dozen goats and an angry hen that only laid when it suited her. Yesterday the scouting group had reported seeing a flock of sheep that had gone wild and were living in the hills not far away. Bringing them in was at the top of her list of tasks. The sheep would provide a good source of milk, wool and meat.

The work ahead seemed endless, but it was a careful balancing act between gradually bringing in new people and growing too quickly. Their new community had gone unnoticed so far, but she realised that would eventually change. Her people had seen groups of bandits, but so far there had been no confrontations. When people inevitably found out about this community she wanted their new home to be secure. She hadn't anticipated bringing in anyone new for a while, but the decision had been taken out of her hands.

Wren got Laila settled in one of the dormitories and left her to get acquainted with some of the other students before going in search of Danoph. She found him in one of the storage sheds hanging batches of herbs from the rafters to dry out.

"So, what's your first impression of the new arrival?" he asked without turning around. He was busy bundling together another batch of willow bark which Morag, their resident herbalist, had told them was good for treating pain.

"You ask me that every time," she said.

"Because you always have a different answer, and first impressions are important."

"I believe that less every day," admitted Wren. She immediately regretted saying it as she didn't want to make this about her. "Actually, I wanted to talk to you about Laila, and the others."

"No one expects you to be perfect, or have all the answers," he said, seeing through her as usual. Wren squirmed uncomfortably and tried to steer the conversation back towards him.

"Let's talk outside when you're finished," she said, suddenly finding the shed claustrophobic. By the time Danoph emerged she felt ready to talk about what she'd been avoiding since leaving the school.

"Tianne should hear this as well."

They found her in the stables brushing down one of the horses but she followed them outside. Wren led them both to a quiet space away from everyone on the edge of the forest.

"Tell me about your dreams," Wren said to Danoph, before they could ask her anything.

"They still haunt me," said Danoph, staring into the distance. "Even now, when I'm awake, I can see some of the images."

"They're not just dreams, are they?" asked Wren, hoping he had intuited something from them.

Danoph's eyes were still unfocused. "No, they're something else. It's hard to describe but I have this feeling." He clutched his shirt, idly tugging at the material. "It's like I'm being pulled in several directions at once."

"What's all this about?" asked Tianne.

"Just before we left the Red Tower, Garvey told me something."

"You can't trust him," said Tianne, rolling her eyes. "Don't you know that by now?"

"I don't trust him, but this is different. I had my suspicions before we left and when I confronted him about it he told me the truth."

"Wren—" said Tianne, but she cut her off.

"The Grey Council knew the school was going to be attacked." Both of her friends stared at her in silence, slowly digesting the words. "That was why Eloise had been meeting with the Jhanidi for months. It's why all of the teachers were so preoccupied and kept going away on secret trips. They were preparing for the day when it happened. It's also why I was the last student to join the school."

A range of emotions flickered across their faces. Wren

watched as they went back through their memories, going over everything they'd seen in the last few months at the school. There were a hundred questions they could have asked but there was only one that really mattered.

"How?" asked Danoph. "How did they know?"

"The same way I knew how to find Morag and Laila. It's because of your nightmares. The dream you kept having about a fire wasn't from the war. It was the Red Tower, burning on the horizon. Danoph, you're an Oracle."

Oracles were rare magic users whose connection to the Source enabled them to make prophecies about the future. At least that was the theory. Most of them were mad, gibbering creatures who lived in their own filth, worse than any animal. Several teachers had spoken of their disdain for Oracles as all of their vague predictions could be twisted to match recent events.

The most famous prophecy, the Opsum, spoke of a child with magic who would reshape the world for centuries. It was why the Grey Council of old had abandoned their posts leading to the downfall of magic and the abandonment of the Red Tower.

But Danoph was different and the new Grey Council had known for a long time.

Tianne started to protest and probably claim it was ridiculous but a peculiar stillness had fallen over Danoph. He was looking inwards again, probably studying the images he'd seen while asleep. Most recently his dreams had been about a girl being burned at the stake for using her magic. Wren had listened closely to what he'd told her for a week before having enough information to send out a search party. Tianne and the others had been told to ride south and look for a village where they could gather supplies. Instead they'd found a suspicious community getting ready to kill one of their own children.

"I don't know what to say," admitted Danoph.

"I didn't want there to be any secrets between us," admitted Wren. "You deserve to know the truth. I wanted to tell you sooner, but we were travelling and then busy setting up this community, but those are just excuses."

"What will you do now?" asked Tianne.

Danoph shook his head. "I don't know. I just don't know."

"People keep asking me what's next for our community. They're all looking to me for answers, but I'm just making it up as we go," confessed Wren. Normally she wouldn't feel comfortable talking about such things, but it was easy in their company.

"We know that," said Tianne with a wry smile.

"I need some time to think about this," said Danoph.

"We all need to think about the future, but there's one thing I'm certain about," said Wren. "I would like you both to be part of this community. You came here because of me, but now you need to decide for yourselves. This place will grow and there will be some difficult times ahead, but this is where I need to be. Is it the right place for you?"

The idea of not seeing either of her friends every day was hard to contemplate but they needed to choose for themselves, without thinking about her or anyone else. Danoph finally knew the truth and Tianne had to make up her own mind, rather than following others because it was easier.

Even if she couldn't admit it out loud, Wren knew the real reason she'd delayed telling them. She was afraid of being alone. But she was loath to manipulate them, even a little, after how Garvey had done it to her.

For now Wren decided to enjoy the time they had together while it lasted because she knew dark times lay ahead. Danoph had foreseen more than she'd told them. Events were going to get much worse and a lot of people were going to die. The question then became would she, or her friends, be among the victims?

CHAPTER 4

Regent Choilan managed to remain in control until he was alone in the royal wing of the palace. He closed the doors to his rooms and those to his bedchamber before falling into a chair in a fugue state.

His left hand began to shake and he gripped it with the right, trying to calm the fear racing through his body. For the first time since wrestling the throne away from the grubby hands of his rivals, Choilan was unsure of himself. Always a decisive man, he now faced a situation for which he was utterly unprepared. His Ministers had offered their best advice, but ultimately it was useless. Normally his clerks and discreet agents had more useful ideas, but even theirs had been insufficient. Any sort of definitive solution eluded him, leaving him feeling powerless and inept.

The guards and servants were whispering every time he passed them in the corridors of the palace. No doubt it would be the same across the city and there would only be one subject anyone cared about. Other minor worries and appeals had fallen away in its wake. Now the line of people requesting an audience every day was all focused on one thing.

Garvey.

Twice the rogue mage had crossed the border into Zecorria. Twice he'd brazenly walked into a village with his followers and acted as if he hadn't erased an entire village only a few weeks ago, murdering everyone who lived there. The second time he crossed into Zecorria he'd spent the night at the village tavern. The local people had been terrified of what he might do to them if they refused to serve him and the others. Afraid for their lives they'd given Garvey and his followers food and drink, drawn them baths and provided them with rooms for the night. One man had described the experience as if everyone in the village had been balancing on the edge of a sword. It would only take one look, one wrong word and they'd all come tumbling down and be cut in half. Garvey had even paid for the rooms, as if he and the rest were normal patrons. Miraculously nothing happened and no one was killed. That hadn't stopped people from demanding that he, as their Regent, do something about the rampaging menace.

It was small comfort that before Garvey had started his killing spree the national ban on Seekers had, apparently, been working. There had been no reports from his people about children exploding when they discovered their magic. Then again he'd not seen any recent reports about children struggling to control their magic. To that end Choilan had several agents discreetly visiting remote villages, disguised as merchants, to make sure that the locals had not decided to take matters into their own hands. So far there had been no rumours of children mysteriously disappearing. He suspected for the time being any child who had developed magic had simply become more adept at concealing it.

In the long term it was a serious problem that needed to be addressed. But right now he needed to find a way to deal with the current threat.

So far Garvey had destroyed two villages. One in Zecorria and one in neighbouring Yerskania to the south. On both occasions every person had been murdered and every building turned to dust. The corpses were left where they fell in the streets, a feast for crows. Those remains able to be recovered had often been chewed and mauled by hungry animals.

While the dead couldn't appeal for justice, scores of relatives queued up in the palace day after day, screaming for bloody vengeance. The Minister of Defence was calling for him to mobilise the army. To take the fight to the rogue wizards and kill them all on the battlefield. Sadly, the Minister seemed to have forgotten his recent history and had learned nothing from it. Choilan understood the futile nature of such a decision but most people didn't seem to care.

The people of Zecorria were afraid and they were quickly losing faith in him as their leader. To them his inaction spoke of weakness. As ever, they were not interested in the reasons for his indecision. Results were all that mattered.

The doors to his bedchamber opened and Selina, his first wife, entered without invitation. She was one of only three people allowed in here and he insisted his other two wives knock first. A tall woman, only a few years younger than him, these days she was often called handsome rather than beautiful. Her dark eyes were a little too large for her face. Her cheeks sharp and angular and her eyebrows constantly drawn into a perpetual frown. His other wives were significantly younger and they often warmed his bed, but he never sought their advice on serious matters. Marrying Selina had been a political move but over time they had developed a mutual admiration of each other's strengths. While never friends, and these days never lovers, their partnership had endured much and was stronger for it.

With a look and the slight raising of one eyebrow, he felt her assessing his slumped posture and the defeat on his face. Despite the early hour she poured two generous measures of kirsch and passed him a glass. As he rolled the colourless liquid around, inhaling the rich scent of cherries and almonds, she pulled up a chair and sat down opposite.

"To health," she said, sipping at her drink for taste before draining the glass. Choilan gulped his down, savouring the burning in his throat and stomach. This was a harsh distillation, taken from the poor area where he was born, but he insisted on keeping a bottle from the region in his rooms at all times. It served as a reminder of his past. It was a way of grounding him to show how far he'd come since those early days of fighting for every mouthful of food. "Vile stuff," said Selina, selecting a bottle of amber whisky and pouring them both another measure. This was something else. Aged for many years in oak barrels until it was smooth as silk and so expensive few could afford it. Instead of drinking it the Regent merely inhaled the rich flavours while Selina sipped at hers.

"Tell me" was all she said. So he laid it all out for her, piece by piece. The Seekers. The national ban. The fall of the Red Tower. Garvey on the rampage and the destruction that followed in his wake.

"I remember what one mage did during the war," said Choilan in conclusion.

"Which one?" asked Selina. "The one who forged the west into an unholy alliance? Or the one who defeated him in battle?"

"Both," he conceded. "One well-trained mage can kill hundreds of soldiers with just a thought or a gesture. How do you fight something like that?"

Selina raised that eyebrow again. "How did Seveldrom fight the Warlock?"

"With mages of their own."

"Then there is your answer." She said it so simply. As if the solution was just that easy. As if he could snap his fingers and solve it, just like that.

"Do you hate me so much that you take pleasure in tormenting me?"

"No, dearest," she said, putting aside her glass and surprising him by holding one of his hands in both of hers. "I was being sincere. You should have mages of your own."

"How? After getting rid of the Seekers, and playing into the people's fear of magic. It would be almost impossible."

"Almost," agreed Selina. "But not quite."

"You want me to hire a mage? I do not think anyone would come to defend us now, no matter the price that was offered. Garvey is also a member of the Grey Council and is known to be extremely powerful. Besides, how could I possibly trust a mage not to betray me?"

"That is the key," said Selina, squeezing his hands. Her fingers were warm but the palms were calloused. She hadn't always worn silk and lived in a palace. Her own path to First Wife of the Regent was no less challenging than his own. "Trust."

"A loyal mage. A mage of my own," he pondered. "A royally appointed mage to the court?"

"Perhaps in time," she conceded. "But look to the far east. In the desert kingdoms they have warrior monks who are mages. They serve the King as his trusted eyes and ears. They carry out his will and wherever they go, the people know them and respect them as honoured guests. To displease them is to displease their King and his punishments are said to be severe."

"The tattoo," said Choilan. Over the years he'd seen a few Jhanidi in his capital city proudly bearing their tattoo which ran down one side of their face. It sent an instant message to anyone they met what they were and who they represented.

"They are loyal patriots, but trust must be earned," said Selina. "In this way Garvey, and his band of murderers, may even be useful."

Choilan was starting to see where she was leading him. "A cadre of my own."

"He is the invading foreigner. A rogue mage and a danger that threatens us all. We need loyal patriots who are willing to stand up and face him. Proud Zecorrans who want to defend their homeland."

"Are you suggesting an amnesty for Zecorran mages?"

Selina shrugged. "Perhaps, although I doubt there are many of worth living in secret. They've probably muddled along, not been properly trained. But we can use the fall of the Red Tower to our advantage. Recruit the children."

"An untrained, untrustworthy child, against Garvey," scoffed the Regent, starting to pull his hand away. "It would be like a bee trying to sting a bear."

"But a swarm of bees can kill anything," said Selina, crushing his hand until he winced. "It will be a show of force that may keep him from our borders. Soldiers working in combination with them would calm the people as well."

Finally she relented and let go of his hand but remained hunched forward, their faces close to one another. He'd forgotten about the vein that throbbed in her forehead when she was annoyed. It made him smile despite the situation and she pulled back slightly, misinterpreting his expression.

"How could we trust them?"

"They are just children," said Selina. "They are lost, without a home or their leaders. They need guidance and strong role models. Better us than they become rogues like Garvey or worse, they join a criminal band and disappear into the underworld."

"I've been pushing hard about the danger of Seekers. It helped soothe the people when the ban was brought in, but now magic is on their minds again."

"Shift the fear to the Red Tower," suggested Selina. "It was responsible for the Seekers. It created the menace of Garvey. The students are just children. Lost little lambs who don't know any better."

"But we will teach them," said Choilan. He briefly shared a smile with his first wife.

"If the children are young enough we can mould them into loyal patriots who will serve their country without question."

"What if they prove disloyal?" asked the Regent. "Or they're too old to be moulded?"

"I'll leave it up to you to decide how you deal with those people," said Selina, running a hand up his thigh. "But remember, there are many ways to motivate young, curious minds. Just ask your other wives."

The shiver of pleasure from her touch faded and he grimaced. "I deserved that." She withdrew her hand and sat back to sip at her expensive whisky. It was at times like these that he remembered why she was still alive. At one point, only a few months ago, he'd been plotting for her to have an accident. Choilan was suddenly glad that he'd put the plan on hold.

"And if those methods fail to motivate them, there's always the torturer's blade to break their spirit. Then you can rebuild them from the ground up." She said it with such dispassion he was suddenly reminded why they rarely shared a bed any more. Every time they did he was sure he'd wake up to find her hands around his throat. Selina regarded him coolly over the rim of her glass as if she could read his thoughts. A small and dangerous smile played at the corners of her mouth.

"The children must be taught, to make them stronger, but

that is a concern for another day. For now I think thirty children, sworn to the throne of Zecorria, would make even Garvey pause."

"I believe you're right," he agreed. "And once again, we can be seen as the example that others in the west should follow. Just as it was with the ban on Seekers."

"Let them worry about their own problems. They may not use the same methods, but that could also be turned to our advantage in time."

Choilan imagined what it would be like to be surrounded by a dozen strong and loyal mages. An immeasurable powerful force that would fight to defend him and give up their lives for him. A cadre that could defeat entire armies. One that he could even loan to his neighbours if they chose not to adopt the same methods.

"It will have to be worded carefully," he mused.

"You have people for your speeches, do you not?" she asked. "Let them earn their coin. It needs to be a powerful message."

"I will get them working on it immediately," he replied and Selina stood up to leave. "Do you have to go?"

Her expression was cold and haughty as she stared down her nose at him. "You have your other wives for that."

He shrugged. It was true. They were younger, and more agile, but sometimes it was nice to be challenged by someone who was his equal in the ways that mattered.

"Do you want me to get rid of them?" he asked, wondering if she was genuinely jealous, although that seemed unlikely.

"You flatter yourself," she said. "No, you should keep them. They stop you from trying to climb into my bed every night when I'm trying to sleep."

Choilan felt his shoulders slump in defeat. It had not always been this way. Once he had been as passionate about her as he was his other wives. Marrying the others had also been a political move upon taking the throne. To ensure that his line continued and to honour the families who had lent him their favour during his campaign. With daughters one step away from the throne they were raised higher than their peers and could ask for more favours.

"Did you seek me out for a reason, or were you just bored?" he said, returning to the pleasures of his whisky since her body seemed beyond his reach.

"A trifling matter, but I can deal with it myself."

"It cannot be that insignificant if you came to me with it," he pointed out. "You're perfectly capable of dealing with most things by yourself."

"Flattery will not get you into my bedchamber tonight."

"I was being honest," he replied. "So, out with it."

Selina sat down again but she remained pensive. "Some of my people have gone missing."

Although the Regent had his own network of agents who worked at home and abroad, he indulged all of his wives in different way. His third wife delighted in fashion. His second in caring for animals and his first wife in spying. He had allowed her to recruit a dozen individuals to gather information. Unlike the hobbies of his other wives Selina's favourite pastime yielded something of real worth. Often her people uncovered titbits of information that eluded even his most trusted agents.

"Missing? Or silent?" he asked.

"Missing. I've sent people to investigate and no one has seen them for days. Not their families or friends. They've simply disappeared."

"How many of them?"

"Eight," said Selina with a grimace.

Choilan whistled through his teeth in surprise. One or two

might be considered a coincidence. Perhaps they'd grown bored in their dual roles and decided to move away and live elsewhere. Sometimes an agent dug themselves into trouble and would disappear, only to turn up floating in a river or lying in an alley with their throat cut. For so many of them to vanish without a trace was highly unusual.

"Send their names to Bettina and she'll have someone look into it."

"Thank you, Choilan," she said, forcing a smile onto her face.

"Thank you for the idea," he replied. "At times like these I'm reminded why you're my First Wife."

He expected another tart response, brimming over with vinegar, but instead she merely bobbed her head and went out of the door. As the silence returned the Regent turned his mind back to the problem of Garvey.

He still needed the people to see that he was doing something about the rogue mage and his followers. A show of force and gathering some soldiers would appease the people, but it wouldn't change the outcome if they were ever to face the mages. Then again, if the worst should happen, perhaps a stray arrow might catch one of his followers in the neck. It had happened in Yerskania during the destruction of a village. Nevertheless, merely giving the order and making it publicly known that he was amassing a force would reassure some who thought him frozen with fear.

The wolves were at the door but he wasn't done yet.

CHAPTER 5

Akosh maintained her rictus grin as Bollgar stuffed another pastry into his face before licking each of his fingers on that hand. His other held a pen which hovered over a ledger filled with pages of numbers in orderly rows. The page was pristine, as was every ledger on the shelves. The books were completely at odds with Bollgar's appearance.

Severely overweight, balding and with several chins and no neck to speak of, Bollgar wore only a stained orange robe in a poor imitation of a monk. As his bulk had increased over the years finding clothes to fit had proven increasingly difficult. In the end he'd taken to wearing loose robes. The latest was plain and inexpensive, marked with grease, crumbs and dried bits of old food.

When she saw he was contemplating another pastry, Akosh cleared her throat loudly, drawing his attention back to the matter at hand. If he hadn't been one of her children she would never have dealt with him.

"Apologies, Mother," he said, wiping his fingers across his chest, leaving more grease marks on his robe. "Where were we?"

"Morrinow," she reminded him.

"Ah yes." He leaned backwards in his chair, which groaned

alarmingly under his immense weight. He retrieved another journal from the bookshelves behind him that filled the wall, floor to ceiling. When not distracted by sweet delicacies Bollgar had a remarkable mind for numbers. Officially he was just a bookkeeper for half a dozen shops on a small side street in Herakion, the capital of Zecorria. Unofficially he was responsible for the money for several less reputable organisations, including various criminal enterprises in Zecorria. What even they didn't know was that hidden among their own numbers was a set of ghost transactions he monitored on behalf of Akosh. Money donated by her children which was then given to orphanages across Zecorria and Morrinow.

Bollgar laid the journal on the table and carefully cleaned his hands on a wet cloth then dried them on another. Only then did he open the book. He didn't care about his appearance, but no one was allowed to touch his books. Every page was spotless, which was remarkable given the quantity of crumbs hiding in the folds of his robe waiting to leap onto the paper.

The fat man muttered to himself as he ran a finger down a column of numbers. "I'm afraid to say it's not good news. The contributions from the Morrin were always low, but they've dropped to almost nothing in the last year."

It was as Akosh had expected. Setting up orphanages devoted to anyone except the Blessed Mother in Morrinow was always going to be a tricky idea. However, with patience and persistence, she had succeeded in a few of the smaller towns that were often overlooked by the capital.

It had been a little easier during the war, and then shortly after during the civil war in Morrinow where old ideas were being challenged. Now that the civil war was at an end many of the traditional values in Morrin society were being reasserted. This included a national focus on religion and the country was slowly edging back to a theocracy in all but name. Gradually she'd been eased out as devotion to the Blessed Mother was not only expected but required, and the punishments for being different from the norm were severe.

"Close the accounts in Morrinow," said Akosh. "It was a nice idea, but I suspected it wouldn't last. Focus on the accounts here in Zecorria."

"As you wish." He scribbled a few lines on a separate notebook and returned the Morrin journal to the shelves.

"How are the funds in Herakion?"

Bollgar didn't even need to look at a journal for that. The figures were all in his head. His wide grin told her everything she needed to know before he even spoke. "Steady. But the numbers for this month are lower than last month. However, there is plenty of extra money sitting idle if you're considering further expansion."

"It has crossed my mind," she admitted. "In fact I'm just on my way to visit an orphanage I recently contacted. If they agree today, I'll want you to send a monthly stipend to them like the others."

"Of course," he said, making another note in his neat script. "Send me the details."

Despite his indulgent appetite Bollgar had never let her down in thirty years. He was one of the first children she'd seen in the first orphanage she'd supported.

"You've been loyal and I value what you've done over the years," she muttered and he flashed a grin, although his eyes strayed to the pastries again. "I would be displeased if you suddenly died because of a weak heart."

Bollgar's eyes snapped back to her and he seemed suitably abashed. "I'm trying to ration myself, Mother, but it's my only real pleasure."

She had a few vices of her own but none that were likely to kill her as quickly. It was possible he could die tomorrow. With a grimace she stood up and put a hand against his forehead. Bollgar closed his eyes at her touch while she used a small portion of her power to study him beneath the skin. After a moment she withdrew her hand, wiping the sweat away on her trousers.

"Thankfully your heart is still strong. I urge you to take better care of yourself," she said.

"Yes, Mother," he said, although she noticed he didn't make it a promise.

If he died it would be a problem only because it would take someone months to decode his journals. Akosh smiled, letting him think it was because she cared. She had grown soft. It was time he took on an apprentice or two, just in case he died in an accident, or she snapped his neck in a fit of rage. He wasn't her only bookkeeper in Zecorria but he was the best. Even so it paid to plan for contingencies.

Akosh left him alone with his pastries and neat rows of numbers. She retraced her route from weeks ago and returned to a once grand part of the city in the east. The hand-drawn sign on the front door of the orphanage had been replaced with a neat wooden plaque and the exterior made brighter with a recent coat of paint.

On her first visit she'd seen mostly empty rooms with children amusing themselves using the barest minimum, but already there were a few noticeable changes.

As soon as she set foot inside the orphanage Akosh smelled fresh bread. In the first room off the entry hall she saw a group of children eating their lunch, happily stuffing bread smeared with butter into their fat little faces. A steaming bowl of thick stew also sat in front of each child. There was no fighting, no jealous looks at someone else's portion, just contented munching sounds. She left them to their lunch and stepped into the room beyond.

Akosh found two neat rows of battered and worn desks, likely salvaged from an old school, being put to good use. Twelve children were focused on the teacher at the front of the classroom. The man was running through the alphabet on a scarred blackboard with the children repeating each letter after him. Some of the students were a lot older than the others, suggesting a life spent on the streets where reading and writing were not particularly valued. Being quick with your fingers and your feet was far more useful to criminal gangs. It might be too late for some of them, but the orphanage gave all of them a chance at a new life if they wanted it. All they had to do was obey the rules and adopt the one true faith: hers.

In one corner of the room sat a small wooden crate of toys and a neat stack of books. She searched for a prayer corner and any votive lamps or candles, but couldn't see any. The teacher spotted her by the open door but didn't seem alarmed. He merely gestured with his head back the way she'd come. Akosh took the hint and went in search of Jille, the administrator.

At the back of the building was a small office. She knocked on the door and almost immediately Jille opened it and stepped back in surprise. Akosh noticed she'd put on a little weight and the bags under her eyes had faded. True to her word she'd been taking better care of herself as well as the children.

"I wasn't sure we'd ever see you again," admitted Jille. "Please, come in."

The office was unchanged and as Akosh sat down on one of the battered chairs she thought she smelled damp paper. Jille saw her wrinkling her nose and gestured at a pile of books.

"A nearby school recently closed. We managed to salvage

some desks and books, but they're a little damp. We're just drying them out."

"You don't need to do that," said Akosh. "You have money for new books."

Jille shrugged her thin shoulders. "We didn't know if we'd receive any more money. So we're trying to make your donation stretch as far as possible."

"What else have you spent the money on?"

"Food, clothing and blankets mostly. We also hired a new member of staff. He's focusing on teaching them to read and write. People always need scribes, messengers and bookkeepers."

"Have you spoken to any of the other orphanages where I'm a patron?" she asked. Jille squirmed in her chair but eventually answered.

"I visited one of them and the man running it let me see inside."

"You seem uncomfortable," said Akosh. "Did you see anything untoward?"

"Oh no," apologised Jille. "All of the children were well fed and happy. I spoke to the staff and they were wonderful."

Akosh folded her arms and leaned back in her chair, baffled by Jille's reluctance. Normally these meetings were over very quickly. The offer of free money for the children, on a regular basis, should not have been a difficult decision. And yet something about all of this had made Jille uneasy. "I'm getting the feeling you've made a decision and it's not one I'm going to like."

"Your offer is generous, and we're grateful for the money, but I must turn it down. We're going to teach the children about the Maker."

Akosh took a deep breath and counted to twenty slowly in her head before speaking. "Why?"

"The Maker is a safe choice. We can ask at several churches

for donations and they're not going to disappear. I spoke to a few people and not too long ago no one had ever heard of Akosh."

On the one hand she couldn't blame Jille. Things could change rapidly. Now every church of the Holy Light was dedicated to the Lady of Light. No one prayed to the Lord of Light any more. He'd only been gone for ten years, but already was being quickly forgotten. His sudden absence served as a constant reminder to Akosh that she needed to move slowly and with caution. One of her brethren, someone with significant power, had eliminated the Lord of Light for interfering with the mortals. Akosh was very aware that if they found out what she was doing in ten years' time no one would remember her name either. Despite knowing all that she sensed something else had changed Jille's mind.

"Are you sure?"

"My mind is made up," insisted Jille, although she didn't look very certain.

"I want you to think carefully about this, Jille. Your decision will affect a lot of children and their future."

"If this is about the money, we still have some of it left," said Jille, pulling open a desk drawer.

"I don't care about the money. Keep it. Did someone say something? Has someone approached you?"

Jille shook her head but she refused to make eye contact. So someone had spoken to her. Perhaps they'd threatened her or the children. The question was, who? A priest from another faith? An agent representing one of her unusual siblings? Or someone else? A human group?

"Who did you talk to?" asked Akosh. Jille was sweating now and she seemed to have decided that silence was her best defence. "Tell me."

"I think you should leave."

"I can make you tell me," promised Akosh. She didn't need to draw a weapon. It would only take a little pressure to break her. Breaking a couple of fingers usually did the trick. Failing that dislocating a joint was enough if they didn't faint from the pain.

"Is there a problem?" said a new voice, startling them both.

A tall man with beady eyes and trousers that were too short for his gangly frame stood in the doorway. Jille relaxed at seeing a friendly face, but Akosh wasn't done. This was perhaps her only opportunity to find out who was interfering in her business.

"I'm still waiting for an answer," she said, ignoring the newcomer.

Jille stared at her friend, silently beseeching him to help her. He came into the room and even went so far as to put a hand on Akosh's shoulder.

"You're making her uncomfortable. You need to leave."

The way he said it sounded unusual. As if he'd been rehearsing it. Perhaps he wanted to impress Jille and make himself the noble hero of their little story. She wondered if this was some kind of scam. There was definitely more going on than she'd been told. Finding out what, without killing at least one person, was becoming increasingly unlikely. Dead bodies would attract the attention of the authorities and there were always ripples from unsolved murders. Enough of those and the people she wanted to avoid, her siblings, might start investigating.

Caution. It was the first and most important lesson she'd taught herself in the last few decades.

Jille's friend took her hesitation as reluctance to leave and dug his fingers into Akosh's shoulder, trying to get her to move. Caution was important, but sometimes others took the decision out of her hands.

Akosh grabbed him by the wrist and twisted it sharply to the right. He dropped to his knees as she stood up, angling his arm to try and relieve the pressure. Instead of crying out in pain as she wrenched his arm, he grinned and reached for something behind his back. It was when he drew the dagger that she finally noticed his boots. His clothes were old and ill-fitting, the trousers too short and threadbare, as she'd expect for someone in his position. But his boots were new and had been polished until they shone. He loved those boots and took very good care of them. Whatever his purpose in being here, he'd exposed himself by being unable to fully commit to the role of penniless teacher.

He slashed at her with the blade and Akosh was forced to release his arm and step out of the way. The back of her knees collided with the desk and she glanced over her shoulder. Jille was pressed against the far wall, wide-eyed with terror. Whatever was happening she wasn't involved. She didn't have the guile and was terrible at lying but Akosh still didn't know who had coerced her into rejecting the money.

"Who do you work for?" asked Akosh, but the man just grinned, showing off even white teeth.

"Help! She's attacking Jille!" he shouted over his shoulder. There was only one door out of the cramped room and the space was already crowded with three of them. If anyone else came into the room it would be difficult to escape.

Akosh rushed the man, dodging a slash and shoulder-barging him to one side. The back of his head collided with the wall and he started to fall, but stuck out a leg on the way down. She tripped and went skidding into the hallway on her stomach.

As she scrambled to her feet Akosh heard children crying and screaming. The teacher was staring at her with alarm but his eyes widened in horror as he stared over her shoulder. The tall man came out of the room with blood dripping from a gash in his forehead, stumbling for dramatic effect. The back of his head had struck the wall and yet somehow his face was bleeding.

At the sight of blood the children's wailing increased in volume and now the teacher was trying to shield all of them with his body, arms held wide. The tall man was edging closer, looking disoriented and groggy. He was making a heroic effort to keep Jille safe and it looked convincing, until he winked at her.

"Take whatever you want, just don't hurt the children," he shouted, holding up his hands in surrender. A smile quirked across his face and then it was gone.

Despite the situation Akosh had to admire his performance. He was good. Playing the victim and scaring the children at the same time. Whatever she did now or said, she'd never be able to come back to this orphanage. Even working through a surrogate Akosh knew she could not be their patron. Someone had outmanoeuvred her.

Part of her wanted to stab him over and over again for interfering in her plans. A larger part wanted to break his bones, one at a time, until he told her everything. Then she'd find out who he worked for and what they were planning. She teetered on the edge, having to work hard to fight her violent instincts, but in the end she withdrew. She calmly walked out of the building, clenching her jaw to stop herself saying something.

Akosh watched the orphanage from a secluded corner a few buildings away to see what happened next. A small boy hurtled out of the front door and raced down the street. A short time later he came back with some city guards in tow.

Maybe she should have just killed them all. She wondered how far it would go. One alleged assault shouldn't be enough to cause any real problems. Even so she would get some of her people to quietly look into it. She wasn't afraid of the authorities, but all of this would leave a trail.

Snarling with frustration she walked away from the orphanage, wondering about the ripples this would cause and who might notice them.

CHAPTER 6

It had been a few years since Balfruss had last seen Tammy but on the surface she looked much the same. A little leaner in the face perhaps. Tired and tense but that was to be expected given her new role and the pressure that came with it. When he'd heard about her promotion it hadn't really surprised him. Her determination was unparalleled.

"Congratulations, Khevassar."

"Thank you."

"It suits you," said Balfruss, gesturing at the Guardian jacket. "It's the first time I've seen you in it."

"Voechenka was a long time ago," she said, recovering quickly from her initial surprise. "But sometimes it feels like only yesterday. It still haunts my dreams."

"Mine too," he said, forcing a smile to try and drive away the mental imagery from their shared time in the haunted city. "I came hoping you had some good news about Habreel and his network."

Tammy hesitated before answering, showing a level of caution he'd not seen before. Balfruss didn't know if that had developed because of her new role or a shift in their friendship. He hoped it was the former. "I have news, but little of it is good."

His fledgling smile faded. "Do you know what's happened?"

"I do. How is Munroe?"

Balfruss stared into the distance, trying to put her grief into words. "For the first few days she was barely holding on. She didn't move, didn't speak. She was consumed by her loss. I thought she was going to die. Two weeks ago she came out of her fugue. I tried to stop her but she insisted on going back to the Red Tower. She wanted to see it for herself and look for any clues about her family. She's due back any day and, unless I can give her some good news, I'm worried what she will do on her own."

"I'm so sorry," said Tammy.

As a father Balfruss couldn't even contemplate what he would do if something happened to his child. It was a nightmare he couldn't dwell on. Thinking about his daughter always came with mixed feelings, but it was better than the overwhelming grief he'd seen in Munroe's eyes. At least his child was still alive.

"Right now, though, I'm concerned about you," she said.

"Me?"

Tammy folded her arms and leaned forward on her desk. "Are you going to seek retribution for the Red Tower?"

Balfruss shook his head. "We may not have spoken in a few years, but I haven't changed that much."

Tammy sighed and sat back in her chair, scrubbing a hand across her tired face. "I'm sorry. These days it's difficult to know who to trust."

"There are some things that I cannot tell you and others I will not," said Balfruss, knowing they both had secrets they couldn't share. No one on this side of the Dead Sea knew about his daughter and despite trusting Tammy, he would not tell her. The less people that knew about her the safer she would be. "But I will not lie to you and I'm still your friend."

"I know."

"Good. So, do you have some news for me?" he asked.

"We have Habreel in custody and he's been helping us locate his lieutenants. They were coordinating his network of followers to stir up trouble against the Seekers. One of the six lieutenants is in the cells below, one is dead and unfortunately we can't locate the other four."

"Still, that sounds like a good start," said Balfruss, puzzled by her lack of enthusiasm.

"It would be, if Habreel and his people hadn't been pawns for someone else. A larger group. He was working with a woman named Akosh, and she was using his group for her own ends. So, now we're trying to track down her and we don't know anything about her agenda."

"There's something else. I can hear it in your voice," said Balfruss.

Tammy's job often required her to conceal her true feelings, but after enhancing his senses with magic for many years, it had made Balfruss adept at reading people.

"Akosh is some sort of cult leader. We questioned one of Habreel's people, Grell, and he described her as an assassin, but he also said she had some kind of magic. She has a following and she funds several orphanages here in Perizzi. One of my Guardians, Brook, killed Grell for saying too much. It turned out Brook was part of the same cult. We found an idol in her home." Tammy fished around in her desk drawer and pulled out a small stone statue. Balfruss held up the idol towards the light. It was crudely made but clearly represented a benevolent woman, probably a mother, caressing the cheek of a small child held in her arms. A symbol of love and affection at first glance, but perhaps it represented something more sinister. Absolute obedience.

"Five orphanages in the city have the same idols and a holy

book. They all receive regular donations from former orphans, and apparently someone claiming to be Akosh visits them in person from time to time. Some of my people are watching the orphanages in case she shows up."

"How old was Guardian Brook?" asked Balfruss.

"Almost forty, why?"

A disturbing idea was starting to form at the back of Balfruss's mind. He and Tammy had shared much during their time together in Shael, but this was skirting close to a subject he'd kept private. It was something he was still struggling to accept and had yet to tell anyone about it after all these years. Few people knew the truth about Vargus, although many like Balfruss had fought beside him during the war. They thought that he was only a veteran warrior who had died defending Seveldrom. If that had been the end of his story it would have been a lot simpler.

"Be very careful," Balfruss warned her. "If your people see Akosh, I would strongly advise them to keep their distance. Tell them not to interfere with her, merely observe and report back."

Tammy folded her arms. "I'll need a little more to go on. Are you saying she's really a mage?"

"I'm not sure," he admitted, shaking his head. He needed more evidence before he could be certain. "Either she's a mage or something else. Something we've not seen before."

Over the years Balfruss had come to realise that while others considered him knowledgeable about the world and its mysteries, he knew far less than people believed. Maintaining the lie massaged his ego a little, but it also protected them from horrors they'd never considered and were better off not knowing about. Tammy had been with him in the labyrinth beneath Voechenka where they'd fought the brood mother. There were many terrors lurking in the dark, waiting for their chance to strike. Most of the time ignorance was bliss.

His instincts were telling him that Akosh was either something new or something very old.

"I recognise that expression," she said and Balfruss guessed her mind had also gone back to Voechenka and the labyrinth.

"I don't think it's the same, but my gut is telling me she's incredibly dangerous. I know someone who might be able to give me some answers."

"I'll make sure they keep their distance," promised Tammy. "I also have people looking into Akosh beyond the capital in Yerskania and abroad. I'm beginning to wonder how far this cult of hers extends."

That was a worrying thought he'd not considered, but it made sense if his theory was right. "I'm staying in the city at the moment. I'll come by with any news as soon as I have it."

"There's something else we need to talk about," said Tammy. "Garvey."

The name echoed around the room and then dropped like a stone. In the last month he'd been helping the students who had forsaken their magic settle into new communities. It often meant him travelling to remote towns and villages, but even in those quiet corners he'd heard the stories. He knew what Garvey and his band of rogue mages had been doing. The lives they'd taken. The homes and communities they'd destroyed.

It seemed impossible that Garvey was responsible and yet, no matter how much he didn't want to believe it, deep down he knew that it was true.

His friend was gone. Twisted by his experience, angered by the fear and violence people directed towards anyone with magic, Garvey had finally snapped. He wanted to live free but if anyone got in his way or disagreed with him, he killed them.

"What he's doing," said Balfruss, his hands curling into

tight fists, "it goes against everything we tried to do at the Red Tower. Everything we stood for."

"We need your help to stop him."

Balfruss shook his head. "You don't know what you're asking me to do."

"He's dangerous. He's murdering people and destroying whole communities. What else do you need to know?"

"He's angry." Balfruss took a deep breath and then another, forcing himself to calm down. Despite all of their preparation and planning, so many people had still died during the evacuation. Their work over the last few years at the Red Tower had been undone in less than a year. Eloise was trying to salvage what remained with the Jhanidi, while others were being forced to hide their power, just so they could live in peace. Seekers had buried or destroyed their masks to protect themselves and now, if a child came into their magic, he had no idea what would happen to them. The fear of being cast out by their community, or worse if they were discovered, would make them bottle it all up. Instead of reaching a place where magic was respected, they were moving towards a new dark age of fear. One where anyone connected to magic would be exiled or killed. He shared some of Garvey's anger about what had happened but knew killing innocents only fed into their belief that all magic was dangerous.

"He's my friend. You know how rarely I used that phrase."

Balfruss had now reached the age where he could count on one hand the number of people he would call true friends. These were people he could turn to in any circumstances and they would be there for him without question. Some friends had died, others had changed over the years becoming people he barely recognised any more, and some had drifted away when their lives went in a new direction. He'd thought of Garvey as a friend, despite all of the changes he'd gone through, but recent events were making him question his judgement. The man he knew, no matter how damaged and angry, could not have committed such atrocities.

He expected Tammy to ignore him but she considered his words carefully before replying, her words echoing his thoughts. "He isn't the same man you knew. Events have changed him."

Balfruss sat back in his chair and closed his eyes for a moment. He knew she was right but there was so much to do. He was doing his best to stop Munroe from going on a killing spree of her own. He'd managed to rehome all of the students who had given up their magic, but being accepted as a member of the community did not happen overnight. And now he needed to contact an old friend about Akosh. And if he was right about her the possible repercussions would force him down a new path.

"I want to help, but I have my limits. The Red Tower is gone and so are all of its students. All of the mages I could call on are scattered to the winds, living in hiding. Garvey has at least a dozen students with him. I wouldn't stand a chance against them by myself."

"Do you think he would kill you?" asked Tammy.

Balfruss considered it. "No, but his followers may have no such compunction. They may have acquired a taste for killing, and, as someone capable of fighting back, I would present them with an exciting challenge."

Balfruss knew his answer was disappointing, but they would have to deal with Garvey by themselves for the time being. Without some guidance he was afraid of what Munroe might do. If she went on a rampage it would make Garvey's seem minor by comparison. Without a doubt she was the most powerful mage he'd ever met and right now she was incredibly unstable.

Tammy didn't push him any harder on the subject, for which he was grateful.

"I'll speak to my contact about Akosh and let you know if I find anything."

"I'd appreciate that," she said, coming around the desk to see him to the door. "Despite everything, it's good to see you."

She hugged him tightly for a moment and then let him go. As Balfruss walked through the outer office he looked back through the door and saw Tammy return to her desk and the mountain of paperwork.

When Balfruss entered his room at the inn he was briefly surprised to see someone sitting beside the window. Munroe looked very small in the large chair with a blanket across her lap. The room was in darkness and she was staring out at the night sky, oblivious of her surroundings.

He moved around the room, kindling the lanterns and starting a fire to drive away the chill in the air. Munroe barely noticed and didn't react to anything he did. She'd been like this at the beginning, numb to everything except her pain.

"When did you get back?" he asked, settling into the chair opposite.

"Tonight," she murmured, her eyes still distant. "Do you think it would have made a difference, if I'd been there?" asked Munroe. She'd asked him the same question several times before but he wondered if she remembered.

"I don't know. Perhaps." It was the same answer he'd given her the last time as well, because there was no way to know. If she had been at the Red Tower it could have made things better or far worse. Whatever answer he gave it wouldn't restore the dead.

"What did you find? Was there anything left?" he asked. Part of him had also been tempted to travel back to Shael to visit the school and see what remained. The more logical part of his mind had warned him against it. Such a journey would only bring him heartache and make him angrier. Heeding the wiser voice inside he'd remained here while Munroe had gone in search of answers about her family.

"The school is gone." Her voice was flat and lifeless. "Every building is a pile of charred timbers. There were bodies, too, burned things, just lying on the ground. Even the crows won't touch them they're too far gone. The tower itself is still there. I could see where they'd tried to burn it. The earth all around is blackened, but there's not a scratch, not a single mark on the stones."

It was a small relief but again not unexpected. The tower was centuries old and he had no idea who had built it or how it had been done. As a boy he'd asked a member of the old Grey Council if they knew its origins, but they were also in the dark. Its creation was another secret that had been lost.

From the moment he'd seen smoke on the horizon Balfruss had known the school was gone. But he'd put on a brave face and kept the students marching, kept their minds and their hands occupied so they didn't dwell on the past. But Munroe hadn't gone back to Shael to check on the school. She'd gone in search of her loved ones.

A long painful silence settled on the room. He didn't want to ask and she didn't want to speak about it, but part of him needed to know. This time, ignoring the wiser voice, he broke the silence and opened himself up to the pain.

"Did you find them?"

"I searched everywhere but found nothing." Balfruss felt his heart lift at her words until he saw the misery etched into her features. "So I spent several nights listening to drunks tell stories in taverns. In dark corners, in whispered voices, several people spoke about chasing an injured man and a boy on horseback. They pursued them down to the river, only for a green monster to rise from the water and scare them away." Balfruss tried to speak. To offer her a glimpse of hope. A sliver of denial that, perhaps, all was not as it appeared. But she wasn't finished. "I went down to the river, to his cabin. And there, soaked into the boards of the pier, I found blood. There was so much."

There were no words he could offer to soothe her agony. Nothing he could do that would change what had happened. Her family was truly dead. Balfruss wondered who was sitting across from him. How much of the person he knew had died with them beside the river?

Her eyes roamed about the room before finally settling on his. For a little while she seemed to be with him in the room. "You look tired."

"It's been a long day," he said, trying to remember the last time he'd slept for more than a few hours.

"Did you visit Tammy? Did she have any news about who killed my family?"

"No. The person we thought responsible was merely a pawn for someone else."

Balfruss saw something dangerous flicker behind her eyes. "I want a name," said Munroe.

"Habreel was being played the whole time. His group of followers were just one branch of a much larger cult."

"Who killed my family?" she asked again.

"Give me some more time," he said. For a brief moment he thought she might concede but then the steel crept back into her gaze. Her posture shifted, shoulders hunching and hands curling up into tight fists. She was out of patience and he was out of time.

"Give me a name," said Munroe.

"Akosh. Her name is Akosh."

"I've heard the name before." Munroe silently moved about the room gathering her belongings.

"We don't know much about her, only that she's been working from the shadows for a long time. She's also the leader of some kind of religious group."

"I know. I was the one who questioned Grell before he was murdered."

Munroe stuffed the last of her clothes into her bag then strapped on a bandolier of daggers around her chest.

"Some claim she's an assassin, but I think she could be a mage."

"That's something we have in common then," said Munroe.

"No matter what I say, it's not going to make any difference, is it?"

"No," she replied.

"Then there's something else you should know. There's a chance Akosh might not be mortal."

Munroe glanced around the room, looking for any items she might have missed before briefly sitting down on the edge of her seat. He knew she was going to leave but, hopefully, would still listen to his advice as it could help save her life.

"What does that mean?"

Balfruss wondered how much he should tell her, but in the end he settled for the simplest version of the truth. "In my travels over the years, I've met certain ... beings. They're not like you and me. They have much longer lives and enormous power. Not power from the Source. It's something else that's hard to explain."

Munroe cocked her head on one side. "Can they die?"

"I honestly don't know. I understand so little about them."

Munroe picked up her bag and moved towards the door. "When I meet this Akosh, I'll let you know. I will make her pay for what she's done."

There was nothing dull or flat in her voice any more. Her eyes burned with hate worse than any he'd ever seen before. He knew Munroe's thirst for revenge would not be quenched until Akosh lay broken and dying at her feet.

He pitied anyone who stood between Munroe and her target.

CHAPTER 7

Danoph tried to focus on the activity around him but his gaze kept drifting to the west. Something out there was calling to him.

With Wren's revelation about his ability the nightmares had started to change. Or perhaps it was simpler than that. He knew they were no longer random images from his brain designed to torment him. They were messages that needed to be studied. Even when they were disturbing there was a reason.

By accepting his Talent as a gift, he thrashed about less while asleep, letting the images wash over him as he tried to study them with a critical eye. Many of them were unpleasant and he saw death, disease and murders both foul and disturbing. But there were also images of hope, love, friendship and sacrifice. A young boy pushing an old blind man out of the way of a runaway horse. A pair of lovers covered in sweat, their bodies intertwined in passion. Old friends meeting up after twenty years apart and talking as if no time had passed.

Sometimes the dreams were easy to interpret, such as finding a young person before they were injured by their community, as they'd done with Laila. At other times the flashes were so fast it took him several nights before he saw them clearly. Or they could appear as nothing more than a random series of images that had no apparent connection. Those were the dreams he pondered on the most during the day.

With his new awareness the texture of his dreams changed as well. More often than not they felt as real as if he were awake. Sometimes he saw familiar places and people he knew from his childhood. Other times it was strangers or those he'd only heard about but could recognise them because of the trappings of their office. And yet with all of them he felt as if he could stretch out his hand and touch the people.

Often he saw a tall, blonde Seve woman dressed in a Guardian uniform. Once or twice he recognised a woman who had to be Queen Olivia of Shael. She was a slight woman with a swollen belly, standing beside her broad-shouldered husband from Seveldrom. Three times now Danoph had dreamed of his mother and the village in which he'd grown up, but he didn't know what any of it meant.

They were just brief moments in time, as if he was standing outside, peering in through a window as the lives of other people unfolded before him. At times he sensed they were glimpses of the future, but there were also images from his past as well.

This was only the beginning. It was something that would take him years to master before he was truly skilled at interpreting his dreams. But at least he was now aware and could start trying to decipher the images.

Danoph had started experiencing unusual sensations when he was awake as well, although he'd not told anyone about those. Wren had good intentions but she was overprotective and already had too much on her mind without him adding to her burdens.

His gaze drifted west again. His instincts were telling him

something important was going to happen in that direction. Danoph had a strong compulsion to get on his horse and ride that way.

"Danoph, are you all right?" asked Wren.

He turned back to face her and the others, forcing a smile. "Fine. Just watching for raiders."

The ruins of another abandoned village lay spread out around him. A gentle breeze rattled the windows and doors, swirling dust around the empty street. The front door of one house repetitively banged open and closed, open and closed. There wasn't so much as a stray dog running along the streets. Dust lay on every surface and an air of forlorn abandonment filled every house. No one had died here. They had simply walked away before the war arrived as they were no longer safe, leaving behind most of their belongings. He wondered how many of them had found better lives and how many still dreamed of returning here.

Now he and the others had become ghosts, haunting the ruins of someone else's life, trying to find something they could salvage for their community.

Wren and three others were busy removing several panes of glass from one of the last houses that hadn't already been stripped of its windows. They'd also gathered up a lot of clothes, a couple of bolts of cloth and more blankets, which would be vital to get them through winter.

Other groups had come to this village before, but there was only so much each could carry on horseback without a cart. Wren had considered asking the blacksmith and others to build one, but then changed her mind. It would be easier for others to track them back to their community and it would be a much slower way to travel. That would normally limit them from carrying heavy objects back home but magic provided them with a way to overcome that restriction.

All of the heavy items, plus several windows padded with blankets, had been laid out on an old sheet. Working together, two of the group created a solid plate of force with their willpower which they slipped under the sheet and then raised off the ground. Maintaining the floating cart bed took considerable effort and concentration, but working in pairs and swapping over after a couple of hours made it easier. Wren was embracing the teaching styles of many magic users and it was starting to pay off. By using it every day the young mages in their community were not only becoming stronger, but also more comfortable and familiar with their magic. It also meant that Talents were starting to emerge, not by hunting for one, but simply by getting involved with a variety of tasks. Their dowser, Helsa, had simply found the water by focusing on their need and following a strong urge. As it turned out her ability didn't only apply to finding water. Now she was being used to find more wild sheep to increase the size of their flock.

Danoph turned west again and felt a stronger pull. Perhaps this was what it felt like for Helsa. He wheeled his horse around to face in that direction before he realised what he'd done.

"What is it?" asked Wren, but he barely heard her. It was calling to him and he felt a growing sense of urgency. Sensing his need, Danoph's horse actually took a few steps forward. "What's wrong?"

"There's going to be smoke over there," he said with a vague gesture towards the west. "People are going to be hurt."

"I don't see anything," said Wren, squinting into the distance.

"That's because I don't think it's happened yet," he said quietly, glancing around to make sure the others hadn't overheard.

Wren stared at him in silence for a long time. He knew she was considering their options and the potential repercussions of doing nothing versus getting involved. When the others were ready she signalled them to lift the goods off the ground and head towards home. The horses could only move at a walk, reins tied to a horse in front, while their riders focused all of their attention on keeping the burden afloat. Any faster and it became impossible to maintain with two people lifting the weight in unison.

He and Wren followed the group at the rear, keeping an eye out for raiders. With every step they took towards the village Danoph felt a growing sense of panic and unease. His skin became clammy and hot. Bile rose up in the back of his throat and he smelled smoke and tasted fresh blood.

They were too late. It was already happening.

On the horizon a thin strand of grey smoke rose up into the air. Danoph gently pulled on his horse's reins until it came to a stop. The others had spotted the smoke as well but they kept moving. At his side Wren was watching him and this time she didn't hesitate.

"We'll catch up," she said to the others, turning her horse to the west.

They rode hard but by the time they arrived it was already over. A group of travellers, six carts in all, loaded with all their worldly possessions, had been murdered. The wagons had been torn open, their contents scattered across the ground and ransacked for anything deemed valuable. Musical instruments had been reduced to kindling. Paintings slashed and trinkets trodden into the mud. The horses were all gone but one lay dead by the creek, two arrows in its neck, thick blood turning the water red. And then there were the bodies.

Men, women and children, reduced to ragged, bloody things. Pierced, torn open and left for the gathering flies and circling birds. Three wagons had been set ablaze and were now so far gone the wood was folding in on itself, fuelling its own destruction. The others were smouldering but with just a wave of her hands Wren quenched all the flames. Danoph felt a brief surge of power and it was done. His warm breath frosted on the suddenly icy air. For a little while it hurt to breathe, but slowly the temperature rose as it returned to normal. Even then, staring at the destruction, his chest still hurt.

In the silence that followed the cooling wood cracked and popped as it settled. Wren dismounted and approached the first of the bodies, her hand hovering over the face of the young woman who was about their age. He could see Wren's lips moving in what he thought was a quiet prayer. Not far away the girl's parents lay dead, throats and stomachs torn open, ropey red innards strewn across the ground. The anguish stamped on their faces suggested they'd watched their own child die in their final moments.

"What's the custom in Shael for dealing with the dead?" asked Wren.

Many people followed the Blessed Mother in Shael, but not all of them. Danoph remembered hearing about the pyres during the war where mountains of dead bodies had been burned. Normally the deceased was raised off the ground and the special platform was set alight, so that every part of the person drifted away on the wind. The tradition had somewhat fallen out of fashion these days.

"I think we should bury them," said Danoph. "The scavengers are already gathering," he said, gesturing at the birds circling above their heads.

A faint groaning drew their attention and a moment later they were both scrambling towards one of the wagons that had been set on fire. The sides were blackened but more or less intact, holding in the mountain of possessions that had toppled over into one huge mound. Peering in the back of the wagon Danoph saw a hand sticking out of the pile.

Working together they started throwing items aside, clearing debris until they found the arm and then the shoulder of a young woman. When they tried to pull her out the whole pile wobbled, threatening to come crashing down, forcing them to remove items one by one. Eventually they uncovered her head and shoulders and were able to risk dragging her out very slowly.

"My daughter" was the first thing she said. A quick glance at her injuries showed one of her legs was bent at a peculiar angle and she was having some difficulty breathing. Danoph wasn't an expert and still couldn't heal, but he didn't think she was in any immediate danger of dying. He gave her some willow bark to chew which numbed the pain. A short time later her eyelids fluttered closed and she slept. He covered her with some blankets to keep her warm and they returned to the wagon, painstakingly removing objects from the top one at a time. Wren was now stood inside the wagon, passing boxes out to him when he heard her cry out. A moment later she emerged, carrying a small girl in her arms. There was blood on the girl's face and a cut in her hairline.

"I don't know if she's breathing. What do we do?" said Wren, starting to panic.

"Put her down," said Danoph, spreading out another blanket. He tried to ignore the wet bloodstain on the cloth and focus on the girl. Bending over her chest he listened for a heartbeat and felt for a pulse on her wrist. At the same time an awful creeping sensation started running up and down his arms and legs. A gnawing sense of fear clogged his throat like a fat maggot, making him gag with despair.

This wasn't supposed to have happened. The girl should have lived. He felt a convergence of possibilities swirling around her.

He heard a faint heartbeat but Danoph didn't think the girl was going to live for much longer and that scared him.

"She's alive, but we need to heal her," he said, knowing what he was asking Wren to do.

The girl's mother was still drifting in and out of consciousness. So she wasn't aware that they'd found her daughter and that she was still alive. Perhaps that would be a small blessing if this didn't work.

Danoph knelt down beside the girl but made no attempt to try and help. He had no ability to heal at all. No matter how hard he tried it simply didn't work. His abilities lay elsewhere and only now was he starting to realise it wasn't limited to nightmares about the future.

There was a randomness to everything. A swirling sea of choices and thousands of crossroads every hour of every day that defined a life. But some decisions were more likely than others. Some roads seemed free of clutter and at this moment the girl's future was bleak. He saw only two roads in her future and one of them was quickly fading. This should not have been the end of her story.

"I've never been able to do this," said Wren. "What if I kill her by accident?"

Danoph didn't want to add to the pressure but if he said nothing Wren might remain frozen and then it would be too late. "If you don't at least try, the girl will die."

The finality with which he said it seemed to strike a chord. Wren took the girl's hand in both of hers and bowed her head. He sensed her embrace the Source and tried to remain perfectly still and silent. He couldn't see what she was doing but he felt a tightening across the skin on his face and a prickling in his fingertips.

The distant sounds of the crows faded into the background

and then disappeared. After a while Danoph could only hear his heartbeat. The rest of the world became insignificant until the only things that mattered were Wren and the dying girl. Time crawled by. The only way he could tell that time was passing was the slow movement of the sun behind hazy clouds.

Wren remained frozen in place, head bowed, hands tightly clutching the girl. He checked that the woman was still alive and found her breathing was slow but steady. Unable to help Wren he moved away from her and started digging a grave for the dead.

Even with his rudimentary control of his magic it seemed to take Danoph a long time to gouge a trench in the earth. Several times he felt his control slip and the Source drifted away from him as if he'd never sensed it. When others embraced the Source they always spoke about a heightening of their senses but he didn't feel that at all. Something was changing within but he didn't understand why it was happening now or what it was.

With sweat streaming down his face he stubbornly persisted, raking the earth with his magic until he was sure it was deep enough to hold the dozen or so bodies. It would have been easier to lift each body with magic but it seemed inhumane not to physically carry them. In the back of one of the wagons he found a stack of bedsheets, neatly folded and only a hand's breadth from the owner's corpse. Wrapping each body in a sheet he carried them one by one before setting them down in the grave.

When he was finished Danoph sat down next to the grave and contemplated what to do with the dead horse. In the end he decided to leave it where it had fallen. The patient birds and other scavengers deserved at least one meal. He didn't know if the deceased had followed the Blessed Mother or not, but he took the time to say a prayer over them that he'd been taught as a young boy. Just to be safe he muttered a short prayer to the Maker to watch over them and give them peace.

By the time he was done his back ached and he felt weak and a little dizzy.

With a groan of pain and cracking of limbs, Wren came out of her trance, stumbling to her feet. He helped her stand upright and she glanced up at the sky, trying to work out how much time had passed.

"It's been at least a couple of hours," he said, helping Wren walk in a circle to restore some circulation to her cramped legs.

"Will she live?" she asked, clutching tightly at his arm. Her skin was pale and there were deep shadows under her eyes that had not been there earlier. She was trembling slightly and he could hear her stomach rumbling. Trying to heal the girl had taken a great toll on her. They walked back around to the girl and Danoph knelt down beside her.

Without really knowing how or what he was doing, he focused on the girl and opened himself to exploring her future. Only one road ran into the distance for a while but then it came to an abrupt halt and there was nothing ahead, only darkness. She would live, but only for a short time unless something more was done. Despite all of Wren's efforts it had only provided the girl with a short reprieve.

Forcing a smile he congratulated Wren and then left her wolfing down food from her saddlebags while he fashioned a sling. There was a lot that could be salvaged from the wagons but that would have to wait. Unless they got the girl back to Master Yettle he knew she would die. Danoph thought both the girl and her mother were too fragile to ride so he created a pouch which hung between their saddles. It was crude and the horses didn't like it but they would have to cope for the time being. Even though he knew it would leave tracks that would be easy to follow, he'd considered taking one of the wagons. In the end he decided against it as it would slow them down too much and they needed to set a fair pace back to their community. He didn't know exactly how long the girl had and didn't want to take any chances.

When Wren saw what he'd done to bury the others she embraced the Source and began to fill the grave. Sweat trickled down the sides of her face from the effort, but with one smooth movement she covered the bodies with loose soil. Normally such a task wouldn't have been difficult for her, but she was already exhausted and moving the earth seemed to drain her remaining stamina.

With Wren dozing in her saddle and the others still comatose it was up to Danoph to lead the horses towards home. Left only with his thoughts for company he focused on the strong impulse that had drawn him here. The sense of despair had faded a little. It was too late for the others but a splinter of concern lurked at the back of his mind for the girl. She was still in danger. He didn't know if she was special, only that he'd not been able to save the others but she still had a chance. Her road was still there, running into the distance, for now.

CHAPTER 8

With a grunt of pain Balfruss got up from the floor of his room where he'd been kneeling for a few hours. His knees creaked and popped alarmingly and pain shot down his back. He walked around in a circle for a while and eventually the aches faded. It was another uncomfortable reminder of his age and the relentless march of the years.

Disappointment washed through him as he cleared away the candles, incense and washed away the chalk symbols he'd scrawled onto the wooden floor. After replacing the thick rugs he carefully checked to see if he'd left anything that might look suspicious. In the past it wouldn't have mattered, but at the moment fear of magic was so great he didn't want to take any chances. The last thing he needed was the maid spreading gossip about something she'd noticed when she came to change the sheets.

Dark thoughts about magic inevitably led to the fall of the Red Tower and Garvey's apparent descent into madness. He couldn't deny the truth. The man that he knew was gone and he'd lost another friend. On days like these, when he truly felt alone, Balfruss wondered if he should have remained in the far north across the Dead Sea.

He'd been cooped up alone in his room for too long. In need of company and a distraction he went down to the common room which was busy with people eating and drinking. Their conversations washed over him but Balfruss wasn't really paying attention as his thoughts remained elsewhere. He found a quiet table and absently ordered some food and a drink while pondering what had gone wrong.

Summoning was not something he'd even been taught at the Red Tower. Nor was it a topic ever mentioned in public as the old Grey Council had forbidden its practice. As a student he'd heard rumours about why it had been banned but they'd never been confirmed. Allegedly a student had accidentally contacted an entity beyond the Veil and the consequences had been dire. He'd not given it any further thought until a few years ago when he'd journeyed across the Dead Sea. The tribes living in the emerald jungle had shown him many forms of magic that he'd never imagined, including summoning of a different sort. One that requested the presence of the spirit of a place, a genius loci.

What he'd attempted tonight was a little different, but he'd been following the same principles. Balfruss had hoped there was a chance of it working. After hours of preparation and meditation all he had to show for it was two stiff and painful knees.

As he ate his meal of spicy beef and red beans in plum sauce, he focused on the conversation around him for the first time. There was only one topic on everyone's lips. Garvey. They were scared. Rumour had it that he was travelling north towards Zecorria but it was all speculation. No one dared get too close to the group. What if he decided to stay in Yerskania? What if he came south again instead and marched towards the capital? Who here could stop him and his band of rebel mages?

Balfruss had told Tammy that it wasn't his responsibility to deal with Garvey, which was true. Even so he knew that it was not something he could ignore. If magic was ever to be seen as a force for good then Garvey needed to be stopped. The only way that would happen was if another powerful mage got involved. With Eloise halfway around the world in the desert kingdoms he was the only one left.

At another table in the room a merchant from Zecorria was explaining Regent Choilan's new declaration. He intended to create an opposing force comprised of patriotic mages, but those at the merchant's table thought it would be too little too late. Soldiers and steel couldn't stand up to a mage and yet both Queen Morganse and the Regent were mobilising their armies. Balfruss also overheard a local woman talking about the increasing number of attacks on merchants travelling into Shael. Rooke, the western district, was still a lawless and abandoned wasteland that had been made worse by a new group of murderous bandits. The woman claimed they even had a mage working with them, but to Balfruss it sounded like more fearmongering. Everyone knew the Red Tower had been destroyed but there was a peculiar absence of conversation in the room on that subject.

"It looks like you've got a lot on your mind," said a familiar voice. "Mind if I join you for a drink?"

Balfruss's mouth fell open in surprise and he stared in silence like a simpleton. Vargus sat down opposite and waited for him to recover, sipping at his ale and glancing around the room at the crowd. It had been many years since he'd last seen Vargus, in a nowhere place between moments of time, and yet he'd not aged a day. If anything he looked a little younger than at their previous meeting. His hair had touches of brown in it, where once it had been mostly grey and silver. The backs of his hands had been covered with liver spots but now the skin was clear and tight.

As before, he resembled a battered old mercenary or a weary caravan guard, dressed in worn leathers with a blade slung across his back. There were a dozen others like him in the tavern, which was why no one gave him a second glance. To them he was just another sword for hire.

"I didn't think the summoning had worked," said Balfruss, still struggling with his surprise at seeing Vargus.

The old warrior offered him a wry smile. "It didn't, at least not in the way you're thinking. It's been a long time since anyone tried to contact me like that, which is why it caught my attention. I'm not a spirit of the earth or the air. You can't bind me and call me by name."

"Then what are you?" he asked, and immediately regretted it.

Vargus put down his ale and the genial expression trickled off his face. "We talked about that a few years ago. I once told you a little about what I am. Do not ask for more."

Balfruss was still reeling at seeing Vargus in person. He took a long gulp of ale and tried to gather his thoughts. "That might not be good enough any more."

"Why do you say that?"

"Do you know what's happened to the Red Tower?" he asked and Vargus nodded grimly. "We lost a lot of good people. They were murdered by an angry mob."

"I'm sorry, but I cannot help you with that. My kind has only one immutable rule. We are not allowed to directly interfere in the affairs of mortals. If that's why you asked me here, then I'll leave now," said Vargus, draining the last of his ale.

"That's not the reason," said Balfruss, trying to stop Vargus from leaving. "Although it's related. Does the name Akosh mean anything to you?"

Vargus froze, half out of his seat, one hand resting on the back of his chair. Moving slowly he lowered himself into his seat again. He gestured at the bar for two more drinks and waited until they'd been delivered before speaking in a low voice. He spoke so quietly his words would be swallowed up by the noise in the room, preventing anyone from eavesdropping.

"Tell me everything," said Vargus.

Starting with Danoph's visions of destruction, Balfruss told him about the seemingly inevitable fall of the Red Tower. Despite their best efforts to change the course of events the mob had arrived at the gates with burning torches. Anger warred with sadness inside when he thought of all that had been lost. It wasn't just the school as buildings could be rebuilt. The children had been robbed of their future. Now most of them had been shipped off to a foreign country to start all over again. Learning how to master their magic would be difficult enough without having to adjust to a new culture with its own peculiar quirks and restrictions.

"Most of our preparation paid off, we saved many items that have been placed in storage, but there was still a high price to pay. Some people stayed behind to give the rest of us time to escape with the children. Most of them died, including my friend, Choss, his mother-in-law and his son."

Vargus rocked back in his chair as if he'd been slapped. "I know him," he said and then corrected himself. "I knew him. He was a good man. A champion."

"Now his widow, Munroe, is bent on revenge. I've been working with the Guardians and they discovered a spider, lurking in the shadows, manipulating others for her own ends. Akosh."

Vargus took a deep breath and crossed his arms over his chest. He stared off into the distance and Balfruss could see he was chewing something over, probably deciding how much he could share.

"Are you certain she was responsible?" he finally asked.

"She's involved," said Balfruss, before going on to tell Vargus about the orphanages and how Akosh was both their patron and the head of a cult devoted to her. "I don't know how many orphanages she has, or where they're located, but she and her people have their own hidden agenda. There was even a Guardian who followed Akosh. She killed a witness and then herself rather than be questioned about her involvement."

"So that's how she did it," muttered Vargus.

"Did what?" asked Balfruss, knowing that he shouldn't ask but he wanted some answers. Vargus didn't say anything for a while, just sipped his ale, but he seemed to be considering something. Eventually he came to a decision. He leaned forward across the table and gestured for Balfruss to move closer.

"I want your word. What I'm about to tell you must never pass your lips again. Not to a future wife, a child and not even on your deathbed many years from now."

"I swear it," he promised.

"I'll hold you to that," said the old warrior and Balfruss believed him. Vargus took a moment to settle himself before speaking. "For all things there is a season. Even the ancient tree, that has been a mute sentinel for centuries, witnessing the rise and fall of countless empires, must one day return to the earth. But it can bear fruit and be reborn anew. So it is with my kind. But unlike the tree, we can change. A long time ago, they used to call me the Weaver, but that power and the mantle now belong to another. Today I am a warrior and brother to all men and women who carry the sword. It began with the war and the Brotherhood. That is my path, for now at least."

Balfruss considered his words and thought back over all of the conversations they'd had in the past. He'd heard about the Brotherhood during the war and how it had bound the Seve warriors together into a united fighting force. It may not have changed the course of the war but it had given warriors hope and the will to keep going in the most desperate circumstances. The tales of sacrifice in Seveldrom during the war had even travelled as far as the west. In the last few years soldiers and warriors in other countries had also adopted the tenets of friendship, honour and sacrifice.

The name Weaver tickled something at the back of his mind. A scrap of information he'd read in a dusty old book of ancient history. During the war he and Vargus had spoken about ancient religions, including the Twelve and their predecessors the Triumvirate. Balfruss thought one of the Twelve had been called the Weaver. For all he knew, that might have been Vargus in a former life.

"Akosh reinvented herself," said Balfruss, fumbling along. The old warrior said nothing, which he took as consent to continue. "She created a new religion in her own name."

"She used to be a patron to assassins," said Vargus with a snort of derision. "For the most part they're a mercenary and sociopathic bunch. Few wanted to believe their good luck was due to their devotion and prayers. It was expected that she would wither and die early on the vine, but she adapted."

"What can we do about her?"

"You will do nothing. She will be dealt with by me," said Vargus, in a voice that brooked no argument. "A rebirth was necessary for her to survive, but to use her followers to change the natural order is not permitted. It sounds like she is trying to shape the course of events."

"How will you—"

"Do not ask that question," said the old warrior. For a brief moment Balfruss was reminded that he wasn't a man. He wasn't even human. The power he glimpsed behind Vargus's eyes made the Sorcerer turn his face away in fear.

The conversations continued to flow all around while the two of them sat in a bubble of silence, both dissimilar from everyone else in their own way.

"I have a suggestion," said Vargus, breaking the hush hanging over their table. "Encourage the orphanages here in Perizzi, in the strongest terms, to consider a more stable faith. One which is likely to still exist in a few years. The Maker or the Blessed Mother."

"I will pass that on."

"How you deal with her mortal followers, and those involved in the fall of the Red Tower, is entirely your decision. Leave Akosh to me."

"I will, but you should know Munroe will not be easily side-tracked. She's out for blood and I know of no power that can stop her," said Balfruss. "Not even me."

He thought Vargus would ask him to speak to her again. Instead he merely frowned and shook his head. "That is her choice. I cannot interfere, but she will find no peace. Revenge will not bring them back." Vargus took a few long pulls on his second ale and Balfruss knew he was running out of time.

"What if I need to find you again?" he asked.

"I will find you," said Vargus, and Balfruss wasn't sure if that was a threat or a promise. Without another word the old warrior passed through the crowd and went out of the front door. Few noticed him leave and no one turned their head to watch his progress.

It made Balfruss wonder how many others like Vargus were out there, walking among them, living ordinary lives, and if he'd met any of them before.

CHAPTER 9

It had been many years since Munroe had crawled over the rooftops of Perizzi, but thankfully she had not forgotten all of her lessons. Her attempt to join the Silent Order, an elite group of assassins in Yerskania, had required months of training which often involved scrambling up and down walls or tiptoeing across rooftops without falling to her death. Unfortunately her assessment had not gone well and she'd been rejected as a suitable candidate. This was long before she'd learned how to fully control her Talent. The result had been some of the most unusual and improbable accidents that the authorities were still struggling to explain. At the very least her experience had taught her how to move quietly and go undetected.

It was a long way down to the street and a fall from this height would break her neck. If the worst happened she could use her magic to cushion her fall, but she was trying to remain unnoticed.

Tonight the city reeked. She'd forgotten about that in her time away. When the wind blew in the wrong direction it dredged up a stench from the port, flooding the streets with the smell of rotting fish, ripe piss, stale beer and suspicious meat sold by street vendors. She may have forgotten about the smells, but with them a flood of old memories returned. She remembered wasting countless hours in the Emerald Dragon, in a permanent alcoholic haze, trying to numb her boredom and self-pity. She remembered a month of cold and wet nights scrambling across the city with a man named Ben as part of her training to join the Silent Order. Mostly the smell made her remember the long and lonely nights when she'd lain in her bed, staring out of her window at the stars, hoping for better days and an end to her isolation.

Her better days had been and gone. They'd died with her family. Now she was caught in between. Unable to move forward. Unwilling to step back in time and become the person she'd been before Choss. But not everything from her old life had been terrible.

Munroe wasn't properly focused on the task at hand and she mistimed a jump between buildings. Her left foot slipped on some wet roof tiles as she landed, sending her off balance. Before starting to slide down the roof, she dug her fingers into the pitted stone and quickly righted herself. She took a moment to catch her breath and check her route before proceeding again with a bit more caution.

This part of the city was not one she'd visited often. The buildings were all comprised of shops and small taverns on the ground floor with apartments above the businesses. Many of the well-tended homes belonged to shop-owners but some were privately owned. It had taken Munroe two days of staking out Unity Hall to find who she wanted and another cautious night to find his home.

Counting the windows she bypassed the first three and focused on the last two on the top floor. At this hour all of the windows were closed and there wasn't a flicker of a candle or lantern from within. She could hear someone snoring loudly and a few creaks as the building settled but nothing else. The street below was deserted but just in case she kept low and spread her weight evenly across the roof.

There was no way of knowing if the building was being watched. The Guardians, the Watch, someone from one of the Families, or even one of Akosh's followers might be lurking in the shadows. It was possible that any one of them could be following her. Munroe realised it was a little paranoid, but she needed to stay invisible until she found Akosh.

Part of her realised that if she hadn't been working alone this would have been a lot easier. She could have posted several lookouts to warn her if she was being followed, or if anyone was showing too much interest in the building. With a team behind her she could have just walked up to the back door and picked the lock. Instead she'd spent the first hour taking a strangled route across the city to lose any watchers and the next hour dressed in black crawling across rooftops.

After securing her rope in two places she slowly eased herself down the sloping roof on her stomach. The window was latched on the inside but with a quick flick and twist with a narrow metal file it sprang open. Munroe eased open the window and slid into the room.

She lay there for a while in the dark, listening while she kept her breathing shallow. The apartment was silent and still. Taking a small risk she embraced the Source and waited to see if that disturbed anyone nearby. As her senses were enhanced the black shadows became brown and then grey smoky outlines that revealed objects in the room.

She was lying on the floor in the kitchen between two tall rows of cupboards. Something grainy was digging into the bare flesh of her back where her shirt had lifted up. After sitting up slowly she inspected the floor and realised she'd been lying in a small pile of spilled rice. To her left she could see a silent procession of tiny black ants going in and out of a food cupboard. Leaving them to their midnight robbery she scuttled across the floor, trying to be as stealthy as them.

Through the open doorway she spied the main room and an array of furniture. It was empty of people and in total darkness but her enhanced vision allowed her to move through the room without walking into anything. The door on the far side was closed and, putting an ear against the wood, she could hear someone inside the bedroom. Their breathing was deep and even, suggesting they were asleep, which actually disappointed her a little.

Munroe eased open the door and peered inside. To her surprise she found Guardian Fray sitting up in bed, staring at her with a sword resting across his bare chest. Even though it had been almost ten years since they'd seen one another it only took him a few seconds to recognise her.

"Munroe?" he said with a hint of uncertainty. He knew all about her past and was probably wondering why she'd broken into his home in the middle of the night dressed all in black. Maybe he thought she was an assassin and had come to kill him.

"I'm just here to talk," she offered, stepping back from the door to show she wasn't armed.

"Then why break in? Why didn't you come to see me at Unity Hall?"

Munroe sighed. "Lots of reasons. It's a long story." She didn't want to tell him. She wasn't even sure if she could say it out loud, but he needed to know some of it otherwise he wouldn't help her. "I'll wait for you out here," she said, gesturing at the main room.

She sat down at his table with her back against the wall,

giving her an ideal view of the whole apartment. A few minutes later he emerged, dressed in a loose pair of trousers and a long shirt that was half open. Fray confidently moved about his apartment without any light, suggesting he'd been living here for a while, but when he reached for his flint and tinder she cleared her throat.

"Don't."

"Why not?"

"I don't want anyone to know I'm here."

Fray sat down at the table but she noticed he rested a sword against his chair. Channelling a trickle of power from the Source into the palm of her hand, Munroe summoned a small mage light. The pale blue globe provided enough illumination for them to see each other clearly, but she didn't think it would show through the curtains.

For a while neither of them said anything and just looked at each other. She wondered what Fray saw when he stared at her. Could he see the rage and the agony roiling inside her? Had it marked her physically in some way? Or was there a more subtle tell behind her eyes?

After a little while Munroe picked out a few details she'd initially missed. Fray was leaner than she remembered. Much of the fat of youth had been leached away from his face and it was now weather-beaten from years spent working outdoors. But then he'd been a Guardian for years now, walking the streets and solving crimes in Perizzi. There was also a touch of white in his hair over the ears and in his beard. It was behind his eyes where she saw the biggest change. He regarded her with caution and some suspicion. The city, the people that he dealt with every day in his difficult job, plus the sword at his elbow, spoke of lessons learned the hard way.

"I'm not here for you. I just want to talk," she said again, trying to reassure him. Fray gestured for her to continue, but she noticed he didn't relax.

"Then talk."

"Have you heard about what happened at the Red Tower?" she asked.

"I have," said Fray, and for a second she saw a familiar rage behind his eyes before he got it under control. He'd been a regular visitor to the school. After almost a decade the Grey Council were still no closer to unravelling his rare Talent. It gave him a unique edge that other Guardians lacked, but only a few people knew that he had any magic. It was safer that way, now more than ever, when anyone connected to magic had been vilified. In return for letting them study his ability the Grey Council had been teaching him about magic and the Source. "Did many survive?" he asked.

Munroe felt as if something had grabbed her heart and started squeezing. She couldn't breathe. She couldn't speak. She opened her mouth to answer him but no words emerged. When his hand closed over hers she jumped back in surprise, her chair hitting the wall. Her heart was pounding and her hands were shaking, but slowly she realised there was no immediate danger. Taking a few deep breaths she sat down again and he gave her time to regain her composure. When she felt calm enough to talk Munroe tried to keep her voice even but it still wavered from time to time as the wound was still raw.

"All of the students survived, but many lives were lost buying them time to escape. My son, my mother and my husband, Choss, are gone."

She looked up in time to see the horror sweep across Fray's face. He'd not been a large part of her old life, but towards the end he'd known her and Choss. Together, the three of them had freed the city of Perizzi of an inhuman terror she still barely understood.

"Oh Munroe," he whispered, reaching for her hand again and then stopping halfway across the table. She grabbed hold of him, squeezing his hand tight to stop herself drifting away on memories again. She needed to stay in the present with him. She needed to do something to stop the pain.

"I need a favour."

"Anything. Name it," he said without hesitation which made her smile. It was good to see his years as a Guardian had not stripped him of compassion.

"I need to speak to them," she said, fishing out a piece of cloth, an ivory comb and a small wooden horse from her pocket. The cloth was part of a shirt Choss had left at the cabin. The comb was her mother's and the horse one of Sam's favourite toys. It was fairly crude, and only vaguely resembled a horse, but Choss had been so proud of his handiwork. Sam had loved it because he'd seen it taking shape over the course of several weeks.

Munroe squeezed Fray's hand and he winced but didn't complain. It was so hard to focus. She just wanted to lie down and wallow in her memories. To live with them in the past for ever. A warm bath, a razor, a bottle of whisky. She'd considered it many times over the last few weeks. But not yet. She needed to know they were at peace. She needed to find the one responsible and snap her neck. Then she could rest.

"Can you do it? Can you summon them?" she asked.

Fray's unique Talent was that he could summon and talk to spirits of the dead.

No one really knew what happened after you died. There were a dozen religions and hundreds of stories, but all of it came down to belief. Spirits were something else entirely.

She'd once heard Fray explain it to the Grey Council during one of his visits. Some mediums claimed to be able to talk to anyone who had died in all of history. Fray made no such claims and thought most mediums were frauds as not every person became a spirit.

A spirit that stayed behind was a piece of the person they had been in life. They were always tethered to items and those they had known in life. Usually they only stayed for a short time before fading away and moving on to whatever came next. And there was always a reason for them to linger. A sudden and unexpected death could cause it, but often that wasn't enough. A strong will in life wasn't always enough. It was often about unfinished business. A task, or a message that bound them to this realm of flesh until the message was delivered. After that there was no need to hold on so tightly and they moved on.

"I've never tried it with someone I knew well in life," said Fray, but she thought he was lying. His father had died many years ago, and more recently his mentor, Byrne, had been killed in unusual circumstances. If Munroe had his power it would've been one of the first things she'd tried.

"I need to speak to them," she said, sliding the items across the table. She released Fray's other hand and saw the red marks she'd left on his skin but he didn't notice. His gaze had turned inwards as he stared at the piece of cloth, the comb and the toy. One of his hands hovered over the items but then he pulled back.

"Are you sure?" he asked. "If I do this, then you need to understand it won't be them. Not really. It's just a shadow that's been left behind."

"I need to see them."

Fray said nothing for a while and just studied her. She met his gaze hoping he could see her resolve and that she'd buried her fear. There was nothing more she wanted in the world than to see her family one last time. However, the thought of it also terrified her worse than anything in the world. What if they blamed her? What if their spirits showed the wounds of their death? What if Sam cried and called out for her? What if they weren't at peace?

"I need to see them," she said, more to herself than Fray, but he took it as her final decision. He picked up the piece of Choss's shirt and wrapped it around the comb and Sam's toy, while she braced herself for the worst.

Even though Munroe knew the theory she couldn't follow what Fray was doing. She sensed him opening himself to the Source, but not in a way she recognised. Like flexing a muscle a Talent came instinctively and without thought. One moment his eyes were green and the next they were the colour of old pennies.

Fray gripped the cloth tightly in one hand while he stared past her, through the wall, at something beyond the city. His brow furrowed and he made a small beckoning gesture with his free hand, perhaps inviting the spirit to visit them. Her heart was racing again, her palms sweaty and she forced herself to breathe steadily. Tears ran down her face but she couldn't stop them.

His frown deepened and Fray held the material tightly in both hands. As he focused Munroe sensed a wave of energy passing through her. She could feel him drawing more heavily from the Source as well. With a gasp he released the cloth and sat back, his eyes quickly changing colour back to normal.

"What happened?"

"There's nothing there," said Fray, breathing hard from his efforts. "I can't find them."

"What does that mean?" asked Munroe.

"Are you sure ...?" said Fray, trailing off before starting again. "Are you sure they're gone?"

She'd heard the stories about a group of people chasing Choss and her son to the pier. She'd seen the blood. "I'm sure."

"Then their spirits haven't lingered."

"What are you saying?" asked Munroe. She knew what it meant but didn't accept it. They were gone. Truly gone. "How can that be?" she asked, but Fray had no answers. Why hadn't they stayed? How could Choss not have any unfinished business with her? And Sam was only a small boy. He still had his whole life in front of him. Her mother had made peace with her death, so part of Munroe could understand her absence, but not the others. Why had they left her alone?

Without really thinking about what she was doing Munroe gathered up the belongings and walked back to the kitchen. She snuffed out the mage light and embraced the Source, using her enhanced senses to navigate around the apartment.

"Wait. Don't go. Stay and talk," said Fray, but she ignored him and reached out of the window for her rope.

"Tell no one I've been here. It's not safe," she said, glancing over her shoulder at Fray. She should have just left without stopping, for in that final look she saw his anguish. His pain was a fraction of her own but it was enough to make her sob. Choking it down she scrambled out of the window and across the roof as hot tears ran down her cheeks.

The next morning, a short time after dawn, Munroe was watching a different quiet street in another part of the city. She waited until the old Drassi Swordsmaster had left the building and disappeared around the corner before approaching the front door. Moving slowly, but making no attempt to be stealthy, she opened the door and entered the building.

The dance studio was empty at this hour, making it easy to search the building quickly. In a small room at the back she found the wooden floor had been covered with thin padded mats which its sole occupant was gathering up and stacking in one corner.

"Did you forget something?" asked Tammy, without looking around.

"Not really," said Munroe. Tammy dropped the mats and spun around in surprise, reaching for her sword until she saw who it was. Munroe felt a small pang of satisfaction at having caught the Guardian unawares. It was only fair after she'd sneaked up on Munroe a few times.

"You could have visited me at Unity Hall. So why are you here?" asked the big Guardian.

"Because I have a proposition for you, and the fewer people who know about it, the better."

"I'm listening," said Tammy, before going back to stacking up the mats.

"Balfruss told me you're going after Akosh and her network. But I also know there are some things you can't do. That's why you let me question Grell."

Tammy paused in what she was doing and Munroe could guess what she was thinking. That letting her question a suspect had been a mistake. But she wasn't responsible for his death. If she hadn't pressed him for an answer they wouldn't have Akosh's name. Her actions had also forced Guardian Brook to reveal her true loyalty. On balance Munroe thought the good outweighed the bad.

"It was a mistake," said Tammy.

"Perhaps," conceded Munroe but she would not be deterred. "But I'm not a Guardian and I'm better suited to direct action. Give me a name and a target. I'll find them and bring them back to you for questioning. You know I can do that. Let me help you destroy Akosh's network."

Tammy finished stacking the mats and then sat down on top, wiping a towel over her bare arms and face. "I'm tempted. I really am, but I also heard what happened to your family."

"Then you understand that I won't give up. That nothing will stop me."

"The problem is, I also saw what happened to Grell," said Tammy, taking off her vest and pulling on a clean shirt.

"I don't understand," said Munroe.

"The coroner showed me his body. Brook's stab wound was what killed Grell, but he also had a lot of other injuries. Bruises, broken ribs, burns on his leg."

"So what?" said Munroe, refusing to apologise. "He would have lived."

"I'm not saying what you did was wrong. I needed information and I knew what could happen when I sent you in there."

"Then what's the problem?"

Tammy pulled on her Guardian jacket and stood up. "You are." The famous uniform had never been a problem before but now it had become a barrier between them. "Grell wasn't a threat to you, but he managed to get under your skin, didn't he?"

"I didn't kill him."

"No, you didn't, but that was before someone murdered your family."

"Be very careful," said Munroe, feeling her temper flare.

"Grell was an idiot. What happens if I send you after someone much smarter? How long will it take them to bait you?"

The pulsing of the Source at the edge of Munroe's perception was getting louder. It was making it difficult to hear what was being said. "I can handle it," she said through gritted teeth.

"What if they tell you the person you're going after was there at the Red Tower that day? What if they saw your family die?" whispered Tammy. "What if they were responsible?"

Flames erupted along both of Munroe's arms, engulfing her in blue fire. It wreathed her head and shoulders like a crown, dancing around her features without burning her hair or clothes. She was aware of the heat but it didn't touch her. More of it spread out across her body, running down her arms to pool in the palms of her upraised hands until it spilled over to the ground like water. The fire sizzled as it struck the wooden floor, instantly turning it black and then it began to smoulder and burn.

Tammy grabbed one of the mats and tried to smother the fire before it spread. Smoke rose from the burning floor and Munroe squeezed her eyes shut, closing herself off from everything in the world. With a huge wrench of effort she swallowed her anger and cut herself off from the Source. The flames across her body faded and then vanished, leaving only a few patches of fire that Tammy quickly dealt with. They opened the windows and when the smoke had cleared Munroe saw two large charred circles on the floor.

"You're too close to this," said Tammy, once she'd finished coughing. "That burning rage you're carrying inside will eat away at you. It also makes you vulnerable."

"Are you going to help me or not?" she asked and Tammy just shook her head. Whatever burgeoning friendship had been growing between them died in that instant. She wasn't even Tammy any more. There was only the mantle of the Khevassar. "I'll do it by myself," said Munroe.

"You can't, and you know it. That's why you're here. You need some time away, to clear your head and to mourn."

"What would you know about it?" said Munroe.

"Nothing," said Tammy, refusing to make eye contact. "We'll bring them to justice and destroy her network."

Munroe laughed bitterly. "You do that. Seek out your vaunted justice, but I suggest you do one thing for me."

"What's that?" asked Tammy.

"Stay out of my way. I don't care about her network. I just want Akosh. And when I find her, I won't stop until she's dead."

Munroe didn't want to hurt Tammy, but she would if it was necessary. Part of her expected a lecture or sermon about the price of revenge, but Tammy offered neither. Perhaps she knew a thing or two about it after all.

As she walked away from the building Munroe grudgingly admitted that Tammy had been right about one thing. She already knew she couldn't do this alone. If those working within the confines of the law couldn't help then perhaps it was time to cross over to the other side of the street.

CHAPTER 10

Bettina, clerk and agent for Regent Choilan, left her meeting with an expression that bordered on a smile. As she passed one of the many expensive mirrors in the palace she paused and made sure no one was around before looking at her reflection.

The high-necked grey dress was long on the arms and it trailed on the floor covering up as much exposed flesh as possible. She pulled up the collar to make sure it concealed the marks on her neck before continuing to her office at a brusque pace.

The reason for her near-smile was that the inevitable had finally happened. The blubbery Minister of Trade, who had been so close to having his neck on the chopping block, had died. The method didn't really matter to her, the headsman or in this case in bed with his mistress, only the facts. He was gone and his widow, Daria, had been appointed to the position in his place, something that the Regent had been considering for a while. The mistress would vanish and everything would go back to normal. Order would resume, just as she liked it. Everything neat and tidy.

The Minister had been erratic, driven by passions and was

someone who could change his mind overnight. Bettina would order scribes to produce a document only to be told days later by the Minister that it wasn't needed any more. She didn't care personally about the scribes, but she hated the time and money that had been wasted producing something that later wasn't needed. Daria was much more stable, described by some people as cold and aloof, but Bettina recognised something familiar in the other woman. Order. Structure. Stability.

That almost-smile tugged at the corners of her mouth until she reached her office door and saw that it was slightly ajar. With a snarl she burst through the door. She was ready to berate whoever had the impertinence to barge in without invitation until she saw the room's occupant. Her usual icy mask returned and she made a low and deep bow, as was fitting for the Regent's first wife.

Despite being fairly tall herself, Selina towered over her. Few people made her feel small and vulnerable. Part of her favourite pastime was doing that to others, but for some reason Selina intimidated her. Her dealings with the Regent's other wives were far less uncomfortable. Bettina often had trouble getting a word in while they babbled on about nothing of value. Not so with Selina. Silence was her favourite weapon.

"My Lady, how may I be of service?" she asked.

Selina moved from where she'd been standing at the window to take a seat in front of the desk. Bettina waited until she'd sat down before sinking into her chair. Even with the desk between them, and in the familiar surroundings of her own office, the other woman's stillness bothered her. Perhaps it was her frown. Bettina liked a good scowl but Selina's seemed to be carved from granite. Even when she spoke her eyebrows barely lifted.

"Do you have an update on the agents I requested?" she asked.

The Regent had asked Bettina to investigate the eight missing agents and so far her contacts had found seven. All murdered. They had been killed in a variety of mundane ways, and Bettina believed the eighth would be discovered in a similar state. In fact she would insist that the last body was found. She couldn't stand loose ends. One of the Regent's agents was looking into who was responsible for the murders, but so far there were no suspects. Right now the why was unimportant. The agents needed to be replaced.

Bettina had supplied Selina with a list of potential replacements and a few days ago she'd chosen eight from the list.

"I've had responses from seven of the eight names you requested, my Lady. I'm just waiting on the last. I believe he's called Doggett." All the names were fake, of course. It came with the job of going unnoticed. "I'm confident I'll hear from him soon."

"I hope you do," said Selina.

Bettina couldn't interpret her meaning as her expression and tone of voice gave nothing away. She didn't know if it was a threat and promise that something unpleasant would happen to her if she didn't hear back from Doggett, or if Selina genuinely wanted a response. Instead of replying she said nothing.

After a while the silence in the room rang in her ears and she couldn't help fidgeting in her chair.

"You're obviously busy," said Selina, gesturing at the neat stack of notebooks laid out in a precise grid on the desk. Each was exactly equidistant from the other and only those of the same colour were touching one another. "I await your response."

"My Lady," said Bettina, standing up and bowing again as the first wife left her office. She carefully closed the door and resumed her seat, resting her forehead on the cool surface of her desk. It helped to calm the buzzing of her thoughts and bring them under control again. A dull ache was forming behind her right eye which she hoped wouldn't develop. She desperately needed to vent her frustration at such an invasion of privacy. The imbalance it caused inside ate away at her. Those she subjugated tonight would receive additional lashes until she was at peace.

There was a brief knock on the door and she barely had time to compose herself before an unremarkable man entered without invitation. Bettina dug her nails into her right thigh until the pain made her discomfort begin to ease.

"Who are you?" she asked in a calm voice, making a note of the man's plain, worn clothing. He didn't look familiar and everything about him, from his clothes to his features, was ordinary and easily forgettable. Bettina was good at remembering names and faces but had no recollection of meeting him before which she found more than a little troubling.

"I'm Doggett," said the man. "My answer is yes. I'll take the job."

Bettina held up one finger, opened the relevant notebook and crossed off his name. Despite the irregularity of entering her office without being asked at least this was one list she could mark as finished. The completeness of it eased the muscles in her shoulders and she stopped gouging her leg.

"Good. You will receive instructions in three days' time."

Doggett gave her a peculiar two-fingered wave and went out of the door, leaving her alone amid tidy shelves of notebooks.

Doggett left the palace via one of the many entrances disguised as a servant. The guards on duty had seen him coming and going for the last week so they paid no attention to him. They probably didn't even remember his face. Being easily forgotten had been something he'd initially hated, until as a young boy he'd realised its potential. He was invisible.

Small thefts and petty crimes were blamed on others who were inevitably punished in his place, until he escalated to his first murder. At that point not even his ability to blend into a crowd could hide him, but thankfully someone else found him before the authorities.

Since then he'd always been working behind the scenes, often alongside people in power who didn't even know he was there, watching, listening and reporting back to others. He was a faceless and nameless man.

Once he was a few streets away from the palace he dumped the empty package he was carrying, stripped out of his servant's coat, pulled off the palace stars he'd pinned on and tossed everything at a beggar. He picked up his own coat and weapons from where he'd stashed them, feeling more comfortable with their familiar weight and smell.

Doggett strolled through the city, apparently at ease, often stopping to chat with merchants and peruse their wares. In truth he was checking to see if anyone was following him. After an hour of wandering he set off for his real destination. Such precautions were necessary, now more than ever before with the stakes so high. Taking a winding route he finally arrived at the tailor's shop.

The owner wasn't part of the organisation but they had an arrangement. She looked towards the ceiling and held up one finger. Doggett thanked her and went upstairs, knocking loudly on the door before pushing it open. At such meetings it was always better to announce your arrival than end up with a dagger in the eye for barging in.

The new Minister of Trade, Daria, who had taken over from her late husband, sat waiting for him sipping tea opposite someone he knew very well. He knelt before her and reached out to take her hand reverentially.

"Mother," he whispered, waiting until Akosh touched him on the back of the head before standing up. "I didn't expect to see you here."

Akosh grimaced and it hurt him to see her so upset. "My plans were forced to change after the incident at the orphanage."

"I've investigated what happened. No one knows who the new teacher works for but I'll keep digging. For now we have someone following him."

She waved it away. "It doesn't matter. We have more important things to discuss."

Daria bowed in her seat. "What are your orders, Mother?"

"I know you've been very patient, Daria, and I appreciate your sacrifice," said Akosh. Doggett had not expected the Minister of Trade to last more than a month with such an enthusiastic and energetic mistress, but he'd proven them all wrong. Somehow he'd managed to last six months before his heart had finally given out. All the while Daria had played the role of the disrespected wife. She had originally married him out of affection, but any such feelings were secondary to their Mother. Judging from Daria's cool expression Doggett guessed that she and her husband had grown apart over the years.

Daria shrugged, confirming his suspicion. "He wasn't the man I married."

"Even so, I expect you to continue to play the role of the wounded widow in public," Akosh reminded her.

"Yes, Mother," said Daria sincerely and Doggett knew her obedience was absolute. "What do you want me to do about the Regent?"

"Nothing. He knows you're thankful for the appointment and he'll expect absolute loyalty in return. That will suffice for now. Don't try to wheedle your way into his good graces. Just do your job as well as possible and that will be enough. Your late husband was incompetent, so your best will be a hundred times better and that will get you noticed."

Doggett knew that Regent Choilan was a cunning man to have clawed his way to the top, driving off or killing others competing for the throne. Now that he was there he intended to hold on for as long as possible. Everyone knew blood relatives of their late King were grooming a young boy to take the throne, but that was at least fifteen years away.

That meant for now the Regent had time to create a legacy for himself and his family, but only if he managed to hold onto the throne. The Regent was cautious and it took him a long time to trust someone. It took even longer for them to become a part of his inner circle, like Bettina. Most thought she was simply another scribe but Doggett knew she was one of a handful in the palace that had other duties. Daria would have to be patient as well and slowly earn his trust.

"In time the Regent will come to rely on you," Akosh was saying. "Yerskania might be the trading heart of the west, but they don't have adequate protection against Garvey and his ilk. Soon the Regent will have an incomparable force on hand and I can foresee a time when he may want to loan them to others."

One of the many things Doggett loved about Mother was her ability to think long-term. She did her best to guide events to benefit certain parties, but the appearance of Garvey was something no one had expected. Nevertheless, she had found a way to turn it to their advantage.

"What about the Regent's wives?" asked Daria.

"Let Doggett and the others worry about them," said Akosh. "Only the Regent's first wife has any brains and we'll keep her busy. Focus on your duties for the time being."

"As you wish, Mother," said Daria, bowing again before leaving via the backstairs. He heard her leave the shop via the back door and knew she would take adequate precautions to ensure she wasn't followed before returning home.

"What are your orders for me, Mother?"

Akosh gestured at the chair opposite and he sat down, perched on the edge, alert and attentive. "Have they found all of the bodies?"

"No, Mother. I still have the last one in a secure location."

"Make sure it's discovered and someone is found to take the blame. Perhaps a foreign agent? Someone from Yerskania? There are too many of them in the city for my liking."

As far as Doggett knew there were nine agents but he would bet the true number was probably double that. Ever since the war Queen Morganse had been paying very close attention to her northern neighbours.

"I have someone in mind," said Doggett, who had been planning this for some time. "Do you need anything else?"

"Make yourself indispensable to the Regent's first wife. She's always dabbled in spycraft, but give her some real meat. Dig up a few foreign agents and send them her way. I want to see how far she's willing to go. That will determine our next move."

"Yes, Mother."

"Is there something you wish to tell me?" she asked.

"I've been told the Regent and one of his aides, Bettina, are looking into the disappearance of Habreel."

Akosh grimaced. "I was expecting this. Drip feed them clues about him being in an asylum. That should be enough, but keep an eye on them."

"Yes, Mother." A crease marred her forehead and his concern made him speak out of turn. "Are you well, Mother?"

Akosh raised an eyebrow at the question but she let it go. "No, but I will be, once we secure the Regent's loyalty and then, one day, Zecorria."

Doggett smiled as he pictured what that meant in the future. A nation of their own. One where every church in every village, town and city was devoted to Akosh. It would be glorious.

CHAPTER 11

Tianne had been putting off her decision for nearly two weeks. But she'd finally found the right moment to tell Wren that she was leaving.

Until today there had been one crisis after another and Tianne didn't want her friend to feel like she was being abandoned at the worst time. It had started with the arrival of the injured girl and her mother who'd been attacked by raiders. Despite Wren's efforts the girl's wounds had been severe and if not for the expert skills of Master Yettle, she would have died. Tianne knew that Wren had tried her best to heal the girl but from what Danoph had told her it had made little real difference. Healing was one of the most difficult skills to master as a mage and few of the students were making any real progress.

There had been some damage to the girl's head, bleeding inside the skull, and Master Yettle had prepared everyone for the worst. There was a chance the girl would wake up and have some impairment, but it was also possible she'd just die in her sleep. Tianne had stayed busy throughout the day, organising other students, making sure classes ran on time and doing her best to pretend that nothing was amiss. Everyone was enormously relieved when the girl woke up and was completely healed.

The next crisis after that was one of their newly caught sheep had gone missing. A thorough search the following day revealed half of its carcass wedged up a tree. They found a few other bits not far away, mostly bones and gristle, that showed signs of being gnawed on by something with big teeth. Something living in the nearby hills, probably a mountain lion, had come down in search of a tasty meal. That meant another busy day was spent building an enclosure for the sheep at night. Now they assigned two armed shepherds during the day to keep watch, especially when their sheep were taken out of the valley to graze. Thanks to the help of their dowser, Helsa, they'd also increased the size of their flock to almost sixty. The number of sheep left to roam wild was an uncomfortable reminder of the number of settlements that had been abandoned in the district.

Another problem with their busy and growing community was the amount of work they faced every day. Unfortunately Wren had difficulty delegating tasks and trusting people, but as her closest friends she often turned to Tianne and Danoph for support. She was happy to help and it was nice to feel needed, but with every day that passed Tianne began to realise that her future lay elsewhere.

When they'd fled the Red Tower it had all happened so quickly. With little time to think about her future Tianne had chosen to stay with her friends. Now, after a few weeks of relative peace, and having spent some time alone with her thoughts, Tianne realised she'd just taken the easiest road. Staying here would be safe. This community was Wren's dream, and, as much as Tianne admired what she was trying to achieve, it didn't feel like home. When news came from the north she knew it was what she had been waiting for.

Finally there had been no major incidents for three days. Tianne realised it was time to tell the others before something else happened that would force her to make another delay.

She'd just finished milking their surly goat when she spotted Wren showing the latest new arrivals around the valley. The man and his wife were refugees who'd fled their remote home in the hills after being attacked by raiders. They'd survived the war ten years ago and all of its horrors, only to be driven out of their cabin by bandits. Grief clung to both of them like a heavy cloak and Tianne knew they'd lost friends and family. The woman was at least six months pregnant and both were exhausted.

Tianne caught Wren coming out of the dormitory, nearly walking into her. "I need to talk to you and Danoph. It's important."

"Can it wait?" asked Wren. "I'm supposed to be helping Leonie with something."

Part of her was tempted to say yes but she firmly shook her head. It wouldn't take much to lose her nerve and find a reason to delay her decision again. Following other people and letting them dictate everything was safe and comforting, but it was also a trap, one that she'd been living in for too long.

Wren seemed to understand the seriousness as she collected Danoph and together the three of them walked over to the sheep enclosure. Until a few days ago the hardy animals had been surviving by themselves on the hills. Their coats had been matted and filthy, but otherwise they'd adapted to their new environment. Now they seemed completely at ease among people being herded around. Perhaps it was simply easier for them as well to follow and be part of the crowd rather than choosing for themselves.

"I'm leaving," said Tianne, knowing that she needed to say it up front.

For a while Wren was stunned into silence but Danoph didn't seem surprised. Perhaps he'd already seen this moment in a dream.

"Where are you going?" asked Wren, surprising Tianne by not asking why she was leaving.

"Home. To Zecorria." Tianne hadn't thought of it as home in a long time, mostly because she'd planned never to return. Her early memories were a pitted landscape of embarrassment, bullying and constantly feeling like an outsider. None of that mattered now. She was needed.

The Regent had declared an amnesty for all Zecorran mages. Garvey and his band of followers were a serious threat and the Regent needed loyal patriots willing to return home and defend their country from harm. Soldiers and steel were not enough. He needed magic. He needed her.

King Matthias had put out a similar call to arms at the start of the war and Battlemages from around the world had answered, including Eloise and Balfruss. This time there wasn't a war, not yet anyway, but she would return home with her head held high to defend her country. None of those who'd scorned or mocked her before she went to the Red Tower were worthy.

"Are you sure about this?" asked Wren.

"I am." Tianne hoped she sounded confident and the others didn't notice the quiver in her voice. "What you're building here is important and it will make a difference to the lives of many people in Shael. I can do that for my people in Zecorria. They need me."

"You are needed here," said Wren, turning to Danoph, perhaps in the hope that he would agree but he remained silent and watchful. "I need you," added Wren.

"You asked us to decide if this was the right place for us.

Perhaps one day it will be my home as well, but not yet." Tianne felt safe in the community, surrounded by the others, because there was no risk. The community didn't lack for excitement, but here she was accepted by everyone for who and what she was. Returning to Zecorria meant it would be challenging, but it was also possible she could change how people viewed mages. Someone had poisoned people in every country against magic and it had led to the destruction of the Red Tower. The amnesty gave her the perfect opportunity to show people that not all mages were like Garvey and that in the right hands magic was a good thing.

"I think it's a mistake," said Wren, stubbornly folding her arms.

"I can help people, Wren. The Red Tower was always so mysterious and far away. It scared people because they didn't know what went on inside the school. Every day in this community we use magic in plain sight. There's no need to hide. It can be the same in Zecorria. I can show people that magic is amazing and you can do so much with it."

"You have no idea what the Regent really wants. It might be a trap."

"A trap?" said Tianne, raising an eyebrow.

"He was the first to bring in a national ban on Seekers. It also appeared that he was going to ban all mages until Garvey went on his rampage. This amnesty could just be a ploy to imprison and kill all mages."

"I don't think that's likely."

"But you don't know," insisted Wren. "You know nothing about the man."

"I know enough," insisted Tianne.

"You're being naïve."

Tianne had expected Wren to try and talk her out of it, not to attack her personally. Instead of replying she turned to Danoph. "Nothing to say? Or have you already seen this moment?"

Danoph shook his head. "I've had no visions about this, but you both make valid points."

"Thank you," said Wren, naturally thinking he sided with her.

"I said both," said Danoph, holding a finger to forestall further interruption. He waited until Wren had closed her mouth before he continued. "You asked us to decide for ourselves about remaining part of this community and Tianne had chosen. You need to respect her choice. However, some caution would also be wise. This request could be both noble and sinister in nature."

It was the most Tianne had ever heard him say. Danoph seemed exhausted by the effort as he fell silent and seemed to fade into the background again.

"I will be careful," she promised, making a small concession to Wren. "Wouldn't you go back to Drassia if the leaders there made a similar request?"

Wren shook her head. "No, I wouldn't, it's very different in my country. Magic has no place there, but Danoph is right. I may not like it, but I will honour your decision. But that doesn't mean I'm not going to miss you."

"Oh Wren," said Tianne, gathering her friend into a hug.

"I'm just worried about your safety. I didn't mean to offend you," she apologised.

"I'm going to be in the capital. I'll be surrounded by thousands of people," said Tianne, trying to recall her memories of Herakion. It had been a long time since she'd visited the city. "I'm more worried about you, out here on the borderlands with the raiders. They've been getting closer and their attacks more violent."

Wren shared a look with Danoph who just shrugged. Tianne wasn't sure if there was something going on between the two of them, but they did seem to be developing their own silent language.

"We will deal with the raiders," promised Wren.

Wren was always planning ahead. Tianne hoped she could come and visit the community in the future. By then it would probably have grown into a city with Wren at the reins. In her own way, Wren had been preparing for a challenge like this her entire life. Instead of running a Drassi clothing empire like her mother had wanted, she was creating something that was completely her own from scratch. She was living her dream. It was time for Tianne to chase hers.

Tianne turned to Danoph. "Take care of her."

"I will, for as long as I am able," he promised, which would've sounded peculiar coming from anyone else.

After that there wasn't much else to say. Tianne packed her bag and the following morning everyone gathered to say their farewells. Although the community couldn't really spare it, she was given a horse for the long journey north. The saddlebags were bulging with provisions and Tianne also received a coin purse from Master Yettle.

"Keep it," he said, when she tried to give it back. "Show them what it means to be a real student of the Red Tower."

There were lots more hugs and a few tears but then she was out of excuses. Tianne felt terrified that she was making the worst decision of her life, but it was too late to turn back. Part of her wanted to say she'd changed her mind and that it was all a mistake. She knew the others would smile and accept it, allowing her to fall back into the comfortable rut. It was the thought of getting stuck in that trap again that spurred her on.

When the Grey Council had asked her to choose, Wren had forged her own path. Now it was Tianne's turn to find her place in the world. With her stomach churning and with sweaty palms she mounted up, gave everyone a last wave and rode away from the community towards Zecorria.

It was time to go home.

CHAPTER 12

Using her set of master keys, Tammy opened the locks to the remote cell block and out of habit locked the door behind her. There was only one prisoner on the corridor but she didn't trust him. That was why she had two armed members of the Watch guarding him at all hours despite his willingness to cooperate. Even though he was locked in an isolated cell, under Unity Hall populated by several dozen Guardians at all times, Torran Habreel was still a dangerous man.

Inside his head were the answers to a hundred questions she'd yet to ask and, if she wasn't careful, someone might break open his skull to stop them spilling out.

There was also the possibility that Brook was not the only Guardian loyal to Akosh. She'd asked Faulk to make subtle enquiries into the religious background of all Guardians, but it was delicate work that couldn't be rushed. Most of her people claimed to follow the Maker, the Blessed Mother, or the Lady of Light. But it wouldn't be difficult to lie about it in order to blend in. Yerskania was famed for being open and inclusive and that included the Guardians. No one was banned from joining the Guardians because they followed a particular faith. It was all down to skill and merit. But Tammy needed to be able to trust her own people with the difficult tasks ahead. Suspicion was a natural part of the job, but as the new Khevassar she needed a solid foundation or else it would all topple over like a house of cards. She really hoped Faulk didn't find anything in his search.

As the silence of the isolated cell block enveloped her, a vicious part of Tammy considered putting Habreel in with other prisoners. During his time as a Guardian he must have arrested dozens, if not hundreds, of criminals and they rarely missed an opportunity to get some payback. But she needed him alive and able to speak. So for now he would have to stay in isolation for his own protection. He would eventually be punished for his crimes according to the law and justice would be served. Vengeance was something she had to leave behind but sometimes it was a struggle. The memory of what she had done to Don Lowell was still fresh.

By the time she'd unlocked his cell door Habreel was standing at the head of his bed, waiting for her. It felt as if this was a cell inspection with her playing the role of a prison guard.

Despite having few personal belongings, the rigid organisation of Habreel's cell spoke of a military background and logical mind. The bed was perfectly made with the sheets pulled tight. The small folding table they'd allowed him had a neat pile of papers and two pens. Four books, the largest at the bottom and the smallest on top, formed a pyramid in the middle of the table. Even the comb they'd given him sat precisely in the centre of his shelf.

Habreel had fallen back into old ways after turning up injured and lost on her doorstep a few weeks earlier. Led astray by a manipulating being of indeterminate power and betrayed by his closest friend, he'd been left with nothing. No pride. No home. No faith. The only thing he claimed was a stack of crimes and a growing list of murders with his name attached to each corpse.

They'd healed his physical wounds and given him the barest minimum of space and belongings. In return he was doing his best to be helpful in her investigation of Akosh, but eventually the time would come when he'd outlive his usefulness. Tammy would relish the day when it happened as he would be put on trial for his crimes. Soon after he'd have an appointment with the headsman and then an unmarked grave.

Others might have found the isolation, silence and incarceration difficult to tolerate, but Habreel seemed to have flourished, or at least partially recuperated. The Old Man had told her as a Guardian he'd been outspoken, verbose and possessing a dry wit. He wasn't exactly chatty, but was a long way from the trembling shell of a man she'd first locked in a cell. With so little that was in his control, and so few choices available, he seemed to be enjoying the relinquishment of power.

"Ah, Khevassar, nice to see you," he said, watching as she moved the chair from the corridor into the doorway of his cell. Habreel waited until she was seated before sitting down again on his bed. It was little more than a stone shelf with a thin straw pallet, but he'd not complained. "I've made some more notes on what I can remember about Akosh and her movements. Hopefully there's something in there that's of use to you."

"I'll take a look at them later, but I have a few more questions in the meantime."

"Go ahead," he said, eager to please. If they had met in other circumstances she would have found his sycophantic nature very creepy. Knowing all that she did Tammy struggled to hide her revulsion at being so close to him.

"Did Akosh ever mention anything about orphanages in Zecorria to you? Either in the capital or anywhere else."

Habreel took his time and went through his memories with his eyes closed. "No, she never mentioned it," he said, coming back to the present. "Has something happened?"

Like most of the questions he asked, Tammy ignored it. He couldn't help asking. It was natural that he was curious about the outside world, and he'd also been a Guardian for a long time. But she was here to question him, not pander to his needs.

Habreel sat up suddenly. "Actually, she did say something unusual, towards the end."

"Tell me."

"She sent one of her people, a mage, to Gorheaton. He was going to pose as a Seeker and I heard he killed everyone, then blew himself up. Of course, the blame fell on the Red Tower. When I asked her about it she claimed to have taken him in as an orphan and raised him." Habreel shook his head. "She was clearly confused as they were almost the same age."

Tammy said nothing, thinking back to her meeting the previous night with Balfruss. It had been slightly less tense than his last visit and he'd been happy to share information. A reliable source had told Balfruss that Akosh sponsored six orphanages in the capital city of Zecorria and she had several others abroad. He'd also told her that his suspicions about her being more than human had been confirmed, although Balfruss had been unwilling to clarify what that meant. All Tammy knew at this point was that Akosh was extremely dangerous and that her people were not to try and apprehend her directly.

So if everything Balfruss had told her was true then it was possible that Akosh had raised the mage who went to Gorheaton. At the very least she had been the patron of an orphanage where the boy was fostered and taught to worship her above all others.

"Didn't you say something about Dannel being an orphan?" said Tammy.

For the first time in days Habreel's façade cracked and sorrow rushed in to fill the void. "Akosh claimed he was one of hers as well. What does it mean? What's really going on?"

His old instincts were kicking in. Habreel was probably starting to wonder if there was more to Akosh than a confused mind.

"She's far more dangerous than you realise," said Tammy, telling him little more than he already knew.

"You need to be careful," warned Habreel. Tammy was ready to laugh at his warning until she saw the look on his face. "I saw Dannel's utter devotion to Akosh. Whatever she really is, a mage or something else, to them she's their entire world. He called her Mother and would do anything for her, without hesitation. Even if that meant killing other people, or even himself, like that poor fool in Gorheaton. Make sure you can trust the people you're working with, otherwise the walls might have ears."

Tammy took the notes he'd made and left the cell without another word. If Akosh's people were as devoted as he claimed, then Guardian Faulk's investigation was even more critical than she realised. Guardian Brook had shown how far they were willing to go. She couldn't afford to lose any more of her people. Only the best were selected to join the Guardians and it took several years before novices were trusted to investigate crimes by themselves. Not for the first time Tammy wondered how the Old Man had managed to do the job for all these years. It had only been a few weeks and she was already exhausted.

As she made her way back to the office, Tammy considered her next move. She had people watching the orphanages but it wasn't enough. All her information about Akosh came from other people. Tammy needed to speak to one of Akosh's followers. Finding one would be a challenge and getting them to talk would be even more difficult.

As soon as she walked into the outer office Rummpoe came out from behind her desk, which made Tammy pause. It was like seeing a turtle crawl out of its shell and go for a stroll.

"I couldn't stop him," apologised Rummpoe. "He went straight in and said he'd wait in your office."

"It's all right," said Tammy, soothing the flustered young woman. "I'll take care of it."

There were few people who would be bold enough to enter her office without her invitation. As she'd expected, Guardian Yedda was waiting for her inside. He was lounging in one of the chairs in front of her desk, one of the Old Man's private journals open in his lap, although he wasn't even reading it. He just wanted to show her how little regard he had for her office and authority over him as Khevassar.

Ignoring the slight Tammy closed the door and sat down behind her desk. She stared at him and waited. He tried not to be unnerved by her stillness and silence, but as the moment stretched on he began to squirm. Tammy glanced at the shelves and then expectantly at the book in his lap. Only when he'd returned the journal to its rightful place and sat down did she relent.

"Report," she said, her voice calm and without inflection.

"I investigated the Minister's death, as you requested." Yedda pulled out a notepad and flicked through a few pages.

The Minister of Trade had been in his late fifties and severely overweight. He'd been widowed five years ago after being married for thirty-one years. Six months ago he met a woman in her early thirties and they were married after just two months. Last week the Minister died and his wife inherited his wealth, much to the displeasure of his three children who were of a similar age to their new stepmother.

Normally the Guardians wouldn't get involved in such a case, but because he was one of the Queen's Ministers it was standard practice. The Old Man had insisted on it to make sure no one was trying to rig the system.

"And?" asked Tammy.

"It seems fairly mundane."

Tammy folded her arms and leaned forward across the desk. "What was the official cause of death? Have you spoken to the coroner? Or the wife? Or the children? How about his assistants in the Ministry?" With each question Yedda flinched as if he'd been stung. He probably thought this sort of case was beneath him, or perhaps he'd believed that the Old Man would choose him as Khevassar. "If you're unable to investigate this case, I can give you something more suitable to your skills. I believe we've been asked to find a missing dog. It has three legs and one eye."

Yedda ground his teeth and she raised one eyebrow, daring him to say something. Just one word. She could demote him to the Watch or give him all of the worst cases for the rest of his life if he continued to disrespect her position. Yedda knew this too and was slowly beginning to realise that he worked for her.

"I've spoken to several people in his office," he said eventually in a strained voice. "And someone called Tovin seems the favourite to take over as Minister. I've asked for background on him, to make sure he wasn't responsible."

"The Queen will personally see your report on this case," said Tammy, which caught Yedda's attention. She decided to switch tactics and appeal to his vast ego instead. Yedda had deep familial roots in the city's aristocracy and as such he was the epitome of entitlement. He probably spent as much time as she did at the palace attending the Queen's functions alongside other wealthy families. As such he was constantly scrambling to impress the Queen for the benefit of his family.

The truth was that Morganse probably wouldn't ask and would be happy with a verbal report about the Minister, but it had made him sit up straight. "I chose you because the Queen cares about her Ministers and I want it done right. But if you'd rather—"

"No, no. I'll see to it immediately."

"Are you sure?"

"Absolutely," he said, suddenly a lot more interested in the case than when he'd entered the room. "I should go. Thank you, Khevassar," he said, rushing from her office. He was in such a hurry he left her door open and Rummpoe stuck her head around the frame.

"If he does that again, you've my permission to have him dragged to a cell," said Tammy.

Rummpoe gave her a wry smile that turned vicious when she realised Tammy wasn't joking. A short time later there was a knock on the door and another Guardian came into her office. She'd sent for him and judging by his expression he was puzzled about her request.

"You wanted to see me?" said Guardian Fray.

"Come in, Fray. Close the door." Even though he'd been in the job a few years she still thought of him as new to the uniform. It came from spending so much time away from Perizzi. But Fray had been tested by the fire several times, in Voechenka before she went there, and since then here in the capital city. The scars of his trials showed in the furrows on his forehead. At some point he'd grown a beard and there were a few patches of white. "I need your help with something. It's a little unusual."

"Whatever you need, Khevassar," he said. It still felt a little peculiar hearing people call her that. At the moment it still made her think of the Old Man.

"We're investigating someone very dangerous. She's a cult leader who holds enormous sway over her people. As a result they're all closemouthed and getting any of them to talk is proving difficult." She was skirting around some of the details, as he really didn't need to know and it would only make things more complicated. She wondered how often the Old Man had done this before her. Parcelling out information on a need-to-know basis. Almost daily she had a new level of appreciation for what he'd achieved.

"Everything I know about this cult leader is second-hand. I need to find some answers for myself."

"I can question the suspect if you want," he offered.

"It's a bit more complicated than that," she said, taking a deep breath. "We can't find any of her people, but I know where one of them is currently, and she's not going anywhere."

"Then why did you ask for me?" asked Fray.

"Because she's dead. I need you to summon the spirit of Guardian Brook so I can interrogate her."

CHAPTER 13

Vargus thought the meeting was never going to end. As ever, it could have finished in half the time but there was a lot of posturing, mostly from the youngest who were keen to prove their right to be at the table. Several were showing off in an attempt to appear wise. Perhaps they hoped to impress some of their elders and curry favour, but it was having the opposite effect. Nethun rolled his eyes more than once and Vargus turned his face away to hide a smirk.

Those at the far end of the table beside him, Nethun, the Blessed Mother, the Lady of Light, Winter and Summer said very little. Winter drummed her ice-blue fingernails on the table and the rest seemed equally bored.

They offered neither praise nor criticism to the speaker as either could be misinterpreted. As ever Elwei said nothing unless called upon but he was always watching and listening. More than once Vargus saw his head turn slightly to regard the empty chair at the far end of the long banqueting table. He'd also noticed Akosh's absence.

At one point Elwei turned his head so that Vargus could just make out one eye regarding him from the depths of the old pilgrim's headscarf. There was a slight shifting, a raised eyebrow perhaps but a question nonetheless, and Vargus just nodded. He'd noticed her absence too and was looking into it.

There was one figure at the table who most people were doing their best to ignore. Kai. He unsettled a lot of the youngest, and many others to be fair.

In this nowhere place, between moments in time, only the table and chairs were real. The rest was an illusion and it had not escaped Vargus's notice that all of them chose to appear as human. Here, they were the best version of themselves, but even in the real world their human bodies were merely vessels for their true nature. Kai appeared as a handsome, blond-haired man with a warm smile and kind face. Out of them all his mask was the biggest lie. If Vargus focused on an individual he could look through the illusion and see their true nature, but there were some things he would prefer not to see again.

A relic from another time, when the mortal races had been more brutal and bloodthirsty, Kai represented an era most would rather forget. But he had endured, although most of their brethren had no idea how he had survived for this long. Vargus knew for certain there were no more temples devoted to the Watcher and the number of followers, who remained faithful Eaters, dwindled every year. Nevertheless, he was slowly building up his power again, within the rule thankfully, or so it seemed. Vargus was doing his best to keep an eye on Kai, just in case.

Normally generous and warm, Summer was starting to look annoyed at the waffling from the far end of the table. Even the Blessed Mother, the epitome of patience, was getting irritated.

"That's enough," said Nethun, cutting off one of the youngsters who was prattling on about the importance of cow's milk and the sanctity of the land. The short, rotund man, who had something to do with cattle and farming, was about to protest when someone beside him yanked firmly on his arm. He took the hint and sat down, doing his best to hide his disappointment.

"Is there any important business to discuss?" asked Nethun, raking the far end of the table with a glare that few would meet. Those who had been planning to make a speech similar to their rotund friend suddenly changed their mind, shaking their heads. "Then we're done," said the sailor, dismissing everyone with a wave of his meaty hands.

Most vanished immediately, going back to whatever they had been doing before being summoned, but a few stayed behind to talk. Most of their kind didn't meet in person very often, and never more than two or three at a time. Everyone at the table was so different from one another that even a small group coming together would raise a few eyebrows and cause ripples they wanted to avoid. They had learned that mistake from their elders. Some of the earliest meetings had been in person and there were still mentions of them in a few history books that Vargus was waiting to fall out of print.

Further down the hall he saw Nethun speaking with a couple of the new faces, doing his best to appear genuinely interested. After a while the others began to disperse until only he and the old sailor remained.

"Finally," huffed Nethun, moving to stand in front of one of the large fireplaces. "I thought they were never going to leave. I won't be sad to see some of them disappear into the Void. They talk too much."

"Well, no one could accuse you of that, old friend," said Vargus, earning himself a brief grin.

"You said it was important."

"You couldn't come in person?"

Nethun shook his head. "No. I'm at sea." As Lord of the

Oceans and patron of all sailors, as well as the Vorga, Nethun spent at least two thirds of his time on the sea or under it.

"Did you notice who was absent?" asked Vargus.

"Akosh. I assume there's a reason she ignored the summons?"

"Yes, there is. Given what I recently learned from Balfruss, her absence was expected."

Nethun's expression turned grim. "Tell me."

"In part, she's to blame for the fall of the Red Tower. Her people have been posing as Seekers, killing children, stirring up trouble and shifting all the blame to the mages," said Vargus. He went on to tell Nethun about how she had been using her followers, seeded across the west, to foster greater fear and hatred of magic and those born with it.

The one rule passed down by the Maker was that their kind was not supposed to directly interfere in the affairs of mortals. They could not change the natural course of events, even if in doing so it would save many lives and avert a disaster. Despite their power and knowledge, it was not their place to right their wrongs.

On a few rare occasions they had bent the rule, but it was always done with the full knowledge of everyone and never by an individual working alone.

The Lord of Light, now all but forgotten by the mortals, had tried it. His attempt to grow his power base had led a large portion of the world into a pointless war where thousands of mortals had died. Akosh's plan appeared more subtle and beyond causing chaos her goal was currently a mystery. But because of her actions the fear that had always been bubbling under against mages had come to the surface.

Whole communities had torn themselves apart searching for the perceived threat of a Seeker in their midst. On top of that children had been killed or driven out of their villages and anyone openly using magic was either shunned or attacked. Others had blown themselves up after being egged on by Akosh's supporters, killing themselves and many others. Chaos might be all she wanted, in order to build her power for the future with more orphanages, but Vargus suspected there was something else as well.

"Does the Grey Council know it was Akosh? Do they know what she really is?"

"Balfruss does. He attempted to summon me," said Vargus with a lopsided grin but it quickly faded as he thought about those who had died defending the Red Tower from the mob. "Do you remember Munroe?"

Nethun shook his head. "I don't keep track of those who aren't mine. They come and go so quickly, and in this age there are so many humans."

"A few years ago she defeated the Flesh Mage in Perizzi. She also helped close the rift."

"Ah. Her, I remember. Small woman, powerful mage. Swears like one of my sailors."

"That's the one. Her family was murdered when the Red Tower fell. She's going after Akosh and wants revenge."

Nethun sucked his teeth. "As much as I want to, and I suspect you do as well, we cannot get involved. It will play out how it must."

"Sadly, I agree," said Vargus, although he'd hoped Nethun might say something else. "But Akosh has broken the rule and must be dealt with."

"Vargus, we've known each other for a long, long time. So, I know you wouldn't have come to me with this unless you'd already taken steps."

"I've tried to find her, but had no luck. I think she's in Zecorria or Yerskania, but can't be sure. So, I'm doing what I can to draw her out of hiding."

"How?" asked Nethun, raising an eyebrow.

"Apparently, someone is about to persuade all of her orphanages in Rojenne and Perizzi to change patrons to the Maker or similar. The rest in Yerskania will follow suit after that. It won't stop her right now, but it will create ripples and a problem for her in the future."

"Thinking long term as ever," said Nethun. "Do you think it will be enough to draw her out?"

Vargus shrugged. "If I start enough fires then eventually she'll show up in person to try and put them out. Either that, or she'll hide in one place surrounded by her own people."

"What if she runs?"

"She won't," said Vargus. "She's invested decades in her orphanages. She won't just walk away from all of that now and try to start afresh."

"What else?"

"The Guardians are looking into her network in Perizzi. Munroe is searching for her, and I suspect various foreign agents will be keen to disrupt her plans in the north. She has enemies all over and doesn't realise it."

"The noose tightens all around." Nethun stared intently into the fireplace for a long time in silence. He seemed to be working up to saying something and finally asked, "Does He know what's happening?"

"Who?" said Vargus, but the old sailor just gave him a look.

"Is He even aware?"

Vargus trusted Nethun with more of his secrets than any of the others, but he'd always wondered how much he already knew. It seemed as if Nethun was a lot better informed than he realised about the location of the Maker and what had happened to him. It was one of Vargus's best kept secrets, or so he thought.

It was Vargus's turn to play for time but eventually he answered. "No. He's not aware. He's not ready."

"Then it still falls to us," said Nethun. "You'll take care of Akosh when you find her?"

"I will."

"Good. I'd say the others will learn from this, but it wasn't too long ago we were forced to deal with that idiot lantern boy."

"Just like him, she won't escape either. In a few years' time, she too will be nothing more than a distant memory," promised Vargus.

CHAPTER 14

Wren felt Tianne's absence from the first day after she'd left the community.

It wasn't just that she didn't have someone besides Danoph to whom she could turn for assistance. Laila, who had arrived a few weeks ago, had mastered control of her magic but beyond that her skills were rudimentary. As such she was happy to take on extra work to make up for her lack of progress. Wren suspected part of the reason for Laila's enthusiasm stemmed from her fear of magic, but with luck that would fade in time.

The biggest reason Wren missed Tianne was because she was her friend. She'd been kind and supportive since her first day at the Red Tower. It was Tianne who had met her at the gates and shown her around the school. At times it was difficult to believe that had only been a few months ago.

But there was another reason she missed her friend. Tianne was a gossip. Tianne couldn't help it and thankfully she wasn't malicious. She didn't delight in revealing secrets to the wrong person in order to cause pain and suffering. It was just that she liked to know what was going on at all times in the life of every person around her. That detailed insight had proven valuable to Wren in running the community, but now it was gone. In turn this had forced her to try something new and uncomfortable.

Wren had to go out and talk to other people on purpose.

She was starting to get better at it. There were still some long and awkward silences, but gradually people were starting to open up to her. Tianne had made it look effortless, but it was new and difficult for Wren. Most often she found herself walking up to people only for her mind to go blank. Then she would lurk and try to think of something to say while they stared at her expectantly.

There was no easy way to start a conversation and she couldn't just ask them about their problems with no preamble. In Drassia such conversations took place behind closed doors in private, but here it was different. People spoke about their problems openly and seemed to have no modesty. At times groups of people, women in particular, would sit around discussing very private and intimate subjects that made her want to leave the room in a hurry. There were some things she wanted to find out for herself. Not have them described to her in graphic detail by a gaggle of middle-aged women.

Nevertheless, Wren needed to know what people were struggling with in order to try and help them, but asking them outright was difficult and made her feel uneasy. At times she also thought it had more to do with expectation than reality. When people looked at her they saw first a Drassi which came with its own preconceptions, most of which were wrong. Recently Wren's attempts at small talk, to ease into a conversation, began with her telling them a fact about Drassia. The reality often surprised them which she hoped was a good thing. At the very least it made it easy to then ask them about something more personal.

From her attempts at talking to people she'd found out that

most of the community were happy and staying busy seemed to be key. Thankfully there was plenty of work to be done so no one was ever sitting around idle. Food was a constantly pressing concern, but with the old wood they were never short of raw material for building. Using an old technique she'd learned as a girl, Wren taught the others how to create charcoal which they were stockpiling for winter and to sell.

Their flock of sheep had grown significantly in the last month thanks to their dowser. When the villages in the area had been abandoned they must have turned all of their animals loose. They'd been living wild ever since and the survivors were hardy beasts that were still docile enough to be rounded up.

Although some found it unpleasant, Wren understood the necessity of having a butcher in their midst. They needed the meat and she made sure her unease didn't show on her face when she visited the abattoir.

After discussing it with Danoph she'd finally relented and allowed one of the scavenger parties to retrieve a wagon. Two of their older residents, who had once been farmers, were then able to pose as tinkers and sell charcoal, wool and other assorted items they salvaged to nearby settlements. At her insistence at least two students with a solid control of their magic accompanied the wagon at all times. As well as providing protection for the wagon, it gave her a constant picture of the surrounding area and the concerns of other communities. The most pressing of which seemed to be the roving bands of raiders.

Villagers said that a couple of months before the fall of the Red Tower one or two groups of robbers had started attacking caravans travelling from Yerskania into Shael. For an unknown reason these groups had started working together and since then the problem had grown significantly worse. Wren suspected someone with a bit of insight and a sharper mind had seen the potential of uniting them. More ground to cover and less infighting meant greater profit for everyone. If she were a robber baron that's what she would have done.

So far her people had not come into direct contact with any of them, but it was only a matter of time. Wren had seen first-hand what they did to innocent people without provocation. The girl and her mother had physically recovered from their ordeal, thanks to the skills of Master Yettle, but they were both severely traumatised. Everyone they knew had been slaughtered in front of them, including the girl's father. It was their wagon the scavenger party retrieved, including many of their belongings, but even they had provided little in the way of comfort.

Taking the initiative Wren had started sending out small patrols of her people to watch the surrounding area for the raiders. Several wagon trains passed through the western province every week, taking goods further east into Shael to the capital city and then back out again. All of them were now heavily guarded, either by groups of mercenaries or Drassi warriors, but that didn't stop them from being attacked with varying success. For the time being the raiders seemed content with remote villages in the region which had far less in the way of protection.

Between discreet patrols, groups going out to scavenge from deserted villages and her roaming tinker wagon, Wren could keep an eye on most of the area.

Today it was her turn to ride with one of the patrols. The area was unfamiliar to Wren but with each trip she began to piece together a map of the landscape in her mind. She, Danoph and one other student, named Rue, passed close to a village south of their community called Sour Crown. There were nearly two hundred people living there and none of them were warriors.

They had a few retired soldiers who had made an attempt at building defences, but they seemed crude to her. The wall wouldn't keep out an angry goat, never mind a murderous band of raiders. At least they had people keeping watch which was why she was lying on the ground, looking at the village from a distance.

For once there was a minor technique that she had been able to master. Embracing the Source naturally enhanced all of the senses, but, with a little bit of focus and direction, she could amplify her voice or even sharpen her eyesight.

"What can you see?" asked Danoph, who hadn't yet managed to master long-sight, as they were calling it.

With the Source pulsing in her veins it was difficult for Wren to lay still and not run around to expend the energy, but she forced herself to ignore the impulse.

"A knee-high wall. A woman dozing at her guard post and people working in the fields."

"Then they're safe."

"They're complacent," said Wren. "Perhaps they think the raiders won't come here."

"It's been a couple of weeks since an attack," said Danoph.

"That's what worries me. They should be more concerned, not less." Wren was convinced this lull was merely the calm before the storm. Perhaps the raiders were gathering their forces to attack a merchant train as most of their recent assaults had been repelled. Or they were going to target a larger settlement like Sour Crown.

"Do you want to stay a while longer, or move on?" asked Danoph.

Before she had a chance to reply Rue answered with a wheezy snore from where she lay asleep on the ground.

"We could stay a while and talk," said Wren.

An uncomfortable silence stretched out between them with Wren fidgeting and Danoph utterly still.

"If you want to ask me something you don't need to dance around it," said Danoph.

"Thank the Blessed Mother. I find myself struggling to talk to people. When did it become so difficult?"

Danoph grinned. "It's different, now that you're the leader."

"I'm not the leader," said Wren. "There was no election. I left and people followed. Then they just kept asking me questions and I try my best to answer. I'd be happy to let someone else take over."

In a rare display of affection Danoph laid a hand on her arm, halting her babble. "We followed you because the Grey Council offered us three choices, none of which we found appealing. You created a fourth choice because your path lay elsewhere. It's your community, Wren, and people see you differently now."

"Well, I wish they didn't," she said, lowering her voice. She didn't want Rue to wake up and hear her complaining. "I'm still the same person I was before."

"I know that and they will, too. Just give them time."

"How is it you're so wise for someone so young?" asked Wren with a smile. "Sometimes, in the echo of your words, I hear my grandfather."

Before Danoph had a chance to answer she heard riders approaching fast. A group of five or six horses were moving up the road and they didn't sound very far away. The three of them weren't visible from the village but Wren didn't want to take any chances. She elbowed Rue awake and together the three of them moved further back from the road, hiding in a copse of trees.

They'd barely settled, lying face down on the ground, when six rough-looking armed men and women thundered past, heading straight for Sour Crown. The village guard continued to doze at her post until the raiders were nearly on top of her. Something finally woke her up and at the sight of the riders she yanked on a heavy rope connected to a bell overhead.

The dull clanging seemed to slow everything down. The people in the nearby fields started running for home, picking up tools as they came, but it was clear the raiders would beat them to the village. Others came flooding out of their homes wielding a mix of kitchen knives, spears and several curved Yerskani cleavers.

Wren drew power from the Source and channelled it into her senses, focusing on her eyes and ears until she could see and hear clearly from their hiding place.

The raiders seemed content to wait until everyone had assembled, saying nothing until those from the fields had joined the swelling crowd.

"You're not welcome here," said a stocky man at the front of the crowd. Wren thought he had the build of a blacksmith and might be their Speaker, or whatever it was called here in Shael. The crowd cheered at their leader's words, hefting weapons and waving them in what was supposed to be a threatening manner.

"What's happening?" asked Danoph, squinting at the scene. Wren described what she could see.

One of the raiders, a tall man from Seveldrom with a narrow face and carrot-red hair, raised a hand and slowly the noise from the crowd subsided. "Are you in charge?" he said, directing his question at the blacksmith.

"I'm the Warden," he said, and Wren assumed that meant the leader of a community in Shael. "This is our village."

"It was," said the raider. "Your homes, your fields, your food and all of your lives now belong to Boros. You're alive only because Boros allows it."

The Warden rolled up his sleeves and spat on the ground.

"You might be good at using that," he said, gesturing at the raider's sword, "but there's only six of you and more than a hundred of us. Sour Crown doesn't belong to you."

Carrot-top grinned down at the blacksmith and nonchalantly raised one hand. There was a faint whistling sound and then the woman to the left of the Warden toppled over, a dagger buried in her throat. Blood gushed from the wound, quickly staining the front of her dress while those around her vainly tried to stem the bleeding. The raiders watched dispassionately as the woman gasped her last breath and then fell silent. The mood of the crowd began to change. Instead of anger Wren saw fear sweeping through the villagers. They weren't warriors. Death wasn't something they were trained to cope with or used to seeing up close. With a simple wave of his hand, and lacking any compassion, the raider had killed one of their neighbours. Someone chosen at random they had probably known for years. Dead. Just like that. And any one of them could be next if they resisted.

"We need to leave," said Rue, whispering in Wren's ear. "They're going to kill each other."

"No, they're not," said Wren, scrambling to her feet. "Stay here, out of sight." Before the others had a chance to protest she started jogging towards the village.

Growing up in Drassia she'd heard many stories about this sort of encounter and power play. Those who wore the mask of service often spoke about their work when they retired. Wren had heard countless tales of war, mercenaries, raiders and robber barons. Their ilk had existed for a long time and they were often people unwilling to work hard for anything. In their mind it was far easier to take from others because they were seen as weak.

"You're all dead," said the Warden. "We're not afraid of

you." The crowd behind him started to surge forward. There was a brief surge of bravado but none of the villagers actually attacked. None of them wanted to be the next to die.

The raider was still unusually calm. "You said you're in charge. That means you get to convince everyone to do as you say. You see, if I don't return with all of my limbs attached, Boros will come here in person."

"That name doesn't scare me."

"It should," said the raider. "Boros won't come back here alone. Every single one of us will come here and burn this village to the ground. We'll slaughter you all. Every man, woman and child. Then we'll salt the fields as an example to others who don't listen."

More of the bravado dribbled out of the crowd as the words sank in. There were no children in the gathered crowd, but Wren saw parents glance towards their houses where little faces watched in the windows.

A burning pain began to build up in Wren's side from her prolonged run, but she persisted, keeping the raiders between her and the villagers so they didn't see her coming. So far it seemed as if no one in the crowd had noticed her approach. All their attention was focused on the raiders.

"You're bluffing," said the Warden. "I bet there are only a dozen of you at most."

The raider shrugged his shoulders. "Ask your neighbours."

Wren knew he wasn't bluffing and so did the Warden. Several remote communities in the area had been abandoned in the last few months because of an increased number of attacks. The Queen of Shael and her small army couldn't help this far out. The war had decimated the country and its population, leaving a shattered ruin in its wake. Progress had been made but it was slow.

The communities this far west were on their own and had believed there was strength in numbers. As she came closer to Sour Crown, Wren could see the skeletons of several new houses being built at the far end of the main street. It still wasn't enough.

"What do you want?" asked the Warden, biting off each word.

"A tithe of food and drink every month."

The haggling would soon begin as the villagers tried to pretend this was merely another merchant driving a hard bargain and not a robbery. The pain in her side had increased but Wren pressed on, taking deep breaths to try and dispel it.

A few villagers had noticed her now but they probably didn't know what to make of her. One Drassi girl, running up behind the raiders. They probably thought she was lost or confused in the head.

The Warden and the raider were arguing over terms but even their conversation trailed off when they noticed more and more people staring. One of the raiders turned in his saddle and stared at Wren. She stopped in the middle of the road which had been churned up into a sludgy field of mud. There were no paved roads out here. It was another reminder that she was a long way from home. A long way from anywhere.

"Are you lost, girl?" asked one of the raiders. When Wren didn't respond and barely seemed to blink he turned his back on her. "I think she's a bit soft in the head," he called out to the others who ignored her. Their leader, however, was still looking at her, which is when she raised one hand and made a flicking gesture as if brushing dirt off her sleeve.

Five of the six raiders were flung sideways out of their saddles into the muddy road. They had all moved in unison and Wren hadn't broken eye contact with their leader. Despite what he'd just witnessed the raider tried to draw his sword. Wren just shook her head, ever so slightly, and balled her hand up into a tight fist. The raider gave out a yell of surprise as his sword shattered into half a dozen pieces. The five raiders on the ground tried to get up but she focused more power and kept them pinned down, preventing them from reaching for their weapons or standing up.

"What do you want?" asked the raider.

"Leave and never return. This village is not for you."

Much to Wren's surprise the raider laughed and shook his head. "If I go back without a tithe, Boros will kill me."

"Then don't go back," said Wren. "Whether there's six, or a hundred like you, it won't make a difference. You can't win." To drive her point home, she increased the pressure on the five raiders on the ground. Two were lying face down and she pressed them deeper into the mud until they began to choke. Wren had to work hard to keep her face impassive as images of what had happened to Brunwal flashed through her mind. She eased up a little, allowing them to gulp fresh air into their lungs.

"This isn't the only village that we're visiting. You can't be everywhere at once," said the raider. This time it was Wren's turn to smile.

"Who said I was alone?" she asked, glancing at the uneven land around her which was dotted with lots of hiding places. The raider suddenly sat up straight in his saddle, alert to danger. The day was perfectly still and yet a gentle wind suddenly sprang up. Most peculiar of all was that it seemed to be completely focused on the raider. It buffeted his hair and then just as quickly it was gone. Wren sensed a delicate rush as Rue channelled power from the Source.

She took a few steps back and released the other raiders who slowly climbed to their feet. They glared at her and she saw a few touching their weapons but none of them tried to attack.

"Let's go," said their leader, still looking around for her friends. "This isn't over," he promised Wren, turning his horse and riding away. The others pulled themselves into their saddles and followed after him. The village and the tithe were completely forgotten, for now at least. She waited until they were out of sight before turning back to the gathered crowd.

As she'd expected they were still hostile and holding their weapons with intent. To them, she was potentially more dangerous than the raiders. She hoped for a little gratitude but even that seemed to be too much to ask.

"We don't want your kind around here," said the Warden, making a shooing gesture.

Any thoughts about trying to reason with them evaporated and Wren simply turned and walked away.

She'd saved their lives, for the time being at least, but to them that didn't matter.

The raiders might not return to this village but she knew it wasn't over. At least she had a name. Boros. He would be angry and perhaps take it out on the raiders for returning empty-handed, but she wasn't responsible for their actions. Wren knew she could have killed all six of them, but after what had happened with Brunwal she never wanted to kill again. As Master Yettle had instructed she'd let herself feel all of it. Dwelling on what she had done still brought tears to her eyes, but she forced herself to relive it.

By the time she'd walked back to the others her face was dry and she felt composed.

"It's not over," said Danoph, and she wondered if he'd seen something in a dream about this village.

"I know. We need to find out more about their leader, Boros."

"Can't we just leave him alone?" asked Rue. "He doesn't know where we live."

"We can't just leave these people to his mercy."

"Why not?" asked Rue. "They hate us and would kill us if they had a chance."

Wren couldn't argue with that but she also knew their fear came from ignorance. Despite all that had been done to her and the others at the Red Tower, she couldn't stand idle while innocents were attacked and murdered. She would have to show them through her actions that not all mages were evil or destructive. Not every mage was like Garvey and his followers.

"So far we've not run into the raiders, but it's only a matter of time. We can't just ignore them," said Wren, knowing that a conflict was inevitable.

All she'd wanted to do was build a safe community for people like her, whereas Boros wanted his own kingdom. Perhaps it had been naïve to think she could achieve that without a fight. So be it.

Wren turned her mind towards what she needed to do next. The first step was to know her enemy. Once she understood him she could drive him and the other raiders out of the area for ever.

CHAPTER 15

Feeling as if she were stepping back in time, Munroe found herself sneaking through the streets of Perizzi. Ever since she'd returned to the city she'd done her best to go unnoticed by people from her old life. She wasn't that person any more and wanted nothing to do with them and their criminal dealings. Now she was trying to avoid them and the Guardians as well.

If any of the Guardians, or a member of the Watch, recognised her then word might get back to Tammy. Munroe knew she was only doing her job, but right now she wanted to avoid the Khevassar. If she had any chance of succeeding, then the fewer people that knew she was still in the city the better. That meant a return to the quieter parts of the city, those off the beaten track, where the Families held sway.

Avoiding the prying eyes of former associates was proving to be a difficult challenge. She had hoped that after being away from the city for several years it would give her a degree of anonymity. After listening to a few conversations in bars Munroe realised stories of the Flesh Mage and his downfall were still popular. Although she wasn't mentioned by name Munroe didn't want to take any chances. Instead she decided to assume a role that was familiar. One that would attract attention in a different and predictable way.

The gambling den was not one she'd been to before but after studying the people waiting to go inside she knew it was a good place to start. The customers comprised mostly merchants and business owners, those with a little extra money to spare. Along with them came a gaggle of working men and women hoping to hook a wealthy trick on a good night. Wooden jackals kept everyone in line and Brass jackals kept watch. It was a fairly middle-of-the-road establishment where fortunes could be won, but losses were not severe enough to result in someone going hungry or losing the shirt off their back.

Wobbling slightly as she approached the front door Munroe smiled at the big doorman on the left and winked at the woman on the right. He merely raised an eyebrow while the woman said nothing and held open the door.

"I hope to see you later," slurred Munroe, waving at the woman as she stumbled inside.

As expected, the furnishings were bright and colourful, giving the illusion of wealth, but a second look showed her they were gaudy copies. The crystal lanterns overhead were made from coloured glass and the multi coloured carpet underfoot was worn thin in places and patched in others. There were a couple of paintings on the walls and a few exotic plants dotted around the room, but they, too, were fading and withered from lack of sunlight. Thirty years ago it might have been glamorous. Today it was merely sad and dilapidated.

Most of the people here didn't really care and wouldn't be able to tell the difference between the real thing and a forgery. Drinks were cheap and plentiful and the room was alive with the rattle of dice, cries of disappointment, cheers, laughter and faint background music coming from a tired old man on a fiddle.

Easing her way through the crowd Munroe went straight to the bar and ordered a couple of drinks, draining one quickly in two gulps. After giving the barman a little wave of thanks she shuffled to the first table and cheered on a Morrin woman doing rather well at cards. One or two people stared when she shouted a little too loudly, or touched strangers in a familiar way, but they dismissed her as a harmless drunk. A few of the working girls in the room were glaring but Munroe pretended not to notice. After a while, when they realised she wasn't there to steal their business, they also ignored her.

When the Morrin picked up a bad hand and lost half her money Munroe commiserated with her and drifted away to the next table. The hypnotic rattle of dice caught her attention and she decided to have a little fun. After watching a few throws, she put some money down and scooped up the dice.

"So I need three crowns, right?" she said to the croupier. The balding man gave her a thin smile of encouragement. The dice rattled across the table and three crowns landed. "This is fun!" said Munroe, scooping up her winnings.

Long before she'd travelled to the Red Tower to learn how to control her magic, Munroe had used her Talent in gambling dens like this one for many years. Back then she hadn't known it was magic and had thought of it only as a curse. The owners never liked to lose too much money and her innate ability to manipulate the odds, cooling off a natural winning streak, had been in high demand. Of course, much later she'd also discovered her ability to change someone's luck for the better, and do so much more with her Talent, if she focused.

Over the next twelve throws she continued to win at dice, adding more money each time until she had a healthy stack of chips in front of her. Others started to notice her streak and began betting on her to win. A pit boss approached the table, whispered in the croupier's ear, and the dice were switched out. Despite their precautions Munroe continued to win and the crowd around her table swelled in number again. After placing a rather large bet, and then somehow winning once more, she bought everyone a drink with the money.

The dice were switched again and suddenly she had three pit bosses and one of the Brass watching her, as well as several Wooden jackals who were scanning the crowd. They were looking for the con, thinking she was the distraction meant to keep their attention in one place while someone else stole their money. Of course there was no con, other than the fact that she was manipulating the odds with her magic.

"Let's make this one a big one," said Munroe to the people around her. "How about I bet the whole lot on one last throw?"

"I'm afraid you've reached the house limit," said the croupier, sweating under the intense glare of so many people. The crowd booed and swore at the croupier until the largest pit boss at his shoulder leaned over and whispered something in his ear. "However, we would like to offer you access to a special high-stakes game. It's very exclusive."

Munroe pretended to consider it, looking at those around her whose opinions were mixed. By now, despite only sipping at her drinks and spilling the rest, she was actually feeling a little fuzzy-headed. Part of her slurring wasn't an act and the lights did seem a bit too bright.

"That sounds like fun," she said, grinning at the croupier who heaved a sigh of relief. Someone collected up her chips while two large jackals escorted her out of the main room, down a short corridor and into a richly decorated waiting area. Munroe sank into one of the comfy chairs and dozed off for a short time before someone shook her by the shoulder.

"We're ready for you now," said one of the pit bosses, a broad

Seve woman with a nasty scar under her right eye. Her smile was probably intended to be friendly, but it only made her look more villainous.

Tottering along, using the wall to support her, Munroe walked down another corridor into a room at the end. It was gloomy and she ran into the chest of the large man waiting for her. When she turned around she saw there was nothing in the room except three very large jackals, all of whom loomed over her. All had battered faces and were wearing weighted leather gloves.

The pit boss stepped into the room, closed the door behind her and leaned against it, blocking the only way out. "How did you do it?" she asked.

"Annoying, isn't it," said Munroe, dropping the drunk act and grinning at the woman.

"Are you working alone or with a partner?" asked the pit boss, showing no surprise at Munroe's soberness.

"What do you care? Is it your money? Are you in charge?"

The pit boss scratched at the scar on her face, a nervous twitch, before shaking her head. "My employer is not someone to be trifled with. You can see what will happen if you don't tell me everything I want to know." She gestured at the three bruisers surrounding Munroe.

"Is he here? Can I talk to him?"

The pit boss winced and her patience seemed to run out. "Left arm," she said to someone over Munroe's shoulder. Without turning, Munroe waved a hand at the three jackals and all of them stumbled back, seizing their chests. Needles of pain were shooting through their chests and it would feel as if their hearts were about to burst. One fell onto his face and the other two stumbled to their knees, gasping for air.

"Is he here?" asked Munroe, producing a dagger from where

she'd hidden it inside her belt. The pit boss stared at her and then at the three wheezing jackals. She knew what Munroe was and how she'd done it. Munroe could smell the woman's fear. The pit boss winced when Munroe pressed the dagger against her throat hard enough to draw blood. "Last time. Is he here?"

"Yes."

"Show me," said Munroe, gesturing at the door behind her. "But lie to me and I'll do the same thing to you."

Even though it wasn't necessary, Munroe kept the dagger pressed against the back of the pit boss. It served as a reminder of what would happen if she tried anything. She followed the scarred woman down a long corridor and then up a narrow flight of stairs to an office where her boss was sitting behind his desk. He looked up in surprise at the pit boss, a question on his face until Munroe stepped out from behind the large woman.

It had been nearly a decade since she'd last seen the Butcher but in all that time he'd barely changed. Back then he'd been an interloper trying to claim territory from one of the other Families. Ten years on he was part of the establishment and had maintained his fearsome reputation.

He wasn't the biggest man she'd ever seen, but his black vest did show off thick arms that were covered with faded scars. An intricate black tattoo ran up his arm from his left wrist, across his chest and down to his right hand. His head had been freshly shaven and the gleam from the lantern reflected off its surface.

"The beard is new," said Munroe, casually sitting down in one of the chairs in front of his desk. He'd been clean-shaven last time but now had a goatee that was shot through with grey. "But the grey makes you look old. I'd shave it off."

The pit boss was at a loss, unsure of what to do or how much trouble she was in for bringing an armed intruder.

"Leave us," was all the Butcher said, dismissing her with a wave of his hand. She closed the door and he sat back in his chair, crossing his arms over his chest. As he did so the swirling tattoo on his forearms lined up, creating a more complex interwoven pattern.

"That's cute," she said, gesturing at his arms.

"What do you want, Munroe?" he asked. If he was afraid of her at all it didn't show.

"Information."

The Butcher raised an eyebrow. "About?"

"A woman named Akosh. I've gathered a few bits and pieces, but I need more. I want to know where she is."

"I see," said the Butcher, running a hand over his shaven head. He seemed to relax, shaking off whatever had been bothering him. Perhaps he'd thought her visit had been about something else. Right now it didn't matter.

"Can you find her?"

The Butcher got up from his desk, poured himself a glass of water and offered her one which she accepted. Munroe didn't think he would try to poison her but she waited for him to drink before sipping hers.

"Why come to me?" he asked instead of answering her question. "Why not speak to your old friend, Don Jarrow?"

"Because a favour from him would have serious strings attached. You need to understand, I'm not coming back into the business. I don't care about Perizzi or any of the Families. I just want you to find this woman."

The Butcher mulled it over and Munroe noticed he hadn't asked why she wanted to find Akosh. There were a number of rumours about where the Butcher had come from and who he used to be before carving out his own empire in the city, but Munroe didn't care. All of that was also part of her old life and she was not going back to it. The reason she'd chosen the Butcher was his reputation. As well as scaring many people in the underworld, he was known to have a network of contacts beyond the city.

Primarily they gathered information on rich targets coming to Perizzi for his grifters to swindle. Cons took time and patience to set up, which meant he had people dotted across the west, or at least in most of the main cities. If Akosh had a network of her own, via her cult, then it seemed feasible that the Butcher's people could find her.

If she'd gone back to Don Jarrow it would have created a number of ripples and she wanted to remain unnoticed. Finding Akosh not only relied on solid information, it was critical that she didn't see Munroe coming until it was too late. Until she was breathing down her neck.

"Can you do it?" she asked.

"Perhaps, but I want something in return."

Munroe cocked her head to one side. "I thought the stack of gold I won downstairs would be enough."

"We both know you cheated and used your magic."

"I'm not going to owe you a favour," said Munroe. "I won't have something like that hanging over my head."

"No, this is something I need right now."

Despite the circumstances Munroe was curious. "Which is?"

"Protection."

"From who?"

"That's the problem, I don't know. Someone killed Don Lowell and no one knows who did it or why."

Such a bold move was surely a play for his turf, but it was unusual that someone had not taken credit for it. It could be that they were waiting for something. Or it could merely be the start and the Butcher, or one of the other Dons, could be the next target.

"You want me to be your bodyguard?"

The Butcher's smile made Munroe uncomfortable. "No. I have people for that. I just need you to watch my back during a few important meetings. Just in case."

She didn't need to ask why. He could surround himself with a hundred of the best killers in the city. A mage could cut through them like a warm knife through butter.

"Deal," she said, offering her hand and he leaned forward to shake it.

"Akosh. Actually, I've heard the name before," said the Butcher, startling Munroe as she leaned back in her chair. "Don't get too excited. She's not here, but I've heard stories from the north."

"Where?"

"Zecorria. One of my people recently had an encounter with her at an orphanage in Herakion." Munroe twitched at the last word and the Butcher smiled. "Yes, I know about them. She has a few orphanages here in Perizzi, but the Guardians are watching those. She's not been seen in the city for a few months."

"Then she's in the north."

"Maybe, but she moves around a lot. You need to be patient."

Munroe ground her teeth and gripped the arms of her chair. She was beginning to hate that word. Balfruss had asked her to be patient as well. She'd given him a month and he'd not come any closer to finding Akosh. Her family, her world, was gone, and that demented bitch was still alive.

"She's cautious and insulated by her people," the Butcher was saying, noting her demeanour. "Finding one of them willing to talk is difficult. From what I've heard they're all zealots. So getting any reliable information to pin down her location is going to be tricky. I suspect you'll only get one chance. If you go blundering in then she could slip away. Once she knows you're after her, it will be a hundred times more difficult. But it's up to you," he said, putting the choice back in her hands.

Munroe knew he was right and that the Butcher represented her best chance at finding Akosh. She still hated it. The anger inside her was just simmering under the surface and at times she felt as if it were going to swallow her whole. Hate worse than any she'd ever felt burned her inside. Her veins were on fire and she needed to find a way to release the pain before it consumed her.

Slowly, bit by bit, as if she were choking down poison, Munroe pushed the rage down inside her. The Butcher said nothing, giving her time to regain her composure. Eventually she felt calm enough to speak.

"I will try to be patient," she muttered through clenched teeth.

It seemed as if Munroe had no choice. She would stay in the shadows for now, but when the time came there would be nowhere for Akosh to run. Nothing would stand in the way of her vengeance.

CHAPTER 16

This time when Akosh entered Bollgar's office she was pleased to see that for once he wasn't eating. He was still dressed in a loose food-smeared robe, this one a dingy blue, but all his attention was focused on the pristine ledger in front of him.

In a small notebook she watched him totting up a series of numbers with incredible speed before recording the final value into the ledger.

"Apologies, Mother," he said, gesturing at the seat opposite. "I just have a few numbers to check for the local businesses."

"Go ahead," she said. On her way into the building she'd nearly walked straight into a tall, impeccably dressed woman. She recognised her as the owner of the candle shop a few buildings down the street. Her business was one of several that he managed. Akosh knew they found Bollgar distasteful because of his slovenliness, but his accounting was beyond reproach, so they tolerated it. However, they preferred not to visit him in person unless absolutely necessary, as his office did have a certain pungent odour.

"Mistress Valine's candle shop is not performing," muttered Bollgar, feigning a sad smile while his eyes twinkled in delight. "With some reluctance she's accepted a new business partner who has generously paid off her debts. In return they will have a healthy stake in her shop. You should make a nice profit in the coming year, Mother."

She was pleased to hear that he was putting her money to good use, but right now she had more important matters to think about. Such as the possible repercussions from not attending the meeting with her brethren. Last time they had been discussing the problem of magic and Seekers where she had feigned ignorance along with the rest as to the cause. Now she was more deeply invested than ever and Habreel had escaped. It would've been foolish to underestimate some of the older ones, like Vargus and Nethun, and assume they remained unaware of her actions. For now it was safer to be cautious and remain hidden. Money was important but it was only valuable if she was still alive to put it to good use. Her new ally, whoever he was, had promised to keep an eye on her brethren in the meantime. Pavel, the former Guardian, had not made contact with her again, forcing her to assume his Master had no important developments to share.

"You said there was news from Perizzi," she reminded him. He added up one final column of numbers, recorded the result and carefully put the ledger to one side.

"Yes, Mother."

"I've heard some disturbing rumours, Bollgar. Are they true?"

"I'm afraid so. I've been informed there are several people watching the orphanages in Perizzi at all times. I believe they're Guardians."

It confirmed her suspicion that something had gone wrong with Brook's mission to silence Grell. She'd already assumed the worst as there had been no messages from her since then. What a waste. To have used such a unique asset on a minor inconvenience. Now she had no idea what was going on inside

Unity Hall as Brook had been her only loyal Guardian. It would take her a long time to cultivate another.

"What do you want me to do, Mother?"

"You mentioned there was surplus money for expansion. For the time being I want you to keep your focus here. Since my last attempt at patronage was rejected, I want you to establish at least three new orphanages in the city. Hire someone competent to oversee it all. Get them to look after finding the buildings, hiring staff, everything."

It was difficult to tell because Bollgar was always sweating, but she thought he was damper than normal. "That's going to cost a lot of money," he offered tentatively, but she waved it away. She could always get more money.

"Make sure the overseer knows what they are doing. I don't want any mistakes."

"Of course," he stammered, which made her grimace.

"And there's one more thing," said Akosh, getting to her feet. "Take a bath and open a window in here. It stinks."

"Yes, Mother," he said meekly. His weakness made her despise him just a little bit more. The more she thought about it the more she realised the truth. She had grown too fond of them. They were tools to be used. Nothing more. If Bollgar died because he was fat and lazy she would simply replace him. Two apprentices were being groomed and soon they would assist Bollgar with his duties. She knew he would complain about the intrusion, but her long-term survival was the only thing that mattered, not their happiness.

As their god and saviour, a certain level of adoration and fawning was expected, but the familial aspect of their praise was making her increasingly uncomfortable. It was something she would have to adjust in the years ahead.

*

An hour later she was sitting in what had become her favourite tavern in the city, the Golden Goose. The owner wasn't one of her children but, once she'd explained what would happen to his family if he refused her requests, he'd become incredibly compliant. He'd even provided her with a private dining room which she used to conduct her meetings.

Akosh sipped at her glass of wine, delighting in the silky texture on her tongue and the way it clung to the edges of the glass. Her moment of tranquillity was spoiled by a knock on the door and Doggett striding into the room. Today he seemed full of confidence and his disguise was a wealthy merchant of some importance which was utterly at odds with his forgettable face.

"Mother," he said, giving her a slight bow.

"Have you resolved the situation with the orphanage?"

"As requested. Jille the administrator, and the new member of staff, were both murdered. It was made to look like a crime of passion. I provided the breadcrumbs and the Regent's first wife asked her new agents to do the rest."

She had decided to solve three problems at once. Her incident at the orphanage would soon be forgotten in the wake of a fresh murder, and she could test Selina's resolve at the same time. It also allowed her to eliminate the agent at the orphanage who had been posing as a member of staff. It didn't matter who he'd worked for. A blind eye saw nothing and now she was watching for a reaction. She'd soon find out who the agent had been working for.

"How did Selina perform?"

"Exactly as I would. She wasn't squeamish in the slightest." Doggett sounded impressed, which was a rare compliment from him. "She followed the evidence I'd provided and it led her to an agent from Yerskania. Bloody clothes and the murder weapon were found at his home in a hidden cupboard. Under extreme duress he confessed to being an agent of Queen Morganse. He denied all knowledge of the murders at the orphanage, but he did cough up a few names of other agents before dying."

Akosh raised an eyebrow. "He died?"

"The inquisitor was a little too enthusiastic," apologised Doggett.

It didn't matter. What was one more dead human? This latest mishap had been turned in her favour. Selina's new spies had proven to be valuable which meant she would rely on them more in the future. Akosh expected she would pass this latest piece of information on to her husband. All rulers in the west knew other nations spied on them. It was to be expected. But they rarely had the name of foreign agents. Now the Regent and Queen Morganse would be focused on playing their games, watching each other's spies. In the meantime Akosh's people were one step closer to the Regent and more ingrained in the government than before. With more people in key positions who had proven their worth, it would be easier to steer gently whoever was sitting on the throne.

"Proceed with caution," said Akosh. "Continue to prove your worth to Selina. If she wants to play at being a spymaster, then let her. We need to continue poisoning the Regent against Yerskania and their open stance on everything."

The Regent had led the way on magic. He'd been the first to ban all Seekers and the first to declare an amnesty and establish a new way of dealing with young children and mages. If all went as planned Akosh intended to gradually move him in the same direction with religion. She was a long way from having a nation of her own, but this was another small step on the right path. Patience, always patience.

"Don't let her do anything too rash. Tell her to move slowly and keep me updated."

"Yes, Mother," said Doggett, giving her another bow before marching out. Reliable. Precise. Someone who followed orders with no fawning. Perhaps she should have made her religion more martial. Then she could have filled her ranks with soldiers. On the other hand they were less flexible and not as good at blending in as her orphans who could hide in plain sight.

As she was mulling over the future direction of her followers, there was another knock at the door. Akosh took another sip of wine before answering. She wasn't expecting anyone else today. If it had been the simpering owner she would have heard him shuffling about. Whoever was on the other side of the door wasn't moving and seemed content to stand and wait. Akosh drew a dagger and kept it out of sight under the table.

"Enter," she said.

A stout Yerskani man with a thick beard and shaven head came into the room. Much to her surprise he bowed deeply. Expecting mockery, she moved the dagger on top of the table. His eyes tracked the motion as he straightened.

"My name is Bissel. I offer greetings from my Master."

"And?"

"If this is not a convenient time I can come back later," he offered.

She was about to ask who he served when she noticed a familiar mannerism. One of his hands strayed to his chest as if nervous but she could see him playing with something under his clothing. The top two buttons of his shirt were unfastened and in addition to a hairy chest she could just see the edge of a black leather cord. There was something around his neck. A religious symbol, perhaps. The last person she'd seen doing the same was Pavel, the former Guardian.

She hated being in the dark. Without knowing who he served

she had no idea as to their motives for this alliance. For all she knew it could be an elaborate trap.

"Sit," said Akosh and he was quick to comply.

"Let me guess. You're not allowed to tell me who you serve?"

"Apologies. My Master prefers to remain anonymous at this time. He's merely being cautious, which I'm sure is something you understand."

"You've no idea what I understand," said Akosh. She was tempted to pin his hand to the table with her dagger and question him until she had some real answers. The last time his Master had sent one of his followers, Akosh had been tested and she was still annoyed. However, the messenger had helped her realise she'd been drifting off course and getting too embroiled with humans and their insignificant problems. That was the danger of living as one for so long. You started to think like them and feel things for them. They were not equals. They were nothing more than ants, crawling around underfoot.

"As you say. I'm sure I cannot know your mind," apologised Bissel. "As a show of good faith and commitment from my Master, I've been instructed to offer you something." Akosh was only half listening. She was still contemplating how best to vent her frustration on this lackey. Perhaps if she just cut off a few fingers. That would send a clear message to his Master without killing him.

"Go on," she said, choosing which of his hands to start with.

"Torran Habreel."

"What did you just say?" said Akosh, focusing on him fully.

"I know where he is."

All thoughts of dismemberment were pushed aside. "Where?"

"The Guardians have him in a secure cell inside Unity Hall."

It was just as she'd suspected. After everything that Habreel had done he was still a Guardian at his core. He saw himself as a good man and every act he'd taken as necessary to build a better future. His morals could bend, to allow him to commit or give orders that normally went against his beliefs, but he always reverted to form. Such disciplined and rigid men were difficult to control, unless you found their weakness. Habreel's had been his ambition and his prejudice. He'd been so driven he paid no attention to those closest to him. And now he was back home. Akosh had no doubt he would tell them everything, to unburden his soul and to feel good about himself.

"I assume he's cooperating with them."

"He's writing reports and the Khevassar regularly asks him questions."

That would only get them so far. Habreel had been kept in the dark on purpose and didn't know much of her plans. However, if the Guardians kept asking him questions it could reveal some discrepancies surrounding her age, reveal the names of some of her followers and even hint at her unusual "magic". Habreel needed to be silenced before her brethren took notice. After avoiding the last summons they were already on alert.

"What is your Master offering?" she asked.

"To permanently take care of Habreel."

Akosh raised an eyebrow. "He can get someone inside Unity Hall?"

Bissel winced. "I'm afraid I can't answer that."

"Because you don't know or you're not allowed to say?" she asked, stroking her dagger.

"I don't know. My Master appreciates your frustration and he realised you might want to vent, once my message was delivered."

Bissel closed his eyes and calmly awaited his death. Akosh admired the ruthless nature of Bissel's Master, whoever it was. He had no compunction about sending one of his people to deliver a message, knowing full well the peon might die in the process. The anthill did not collapse with the death of one worker.

"Is there more to the message?" she asked, still playing with her dagger.

"I've been instructed to say this favour is freely given. My Master expects nothing in return at this time."

"At this time," echoed Akosh, mulling over the words. Just as Selina would come to rely on her new agents, Akosh was aware she might fall afoul of the same trap if not careful. It was the same trick black crystal dealers had been using on addicts for centuries. One free taste and then they were hooked, usually for life. After that they would do or say anything for another fix. However, right now Habreel was a problem that she needed fixing before he caused any more problems.

Alliances between her kind were rare for a reason. They only had their own best interests at heart. Their survival did not depend on another's, only on worship and belief from the mortals. While their goals might currently align, it was inevitable that with time they would drift apart.

"Thank your Master for this generous gift."

"I can leave?" he asked, surprised that she was letting him go. Akosh merely removed her dagger from the table. Bissel glanced at the door and then back at Akosh, as if expecting a knife in the back.

"Get out before I change my mind," she snapped.

With a short bow he scuttled out of the door and disappeared.

The favour was generous but it was also troubling. It meant Bissel's Master had eyes and ears in Unity Hall. She had no idea how many people he had, or where they were based. Without knowing his identity it made it impossible to guess what he was after.

Bissel was just turning the corner when she hurried out of the front door of the tavern. Akosh took a deep breath and then followed him at a sedate pace.

She needed to find out more about his Master. Her survival hinged on her children and the continued growth of her faith. She doubted he was one of the Elders, which meant he didn't rely on places of worship. Once she knew his identity it would make it easier to find out what he wanted and how to stab him in the back.

CHAPTER 17

The journey had been long and arduous but finally Tianne had made it home to Zecorria.

She was exhausted from long days in the saddle and a lack of sleep, not to mention in desperate need of a bath and a hot meal. Her last brief wash had been in a brook a few days ago, but it had been cut short when she'd heard riders approaching. Thankfully they'd not been after her, not this time at least. Twice on her journey she'd been forced off the road by a group of bandits. They'd been posing as injured travellers who tried to rob her and then followed her when she fled. She managed to lose them after a few hours but they found her trail the next day. Tianne knew it was her own fault. If she'd not used her magic they would never have come after her.

After that encounter she didn't use it again but remained wary of other travellers she met on the road. Her supplies were gone, as was all of her money, but none of that mattered now. She'd made it to the capital city.

As she rode through the streets of Herakion she expected to feel different. A sense of relief, or an easing of the longing she felt inside, but nothing had changed. As far as everyone else knew she was just another traveller coming to the city. But she had an appointment with the Regent. Tianne knew that first impressions were important and she could not present herself at the palace in her current state.

With no money in her pocket she was forced to sell her horse. In exchange for a lower price she made the new owner promise to hold onto the animal for at least a week. By then she hoped to be able to buy him back.

With the money she received Tianne bought some new clothes, rented a room in a modest tavern for the night and scrubbed herself from head to toe in a bath. When the water turned brown she realised why the owner had been wrinkling his nose at her. After she'd dressed in fresh clothes and tied back her hair in a neat ponytail, Tianne treated herself to her first decent meal in days. This time the owner actually smiled and gave her an approving nod when he delivered her food.

That night, despite the softness of the bed and clean sheets, Tianne had difficulty sleeping. She was nervous about the following morning and rehearsed over and over what to say to the guards at the palace gates.

Different scenarios ran through her mind where she encountered a problem and tried to think of a suitable answer. The most important thing she focused on was staying calm. She had every right to be there and didn't want to scare anyone when they found out she was a mage. The last thing she wanted was to cause a panic and be attacked.

At some point in the early hours she passed out and slept fitfully for a few hours. Morning found her groggy and sandy-eyed, but she rose early, ate a quick breakfast and then joined the line of supplicants outside the palace. By the time she arrived there were already at least thirty people ahead of her and she prepared herself for a tedious wait.

After a couple of hours a palace clerk, accompanied by two

guards, walked down the line. Tianne heard him asking each person their name and business before making a brief note in his book. A few people were told their business wasn't urgent and they were asked to come back the following morning. By now the line behind Tianne stretched down the street and she counted over a hundred people waiting. There simply wasn't time for all of them to be seen in one day. Being told to come back tomorrow wasn't a scenario she'd considered and panic began to set in.

The money she'd received from selling her horse would last for a while, but what happened if he sent her away this morning? What happened if they kept sending her away? Eventually the money would run out. What would she do then? How would she survive?

"Name," said the clerk, startling Tianne out of her reverie. He was a short, portly man wearing a stylised grey shirt marked with one red star on the left side of his chest, indicating some kind of rank.

"Tianne," she blurted, giving herself a shake. One of the guards raised an eyebrow and she did her best not to look suspicious. Tianne started fidgeting under the woman's intense stare and couldn't stop.

"Your business?" asked the clerk.

"I'm here because of the amnesty," she said, keeping her voice low. Those immediately around her could hear, but she didn't want everyone knowing her business.

The clerk raised an eyebrow. "The what?"

"For Zecorran mages," she said and now both guards were staring at her. One of them slowly moved a hand to rest it on the sword at her waist. The clerk was less impressed.

"Girl, I've no time for games. Go away and bother someone else."

"I'm serious," hissed Tianne, earning a few startled looks from those nearby.

"Really?" said the clerk with a sigh before gesturing with one hand. "Show me."

Tianne was already drawing attention to herself. The clerk had stopped moving down the line and people wanted to know who was causing the delay. People were turning around to look back at her. "Here on the street?" she asked. "Shouldn't we go somewhere more private?"

The clerk ran a hand through his thinning grey hair and folded his arms. "Here. Now. Or I'll have you whipped for wasting my time."

Taking a deep breath Tianne tried to slow the frantic beating of her heart. She could feel everyone staring but there was no choice. Embracing the Source she trickled a little power into the palm of her hand and created a small mage light. It glowed blue and, flicking her fingers, she made it dance across her knuckles like a coin. Those people nearby in line stepped backwards in surprise and perhaps fear, whereas the clerk didn't seem at all disconcerted.

"Is that all you can do?" he asked. "It's not very impressive."

"I can do a lot more than that," said Tianne, feeling her temper flare. She lifted the clerk off the ground and he let out a squawk of surprise. His head was just above the level of the crowd and he bobbed in the air like a cork in water before she lowered him again.

Both Royal Guards had not drawn their weapons but she could see they were tensed and ready for a fight. A pool of empty space had opened up around Tianne and she felt the uncomfortable weight of many unpleasant stares. The clerk had regained his composure and with a harrumph he gestured for Tianne to follow him to the front of the line. The two Royal Guards fell in behind her, watching her closely. She had the impression they were waiting for her to do something violent so that they could stab her in the back. So far her welcome home was far from what she'd been expecting.

Calm. She told herself to stay calm and that everything would be fine.

When they passed through the first set of palace gates she heaved a sigh of relief at being off the street. There were more people in the courtyard waiting to gain entrance, but none of them had seen or heard what she'd done, so they paid her no special attention.

"Sit over there," said the clerk, gesturing at a bench against the far wall. Tianne did as instructed while he went to speak to another official, this one with two red stars on his palace shirt. After a short whispered conversation, during which both clerks sneaked glances at her, they disappeared through the gates into the palace. The Royal Guards had also spoken to their colleagues as now there were four of them watching her. They hadn't moved from their posts, but all had turned their bodies to face her with hands on weapons. One man strung his bow and casually leaned on it.

Tianne did her best to look unthreatening but the tension of the Royal Guards proved to be infectious. Eventually the other supplicants noticed something was wrong as the low hum of conversation drained away until it was replaced with a tense silence.

When yet another clerk appeared in front of the others, this one with three stars on his shirt, Tianne realised if nothing else they were taking her request seriously. The tall, bearded man had a lean face and stared down his nose at her if she were mud on his shoes.

"Come with me," he said, turning away before she had a

chance to ask any questions. Tianne hurried after him down a
dimly lit corridor. She caught brief glimpses of huge paintings
that showed figures from history, old rulers perhaps, and a
huge worn tapestry of an ancient battle. Following the sound
of his boots she descended several flights of stairs before finally
catching up.

"In there," he said, gesturing towards an open door, and she
went inside without hesitating. It was only when she'd walked
into the room and turned around that she realised something
was wrong. The walls were plain stone and the room was empty
except for a pair of burly men in leather armour. As she opened
her mouth to ask a question one of them punched her in the
face, splitting the skin above her right eye.

Tianne stumbled back, blood dripping down her face. The
heavy door behind her clanged shut. Before she had a chance
to recover the other man rushed in, catching her on the temple
with his fist. She spun around and fell against the wall, dazed
and surprised. Several blows caught her in the spine and she fell
to the ground, curling up into a ball. But they didn't relent and
started kicking her instead.

She did her best to protect her head with her arms but it left
her stomach exposed and soon she was winded and gasping for
air. She tried to reach for the Source but the pain and repeated
kicks broke her concentration. A heavy blow caught her in the
chest and she felt something snap. A fresh spike of pain lanced
up her side and she screamed. Darkness closed in on all sides but
even as she fell into the abyss she could still feel the repeated
assault on her body.

Freezing cold water shocked her awake but her body had difficulty responding as her limbs were heavy and slow. Tianne
was lying face down in ankle-deep dirty water and before she

drowned she managed to crawl on all fours until she reached a wall. One of her eyes was swollen shut but faint light from above showed her four walls of a stone pit or an old well. Ten feet above her head was a heavy metal grille and flickering torchlight. She could just make out several figures in armour and all of them were carrying weapons.

The cold air and frigid water told her she was somewhere deep underground. Probably in the lowest levels of cells under the palace, unless they'd moved her somewhere else when she'd been unconscious. The only way out was to go up, through the metal grille and the waiting armed guards. She was willing to bet there would be more waiting beyond that room. Even if she could somehow use her magic to get out of the cell it would be pointless. She was trapped.

Waves of pain rolled through her body and she felt herself teeter on the edge of consciousness again. Her hands felt swollen, her head ached and it was difficult to catch her breath. Tianne slid down the wall until part of her body was submerged in the water again but she didn't dare fall asleep. She might drown and no one would help her if she did.

The pain in her hands and chest made it difficult to think but as she went over the last few hours she couldn't understand what had gone wrong. The Regent had declared an amnesty on Zecorran mages. He might not have been expecting someone her age, but surely any mage was better than none. Garvey was still a threat and the people needed protection. Magic was the only thing that was going to save them.

Perhaps Wren had been right. All of this had been nothing more than an elaborate trap designed to capture and kill all mages in Zecorria. But if that was the case then why was she still alive? Once she was unconscious it would have been easy for them to kill her.

A horrible thought slithered into the back of her mind. What if she was still alive because they intended to torture her? What if they forced her to tell them where to find the other mages?

It was that thought, more than the beating, that finally broke her.

She'd been so stupid. Determined to find her own place in the world she'd been sure that coming home was the right decision. The brief time she'd spent at the Red Tower had been better than anything that had come before and yet here she was, desperate to return home and impress other people. Growing up she'd been mocked, bullied, ignored and belittled, at times even by her own parents. The new life that she'd built had been one full of wonder and discovery. Even when that had all fallen apart she'd landed on her feet by staying with Wren. Her friend had trusted and relied on her. Tianne had been valued and respected in the new community and people genuinely liked her.

Now all of that was gone. She was alone, with no one to call on, injured and facing impending torture and perhaps death.

Hope abandoned Tianne in the dark and she began to cry.

CHAPTER 18

Balfruss stared at his reflection in the mirror, picking out all the little details that had gone unnoticed until now, as he never spent long looking at himself.

There was far less black in his hair than he remembered and lots more grey and white. Also his face was leaner and more weather-beaten than he'd been expecting. That came from the last few months which had been among the most difficult he'd experienced. Lying to himself wouldn't change the fact. Every day he was beginning to look a bit more like his father.

Putting that distressing thought aside, he focused on the candle's flame while summoning a mental picture of Eloise. Embracing the Source he channelled a small amount of power into the mirror, waiting to see if she was there. This was the fourth time he'd tried to speak with Eloise but she hadn't answered.

As it had been explained to him several years ago, this was a lot like fishing, except it was far more dangerous for him.

He cast out a line and waited to see if Eloise answered. The amount of energy required was fairly small, which meant that normally he could continue this indefinitely. The difficulty came in maintaining his concentration. If his mind wandered and he stopped focusing on her, then his connection would evaporate. The most dangerous part about this type of fishing was that his dangling hook could be snagged by someone, or something, else.

He knew how to create a connection within the mirrors, using the space between, but didn't really understand how it worked. Every time he discovered something new, he realised how much there was still to learn, and how little he really knew.

In the past he'd scoffed at the idea of meditation but now he understood how critical it was at times like these. Without it he wouldn't have been able to maintain his side of the link for long. Munroe had quickly floundered because she lacked the mental discipline to keep her mind focused on one image.

Something unfamiliar brushed up against the periphery of Balfruss's senses but he didn't react. He would instinctively know if it was Eloise and reach out towards her. Whatever else was out there, in the place between, was not her. Keeping perfectly still, and focusing only on Eloise in his mind, Balfruss waited for the other presence to move on. It was impossible to tell its identity, but the vague impression he felt was that its intent was malicious.

Sweat trickled down the sides of his face but he did his best to ignore it. After an indeterminate amount of time he felt the other drift away and heaved a sigh of relief.

Some time later, when the sides of his shirt were damp with sweat, he decided to withdraw his magic and try another day. Just as he was about to let go of the Source he felt a tentative touch that he recognised. Balfruss pressed one hand against the mirror, letting his fingers rest lightly on the surface. The feeling of familiarity increased significantly and he trickled a little more power into his connection. The surface of the mirror rippled as if made of water and then settled again. The glass seemed to frost over, turning black, but only for a moment. When it was gone he was staring at Eloise in the mirror.

She was just as he had pictured her in his mind, except for the loose white headscarf folded around her neck to ward off the sun. Behind her there was an open doorway and through it he could see a painfully bright blue sky. Golden rays of sunlight filtered into the room from somewhere on high, bathing her in its glow. Lots of brightly coloured cushions and a low table were in the background as well, bringing back memories of his time in the desert kingdoms before the war. Back then it had been just the three of them. Eloise, himself and Darius, her late husband. The warmth from his fond recollections faded away leaving behind a sour taste in his mouth.

Balfruss pressed his fingers more firmly against the glass and felt it give until he gripped Eloise's hand. Her skin was warm and he felt a few grains of sand pressed between their palms.

"You look tired," she said.

"It's been a difficult day."

"There have been a lot of those lately."

"How is it, being back there?" he asked.

When Eloise had last been in the far east it had been with her husband prior to the war. Part of the reason she and her husband had come west to fight in the war was to repay Balfruss for all that he'd done to protect the desert kingdoms. They thought returning the favour was the least they could do, but it had cost Darius his life. Most people believed Eloise had died as well, burned up on the walls of Charas by the Warlock and his twisted apprentices. To return now, many years after being presumed dead, was always going to be difficult. But protecting the students mattered more to her than anything else.

"At first it was awkward, and there was a lot of tears and beating of chests." Eloise shook her head and wiped her eyes with her free hand. "Then his mother and aunts wouldn't let me out of their sight. Now they're constantly feeding me, telling me I've not been eating enough."

"They're right. You're so busy I know you sometimes forget to eat."

"Every day they turn up with huge plates of rice and stew."

Balfruss felt his mouth begin to water. "I remember their cooking was delicious. I always ate too much."

Eloise laughed but it was brief and bittersweet. "They ask after you, given that you're family, too."

Balfruss wasn't a blood relative but when Darius had died he'd inherited a large portion of his wealth, possessions and responsibilities, including his wife. As Blood Brother he was supposed to marry Darius's widow. It was another reason that Eloise had gone east with the children instead of him. That was a tangle he did not want to unravel at the moment.

"How are the children?" he asked, changing the subject. Eloise smiled and let it pass, knowing he didn't want to talk about their family any more. Several years on and it was still a difficult subject for both of them.

"They're adjusting. It's taking some of them more time than others, but having structure again is helping. The heat is the most difficult thing for them to get used to, but in time I know they'll manage. I did, even though it took me years."

"How long will you stay?" he asked.

Eloise sighed and nearly turned her head away which would have broken their connection. Instead she slumped forward and seemed to deflate. "I don't know. They need me as an anchor from their old lives. For all the Jhanidi's patience as teachers, it's going to be a long time before the children feel comfortable living here in a temple. In some ways the other teachers from the Red Tower are having a more difficult time adjusting. They can leave the training grounds unattended, but then have to contend with a very different way of life to what they knew. I'd forgotten how different it is out here."

Balfruss remembered when he'd first travelled to the desert kingdoms it had been quite a culture shock. He'd only been a visitor, and could have left at any time, but the former teachers had to live there indefinitely. It would probably be years before they fully adjusted and several more until they thought of it as home.

For Eloise it was equally uncomfortable to be in the desert. The longer she stayed there, surrounded by her late husband's family, the more difficult it would be to leave. But she could not just run out and abandon the children because it was awkward. It was what he'd expected her to say, but a small part of him had hoped that Eloise would soon return to the west. There was only so much he could do by himself and he valued her wise counsel. She was also one of his oldest friends and he missed her.

"How are things there?" she asked, perhaps hoping for good news and it was his turn to look uncomfortable.

"Worse than ever. Munroe is gone. She's bent on revenge and I'm not sure what could stop her. People are increasingly scared and paranoid about anyone with magic and Garvey is making it worse."

Balfruss was conscious of how much time they'd been talking and knew it couldn't go on much longer. Speaking quickly, he filled her in on what Garvey had done with his group of followers. Eloise's expression darkened as he spoke until it was a mix of anger and sorrow.

"I didn't think he'd go that far," she said, shaking her head. "I knew he was on a dark path, but to kill so many innocent people, it's so unlike him. It goes against everything he stood for."

"I'm not so sure," said Balfruss, hating to say such a thing about his old friend, but recent events had made him wonder. "He's changed. He's not the same person I remember when we studied together at the Red Tower."

"None of us are that naïve any more."

"It's more than that. From the first day when I returned to the school he was different. Cold, distant, and he was always so angry. His rage was always there, bubbling away under the surface."

"After everything he was asked to do, I knew he was carrying a great burden, but I thought that teaching a new generation of children would bring him out of the dark," said Eloise. "I hoped it might heal him."

"Me, too," he said with a sad smile. "Perhaps we're both still a little naïve."

"When did you know?"

It was something they'd never spoken about before. For all the noble things the old Grey Council had done before abandoning their posts, there had been a dark undercurrent. Over the years Balfruss had gathered scraps of information, from anecdotes and eyewitnesses, but he hadn't believed Garvey had been involved. Not at first.

"I didn't find out for several years after we'd left the Red Tower," he said, thinking back to that time. Part of him had thought the world had been a kinder and simpler place, but now he knew differently. It was simply that ignorance was bliss. The less you knew, the less there was to worry about. "I heard a rumour about Garvey but didn't believe it. I knew it couldn't be true. I was so determined to clear his name that I visited the village and spoke to some of the locals. After that, any time I heard a similar story I knew it was him."

When Balfruss had left the Red Tower as a young man,

freshly anointed as a Battlemage, he'd gone in search of adventure. His hunger had taken him across the world, to many amazing countries, where he'd lived to the full. Unknown to him Garvey had been led down a different, much darker path, before they'd even left the school.

The Red Tower had always done its best to teach as many children as possible to control their magic and use it to help others. But not every child was found and others evaded the Seekers on purpose, preferring a life in the shadows where their gifts could help themselves and those with less scruples. If these people were discovered by the Grey Council they were not put on trial. Magic left no footprints in the mud, no marks on the skin, no sediment in a liquid. Proving that someone had been murdered or cheated with magic was all but impossible.

The rogue mages received no warning. They were simply eliminated by the Bane. A mage, sanctioned by the Grey Council, to hunt down and execute magic users using their powers for profit. Garvey had been chosen and shaped into a weapon, designed to hunt and kill other mages. When the war began, Garvey had been pursuing a destructive mage and had ignored King Mathias's call.

Garvey was the last in a long line of people to hold the title of Bane. When they'd formed the new Grey Council it was not something they'd reinstated, despite Garvey's insistence that it was necessary.

"Killing all those people as the Bane left a mark on him," said Balfruss. "He may not even have noticed he was being affected, but over time it changed him. It must have. Perhaps he acquired a taste for killing."

"I don't believe it," protested Eloise.

"Then how do you explain what's happened?"

"I can't," she said and Balfruss felt her fingers tighten against his. "Whatever he's become, Garvey has always been a clever man. There must be a reason, but whatever that is no longer matters. He's out of control and must be stopped."

"I must go after him," said Balfruss, tasting bile in his mouth. He'd been putting it off, giving Tammy excuses that held no water. Another reason for hoping Eloise would soon return was that he didn't want to go after his friend alone. He was afraid, not of dying, or being defeated, but finding out that his friend killed people because he enjoyed it.

"Will you be able to stop him?" asked Eloise.

"I don't know. If he's alone, then perhaps, but he has more than a dozen students with him. I need to find a way to separate him." A deep sorrow settled over Balfruss and he felt overwhelmed by what lay ahead. "There are only a handful of people I can truly call my friend. And now, Elwei forgive me, I must hunt down and kill one of the few that remain."

CHAPTER 19

It was late, again, and Tammy was still at work in her office. There didn't seem to be any other kind of night at the moment.

In cutting herself off from all familial connections she realised that the benefits for them were twofold. It protected them from reprisals if criminals sought to get back at her as Khevassar, but it also meant she had no one to let down. If she'd had a family, or someone waiting for her at home, the guilt of never being there would only mount day after day. The excuses about the work being important would soon wear thin, as would their patience. Then she'd end up alone anyway but more heartbroken and distraught than before. It was simpler this way. Easier. At least that's what she told herself as she struggled to focus on yet another report.

Tammy was trying not to think about her family or Kovac and what they were doing.

She pushed her chair back from her desk and took a break, resting the back of her head on the wall. The report in front of her was about another body in the morgue. Another possible murder that needed her attention. This time it was the Dockmaster who had died in what seemed like slightly suspicious circumstances. No one outside the city of Perizzi would ever have heard of him, or considered him an important figure. But as the most senior person in charge of the busiest port in the world, everyone here knew his name.

He could destroy businesses if he wanted, holding cargo indefinitely at the docks for any number of plausible and legal reasons. It was why the person holding the position was closely vetted and all of his dealings were scrutinised, without him knowing of course, to make sure he was beyond reproach. As such his death also needed to be thoroughly checked to make sure foul play wasn't involved.

One of the Dockmaster's few vices was drinking. He never drank to excess but was known to enjoy expensive brandy from around the world. All gifts he received were declared and put up for auction, but he usually ended up buying the best of them with his own money. After all, who would bid against the Dockmaster on his favourite drink? The initial report from the doctor indicated he'd died from excess over many years, but when Tammy had seen him last week, bellowing at a ship's captain, he'd seemed in fairly good health. It was possible that he'd had a sudden and rapid decline in his health, but she needed to be sure.

She rubbed at her eyes and made a note of a couple of names she could assign to the case.

There was a polite knock and Guardian Fray stuck his head around the door. "I'm ready. Let me know when you have time."

"Now," said Tammy, standing up. Her reports would still be there waiting for her when she got back. She collected the items they would need and picked up her master set of keys for the building. "If we don't go right now, something else will distract me."

"I need somewhere quiet where we won't be disturbed."

"Follow me," said Tammy. "I have the perfect place in mind."

One of the many things she'd discovered since taking over the Old Man's position was the secret history of Unity Hall. The one known only to the Khevassar. No other Guardian of the Peace had access to the same information as her. It was not recorded in any of the modern journals and, despite attempts at preservation, the oldest had long turned to dust. The story was one that had been passed on verbally from one Khevassar to the next, down through the centuries.

Most Guardians rightly assumed their organisation had been founded with the earliest settlement in Yerskania for the express purpose of investigating crimes. But there had also been a second purpose that no one knew about. Guarding the peace against other forces. Especially those who used their powers to help themselves while hurting or killing others. Tammy would have thought that the Old Man had finally lost his mind if not for all that she'd seen in the last decade. Magic forces and beings beyond the understanding of most people.

"Tell no one about this," she said, stopping outside a plain wooden door. "I must ask you to swear a blood oath."

Fray swallowed hard, suddenly understanding the seriousness of what she was sharing with him. To his credit he didn't run and quickly swore to keep the secret. Tammy unlocked the door, gestured for him to enter the cramped archive and locked it again behind her. The room was identical to many others, stacked floor to ceiling with shelves containing hundreds of journals. Two small writing tables sat in the middle of the room, surrounded by half a dozen unlit lanterns. Scribes were permanently employed to copy fading, damaged or old journals from previous Khevassars, so that one continuous history of the city was maintained for all time.

At this time of night the scribes were in their beds and the archive was deserted. Tammy lit one of the lanterns and then moved to the back of the room. Taking a small, thick key from her pocket she removed a few journals from the top shelf and slid the wooden panel behind them to one side. The keyhole was small and not easy to see but when she turned the key in the lock there was an audible click.

"Help me with this," she said. Together she and Fray pushed the bookcase into the wall and then to one side, revealing a tall but narrow corridor. Tammy was forced to walk sideways until it opened out onto a set of tight spiral stairs that wound down into the darkness.

They descended into the earth and Tammy lost track of time. She lost count at five hundred steps and they still had a little way to go. This went far below the black cells to another part of Unity Hall that had not been used for centuries.

Finally, the stairs ended at a short corridor that housed seven cells. Six were plain identical rooms but she led Fray to the larger seventh cell at the end of the hall. The Old Man had brought her down here once and that had been more than enough. She'd only peered into the other cells but he'd insisted she set foot in this one.

From his expression she could see Fray was desperate to ask a question but he kept his mouth shut. She walked into the final room without any difficulty but he paused on the threshold and raised one hand.

"There's something here," he said, sounding puzzled. "It's like the air is made of honey. It's thick and heavy."

Tammy said nothing and watched as Fray tentatively stepped into the room. Nothing happened but she could see he was struggling to cope with whatever he could sense. She left him to adjust as she moved around the eight-sided cell, lighting the torches until the whole space was full of warm yellow light.

"What is this place?" he finally asked.

"A long time ago it was used to house difficult prisoners. Those with abilities," she said as Fray gently touched two fingers to the wall. He yanked his hand back as if burned but there wasn't a mark on his fingertips. "Take another look," she said, gesturing at the walls.

More cautiously this time, Fray moved closer to one of the walls until his face was almost touching it. Normally he hunched his shoulders slightly, but now they were almost touching his ears as if braced against a strong wind. She watched as his green eyes changed colour, first to a pale lemon and then turning darker, becoming a rich amber. Fray let out a startled bark and stumbled back until she caught him, keeping him upright.

"By the Maker," he hissed through clenched teeth. Tammy could feel his whole body was rigid with tension.

"Tell me what you see."

"The walls. Even the ceiling and the floor. They're all covered with symbols. I think they're letters, but I don't recognise the language." Fray's voice was a mix of awe and surprise. "There are so many, overlapping each other. There are layers and layers."

The Old Man's theory was right. This cell was designed to contain any number of powerful creatures, including those with magic. She'd seen first-hand how dangerous magic could be in the wrong hands. A long time ago, at the beginning of the Guardians, several mages had worked in concert to create this cell to house the worst of the worst.

Tammy could have simply taken Fray to a quiet storage room and locked the door while they worked to raise the spirit of Guardian Brook. She had the authority to ensure they weren't disturbed. Bringing him down here was a lot further out of the way, but she'd needed to know if the ancient magic was still active. It could prove to be incredibly useful in the days ahead with rogue mages on the loose.

"Will it stop you from working?" she asked, shaking Fray gently by the shoulders.

"I don't know. Maybe."

"Let's find out," she said, opening the bag of personal belongings she'd had someone gather from Guardian Brook's home. One by one she passed the items to Fray who held each one carefully as if it were fragile. When he touched an old patchwork blanket he stopped and tapped the wool with his fingers.

"This one. There's a strong connection."

She set the other items aside and sat down beside him at the centre of the room. Fray bowed his head slightly and let out a long, slow breath. His lips were moving but he didn't speak and he made a small beckoning gesture with both hands.

After a few minutes in silence he sat back and shook his head. "I can't feel anything. It's like there's a huge wall that's blocking me."

Tammy was pleased but did her best not to show it. The magic was still intact.

"Let's try one of the other cells," she suggested, leading him to one of the plainer rooms. She lit the torches and Fray tried again, bowing his head over the blanket.

After only a few seconds the air in front of him flickered and a spectral figure began to appear. At first the person's features were fuzzy, as if hidden behind a thick fog, but they quickly sharpened until Tammy recognised Guardian Brook.

Fray opened his amber eyes and stared at the shade. His expression turned incredulous when he noticed she was staring at Brook. "You can see her?"

"Of course. Why?" asked Tammy.

"That's never happened before," he said, briefly glancing

around the plain room. There was nothing unusual about this cell, but perhaps it was caused by their proximity to the special octagonal cell.

"Ask a question. See if she can hear you," suggested Fray.

Tammy faced the spirit. "Guardian Brook, can you hear me?"

"I hear you," said Brook. Her voice echoed slightly, as if she were speaking to them from another room. "Why am I here?"

"To help me. I need to understand more about Akosh. Is she your patron?"

Brook's natural expression was wary but at the mention of her patron it softened. "She's much more than that. She found me when I was small child living on the streets, abandoned and starving. I was given a home, schooling and a safe place to grow up. Many of those I knew from that time were not as fortunate. Many of them died and others became criminals."

She spoke with such reverence that Tammy knew it would be pointless to try and change her mind about Akosh. Brook had killed herself rather than be questioned about her Mother and risk betraying her. Brook believed she owed everything in her life, and all that she had accomplished, to Akosh. Apparently none of it was due to her ambition or drive. Anything good in her life came from on high. She'd come across other people with similar faith in the past, but none of them claimed to have met their god. Brook's faith would be like a block of granite.

"Did the people at the orphanage teach you about her?" asked Tammy, holding up a copy of the text she'd found at Brook's home. The symbol on the front of the small book was that of a woman caring for a small child. The spirit recognised the stylised image and smiled.

"Not at first, but most of what they taught us was common sense. To care for others and help those less fortunate, just like us. It was only later they told us everything came from the book."

"Is that why you became a Guardian? To help people?"

"Of course," said Brook. "Who are you?"

"Someone seeking answers and a new path," said Tammy, trying to appeal to her religious zeal.

"You seem familiar," said Brook, her face scrunching up in concentration. Fray had told her that the spirits he summoned were incomplete pieces of the person they'd been in life. This was merely a shadow. "I think I know you."

"Can I join your faith?" asked Tammy and the spirit's smile returned. "Learn more about it?"

"All are welcome, but few come to us as adults."

"So it's usually orphans," clarified Tammy. "You're saved at an early age."

"Many on the streets were not as fortunate as me," said Brook, repeating herself. It seemed as if they found the limit to what the spirit could remember from her old life. She'd seen Brook once or twice in Unity Hall but they'd never worked together. Even so, if her mind had been intact Tammy was confident Brook would remember her as she tended to stand out in a crowd.

"The war created so many children without parents, and orphanages are expensive to run," mused Tammy, talking fast to keep her off balance.

"Faith provides," she said and Tammy felt a nerve twitch in her jaw. It was the same horseshit they'd tried to feed her as a child. Her sister Mary had bought into it, but such blind obedience had never made sense to her.

"But it doesn't. You provide. You and the other orphans donate money."

"As I said, faith," insisted Brook. "Giving some money back

is the least we could do for all that we received. Why are you asking about this? Where am I?" Despite being a semi-transparent version of herself, the former Guardian was still quite alert. She started looking around the room and then down at herself with a puzzled expression.

"Hurry up," muttered Fray. "She's slipping."

"How often do you go back to the orphanage?" asked Tammy.

Brook was growing irate and the image of her flickered and then resettled like a candle in a breeze. "I don't visit the orphanage, but what does it matter?"

"Then how do they receive your donations?"

"I'm not going to answer any more questions until you tell me who you are," declared Brook.

"We're done here," said Tammy, talking to Fray. Brook started to say something else, but the words were lost as she faded from view. His eyes flickered and then quickly changed back to their natural colour.

She should have thought of this sooner but had been so busy with a hundred other jobs. Some of her people were watching all the orphanages in Perizzi in case Akosh made an appearance. Perhaps they'd been looking for the wrong person. There was a report on her desk that listed all visitors coming to each of the orphanages. All she had to do was look for any names that appeared on all the lists. If there wasn't a match then she'd have all members of staff followed when they left the buildings to find the common element. Either way one of them would lead her to the money spider sitting at the heart of the web, parcelling out donations from former orphans. Once she found the money spider she could get access to the list of donors. Then she'd have a clearer picture of who she could trust in the city and if any more of her Guardians were followers of Akosh. It seemed unlikely that Brook was the only one.

"Tell no one about what you've seen or this place," said Tammy. "It's part of a highly sensitive investigation."

"On one condition," asked Fray, doing his best to meet her gaze.

She stared down at him coolly for a long moment before slowly raising an eyebrow. "Which is?"

"I want to come back here and study that room."

"Fine," said Tammy, turning away to hide her smile. She'd hoped he would be intrigued by the cell and make this request of her. It was another reason she'd brought him down here. The more she learned about it the better.

"What are you going to do now?" asked Fray as they started back up the winding stairs.

"Follow the money," said Tammy.

CHAPTER 20

Despite Wren's best efforts to keep her community a secret, word was beginning to spread. After what had happened in Sour Crown, as well as foiling several attacks on merchant caravans, travellers were starting to realise the normally dangerous and lawless western region of Shael was a lot safer than it used to be.

No one knew where Wren and the other mages lived and she made sure anyone who left the community was careful upon their return to make sure they weren't followed. The last thing she wanted was for a scavenger party to lead the raiders right up to her front door.

Travellers on the road into Shael understood that Boros and his raiders were still a problem, and that her mages couldn't be everywhere all the time, but anything that disrupted the robberies was seen as a good thing. Even if it was a mage. Wren knew they were still scared of magic and it wasn't a softening of their attitude, merely a reflection of how dire circumstances were in this desolate region. Given the chance they would still kill her or any other magic user. Caution seemed to be the word she imparted most often when speaking to anyone who set foot outside their community.

Wagon trains didn't take any fewer precautions. They were still crawling with mercenaries and sometimes one or two Fists of Drassi warriors, but losses had been reduced. What she found most odd about it all was that some of the travellers left her a tribute.

There was an old stone marker towards the halfway point in what she'd come to think of as her territory. The worn stone circle, once a shrine to the passing of the seasons, was now used to drop off offerings of food, a little money and sometimes children.

The refugees came from all over the west and she suspected many had fled south to Shael to avoid persecution at home. Although no country had brought in a national ban on magic, Garvey's murderous rampage, combined with the problem of Seekers and children exploding, meant anyone connected to magic was still seen as a threat.

Until rumours of her community spread there had not been anywhere that was remotely safe for children struggling with control. Wren felt a little guilty as recently she had been vocal about the shortfalls of the school but it had been a haven. In the years to come Wren suspected there would be many such moments where she discovered the Red Tower had done a lot more than she realised. It had given people hope that the power inside them could be tamed and that it need not be seen as a terrible burden or a curse. With the destruction of the school, and communities turning their back on magic, there had been nowhere to turn. Until now.

After speaking with the children who were abandoned on the road, they told Wren how they'd done their best to hide in plain sight. They'd tried to go on with their lives as normal while struggling to contain the primal forces growing inside them. All of the children found beside the stone marker had their hands and feet tied together, suggesting they'd been prisoners or captured stowaways on the caravans.

So far they'd rescued eleven children and only nine of them had the ability to touch the Source. As for the other two, someone had taken a dislike to them and used the threat of magic to force them from their homes. At least with more people the work in their community was made a little easier.

Delegating had always been difficult for Wren but, after Laila had proven to be so reliable, she was gradually learning to let others share her burdens. In truth it was something of a relief. She wasn't nearly as exhausted all of the time and it allowed her to focus on the issue of Boros.

The houses were being built at an astonishing rate, some cows and chickens had been rounded up and all the students were making progress in their studies. For some that meant going back to basics, learning to read and write, as they'd come from small communities where they weren't seen as a priority. Those without magic were taught alongside everyone else, learning herb-lore, survival skills and how to fight with a sword or empty-handed. The absence of Master Choss during those lessons was particularly noticeable and Wren knew the news about him from other survivors was not good. The last time anyone had seen him was fleeing into the woods on horseback being pursued by an angry mob. She'd whispered a prayer to the Blessed Mother that night to watch over his spirit.

Master Yettle and a few others offered her advice on decisions that affected the community when she asked, but a lot of Wren's time was now taken up with keeping the peace in the region and planning how best to tackle the raiders. So far Boros had done little that was different. It was as if her confrontation with the raiders in Sour Crown hadn't happened, or the message she'd delivered hadn't reached him. Whatever the reason his people had not returned to the village to exact revenge. Not yet at least.

In the last week there had been two attacks on merchant trains and one on a village where some of Wren's people had been only an hour before. They'd barely left and had doubled back, injuring several of the raiders who quickly fled.

"Perhaps they're scared," said Laila, who'd taken to walking with her and Danoph early in the morning. Wren liked to see how things were progressing in the community and it gave her a chance to talk things through with her friends.

"No. It's something else."

"A test," said Danoph, reminding Wren once more of his unusual insight. It wasn't just his visions that allowed him to see what was to come. He was only a year older than her and yet at times he seemed so much older, or at least significantly wiser than her. Maybe being exposed to brutality from such an early age gave him clarity when it came to violent criminals and their deeds. Whatever the cause, she'd learned to trust his instincts.

"Exactly. I think it's a test," she agreed, but her feeling did not come from her intuition. It was from long experience, but not hers. Old men loved to talk and children often went unnoticed in a crowd. Wren had grown up around craftsmen who, in their youth, had been Drassi warriors who wore the famous mask. They had travelled to every land, fought for and against every kind of soldier and warrior, and lived to tell the tale. They were veterans of wars and countless battles most people had never heard about. In every tea-house and whisky bar across Drassia they reminisced and spun stories for attentive audiences. Before his passing her grandfather had sat her on his knee and told her hundreds of stories about his life as a young man. Wren remembered his tales and those of other warriors because they were full of exciting adventure and heroic deeds.

Once Wren's mother learned of her interest in these stories she had tried a similar approach, with less wondrous tales about their family's clothing empire. However, she gave up when she realised Wren retained none of the facts about the less exciting history of silk and its arrival in Drassia.

After going over many of the stories she remembered, Wren came to understand one thing. There was nothing new that Boros could attempt had not been done before by someone else.

Every scheme, every ploy and tactic had been tried in the past. She just had to hope the stories she remembered included how to beat whatever he was planning. At the same time Wren was under no illusions about her skills and made sure she talked through everything with the teachers before making any important decisions. She made no attempt to hide that she was speaking to them and yet everyone assumed the plans were hers alone. Master Yettle had even encouraged her not to dissuade others from thinking this. She was the founder and figurehead of the community and people needed someone to believe in.

"What kind of test?" asked Laila.

"I think he's studying us to see how we react. How fast we can travel to the villages and our tactics when we defend the caravans," said Wren. It made sense. After all she was doing her best to learn about Boros, his people and how they fought. "All of this is a lull before the storm."

She had a few ideas about what he would next attempt. It might not happen tomorrow or the next day, but it would come soon. They were on a collision course and only one of them would walk away from it. The thought made her hands tremble but only Danoph noticed.

"Laila, could you please do me a favour?" asked Danoph, holding out his basket of fresh herbs. "Morag asked for these and I have to go and help in the school. Would you mind?"

Laila's smile spoke volumes. Wren had heard some of the rumours about her. A few people thought she and Danoph were more than friends despite her protests. She let it go for now as it gave her some time alone with Danoph. It was clear he wanted to tell her something in private. Laila took the basket without a word but winked at Danoph before she left.

The two of them walked in silence for a while, heading for the sheep enclosure, where one of the new arrivals was being trained to herd the flock. Amos, a grizzled farmer, was teaching the girl how to whistle to control the dog, but they were far enough away to talk without being overheard.

"Have you had another vision?" asked Wren.

"Yes, but it's one I've had before."

She was afraid this was going to happen and knew what it meant. "Was it the one about your village?"

So far he'd had the dream at least five times that she knew about, but was beginning to think it was a lot more.

"Yes. It's coming more often."

"You're going to leave," said Wren, feeling a pain in her chest.

"I am, but not yet," he promised. "I need to go back to the beginning and speak to my mother. She sent me to the Red Tower for a reason, and now I wonder if it was because I predicted something when I was young. I believe she knows more than I've been told. My ability to channel power from the Source is limited, so something must have happened that made her get me tested by a Seeker."

The heartache was spreading and Wren did her best not to let it show on her face. It had been a couple of weeks since Tianne had left and she still hadn't grown used to her friend's absence. Her two friends had helped her survive the Red Tower and losing one of them so soon was bad enough. For her to be without either of them was something she found difficult to think about. Nevertheless, it was not her place to keep him here against his will.

"What's coming with Boros is going to be difficult. Perhaps the most difficult challenge you'll ever face," he said. "I'm not going to abandon you now."

"Did you see something? Is there something I should know?"

Danoph shook his head. "No, I can just see which way the wind is blowing. I want to make sure that when the time comes you won't hold back."

Wren fidgeted and turned away from him to watch the sheep. "What do you mean?"

"You scared the raiders away at Sour Crown, but you know that it won't be enough next time. It may be necessary for you to kill them."

The words hung in the air and Wren struggled to control the emotions roiling inside. Her mind immediately went to the bully, Brunwal, and the way the black motes had eaten through his flesh and bones. The sounds he'd made had been unlike anything she'd ever heard. They'd been inhuman.

The logical part of her mind was reminding her that she wasn't the one who had summoned the thing that destroyed him. All she'd done was defend herself against someone who wanted her dead. The rest of her mind wasn't as calm and rational. It showed her again and again the terror in his eyes as she'd trapped him inside a shield with the pulsating living darkness. Over and over she heard the noises he'd made and some nights it was she who woke up Danoph with her screams.

She had killed him. No matter how she tried to look at it, as an accident or in defence of her life, that one thought was undeniable. He was dead. There was no one else to blame. And now Danoph was telling her she might have to do it again.

"I'm not sure I can," she said finally. "Even to save myself."

"Out here, we're far away from the capital city, but the villagers don't kill their neighbours just because the Queen isn't sending patrols to the area. They don't need to be told. Right and wrong doesn't come from the threat of punishment for not obeying the law, or what's written in a sacred book." From the corner of her eye she saw Danoph shake his head in disappointment. He had little time for religion or those who followed any faith blindly. "Boros and his people chose this place because there are no repercussions for their actions. They can steal and kill and hurt other people and nothing happens." He spoke calmly, neither angry nor sad, it was merely a statement of fact. "The villagers aren't strong enough to fight back, otherwise the raiders would go elsewhere. They're preying on the weak and they like doing it. Even a lion that hunts a herd of deer does it for food, not for fun. The raiders enjoy scaring and hurting other people."

"You want me to kill them? Kill all of them?" asked Wren, her voice turning hysterical.

"I don't, but tell me this. Do you think Boros can be reasoned with? Do you think he will accept a compromise if you offered one? Do you think he would hesitate to kill you?"

She knew the answers to all of his questions. The villagers at Sour Crown had tried to negotiate at the point when they'd already surrendered. The victor did not negotiate with conquered subjects. They made demands and doled out punishment if they were not met. She represented a threat to his control and reign of terror. With her dead, and made an example for others, their fear of Boros would only increase, making it easier for his people to collect their tithe in the future.

"There's no law or justice out here to protect the people. There's just us. You could try to scare them off again with magic, and it might work for a time, but they'll come back."

"You don't know that," said Wren, but she didn't really believe it herself. It hadn't worked on Brunwal and she knew hardened criminals who robbed and killed would not be easily scared away. This remote frontier offered them a chance to live as they chose, outside the law, because if they tried it anywhere else they would be arrested and imprisoned. Killing one teenage girl to keep their way of life wouldn't worry them or cause any sleepless nights.

Danoph took one of her hands in both of his, making her look at his face. "Something in them is broken. I don't know how it happened or when, but at some point they walked away from one path and chose this life. They're scavengers, preying on the weak. They don't have the courage to try something difficult and fail. I may be wrong, perhaps a severe shock will send them in a new direction, but I have my doubts."

"I don't want to hurt anyone," she said, trying to swallow the anguish.

"I know and that tells me a great deal about you, but you need to be ready in case they leave you with no other choice. When the time comes people here will need your strength and leadership."

She knew he wasn't just talking about those in their community. Every person in the nearby villages had been suffering before she'd intervened.

"If the moment comes, and you find yourself facing Boros, then you need to act without hesitation. I know this is a terrible burden, but you can shoulder it," he said, giving her hand a squeeze. "Others cannot. The weight would crush or twist them into something else. Something dangerous and destructive. Those who went with Garvey have shown us what can happen when anger and hatred take over."

"I don't know how to move past this guilt and pain," said

Wren, putting a hand to her chest. It was always there, lurking in the background.

"We'll find a way, together. You're not alone."

"What if, when the time comes, I'm not ready?"

"You will be," said Danoph. He sounded so confident. Perhaps he'd seen a vision of her fighting Boros, or perhaps it was just wish-fulfilment because she needed to be. All she could do was try. Wren decided she could do that much and hoped that when the time came she would be able to do whatever was necessary.

CHAPTER 21

Tianne wasn't sure how long she'd been in the water cell but she'd heard the guards upstairs change over at their posts several times. It felt like days at least.

Sometimes she drifted into a troubled, pain-filled sleep, huddled in a corner of the cell, her feet going numb from the cold water. The gnawing pain in her stomach told her she hadn't eaten in a long time and her throat was parched and raw. There was filthy water all around but she was sure it would do her more harm than good to drink it. Several times she'd called out to the guards but no matter what she said they continued to ignore her.

Escape seemed impossible and so she was left only with time and her thoughts for company. If she'd worked harder on learning how to heal then she could do something about the burning pain in her side, the bruises and her swollen eye. Several times she tried to heal herself but at the Red Tower she'd barely been able to master minor cuts, never mind anything else. The pain made it difficult to embrace the Source but each time she did it provided her with a brief respite. Her physical discomforts faded but, unfortunately, at the same time her senses became more acute. She could pick out individuals in the crowd upstairs and began to recognise certain voices. Out of boredom, and to keep her mind occupied, she assigned names to them and tried to picture their faces.

Tianne's sense of smell also sharpened to the point where it felt as if the stench of the stagnant water was filling her nose and scratching the back of her throat. She tried not to gag but ended up dry retching a few times. Her empty stomach contracted even further but she fought to hold on to the Source as the pain of her injuries was far worse than the assault on her senses.

All too often her physical condition interrupted her reverie and she lost her concentration. Her grip on the Source shattered and the pain and cold rushed in again making it that much more difficult the next time.

At some point Tianne found herself feeling light-headed. A rat had found its way into her cell and it started paddling across the water towards her. When she tried to kick it away the rat vanished. A moment later it reappeared with two more rats, all of them seemingly intent on crawling over her. She was already pressed into a corner of the cell and had nowhere to go. Kicking and punching, she tried to keep the rats away but they dodged back out of reach and then just sat and waited. It wasn't natural. Rats were never that silent and still. Six beady eyes watched her, waiting for her to exhaust herself or perhaps fall asleep.

Despite the danger and the cold, Tianne felt her head dip towards her chest. Each time her head started to nod she shook herself awake, expecting to find one of the rats gnawing on her arm. But they just sat and waited. The next time she felt her head dip forward she stood up, screaming and shouting, waving her arms to fight off something. Her cell was empty and she didn't know if the rats had been real or an hallucination.

Her mind started drifting down peculiar pathways and she found herself full of strange regrets. Her new clothes were torn, wet and ruined. They were only a few days old. Tianne also worried about her horse. The merchant would think she wasn't coming back and by now had probably sold it on to someone else. It could be days away from the city already. She envied that freedom.

Alone in the dark and cold she wondered how long her sanity would last. If they did intend to torture her then perhaps they wanted to break her spirit first. What if they asked her about the location of other mages? What if they wanted to know about Wren's community? But that was impossible, they couldn't know where she'd come from. Unless she'd already told them and just couldn't remember.

Wailing in a panic about her possible betrayal, Tianne instinctively reached for the Source and without realising began to freeze the air. Water began to drip from the ceiling of the cell and a long icicle formed on the metal grille. When something freezing dripped onto her face she thought it was raining, forgetting that she was inside. Looking up she saw the icicle and her connection to the Source evaporated. With greedy, swollen hands she snapped it off and, not caring about the metallic taste, bit off the end. The water was freezing and delicious, easing her parched throat. She crunched her way through half of the icicle before her thirst was sated.

It took a while but eventually Tianne noticed something was different. It was the silence. People talking and moving above her head had become a constant background noise that she'd grown used to, but now it was absent. Staring up at the grille she saw several faces peering at her through the narrow gaps.

"Open it," said a rich, commanding voice and she heard several people scrambling to obey. More light flooded into her watery cell and she had to shield her eyes until they adjusted to the brightness. "Bring her up," said the voice again. She caught a glimpse of a handsome, middle-aged Zecorran man with thick black hair and a brooding expression. Rage flowed off him in waves and everyone else seemed petrified by him.

A rope ladder was dropped into her cell but Tianne was so weak she couldn't climb up. The fingers on her left hand wouldn't work properly and she didn't have the strength to pull herself up the rungs.

"Child, stand to one side," said the voice again in a gentler tone. Tianne complied and a moment later heavy splashes announced the arrival of two large men. When they approached her she panicked and tried to fight back but all she managed to do was feebly flap her hands against them. They ignored her cries and lifted her above their heads. More hands from above grabbed hold of her arms and she was lifted out of the darkness into yellow light that stung her eyes.

"By the Blessed Mother," hissed the man. Tianne felt something warm and soft wrapped around her as strong arms lifted her off the ground.

"Regent, she's filthy," someone protested and was abruptly cut off.

Tianne felt herself being carried and in a daze she saw several corridors fly by. She didn't care what was happening any more. She was warm and this illusion was a lot better than some that had come to her. Tianne decided to embrace the fantasy while it lasted, drifting off into an uneasy sleep.

The next time she woke up Tianne was surprised not to see the familiar walls of her cell. Her feet were dry and had been wrapped up in something warm and soft. She was buried under a heavy sheet and it took her a little while to realise it was a thick woollen blanket. She lay in a plush bed in a comfortable-looking room and not far away the handsome man was tending a roaring fire. Its heat filled the room and her face was hot and flushed. Her eyes were sticky but the swelling over one of them had been reduced. When the man saw that she was awake he came to her side and gently lifted her head.

"Drink this," he said, holding a cup to her lips. "Slowly," he warned her. Tianne gulped down some of the liquid which tasted like a broth of sorts. She felt its warmth spreading throughout her body and after only a few mouthfuls was done. The fire and the blanket and the broth wrapped her in a warm cocoon and she slept again.

For the next few days Tianne drifted in and out of consciousness and each time she woke he would soon appear at her side to feed her and check on her health. Others came and went, treating her wounds and tending to some of her needs, which initially she found embarrassing. Her old clothes were gone and Tianne realised she'd been bathed and dressed in thick woollen garments beneath the blanket. With barely the strength to sit up without assistance, Tianne soon overcame her embarrassment. By the third day she felt more like herself and was sitting up in bed eating unaided, no longer swaddled in woollen clothing and blankets. Her right eye was still a little swollen and sore, but there were no mirrors for her to see how badly she'd been injured.

Much to her surprise she hadn't lost any toes from her prolonged exposure to the cold water. Her feet ached a little when she stumbled around, but she hoped that too would fade in time.

When he entered the room this time she noticed how the guards outside the door bowed their heads, confirming her suspicion about his identity.

"How are you feeling?" he asked, sitting down on the edge of her bed.

"Much better, thank you, Sire," said Tianne, bowing her head.

"Ah," said Regent Choilan, offering her a smile that warmed her right down to her toes.

"If not for you, I would be dead. I don't know how to thank you."

The Regent sadly shook his head and Tianne felt dismayed. The last thing she wanted to do was disappoint him. "I owe you an apology. I'm so sorry for what happened."

Tianne was stunned into silence but eventually managed to speak. "I don't understand."

"It's my fault," he said, taking one of her hands in his. "I had told my people that any Zecorran mages were to be made welcome, but they didn't listen. Maybe some of them didn't think it was real, or their bias made it easy for them to ignore it. I've punished those responsible for what happened to you, but can you ever forgive me?"

She didn't know what to say. The Regent of Zecorria was asking for her forgiveness. In every fantasy and scenario in her mind, not once had this ever come up. "Of course," she managed to babble. "All is forgiven, Sire. It wasn't your fault."

His smile, and the gentle squeeze of his strong hands made heat rise in her cheeks. If he noticed he didn't say anything, for which she was grateful. He gently released her and she felt a jolt of disappointment that he was leaving so quickly. A moment later she realised how stupid that was. He was the Regent of the entire country, not her nursemaid. He'd already made a point of visiting her every day and helping feed her.

Thankfully, instead of leaving he moved to the window and stared out at the city below. As part of her daily routine she was encouraged to walk a little and yesterday she'd made it to the window by herself.

"It was a very brave thing you did, coming home after how I've spoken about mages." Tianne wasn't sure if she was supposed to answer or not. She decided to play it safe and remain silent. The Regent seemed lost in thought, wrestling with something, his face creased with worry. "But all of that is in the past and now we must move forward together. A terrible menace threatens us and I need loyal people like you. Loyal Zecorran mages."

He turned his head slightly towards her and Tianne thought it was a cue. "I still want to help. I came home to protect Zecorria."

"That's generous," he said, favouring her with a brief smile, "but you should know what's coming before agreeing to it. The work ahead is not going to be easy. Most people still think magic is evil and that mages are not to be trusted. I admit, I'm partially to blame for that attitude." The Regent's broad shoulders seemed to sag and Tianne thought he must have a lot of pressures weighing him down.

"It's not your fault," she said, but he carried on speaking as if he hadn't heard.

"Magic is a part of everything and I cannot pretend otherwise. Garvey and his band of rebels are murdering men, women and children. They're destroying whole communities and I need loyal, brave mages that are willing to stand up to him. But wherever they go, people may try to hurt them. It's going to take a long time to earn the people's trust."

"I'm used to it," said Tianne and the Regent turned, sadness and surprise warring on his face. "We fled from the Red Tower because people were afraid and blamed us for what had happened. We could have fought back and easily kept them at bay, but it would only have made things worse. So we ran instead."

"It saddens me that someone so young has had to deal with

so much." The Regent moved to sit down on the edge of her bed again. "After how you've been treated I wouldn't blame you for leaving. You would be given money, a horse and whatever provisions you need."

"This is my home," said Tianne, although part of her knew that was a lie. It hadn't felt like home in a long time. She'd felt more at peace at the Red Tower and later among her friends in the new community. Zecorria was a strange and unwelcoming land but she hoped that, in time, it would start to feel familiar again.

"If you choose to stay, you will become the first of my new cadre of loyal Zecorran mages."

"It would be my honour."

"Thank you, Tianne," he said, touching her hand, which sent a thrill up her arm. "The first step to regaining the trust of the people is to secure the city. There are many here who want to harm me and see chaos in the streets. I need your help to root out those using their magic for ill, scaring, harming or cheating others. You'll be assigned a patrol of Royal Guards to protect you, just in case."

He didn't need to say any more. Just by showing a small bit of magic in the queue for the palace people had been scared. Given what had happened during the war, and recently with Garvey, she couldn't really blame them. It was going to take people a long time to become accustomed to seeing magic being used deliberately in public. But she was determined to show the people of Zecorria that magic, in the right hands, was a wonderful thing.

"It will be my pleasure, Sire," said Tianne, giving him another seated bow.

"I'll come by and visit when I can," he said, getting up to leave. "Make me proud."

Many times she'd regretted leaving the safety of the community and making the long journey here, but now she had a purpose. She would impress the Regent and show him that he'd made the right decision with his amnesty. She wanted to prove that his trust in her was well placed and together they would slowly begin to win over the people.

Despite the perfect picture of the future she was creating in her mind a seed of worry remained. Her thoughts lingered on her arrival at the palace. The dull ache in her feet was a constant reminder of what happened when she trusted people too readily. Wren had been partially right. She had been naïve, but that too was in the past. This time it would be different. She was sure of it.

CHAPTER 22

The second time Munroe went to meet the Butcher her experience was a lot more pleasant. There was no need for the drunk routine or any form of pretence.

A note had been slipped under her bedroom door with a place to meet him. After a hearty breakfast, and remembering to avoid her old haunts, Munroe took a slightly strangled route down to the docks. If Perizzi was the centre of the west then the port was its beating heart. Rivers of goods and information flowed through the city and a hundred new stories arrived every morning via the ships with their diverse cargo. Merchants bartered with ships' captains and dockside workers for better deals while exchanging tales and rumours.

In the short time she'd been waiting for the Butcher she'd heard four stories about Garvey. After his latest attack on a village in northern Yerskania he'd vanished for about a week, only to reappear in Zecorria. The Regent's sudden change of heart and plea for mages made a lot more sense. She would've felt more sympathy for him if not for the fact that he'd been the first to bring in a national ban on Seekers.

One rumour about Garvey claimed that a group of Yerskani soldiers had fought the rogue mages somewhere in the north.

When Garvey and his followers attacked a town the soldiers had surprised them, succeeding in killing one of their number. A variant of the story from a swarthy captain claimed Garvey himself had been injured. For whatever reason all four stories agreed that he and his group had not been seen for eight days before their sudden appearance over the border. They hadn't attacked a settlement recently, which was making patrols in both countries increasingly nervous.

Despite spending several years at the Red Tower, Munroe's first impression of Garvey had not changed. His power and skill as a Sorcerer couldn't be denied, but he was dangerously unstable. Perhaps that was why when she first heard the stories of his rampage it didn't surprise her.

Normally Munroe enjoyed the crowds at the docks. Seeing so many people crawling over the ships made her realise she was just one individual among thousands and it put her troubles into perspective. Today she didn't care about any of them or their problems. Today there was too much noise and too many people for her liking. The only good thing about the crowd was her ability to hide in plain sight. None of Akosh's people knew she was coming after her, and, if she was half as clever as Munroe imagined, she would have several people working in the port. The only problem was she had no idea who they were. The Butcher probably had his suspicions, but she doubted any of Akosh's people would betray her. With a glare at the crowd and the unknown agents hiding within, she drained her glass of ale and went inside the drinking hole to fetch another.

A short time later the Butcher came in and sat down at the bar beside her. He ordered an ale and they drank in companionable silence for a while.

"I received some news from Rojenne," she said, forgoing any

of the usual banter. The crushing weight on her heart was a constant reminder of what had been taken from her. The constant effort of holding back her anger left little room for much else. The drink numbed the pain a little, but it always came back, full of razors and claws, ripping her apart on the inside.

She hated standing still and not being out there chasing down people, but had finally accepted her less than subtle approach would not be enough. Not this time.

"Was this your first official report as Doña Munroe?"

In Perizzi the underworld was controlled by several crime Families, each headed up by a Don or Doña.

She snorted. "Hardly. They don't have crime Families down there. The man I left in charge, Tok, found out she has two orphanages in Rojenne. Both of them receive their money once a month from someone here in Perizzi. It always comes in with merchant trains, so it's well protected. Someone then passes out the gold to the orphanages."

The Butcher said nothing for a while, mulling it over. "Makes sense. Rojenne is a fairly small city and a little out of the way. I doubt she has many people down there. It also lines up with what I've found."

"Which is?"

"A fat money spider," said the Butcher, raising one corner of his mouth in a half-smile.

"Where?"

"Right here, in the heart of Perizzi. The money flows in from all over and then goes back out again, to Rojenne and probably other places in Yerskania I've not found yet."

"Then why are we still sitting here?" said Munroe, getting up from her stool. The Butcher just tapped the bar and looked at her expectantly. Taking a deep breath, she sat back down again, swallowing her bitter frustration.

"If we were to grab the bookkeeper, there's no guarantee he'd know where to find her. However," said the Butcher, holding up a hand before she interrupted. He waited until Munroe had bitten her lip before continuing. "What he does have is a list of names. People and places. Part of Akosh's network. What we need is to get hold of that list, then I can have eyes and ears watching for her in all of those places."

"It's a good thing I never joined the Silent Order," said Munroe. "I don't have the patience for all this crap."

The Butcher raised an eyebrow. "The Silent Order? Never mind, I probably don't want to know."

"So where's the list? In his office?"

"No, I had someone check and that's the first problem. The Guardians are investigating Akosh as well, and they had the same idea. They picked up the accountant a few hours ago."

"What's the second problem?" asked Munroe through clenched teeth.

"He's being held at Unity Hall. It would be extremely difficult and costly for me to get one person inside that place. If I tried, the long-term repercussions would severely outweigh the short-term benefit." The repercussions for breaking into the Guardians' most secure building would be harsh. It was also not something that they would forget. There would be a lasting shadow hanging over everything the Butcher did while the Watch and every Guardian focused their attention on him. The risk simply wasn't worth the reward.

"Shit."

"I had hoped once the Old Man retired the new Khevassar would be more flexible. Sadly, it seems she's just as implacable as her predecessor."

"I know her. She's pretty dangerous."

"Perhaps you could work with her, and the Guardians, to find

Akosh," suggested the Butcher, but Munroe was already shaking her head before he'd finished talking.

"No. I tried that," she said, thinking back to her last meeting with Tammy. "They're too slow and always go by the book. They'll probably try to imprison Akosh. I'm going to rip off her head with my bare hands and piss on her rotting corpse."

"Very colourful."

"So what do we do instead?" asked Munroe. "I swear if you say 'be patient' or 'wait' I'll throw you through that wall and drown you in the river," she said.

The Butcher showed no signs of alarm other than to raise one eyebrow. He considered his answer carefully and Munroe felt herself reaching for the Source. She would throw him through the wall and into the next building and the one after that. There was only so much sitting around and doing nothing she could stomach. She needed answers. She needed an edge. Drawing power into herself she felt it fill her body, making every part of her skin tingle. Her senses were magnified until she could hear the slow and steady heartbeat of the Butcher. It also made her aware of a few other things about him that she'd previously missed.

He smelled of the sea and because he was dressed in a black leather vest she couldn't miss the heavy muscles across his shoulders and down his arms. His vest hid little and showed off his unique tattoos. It would make him a distinctive figure wherever he went. She'd presumed it was because he liked showing off his body, but now she began to wonder if there was another reason.

Wherever he went, people would immediately recognise him. The woman serving drinks behind the bar had steady hands until she came to serve the Butcher. Munroe had also noticed the worried looks other patrons had been giving him since he sat down. People were petrified of him.

It shouldn't matter. She'd left all of the mind games and scheming behind to start a new life and yet here she was, back in Perizzi, hip deep in Family business again.

"Follow the money," said the Butcher.

Munroe eased her grip on the Source, dulling her senses in the process. "What do you mean?"

"A peculiar thing happened in the last few days. All of her orphanages here in the city recently changed patrons. Priests have rededicated them to the Maker, the Blessed Mother or the Lady of Light."

"Someone else is trying to get rid of her in Yerskania," said Munroe.

"I suspect those in Rojenne will soon disappear as well. So, if you were one of her followers, and suddenly all of her orphanages in Yerskania are gone, where do you send the money?" asked the Butcher.

"You said she had orphanages in the north. In Zecorria," said Munroe.

"I have four bookkeepers," he said. "I'd be an idiot to trust one person with all of my money."

"She has another money spider in the north," said Munroe. With the Guardians swarming over Perizzi, and now someone else removing her connection to the orphanages, Akosh would have to be an idiot to return to Yerskania. She still had people in the city, but wouldn't know if they had been bought. And with so many different parties just waiting for her it would be the same as walking into a bear trap with your eyes open.

At the moment Zecorria was a safe harbour where she was still surrounded by people she could trust. The difficulty for Munroe, without having a network of her own, would be finding reliable information in the north. If she started asking too many questions or used her magic overtly it would draw attention.

"I can see what you're thinking," said the Butcher. "Nothing has changed, Munroe. If you go to Herakion, you'll be on your own, in her city. I have a handful of people there, but they're just Ears. They never ask questions and you can't use them for that. Someone might be willing to talk, if you have enough gold, but sifting through the lies will be the challenge."

He was right. Sometimes people would tell you exactly what you wanted to hear for a bit of money. Once people found out she was after Akosh they would come crawling out of the woodwork to feed her information. And in a city teeming with Akosh's people it wouldn't be long before someone tried to cut her throat in the middle of the night. In spite of knowing all of that, she couldn't sit still any longer. She knew it was rash. Balfruss and Tammy would probably say she was letting her thirst for revenge consume her and they'd be right. It didn't matter. Her rage was a living thing inside her. Munroe could feel it hammering against the bars of her restraint like a caged bear. It would only remain in check for so long. After that even she was afraid of what might happen.

"It doesn't matter. I have to go north," insisted Munroe. "She must pay for what she's done."

"There's also the other thing," said the Butcher. "The Regent has banned all mages, except those from Zecorria, who are willing to serve him."

"People in the north don't know me, or how my magic works. I can use it quietly until I find her. I just need some answers."

"If you insist on doing this, then at least take someone you can trust. Someone who will watch your back." Munroe immediately thought of Choss and her heart lurched in her chest again. "You need someone who doesn't stand out."

Tok would be the ideal candidate and she knew he would be reliable. On the other hand, she wasn't sure she could put him at risk. The thought of what it would do to his family if something went wrong was too difficult, and too familiar, to think about. An idea began to form in the back of her mind. People always underestimated her because of her size. She needed someone who could help her who would also go unnoticed.

"I have the perfect person in mind," said Munroe. "I need you to send a message south to Rojenne."

Once her new partner arrived she would travel north and begin her hunt. All she needed to do was find the bookkeeper, or, failing that, one person who was loyal to Akosh. Then she would squeeze them for every drop of information. However loyal the person, it would be meaningless in the face of what she could do to them with her magic.

CHAPTER 23

Akosh took a deep breath and tried to calm down. To distract herself she studied Bollgar's office, making a note of the small changes. He'd hung a few sprigs of dried lavender from the ceiling, giving the room a pleasant floral scent that wasn't overpowering. The stained robe he normally wore was gone and in its place black trousers and a stark white shirt that strained across his vast middle. A navy waistcoat and matching blue hat gave him the look of a retired sea captain, but all of it was a vast improvement from her last visit. He even smelled much better and she could see the skin on his face had been freshly scrubbed. She knew he was sweating, as dark stains were appearing under his arms, but at least the brim of his cap kept his face dry.

"Say that again. Slowly," said Akosh when she felt in control again.

"The two orphanages in Rojenne and all of the others in Yerskania have been rededicated to other gods."

"All of them."

"Yes, Mother. Priests from the Maker and others recently visited."

"When, exactly, did this happen?" she asked.

"In the last seven days."

Someone had been planning this for a while. To have all of them change, almost overnight, was unprecedented. It was possible human agents had been involved in persuading the orphanages, but she knew the person behind them all was one of her brethren. It was probably one of the eldest like Vargus or Nethun. No one else would be so bold. Only they understood what such a move would mean to her in the future.

Without the orphanages she had only one way of identifying those loyal to her in Yerskania; tracking the donations made to Bertran her bookkeeper.

She had far too many followers in Yerskania for her to remember them all. While some of her children might raise their offspring in the same faith, their loyalty was not as absolute. She could ask anything of her followers because she had saved them from a life of misery or an early death. Their children would be less reliable.

In fifty years' time, when all of her children were dead, she might cease to exist. Without followers, without their prayers and focus, her power would dwindle to nothing. She might disappear into the Void and never re-emerge.

In human terms fifty years was a lifetime and so much could change. For her kind it was nothing. A blink of an eye. She needed to find out who was doing this to her and how much they knew about her plans.

To lose everything she had built in Yerskania could not be tolerated. She still had many children in the country who were dormant. They were just going about their lives as normal. Their only direct contact with her might have been at an early age if she'd visited the orphanage. Since then their only connection was a monthly donation to help others. If she could find them, then perhaps now was the right time to test their loyalty and put them to good use. Most of her children in Yerskania were not in positions of power, but as shown with the Seekers that wasn't always necessary.

Whoever was behind this probably expected her to rush back to Yerskania to solve this personally. She had not gone unnoticed for this long by being rash.

"What about Bertran?"

"He's not been seen in Perizzi for days," said Bollgar. "I received a report that mentions the Guardians dragging him out of his shop. I believe he's being questioned by them."

Bollgar swallowed hard and went to mop his brow then remembered his new cap. He was right to be nervous. Bertran had been a loyal servant and an excellent bookkeeper, channelling all of the money into solid investments. The profits went back into funding the orphanages across Yerskania. Unlike Bollgar he had been a soldier as a young man, making him able to resist their questioning for longer. Even so, he wouldn't be able to hold out indefinitely. It was possible they already had a list of his clients and were hunting down her people.

Akosh gritted her teeth in frustration. It was beginning to look as if all of her people in Yerskania were completely lost. At least her followers would continue to sustain her for the short term. Surviving the next few months was the most critical issue. She could look at rebuilding when this crisis had passed.

Bollgar was very aware that if he was captured by the Guardians, or anyone else, he wouldn't last a day in their less than tender care. Perhaps from now on that might persuade him to behave in a more friendly fashion towards his two apprentices.

Akosh was getting annoyed at the Guardians and their constant interference. They were always sticking their noses into other people's affairs. If it was limited to Yerskania, that would be bearable, but sometimes they were invited abroad to solve difficult cases. For all she knew they could be petitioning the Regent right now to continue their investigation here in Zecorria.

"Has the money been redirected here?"

"Yes, Mother. A number of anonymous individuals have sent me their donations. I might be able to identify them, given enough time."

"Make sure half of the new donations are sent to Nazren."

"Yes, Mother." He managed to keep the sneer from his face, but not out of his voice. She had none of Bollgar's problems and was equally brilliant with numbers and investments. It was far safer to split the money in case Bollgar's heart finally gave out.

"What do you want to do about Bertran?" he asked.

It was a good question. As had been promised, Habreel had died in Unity Hall and it had been made to look like suicide. So far her ally was as good as his word. It would be very easy to reach out and ask him for another favour. Akosh was confident arrangements could be made so that Bertran suffered a similar fate to Habreel. But she needed to avoid relying on her ally.

As for Bertran it was already too late. She had no way of knowing how much he'd already told the Guardians. The damage had been done and her network in Yerskania had been compromised. Only a few months ago she would have wasted resources on trying to retrieve him and would have felt guilty if the attempt had failed.

"Nothing. Let him rot in a cell. He failed me," said Akosh.

"Yes, Mother," whispered Bollgar, avoiding her gaze.

"What's happening with the new orphanages here?"

"They're in hand," said Bollgar, pulling down a ledger from the shelf. "We're recruiting staff and should be able to open in a few weeks. Do you want the details?"

Akosh waved them away. If Yerskania was lost then at least

she still had a strong foundation here in the north. From it she could rebuild in the west and even look to the east.

Seveldrom had suffered losses in the war and they were almost as liberal and weak as Yerskania. It would be easy to set up orphanages over there dedicated to a god no one had heard of before. The only difficulty was the distance and the time required. It would also mean weeks or even a couple of months away from Zecorria.

A surrogate could be sent in her place, but experience had taught her that absolute loyalty required a miracle that only she could provide. It was a lot easier to believe in a god, follow their teachings and pass that faith on to others, if you had witnessed their power first-hand.

That was a problem for another day. In the meantime, she needed to know who was coming after her.

This time while she waited for Bissel at the Golden Goose, Akosh was relaxing in the dining room with a friend. The young man didn't have a lot to add to their conversation, but he followed every word she said with great care. So far that had consisted of her telling him stories from the early days when she'd been wild and hadn't thought about the future. Newly born, she'd had no doubts about living for ever and had revelled in the murders and the occasional bloodbath. Sometimes literally. Around the world assassins had butchered victims in her name and her power had grown. It was always going to be that wonderful. Until it wasn't.

"I tried bathing in a virgin's blood once. It didn't seem all that different to me. It was just so sticky," she lamented and her companion's eyes widened in terror. "Perhaps I wasn't doing it right. Maybe I should try again, although I think we both know that you're not a virgin any more." She laughed and nudged him with her shoulder in a friendly fashion. Sweat continued to pour down the sides of his face and a single tear ran from his left eye.

There was a bold knock on the door and a moment later Bissel strode into the room. His confidence evaporated when he saw who else was in the room.

"Ah, I believe you two know each other," said Akosh, noting the strong resemblance. They had the same nose, but where Bissel had dark hair his son's was blond.

The son tried to say something, perhaps to bravely warn his father, but the gag in his mouth muffled everything. He strained against the rope around his wrists and ankles but Akosh didn't try to stop him. She enjoyed watching him wriggle about. He was a tall, strapping young man, with balls the size of a horse's. Only a few hours ago he'd tried to seduce her in the tavern, but events had not gone quite as he'd anticipated.

"Join us for a drink," she said, pushing a glass of wine across the table. Bissel remained frozen in the doorway, his eyes flicking between them. "I said sit down and have a drink." The tone of her voice startled him into action. As if in a trance he closed the door and then sat down.

"You'll be all right," Bissel promised his son.

"Really?" she said, drawing a dagger and placing it gently against the son's cheek. He squeaked and tried to shuffle away from her but there was nowhere to go. "Do I have your attention?" Bissel focused on her and she relaxed. As a show of good faith she even went so far as to place the dagger on the table.

"What do you want?" asked Bissel.

"How is the wine?" she asked, ignoring his question. He was struggling to focus on her words but eventually lifted the glass to his lips and gulped some down.

"It's very nice."

"I want you to send a message to your Master, whoever he is. I would like a face-to-face meeting, here, in Herakion." As Bissel opened his mouth to protest Akosh held up a hand and he fell silent. "Choose your next words very carefully," she warned him.

"He won't come."

"Then you'll have to persuade him," said Akosh, affectionately patting his son on the leg. "I know you were ready to die for your Master, but what about your son? What about his life, Doctor Bissel? Aren't you supposed to save lives?"

After the last time they'd been in this room together she'd followed Bissel back to his surgery. Since then some of her people had been gathering information about him. Regarded as an adequate doctor with moderate skill, he lived a comfortable life with his only son after the tragic death of his wife. Unknown to everyone was Bissel's devotion to a new and mysterious god called Akharga. She knew it had something to do with medicine and healing, but the name was also another mask, making it impossible for her to know their real identity.

"I know all about you, Doctor, and what you're wearing around your neck," she said, gesturing at his shirt. It was a crude icon, made to resemble an open eye in the middle of a triangle. So far her people had found six doctors and several apothecarists in the city wearing the same pendant.

"He's not in the city," said Bissel, trying a different approach. "I don't even know if he's in Zecorria."

"Then you'd better send him an urgent message. Until then, your son is going to keep me company." Akosh put one arm around his shoulders as if they were good friends or lovers. This time he was far less eager to get close to her. She could feel him shaking while he whimpered like a newborn puppy.

"Be brave, son. I'll get you out of this, I promise," said Bissel. She didn't bother pointing out he couldn't keep that promise, but she let it go if it meant less whimpering from the son. With a glare and a shake of his head Bissel hurried out of the room leaving the two of them alone again.

He knew she was serious which meant he would do everything to get his Master to visit. Even without knowing the identity of her ally, she could start making preparations for his arrival. She had eyes and ears all over the city.

Soon she would find out who was behind the curtain. Then it would be time to adjust their alliance in her favour. Or end it abruptly if he tried something untoward.

"We're going to have so much fun," she murmured, slapping her companion on the leg. Beside her the young man began to scream around his gag.

CHAPTER 24

It felt strange to be out of uniform but Tammy enjoyed the anonymity it provided. It was a little before midnight and the streets of Perizzi were busy with drinkers and patrols of the Watch scooping up people and breaking up fights before they turned into proper brawls. At one point Tammy was forced to carry a teenage girl to the nearest squad of the Watch. The girl had pretended to be seeking directions, only then to draw a knife and attempt to rob Tammy.

After disarming the girl and putting her on her arse, the sensible thing to do would've been to run, but something in the girl wouldn't quit. Tammy had been willing to let her go, but when the girl came at her with another knife she'd knocked out two of her teeth. Thankfully she only had to carry the girl on her shoulder for a couple of streets. The Captain of the squad recognised Tammy immediately and took the would-be robber off her hands into custody.

Annoyed at the delay, Tammy increased her pace and arrived late at a modest house on a quiet side street. Wedged between a bakery and a cobbler's was a narrow alley that led to a private courtyard. The houses were old-fashioned in design, tall and narrow as if huddled together for warmth. It was secluded but not too far away from amenities and the heart of the city. She also noticed it was only a few streets away from where her sister lived.

After knocking on the door she glanced behind her and studied the windows facing onto the courtyard. All were dark and had the curtains closed but that didn't mean someone wasn't watching. A bit of paranoia in her position was healthy.

The door behind her opened to reveal the Old Man. "Welcome. Come in," he said, stepping aside. Tammy had to bow her head to get through the front door and the next doorway to enter his front room. She could see why the houses in this street might be unpopular with some, but for someone short like the Old Man it was probably quite cosy.

She briefly glanced around the room, noting several chests of personal belongings that had not yet been unpacked. The furniture was old and worn but it was comfortable when she sat down. Her mentor cleared a stack of books from another chair and added more wood to the fire. The room was too hot and almost immediately her forehead was beaded with sweat. Knowing that old people felt the cold more readily she said nothing but took off her jacket and loosened her shirt. The Old Man noticed and a wry smile touched the corners of his mouth.

"It will happen to you one day."

"If I live to be as old as you," she replied.

Before his retirement he'd looked worn out and had collapsed at the palace from exhaustion. Time away from the job seemed to have had a rejuvenating effect as his eyes were clear and focused. He moved with more energy than she'd seen in a long time, fetching two mugs of tea from the kitchen, despite her protest. Once they were both resettled, and she was getting too warm again from the fire and the tea, Tammy tried to find the right words.

He could see that she was struggling with something and gave her time. It was another small delay but curiosity made her ask.

"I noticed we're only a few streets away from my sister."

The Old Man shrugged. "I didn't want to walk halfway across the city every time I want to visit my long-lost family."

"Did Mary believe you?"

"Of course not. She knew exactly who I was. I should have recruited you both," he mused. "That would have been something."

"And the children?" she asked, getting dangerously close to a subject she did her best to avoid thinking about, even when alone.

"They're just happy to have something like a grandparent in their lives again. It's been quite a few years. Mary says I'm spoiling them, but she lets me do it."

A weight lifted off her shoulders. Other larger, more pressing issues still weighed her down, but that thought gave her some relief. She'd been worried Mary would reject the Old Man's offer and their long-term wellbeing had been playing on her mind. It was one thing she could set aside, allowing her to focus on larger concerns.

"I need your opinion on a couple of things," she said, getting to the reason for her visit.

"Always happy to lend an ear."

"Habreel is dead. He was found last night, hanged in his cell."

"I see," said the Old Man. He sounded fairly unmoved and Tammy shared his sentiment. There was a huge list of crimes levelled against Habreel which he'd freely admitted to committing. As result he'd been facing many years behind bars and potentially death by public hanging. "Do you suspect foul play?"

Tammy shook her head. "I had Faulk check into the family history of all the other Guardians. Brook was the only acolyte of Akosh. I also trust everyone who had access to Habreel's cell."

"Then what happened?" he said.

She'd been mulling that over for hours. "I think it was guilt. Habreel still thought of himself as a Guardian. He had a mission and people who shared his ideology, but then he was betrayed. Everything he'd done, all of the terrible orders he'd given, were for nothing. When he arrived at my office, he was a broken man. I thought helping me bring others to justice would be enough for him."

The Old Man sighed. "He had a lot of pride. To find out he'd been outsmarted and lied to for years, by those closest to him, must have been difficult to swallow. In some ways I think it was inevitable."

Tammy was disappointed that Habreel had taken the easy way out instead of accepting responsibility. If it had been up to her she would have had him imprisoned for the rest of his life. That would've been torture for someone like him. To be part of the world, to hear about events, but have no place in them and no way to contribute.

His suicide also meant that she had lost another valuable resource in her campaign against Akosh, which brought her to the other reason for her visit.

"What was the other thing you wanted to speak about?" asked the Old Man.

"All of the orphanages we're watching in Perizzi, and some in the south, receive monthly donations from former orphans. And I found the recipient. A bookkeeper named Bertran. He's currently sat in the black cells waiting to be questioned again."

Finding him had required a few days of following all of the visitors to the various orphanages in the city. Bertran never visited in person, and the money often arrived with other supplies, but with some persuasion her people had eventually found him. A few hours of studying his records had revealed nothing as it was all written in code. It might be possible for one of her people to crack it, but it wouldn't happen overnight. In the meantime, Akosh's network could be putting their plan into effect and she would have no idea about what it was or the repercussions.

Guardian Faulk, one of her most trusted, had spent a few hours alone in a cell with Bertran but surprisingly had produced nothing of value. Physically the bookkeeper wasn't imposing, a spindly, pale man with long, elegant fingers and a balding pate, but his mind was incredibly sharp. Faulk had fenced words with him for a long time, only to emerge with an appreciation of the man's ability to recite and multiply numbers to avoid answering questions.

"What is it you want to ask me?" prompted the Old Man.

"Have you ever had someone tortured for information?"

The Old Man didn't look surprised. In fact his expression seemed to indicate he'd known this was coming. "I'll need something a little stronger than tea," he said, digging around in a box before producing a dusty old bottle. He offered her a glass but she declined and he poured himself a generous portion of a colourless liquid. She could smell it from across the room and guessed it was fairly potent.

"What does this bookkeeper have?" he asked, setting the question aside for now.

"A list of names. People in the network."

"And have these people done anything to harm others?"

Tammy ticked items off on her fingers. "Some of them have spread stories that encouraged violence against Seekers and anyone with magic. Inciting hatred of children and taking part in exiling or killing some of them. I also believe some of them have magic of their own and posed as Seekers to make it worse. You've heard the stories. The Red Tower denies the Seeker in Gorheaton was one of theirs and I believe Balfruss."

"That's a long list of serious crimes, but I noticed you said some of them were responsible. What about the others you've not found yet?"

"What about them?"

"That's why you're here, isn't it?"

"They're dangerous people," said Tammy.

"Ah," he said, holding up a finger. "Potentially they're dangerous."

Tammy had been wrangling with this issue since the moment Bertran had refused to cooperate. More acts of violence and murder were likely, being perpetrated by members of this group, directed by Akosh. Finding her would be incredibly difficult. She suspected most of her people would rather kill themselves than give up any information, like Guardian Brook. However she had doubts about all of them being such zealots.

The worst-case scenario was that Bertran gave her a list of names and they imprisoned all of them. Then it wouldn't matter what orders Akosh sent out if she had no one to execute them. A better scenario was that some of them were willing to talk.

Finding Akosh and stopping her was the end goal, but if Balfruss was right then it might be a better idea to let someone else deal with her. Tammy had no illusions. Her experiences with magic and what had happened in Voechenka didn't make her an expert. She'd survived it, not mastered it and her skills lay elsewhere.

She needed information and Bertran had it. Torturing him would give her the list of names she needed. At the moment it was likely some of the people in Akosh's network hadn't done anything, but it was what they might do if she gave an order that worried her.

"All of these people. They're all part of the same cult," she said, pulling out a copy of a slim book she'd found at Bertran's home. The Old Man opened it and began to flick through the pages, reading passages at random.

It was identical to the one they'd found on Guardian Brook. By itself the religious text was fairly innocuous and not too dissimilar from others she'd read.

The book of Akosh preached a number of values that were common to other faiths, such as compassion, helping others and equality. It deviated in only two significant ways that were potentially dangerous. First, there were no priests or places of worship. People simply prayed at home. Second, every member of the faith was a follower and Akosh, above all others, had to be obeyed. This founding principle overruled everything else. Every law, every tradition, every family value and blood tie, every moral restraint. Normally such a rule wouldn't be an issue as people didn't have conversations with their god. But with no priests all the orders came from just one person.

Whether Tammy believed Akosh was actually a god, or a cult leader who had adopted the name and mantle of a predecessor, didn't really matter. The followers of Akosh believed it and they obeyed her absolutely. So far she knew of at least three followers who had used their magic to kill people and then blown themselves up, despite such an act going against everything in their religious text. Akosh's word had to be obeyed and they had done it, sacrificing themselves because she'd asked.

All of which brought Tammy back to the original dilemma.

"Did you ever have someone tortured?" she asked. The Old Man set the book aside and drained his glass in one go. Something made him wince, but she didn't think it was the taste of the alcohol.

"Yes, and I still carry the memories," he replied. "Getting a confession that way is almost always unreliable, but a few years into the job a day came when I needed information and time was running out."

"Did you get what you needed?"

"I did, and we stopped the ship unloading its tainted cargo." He waved a hand dismissing her next question for more details about what happened. "It's in the past. You don't need to know. No one died. That's the important thing."

Tammy wondered how many times he and the Guardians had averted disasters that now only existed within the pages of a journal in Unity Hall. Only a handful of people would know how many near misses there had been and in truth most people wouldn't want to know. They slept a lot easier.

If she'd been having this conversation with someone else, like her sister, then Tammy knew that right about now Mary would be judging her. But the Old Man knew exactly what she was struggling with as he'd been in the same position, probably more than once. He was, perhaps, the only person who could understand what she was going through.

"I need an inquisitor," she said, coming to a decision.

"I can put you in touch with someone I've used in the past."

The consequences, and the weight of her actions, would be a burden on her conscience, but she would have to find a way to live with them.

CHAPTER 25

Taking a deep breath, Wren embraced the Source, feeling power flood her body until every part of her skin was tingling with unspent energy. On her left Danoph didn't react, but on the other side she heard the others shifting uncomfortably. They could sense it coursing through her and thought it meant that conflict was imminent. Wren was nervous, but as their leader she was trying her best not to show it. With a small amount of effort her eyesight sharpened until the blurry landscape ahead came into focus.

Gillen's Jaw lay before her in the valley below. It was a quiet fishing village located beside a lake that had once been a popular place for anglers seeking a challenge. On the outskirts were a few large houses, the largest of which belonged to the previous Queen of Shael. Since her only surviving daughter, Olivia, had taken the throne the summer home and those surrounding it had mostly gone to ruin. Queen Olivia didn't have money to waste on such frivolities. So the buildings sat idle and became a once-glorious reminder of a better time for the country and the village.

"Why here?" asked Kimme, scratching at her armpits. Wren tried very hard not to wrinkle her nose at the girl. She didn't have fleas, just poor personal hygiene, and would only wash when others insisted the smell kept them awake at night.

"It might not be here," said Wren, which was why she'd sent four groups of students, each under the guidance of a teacher, to watch for trouble at other villages. She didn't have enough people to cover every community, but then again neither did Boros, which was what she was counting on. One raider on a horse demanding a tithe would be chased away from a village, no matter who'd sent him. Boros would have to choose his next target wisely.

"So, can I go to sleep?" asked Kimme.

"Only if you don't snore again," said Wren.

Kimme grunted and turned away. She'd been elbowed awake at various points during the last three days for dozing off. This was the fourth day in a row Wren had been waiting for Boros to strike. She knew it was tedious and required a great deal of patience, which was why she'd rotated those who visited a different village each day. Everyone needed to know what they were fighting for, but it was difficult to remain focused all day with nothing to do.

The first few hours were always tense, with those beside her expecting raiders to come pouring out of the surrounding hills to attack the village. When that didn't happen, the adrenaline began to fade, tiredness crept in and muscle cramps and boredom took its place.

Danoph always came with her. He remained a steady presence that helped her maintain the appearance of being calm. She also insisted on regularly bringing Kimme, despite her pungent aroma, as she was one of the strongest students to arrive. As a farmer's daughter she'd regularly lifted cows and even horses above her head, moving them around like toys, and ploughing fields using only her willpower. If not for a nosey neighbour

who'd rallied the village against her, Kimme would have continued doing the work of five people on the farm. Her parents had
been distraught at seeing her leave, which was a rarity among
children with magic.

"There's movement in the main street," said Wren, watching
as a crowd of adults started walking down the middle. Ahead of
them was a woman dressed in ragged leather armour dragging
a man along by his hair. The raider had a bloody dagger in one
hand and Wren could see splashes of red on the man's face and
chest.

Something flickered briefly in one of the windows of the
old abandoned mansion on the hill and a frown creased her
brow. She gave Kimme an order and the girl happily complied,
scuttling away to the west of their position before circling
back to the village. The two other students with her she sent
to the east, just in case, while Danoph would come with her.
He still had an ongoing struggle holding onto power when
he could embrace the Source, but she didn't need him for his
strength. His instincts for people were especially useful in tense
situations.

Maintaining her grip on the Source, Wren started running
towards the main street of Gillen's Jaw. Slowly the conversation
between the raider and the villagers reached her magic-augmented
hearing.

"You brought this on yourself," the raider was saying, bran-
dishing her dagger. "And every time you refuse Boros it will
cost you another life. Maybe next time it will be one of your
children."

Even though she was still quite far away Wren was able to
reach out and wrench the blade from the raider's hand. It flew
across the street and buried itself in the front door of a nearby
building. There were gasps in the gathered crowd but the raider

didn't seem alarmed. It was almost as if she'd been expecting Wren. Instead of releasing the injured man she drew another dagger and pulled him tight against her chest, pressing the blade to his throat.

Wren stopped a short distance away from the raider and her captive. Danoph stood next to her, silent and watchful. His eyes drifted up to the roof of a nearby building and then back to the street. The gathered crowd were clearly scared for their friend, but none of them said a word.

"Want to try that again?" said the raider. She pressed the blade to the front of the man's throat, wrapping both arms around his neck, almost as if they were lovers. If Wren tried to yank it free it would slice open his neck.

She had thought the raider would be older, perhaps a veteran of the war like many of the others she'd seen. Instead she was facing a young woman from Seveldrom who hadn't seen thirty summers. With wild straw-coloured hair and gentle features, she might once have been pretty, if not for the void behind her wintry blue eyes. Much like other raiders the woman lacked compassion. Her language was violence, used as a club to get what she wanted. Just as Danoph had predicted Wren thought it might be the only thing she understood.

"I could make you drop it, or I could just make your head explode," said Wren, making herself smile.

The raider paled slightly but quickly recovered. "This village isn't yours."

"It doesn't belong to Boros either," said Wren and the raider twitched at the mention of his name. "Leave these people in peace and never come back."

"Or what?"

It seemed as if a show of force was necessary. "Or I'll kill you where you stand."

Much to Wren's surprise the raider grinned, but somehow the smile never made it to her lifeless eyes. Pursing her lips, she let out a sharp whistle and Wren sensed movement on both sides. Looking up at the buildings she saw three archers on either side, but instead of aiming at her they were pointing at the crowd.

"You might be able to stop me, but I doubt you can save everyone," said the raider.

It was a good idea and it showed both forethought and caution. If Wren hadn't showed up Gillen's Jaw would've become yet another village paying a tithe to Boros. But now the raiders had the opportunity to get rid of her at the same time as scaring another community. With so many people witnessing her defeat the raiders wouldn't need to work as hard at intimidating other villages in the area.

Wren thought it might even have worked if they hadn't underestimated her.

"Your move," said the woman.

Never one for dramatics, Wren simply focused a trickle of the power she was channelling on her throat. "Now," she said, the word reverberating down the road. Kimme struck on the left and all three of the raiders on one side of the street were suddenly left clutching a collection of kindling in their hands. A moment later the raiders were thrown into the street, one of them landing badly and breaking an ankle. The other archers followed suit, landing without their bows in the street while people in the crowd dodged the falling bodies.

While everyone was distracted Wren reached out and shattered the dagger then wrenched the raider's arm to one side where she heard it pop out of joint. The villager scuttled away back to the relative safety of the crowd who huddled together like frightened sheep. In other communities the people had shown some defiance, but here it seemed as if they were down-trodden and willing to submit to whoever came along.

"You shouldn't have done that," said the raider between gritted teeth. Her right arm hung down at her side. Her men were all lying in the street, bruised and battered, but she remained defiant. "You can't be everywhere at once."

"Neither can Boros."

"Something is wrong," muttered Danoph. "She's too calm."

The raider gritted her teeth and gestured at the villagers. "Tell her."

A sturdy woman with grey hair stepped forward from the crowd. A creeping sense of dread crept up Wren's spine when she noticed the woman was constantly wringing her hands.

"You need to leave and never come back. We're fine. We don't need your help." She was clearly terrified of something, but Wren didn't know if it was the raider or something else.

"Why are there no children in the village?" whispered Danoph.

Scanning the crowd Wren noticed there wasn't a single child. "What have you done?" she asked. "Where are all the children?"

The raider gave her an awful grin. A mix of pain and triumph. "They're around here somewhere," she said, vaguely gesturing at the surrounding houses. "A few of my friends are keeping them company. To be honest, they're depraved men and more than a little twisted in the head. They have a thing for young flesh and are difficult to control. Right now it must be like a bear finding a whole hive full of honey."

The raider's words carried around the street and there were a few wails of agony from the crowd. Far too late to be of any use, Wren realised their fear was not for themselves. All of this had been carefully orchestrated for her benefit.

"You might be good at pushing people about, or breaking weapons with your magic, but you're not too bright, are you?"

"What do you want?" asked Wren.

"Take your group of freaks, crawl back to whatever hole you came from and pack up. I want you gone. What was it you said?" she asked rhetorically. "That was it. 'Leave and never come back.'"

For a moment Wren considered killing the woman and the other raiders lying in the street. After that, with help from the villagers, it wouldn't take her long to find the children being held captive. The problem with her plan was that if even one of the children was hurt the villagers would never forgive her. It wouldn't matter that she'd been trying to protect all of them.

"What happens to the children after we leave?"

The raider cocked her head to one side. "Whatever I want."

The message was clear. She was in control. It didn't matter if Wren stayed and fought or walked away, the raider would decide the fate of the children.

"We'll leave," said Wren.

After all of her planning, shame at such a defeat burned but Wren knew this wasn't the end. Her community was only a few months old and their numbers and reputation were growing all the time. She hadn't come this far just to give up now.

Even as she and Danoph walked away from Gillen's Jaw a plan began to form in the back of her mind. This had been a defeat, but it had also proven revealing in its own way about the challenges ahead.

The others joined her back on the ridge where they gathered to look down at the village. The crowd in the main street had dispersed but one figure was still standing in the middle of the street, their face turned towards Wren and the others. Even without embracing the Source she knew who it was. The raider stood alone and unafraid in defiance to send a clear message to her.

"What do we do now?" asked Kimme. "Are we really going to leave?"

"No. You and the others are going to go home. Danoph and I will join you soon."

"Where are you going?"

Wren made herself smile. "To face the enemy."

They walked back to where they'd tied up the horses and together she and Danoph watched the others ride away. When they were out of earshot he turned to face Wren.

"For someone who was just outwitted, you seem unusually calm."

Around the world the Drassi were known as peerless warriors who were without fault, but even for the most skilled among her people, victory was not guaranteed. Drassi warriors had been defeated in the past, and there would be more in the future, but the way they maintained their reputation was to adapt.

"Every defeat is a chance to learn," said Wren, quoting her grandfather. "Besides, the raiders revealed a lot more about themselves than they realised."

"Such as?"

"I know a lot more about the tactics Boros is willing to use. I will not stoop to that level, but it doesn't mean I have to keep thinking in straight lines. The normal response would be to retreat as we've been told, and perhaps mount an attack on Gillen's Jaw, in force, at a later date. The last thing the raiders would expect us to do is follow them back to their camp."

Danoph understood what she was planning and smiled. It wouldn't make sense for just two of them to follow the raiders home. So far they'd been able to keep the location of their community a secret and Boros had done the same. Once she had an idea of where to find their camp, Wren could start making a different kind of plan.

"What else did they reveal?" asked Danoph, raising an eyebrow as Wren grinned at him.

"I know more about their leader as an individual. What they're capable of and how far they're willing to go to get what they want."

"Why do you say that?"

"Because we just met Boros," said Wren.

Chapter 26

Tianne stared at herself in the mirror, lingering on the clothes the Regent had provided. It was her new uniform as a mage of Zecorria. The grey jacket was longer than she was used to, extending past her waist, but it was lightweight and made to fit her perfectly by the royal tailor. The single blue star on her chest, over her heart, denoted her rank. She was the first of the Regent's new cadre.

Her white cotton shirt and black trousers were equally smart and the leather of her new boots was soft and comfortable.

There were a few details about her reflection she didn't like, but Tianne thought they would fade with time. Her naturally pale skin seemed washed out from being indoors so much. It was a remnant from her ordeal in the cell and a lack of food. Now she had rich, filling meals every day and never went hungry. Although her cheeks weren't lean any more, there was still a gauntness about her face, mostly around the eyes.

That brought her to the most visible reminder of her imprisonment. Despite the lavish care, and treatment from the Regent's personal doctor, she still had a livid pink scar above her right eyebrow. Shaped like a sickle, it was an ugly, swollen thing that would fade in time, but never truly disappear. She hated it and wished she could use her magic to heal it. Part of her felt like crying about the disfigurement. She told herself not to be so childish and stupid. To be grateful she hadn't died in that cell. She didn't want to think what could have happened if the Regent hadn't come to her rescue.

She tied her hair back in a tight ponytail with a piece of leather, tucking loose strands of black hair behind her ears. Giving her reflection one last look, Tianne wondered if she'd changed all that much. If she met someone from her old life on the street, would they recognise her? Did she want them to any more?

With many questions and no answers, she left her rooms and was immediately shadowed by two Royal Guards. They walked behind her at a respectful distance and Tianne knew better than to try and engage them in conversation. Each of them took their jobs very seriously and she never heard any small talk from them compared with other guards and soldiers around the palace. A pool of silence spread out from each when they were on duty. She hoped they were different people out of uniform, but staring into their hard eyes she saw little in the way of empathy or a sense of humour.

Three more guards joined her at the outer gate of the palace. Even though Tianne was the youngest by many years, the leader of the squad, a tall woman with a scar on her left cheek, deferred to her.

"Shall we proceed?" It sounded like a real question but Tianne had the impression the woman was merely humouring her. If she said no the guard would probably just drag her into the street by her hair. It seemed as if everyone in Zecorria, including the Royal Guards, had a lot to learn about mages. It was up to her. She was the first and had always known it was going to be an uphill challenge. Tianne squared her shoulders and raised her chin.

"Lead the way," she said, smiling to hide her true feelings.

From the moment they left the safety of the palace Tianne noticed people staring at her. At first they watched her with open suspicion and hostility, thinking she was a prisoner of the Royal Guards. When it became apparent she was with them they paid enough attention to notice her uniform. Thinking she was nothing more than another palace servant was liberating and after a while people ignored her completely. It made a pleasant change to the hostile stares and anger she'd experienced a few days earlier. Part of her also felt guilty, that in order to be accepted by her people she had to hide her natural ability. Anything associated with magic was instantly seen as dangerous and destructive. It was going to take a long time to change people's minds.

"This way," said Scarface, gesturing for Tianne to follow her down a side street. She hadn't bothered to tell Tianne her name, so she'd given her a suitable nickname.

"Who is first on the list?" she asked, hoping for some conversation.

For a moment it seemed as if Scarface wouldn't answer but then changed her mind. "Frohake claims to be a healer. He's been charging people a lot of money, sometimes everything they have, in return for a cure. We need to know if he's genuine."

If there was a genuine healer it would be an enormous boon for the Regent, but also mages in general. Learning to heal was incredibly difficult, but if Frohake possessed the skill it would be a positive first step in convincing the people of Herakion that magic could be a force for good.

Tianne knew Master Yettle could cure almost anything, given enough time, and some at the Red Tower claimed Eloise's skill exceeded his. There was even a rumour that she could regrow organs and missing limbs. Tianne wasn't sure if that was true, but there were numerous stories about how Eloise had healed herself after being severely injured during the war. If only she'd been here, or Tianne was better at healing, it would make all this much simpler.

Even at this early hour the line of people waiting to see Frohake extended down the street and then back up the other side. Most of those in the queue were locals, but there were also two Morrin and a handful of stout Yerskani. There were a number of families standing together and people of all ages waiting to be healed. Many of them were coughing or wheezing, others were wrapped in bandages and a few had an arm in a sling or rested heavily on a crutch. The Royal Guards bellowed for them to clear a path down the middle of the street rather than try to squeeze through. Tianne had the impression they just wanted the sick and injured to keep their distance in case they were contagious.

At the front of the line an old man wrapped in a blanket was sitting on the steps. She thought he was asleep but as they approached he stood up suddenly.

"Are you Frohake?" he asked, staring at Tianne with cloudy white eyes.

"No, I'm sorry," she said.

"Royal Guards," said Scarface, speaking over her. "We're here on the Regent's business. Step back."

The old man turned his face towards Scarface. "Need some healing, does he?"

Before she had a chance to answer the front door opened and everyone waiting scrambled to their feet. A tall buxom redhead from Seveldrom came out and everyone visibly wilted when they saw it wasn't Frohake. He appeared a moment later, his arm around another scantily dressed woman who he waved off.

Frohake was dressed only in a pair of loose trousers and his

open shirt showed scratches on his chest from someone's fingernails. Tianne had to admit that he was handsome, with his oiled
beard, luscious curly black hair and swarthy features, but even
before he spoke Tianne knew she didn't like him.

His arrogance was apparent in the way he stood, as if the
whole world owed him a debt. When he scanned the desperate
crowd like a merchant taking a stock count, she knew he had
no compassion. She also didn't like the way his eyes lingered on
the most attractive women. She could guess how he asked for
payment for those without money.

"Are you Frohake?" asked Scarface, and he turned his gaze
on the Royal Guard. If his dazzling smile normally had women
going weak at the knees Scarface was immune.

"Indeed I am," he said, reaching out to touch her cheek, surprising everyone. "I could take care of that scar, if you want?"

"And how much would it cost me?" sneered Scarface.

"For a woman as beautiful as you, no charge."

Scarface snorted and turned to Tianne. "Get on with it."

"Who is this?" asked Frohake, noticing her for the first time.
Tianne did her best to meet his eyes and not stare at his muscled
chest. "What's this all about?"

"We're here to test you," said Scarface with a nasty grin.
"There have been a number of reports that you're a fraud."

It was only then that Tianne noticed two of the Royal Guards
were missing. Frohake's eyes widened briefly but his calm mask
quickly returned. "Is that necessary?"

"Inside," said Scarface, shoving him backwards into his own
home. Tianne went next and two Royal Guards took up their
posts just outside the front door.

The exterior of Frohake's home was modest but inside it
resembled a junk shop as it was littered with piles of random
belongings. There were stacks of silver ornaments, paintings,

expensive silk clothing and dozens of crystal figurines sitting on shelves. No doubt he'd taken them as compensation when people didn't have the gold.

Frohake stumbled into the room and started to move towards the back door of the house when Scarface's voice stopped him. "I've two more guards stationed at the rear. There's nowhere to run."

When he turned around there was still a smile on his face, but it was brittle. "I was just going to get us some drinks."

"Of course," said Scarface with a smile like a cat about to eviscerate a tasty mouse. "Sit." She pointed at a plush chair that was piled high with silk cushions. Realising he was trapped, Frohake sank into the chair trying to appear completely at ease.

Tianne pulled up a plain wooden chair and sat down opposite, just out of arm's reach.

"And what happens now?" asked Frohake, his eyes flicking between her and Scarface.

"Show me," said Tianne, already reaching out with her senses towards him.

"I can't. There's nothing to heal," he said with a peculiar laugh. She gestured at the scar on her face and he just shrugged. "It's barely noticeable."

"Try anyway," she said, sensing a faint echo from the Source. He definitely had some magic, but she wondered about his level of skill.

"Very well," he said, lowering his head and taking a deep breath. With a dramatic wave of his arms colourful balls of red and blue light appeared in the air. They glowed and seemed to be humming at different pitches. Each was smaller than an apple and as they zipped around the room in a whirlwind of light and sound Tianne had to admit it looked impressive. The collection of light globes clustered around her head and she felt a faint tingling sensation as the notes merged into one chorus that was in perfect harmony. Frohake was breathing hard from the strain and after only a short time he let out a long sigh and the lights vanished.

"It's done," he said, wiping at his forehead even though Tianne could see it was dry. "The scar will disappear very soon."

Even Scarface, who had no magic of her own, seemed sceptical. She raised an eyebrow and tilted her head at Tianne. "Well?"

"He's a liar. He can't heal anything."

"This is ridiculous," scoffed Frohake, but now he was sweating. "You've seen my magic. Who are you? Who is this girl to judge me?" he said, addressing the last question at Scarface.

"Apparently, she's a mage."

Tianne considered a snide response of her own but with no witnesses she decided on something more direct to teach them both a lesson. With an unmanly squeak Frohake was lifted out of his chair and sent towards the ceiling while Scarface's feet also came off the floor. The Royal Guard was alarmed and when she saw Frohake's face pressed into the ceiling she turned her steely gaze on Tianne.

"You've made your point. That's enough."

Tianne was tempted to lift Scarface higher but the look on the woman's face changed her mind. She lowered her to the ground but left Frohake pinned for a moment and then cut her connection to the Source. He fell to the floor and landed on his face, groaning in pain.

"It's a light show. Magical sleight of hand," explained Tianne, summoning a larger light globe which brightened the interior of the room. "I can do similar and with enough practice I could imitate his dramatics."

Scarface knelt down next to Frohake who was sweating in earnest now. "Can you do anything useful?" she asked.

"I help people," he said. Scarface punched him on the nose and blood ran down his face. Tianne would've felt some sympathy for him if not for all the desperate people waiting outside for a miracle cure. To be so renowned as a healer he must have cheated dozens of people out of a lot of money, just so he could live in luxury. It made her wish Scarface had punched him even harder.

She raised her fist again and he cowered back. "No, wait! Don't hurt me."

"What can you do?"

"Just the lights," he said.

Scarface put two fingers between her lips and whistled sharply. The front door opened and one of the other guards stuck his head around it.

"Take this one to the cells," she said, pointing at Frohake. "And ask the palace to send a couple of clerks." The guard marched into the room, grabbed the charlatan by the arm and dragged him out.

"What will happen to all of this?" said Tianne, gesturing at all the stolen belongings Frohake had taken.

"It will be returned to the rightful owners. The clerks will sort it out. In the meantime, we have more names on the list for today."

Although Tianne felt a sense of justice in revealing Frohake to be a fraud it was hard to look at all the faces of the people waiting in line. All of them were desperate enough to risk visiting a mage and she had just taken that away from them. As she squeezed past, surrounded by four Royal Guards, she kept her gaze averted.

*

The second person they visited was a card shark who people claimed had been using magic to steal their money. As soon as the man saw the Royal Guards he tried to run but they'd anticipated this and blocked his escape route. While one of the guards held the squirming man by the arm, Tianne tested him but found no echo from the Source.

"He doesn't have any magic," she said to Scarface, who gestured at the guard holding him. "It must be sleight of hand."

"Told you. I'm clean."

Scarface smiled as she approached the man and Tianne felt her stomach lurch in fear. She punched him so hard that he stumbled back and collapsed on the ground. Two of the Royal Guards started kicking and stomping on the man until he was a bloody mess, curled up in a tight ball. Tianne was so shocked she froze. By the time she started to move towards the man the beating was already over.

As the morning wore on and they encountered only more frauds, Tianne began to lose hope of finding someone like her. It should have been a glorious day of new beginnings where she introduced mages to a new way of living, under the protection of the Regent. Part of her had wanted to build a community of her own, much as Wren had done, but this one would have no need to hide. They would proudly walk through the streets of the capital city, but with each beating of a fraud, she wondered again at her decision to return home.

By the end of the afternoon she felt numb and had stopped trying to intervene. The first time she'd tried Scarface had pinned her to the wall and put a dagger to her throat.

"Mind your business or you'll be next," she hissed in Tianne's face.

Dejected and reconsidering her role, Tianne was finally able to rid herself of the two most brutal guards at the outer palace

gate. They had taken great delight in kicking people unconscious while Scarface remained icy and calm throughout. The
only outburst from her had been when Tianne had interfered.
Perhaps Scarface had been hoping Tianne would attack her so
she'd have an excuse to kill her and dump her body in an alley.
It was obvious that she hated Tianne and resented having to
chaperone her around the city looking for others just like her.

In desperate need of a bath she was about to head for her room
when Scarface placed a hand on her shoulder. "Wait here. I need
to report in, then I'll escort you to your room."

She knew it wasn't a request and leaned against a wall in the
entrance hall, idly studying the decorations. The huge paintings
that covered most of the walls in this part of the palace were
ancient, musty and moth-eaten. They depicted rulers from centuries ago, who she couldn't identify because they had faded so
badly. After two insane Kings in a row Zecorria was looking to
the distant past for inspiration.

One servant had told her the palace had been scoured clean
after the death of the Mad King in an attempt to remove any
signs he'd ever been there, but she could still see a few traces.
Deep scoring on stone pillars that had been badly repaired. A
hallway with one dark wall to cover the bloodstains. A bricked-
up door where no amount of fresh paint would remove the smell
inside.

It made her wonder about what kind of a legacy she would
leave behind as a member of the Regent's cadre.

A short time later Scarface appeared, deep in conversation
with a palace clerk, a tall woman with an equally icy disposition.
She stared down her nose at everyone and her severe grey dress
covered any bare flesh that seemed a bit extreme.

"You're not done. Someone was brought in. They're in the
cells," said Scarface, gesturing for her to follow.

Tianne followed the guard through several narrow servants' corridors before descending six winding flights of stairs taking them deep underground. As she stepped out into the dimly lit corridor she started to hyperventilate, thinking back to her own time in the cells. It had only been a couple of weeks ago and she was still struggling to sleep at night. Thankfully the cells surrounding her were different, with only plain stone walls, and each prisoner had a straw pallet and even a bucket for waste. None of those she passed looked as if they'd been beaten and there was a strange feeling of camaraderie, with one pair of prisoners even playing cards and another sitting talking to her neighbour.

"Who are they?" she asked.

"Petty thieves, pickpockets and the like. They'll soon be released with a fine or a few lashes. These cells are just for overnighters. The worst criminals are deep underground," said Scarface and Tianne couldn't repress a shudder.

At the end of the corridor they found a teenage Zecorran girl, who looked about the same age as Tianne, huddled in the corner of her cell. One of her eyes was swollen shut and she had a few cuts and bruises on her arms. When Tianne turned accusingly to Scarface the Royal Guard just shrugged.

"Nothing to do with me. She came in that way. She's accused of being a witch. Cast a spell on someone."

"That's not true," said the girl, showing a glimmer of defiance. Her bottom lip had also been split and as she spoke the scab broke open and more blood trickled down her chin.

"Give me some room," said Tianne but Scarface just folded her arms and leaned against the wall. "Please."

They locked stares but Tianne was the first to look away. She didn't want to challenge the older woman's authority. She just had a feeling that the girl would open up to her without an aggressive audience. With a roll of her eyes Scarface walked down the corridor to chat with one of the prison guards.

Tianne knelt down in front of the bars, getting a proper look at the girl's face. The injuries were fresh but she made no attempt to cover them up, wearing them like a badge of pride.

"I'm Tianne."

"Kalina." As Tianne studied her she could see Kalina looking at her uniform.

"What happened?"

Kalina shrugged, as if her current predicament was normal. "Raslin came into my dad's tavern with some of his friends. He got drunk and tried to bend me over a table in the back room. I wasn't interested so I fought him off and broke his arm. His father is someone important in the city, a Minister or something. Raslin told him what had happened."

"So why isn't he in here instead?"

Kalina grinned. "Because he's got money. And because I threw him across the room and out of a window. His father claimed I'd bewitched his son, so I ended up here."

Kalina wasn't particularly tall and didn't look muscular, but even so Tianne had a suspicion she hadn't done it by hand. She also intuited there was a lot more to the story than had been said. Instead of asking her more questions she decided to try another approach.

She drew power into herself and embraced the Source, feeling its energy wash away her tiredness and the lingering aches in her body.

"What did you just do?" asked Kalina, her eyes widening in awe.

Instead of answering Tianne asked, "How did you throw him across the room?"

"With my curse. They're right about one thing. I am a witch."

"Oh no, you're so much more," said Tianne, summoning a globe of light in her hands. She sent it drifting through the bars and fixed it to the ceiling of Kalina's cell where it filled the space with pale blue light. "I'm a mage and so are you. And it's not a curse, it's a blessing."

"Then why am I in here and you're out there?" she said, gesturing at the cell.

"I'm here to change that. The Regent wants a cadre of loyal mages, to protect the people of Zecorria. If you join me, no one will ever be able to hurt you again."

"Are you serious?"

"I am. I've been recruited to find others like me and chase away the charlatans."

Kalina shook her head. "I'm not like you. It only happens when I get angry."

"I can help you with that. I promise."

"What's going on here?" said Scarface, coming to stand in front of Kalina's cell. "Is she another scam artist?"

"No, she's like me."

Scarface raised an eyebrow. "Really?"

"I can feel her connection to the Source," said Tianne, drawing more power into herself. Kalina immediately reacted.

"I can sense . . . something," she said, squinting at Tianne.

"She wants to keep you here," said Tianne, stepping back and gesturing for Scarface to do the same. "She doesn't believe you have any real power. Remember what he tried to do and how it made you feel. It's your choice. Either you can stay in that cell or you can join me. If you do, you'll never be that powerless ever again."

Kalina gritted her teeth and the veins in her forehead began to pulse. Tianne edged a little further away down the corridor. Sensing something was about to happen, Scarface followed her.

Tianne felt a build-up of power in the air, and her skin began to tingle like the moment before a storm. With a groaning of stone and a clang of metal all the bars in Kalina's cell were ripped from the mortar and flung across the corridor. The sound rang in Tianne's ears and just as suddenly the surge of power was gone. The prison guards came running with weapons drawn and even Scarface was startled as Kalina stepped over the bars of her cell into the corridor. The fierce smile on her face made Tianne grin.

All day she had been dreaming of a moment like this. Of finding someone like her, who she could befriend and coach into becoming a real mage. The dream of a community of Zecorran mages was still a long way off, but, finally, this was a beginning.

"And now we're two," said Tianne.

CHAPTER 27

Garvey let his pony set its own pace as it picked its way down the craggy hillside. He'd been up in the mist for a few hours, enjoying the time alone and the silence of the mountain.

The fog swallowed all sounds below. The only noises above had been the chirping of birds and the sighing of the wind. At the peak of the mountain, even at such high altitude, he'd found an abundance of life. Scraggly green plants with small purple flowers growing up between slabs of stone. Creeping vines, stubby trees and rich grass covered the mountain like a thick cloak. Dozens of gaping holes in the ground revealed pure white rabbits with red eyes and the steppe cats with flat heads and stubby ears that hunted them. A few of the cats had peered at him curiously from behind some rocks but they didn't approach. Walking on paths not even he would risk was an old grey goat, mocking his unsteady feet as it scampered up the rocks.

If only he could stay up here where everything was simple.

Word had reached Garvey a few days earlier from the chatty mouth of a merchant who hadn't recognised him. At times he left the others behind and went unseen into large towns and settlements to hear the latest news. Mostly the talk was about his followers and the atrocities they'd committed, but recently people had been speaking about the Regent of Zecorria's new cadre of mages. It was early days but in time they would be a dangerous force to be reckoned with. Magic needed to evolve beyond the Red Tower. Perhaps this was the start of one pathway.

With a little coaxing the merchant had also told Garvey about a different storm that was approaching.

It was long overdue.

As he came down out of the clouds Garvey thought he smelled smoke. The lower he went the more apparent it became until he could see a thin plume rising up from the village at the base of the hills. He'd left the others only a few hours earlier in good spirits, but it seemed as if the situation had grown worse in his absence. Usually Tahira was able to control the others without him being present.

The first body he came across was that of a young girl, fifteen years at most, lying face down in the street. His pony shied away from her and he steered it around the corpse with his knees. Garvey noticed the lack of blood and the peculiar shape of her twisted and lumpy spine. The girl's eyes were such a vibrant green. Like the rich grass at the top of the mountain.

Further down the street he came across a group of fifty or sixty locals, mostly adults but also at least a dozen children. They were all huddled together on the ground. Many of the children were crying as they stared at the six teenagers standing guard. None of the adults were looking at their captors and did their best to avoid all eye contact. Their eyes were focused on the smouldering ruin of a building further down the street. The fire had been put out but grey ash still drifted on the wind and a faint line of smoke rose up into the lead-coloured sky.

Half a dozen students were standing not far away from the charred timbers and tumbled stone. Tahira was berating someone in a loud voice and as Garvey approached he saw it was Haig. He didn't notice Garvey at first and continued to grin at Tahira and ignore her complaints.

"It doesn't matter. They're just peasants," said Haig, gesturing at the collapsed building. Garvey guessed that he'd brought it down with people inside and then tried to burn the remains. "We have the power to do whatever we want, whenever we want. No one can stop us. When are you going to realise that?" he asked. Haig was without remorse about what he'd done.

In his mind it was fair and just retaliation for the destruction of the Red Tower. The people in this sleepy mining village might not have been there in person, but they'd been complicit in their anger towards those with magic.

Before he'd gone up the mountain the villagers had admitted to exiling one girl of eight and hanging a boy of thirteen for lighting a fire without flint and tinder.

Haig was talking at him but Garvey just blocked out the words. He kept his face impassive and tried to feign interest, but his attention was on the other students nearby. Several of them were agreeing with Haig's rhetoric, smiling and making jokes about those trapped inside, as if they'd killed a neighbour's dog and not humans. As if they were better than everyone else because of their magic.

"How many?" said Garvey, cutting across whatever Haig had been saying.

"At least a dozen," bragged Haig. "One of them was a little boy. He just wouldn't stop screaming. It hurt my ears so badly I thought they were going to start bleeding." He laughed and mimed blood running from his ears. Some of his cohorts chuckled.

Haig's laughter was cut short when part of his head exploded in a shower of gore.

Blood splattered onto Garvey's shirt but he didn't flinch. It was a relief that someone had finally shut him up. Haig made a strange hacking sound as he sank to his knees revealing an axe buried in the back of his skull. As the other students cried out in alarm, summoning shields and scanning the area for the enemy, Garvey felt a smile lift the corners of his mouth.

He turned to the west and waited for his old friend to come into view. Garvey had felt him approaching for some time but the others, despite everything he'd tried to teach them, had remained oblivious. It was only when Balfruss stepped out from behind a veil that they finally realised what had happened. They froze in terror and turned towards him for guidance. It was one thing to fight soldiers and kill innocents who had no chance of fighting back. It was something else entirely to tackle a trained mage, never mind a Sorcerer, and a former member of the Grey Council.

"What do we do?" asked Tahira. Garvey smiled and his mirth seemed to unnerve her and the others.

"Run."

Several of them were already backing away. Two of those guarding the villagers had already disappeared and were scrambling onto their horses.

One of Haig's friends wasn't cowed. "If we fight him together we will—"

"All be slaughtered," said Garvey, cutting him off with a snarl. "I don't need your help. You're only going to get in the way. Leave, before I step on your neck." Garvey stared hard at the boy, daring him to say even a single word. All he needed was the smallest of excuses to rip the boy's head from his shoulders. It was what they had come to expect.

Showing more wisdom than Garvey thought possible, the boy bit his lip and backed away. Most of the others went with him, but a few lingered, staring at Tahira. It made sense. Most would separate into pairs but a few would cluster around her. It would make it easier to hunt them down later.

Garvey turned his steely gaze on her, knowing that she wanted to say something. To praise him, to thank him, maybe even to say that she loved him. It didn't matter. It was all too late. She seemed to deflate then shook herself as if coming awake. Tahira turned on her heel and ran towards the stables.

"Clear the area," warned Balfruss, gesturing at the villagers to disperse. Even without their guards they'd remained on the ground, but now they ran towards the safety of the woods beyond the boundary of the village. Garvey waited until the last of them had disappeared among the trees before turning back to face his old friend.

Balfruss kept one eye on the villagers running for the trees and the other on Garvey. Oddly his old friend seemed completely at ease. His followers were riding hard in all directions, but Balfruss couldn't worry about them for now. He could sense a handful had not fled and were watching at a distance to see what happened next. If he survived then they would become an issue for another day.

When the last villager disappeared, Garvey turned back towards him and smiled. It seemed so out of place. He'd become so used to seeing Garvey's permanent scowl it was unnatural. His whole demeanour had changed and Balfruss barely recognised him.

"I can't believe it's come to this," said Balfruss. "After everything we've been through, how could you do it?"

"They did this. They drowned, hanged or burned their own

children. Then they came into our home, Balfruss, and tried to do it to the rest of us."

"So it's us against them? Everyone? In every country?"

Garvey shrugged. "I told you. I will not hide and I will not run. Not from them. I spent too many years in the shadows as the Bane, protecting them, and this is my reward. How many times will you save them from themselves? How many lives have you saved over the years?"

"I don't keep a tally," said Balfruss. "But this rampage must end."

"Then tell me, wise Sorcerer, what is the answer? What is your solution?" said Garvey, holding his arms wide, his voice booming around the streets of the deserted village.

"I don't know," Balfruss admitted, before pointing at the building that had been destroyed. "But this is not it. We always said we would accomplish great things."

"We were young and naïve," said Garvey, but his voice sounded rough and choked with emotion. Perhaps he was thinking back to when they'd been young men studying at the Red Tower. They'd both had great ambitions about how they would make an impression and shape the world. Create a legacy that would echo down through the centuries. Time had weathered them both, smoothing away their sharp edges, eroding some of their glorious visions for the future, but Balfruss was not ready to give in to apathy and despair.

"Perhaps, but naïveté is better than this brutality and a lack of compassion."

"Talk as much as you want," said Garvey pushing up his shirtsleeves to his elbows. "I'm never going to stop. That leaves you with one choice."

"Don't make me do this," begged Balfruss, but Garvey's face had settled into its familiar mask.

Balfruss was about to make another plea when he sensed a massive build-up of power as Garvey drew heavily from the Source. Instead of weaving a shield Balfruss covered himself in a veil and darted to one side, blending in with the street and the houses behind him. A bolt of pure white energy struck the spot on which he'd been standing, blowing a horse-sized crater in the earth. Another landed to the left and another immediately to the right. Garvey was trying to bombard the area as quickly as possible and catch him before he made it too far.

Balfruss sprinted to his left and skidded around a corner before heading back towards Garvey from behind. When Garvey failed to hit him, Balfruss knew his old friend was trying to find him, via his connection to the Source. All magic users could sense each other when in close proximity to one another because it created an echo. It was how Seekers tested children for magic. But Garvey knew better than that. Balfruss had taught both Garvey and Eloise the ability to mask their connection to the Source. It was something he'd learned from one of the tribes across the Dead Sea.

Holding one hand out in front like a dowsing rod, Garvey turned to his right and let out a shout of triumph. It wasn't Balfruss's connection he was sensing, but the few remaining students who hadn't fled with the others. Too late Balfruss realised what was about to happen as Garvey unleashed a powerful blast of force which smashed the house apart. The walls collapsed and the roof broke into a hundred pieces, blasting the surrounding area with chunks of rock and wood. One student was impaled by a spear of wood through her torso and another was crushed by an avalanche of rocks. The two remaining students suffered minor injuries but fled before they were caught in the crossfire again. Balfruss felt them retreat to a safe distance but unlike the others they didn't keep going. They were waiting for something.

Moving as slowly and quietly as possible Balfruss approached Garvey from behind as he continued to scan the village. Garvey remained in the open, standing in the middle of the street, which was alarming. Either he was more arrogant than Balfruss realised and thought himself unbeatable, or his lack of indifference extended to his own future.

Balfruss edged closer, certain at any moment Garvey would spin around and attack. When he was within arm's reach he dropped his veil and locked his arms around Garvey's throat in a chokehold. Once more his old friend surprised him by not putting up any kind of a struggle.

"It's about time," said Garvey, pretending to wrestle with him but making no real effort. "I've been standing out in the open. I couldn't make it any easier for you."

"You wanted me to stop you?"

Garvey gestured at the space around them. "Can you veil us? Create a distortion so they can't hear us?"

With a series of quick twisting gestures Balfruss created a slow haze around him and Garvey, sealing them inside a bubble. Everything outside appeared the same, but sounds were distorted and the nearby tweeting of a bird seemed to stretch on and on, becoming unrecognisable.

Garvey stared at the fine net he'd woven about them and, turning his head, Balfruss saw him smile. "Can they still see us?"

"Not really." Anyone looking at them would only see vague shapes inside the net, as if they were observing them through a dense haze.

"How much time do we have?" asked Garvey.

Something in his voice made Balfruss release his chokehold and step back. Staring into the eyes of his old friend he saw a glimmer of the man he remembered from his childhood. The

other version of Garvey was there, the cold man fuelled by rage
and without remorse, but it seemed at a distance as if it was a
mask that belonged to someone else.

"What have you done?" asked Balfruss. "Did you plan all of
this? Was it all a charade?"

"Even before Danoph had his vision about the Red Tower, I
knew a version of this was coming," admitted Garvey. "The old
ways of teaching were flawed. We knew that when we left the
school as young men."

"I told Eloise that being the Bane for so long had left a mark
on you. You're sick, Garvey. You need help."

"If only it were that simple," he replied. "When the hatred
began to build, and they started to turn on Seekers and children,
people soon forgot what magic had done for them. The lives that
you and the others saved during the war. The sacrifices we've all
made to protect them over the years." Garvey's nostrils flared
and his hands balled up into tight fists but he didn't reach for
the Source.

"I didn't know," said Balfruss. "It was years before I found out
what they'd made you do. The old Grey Council were wrong to
ask you to take on the mantle of Bane."

Garvey dismissed it with a wave. "If it wasn't me they would
have chosen someone else. Nothing would have changed."

"I could've helped you. I should at least have tried."

"It's in the past. It doesn't matter now. They're killing children, Balfruss," he said, gesturing at the village and the world
around them. "Blaming them for something they're born with.
Magic isn't evil and it's not going to go away. They need to
understand that."

"You've killed hundreds of people . . . "

"They needed someone to hate. A lightning rod to focus
their anger. If my years as the Bane taught me anything, it's

that magic is necessary. There will always be another Flesh Mage, another Warlock. I don't need to be an Oracle to know that, in time, it will happen. What I've done will force them to change. To create new schools and find different ways to teach magic. Children with magic should be nurtured, not drowned or burned at the stake."

Balfruss was struggling to accept what Garvey had done. Not only killing so many people because he thought it necessary, but creating a persona of someone fuelled by rage and living inside that mask. For years he'd isolated himself from everyone and never once hinted at what he was planning. From the first day he'd returned to the school, Garvey had been wearing a disguise. That level of determination and focus was unlike anything he'd ever seen.

"You've been lying to everyone for years. You manipulated us all into thinking you were brutal and unstable."

"Not all of it was an act," admitted Garvey. "But it was necessary."

"You should have told us about your fears. We could have tried something else."

"We did try, old friend," said Garvey, gripping his shoulder. "We worked so hard to try and stop Danoph's vision coming to pass. Once I realised it was inevitable, I knew I had to play my role through to the end. And now, you must play yours."

"What are you saying?"

"There's only one way this can end," said Garvey. "If you kill me then you risk creating a martyr. The rogue mages will unite in my name, creating a whole generation of Warlocks who only want to destroy. Nothing new will be built and magic will be pushed to the fringes. But if you stop me, if you drag me before them in chains, it will be the catalyst others need."

"We're over the border. Garvey, we're in Zecorria. They'll

kill you," said Balfruss, amazed that Garvey could be so calm. But on the other hand he'd been preparing for all of this for years. He must have known this moment would come as well and he seemed willing to accept whatever punishments lay in his future.

"They will try, but it won't be as easy as they think." An unusual serenity had settled over him, washing away all traces of anger from his features. At that moment Garvey seemed reborn. "I am sorry to add to your burdens, but there's something else you must do."

"I'm afraid to ask," admitted Balfruss.

"You must become the Bane, at least for a little while. Those who fled the Red Tower with me must be stopped. They're unstable and they threaten what could be built in the future."

"I cannot," said Balfruss, shaking his head. What Garvey was asking brought up old memories of what he'd done in Voechenka. Years later he still had nightmares about the corrupted children he'd been forced to kill. "Do not ask that of me."

"Then you must find another who will assume the mantle, because we both know that, in time, there will be others who choose the left-hand path of magic. The Bane is a necessary evil."

Balfruss had thought he would face the problem of the rogue students another day, but now he was forced to consider his options. When the Red Tower had fallen they had given the students three choices, but Wren had presented them with a fourth. Perhaps it was not too late for those who had followed Garvey. Perhaps they could be brought back into the fold. Perhaps.

"It's time," said Garvey, taking a deep breath. "Short of death, there's only one credible way they'll believe you captured me."

The full horror of what Garvey was asking him swung into focus and Balfruss was so shocked he involuntarily took a step backwards.

Knowing the reason for his actions, no matter how noble, did not make his crimes any less heinous. He had destroyed entire communities and, at the last count, slaughtered hundreds of defenceless people. He had created a level of fear focused on one individual not seen since the Warlock. Even knowing all of that, Balfruss had been struggling with the idea of killing his old friend.

What he was now asking him to do instead was far worse.

It would cripple him in a way that only a couple of people could heal and both Yettle and Eloise were far away. If Garvey died they couldn't hurt him any more and after that only his name would be cursed. If Balfruss did this it would be in the full knowledge that what lay ahead for his friend was months and perhaps years of torture.

"Do it quickly, before I lose my nerve," said Garvey, staring up at the sky.

With tears running down his face Balfruss embraced the Source and lashed out.

CHAPTER 28

Akosh stared in disbelief at the man seated across the table from her. Akharga.

Finally, after some negotiating about the time and place via his surrogate, Bissel, she was face-to-face with him, in the flesh. Wearing masks and blending in was common to all of her brethren, but she would never have guessed his real identity.

Akharga was Kai. The Pestilent Watcher. The Eater of Souls. And one of the oldest and most dangerous beings she had ever met. He was a monstrous thing from another era who had managed to survive across many long centuries. He was unique, alien and terrifying.

He was also the only one of their kind who had feasted upon his own followers in order to sustain himself. It should have spelled out his doom and yet, somehow, he was still here and flourishing.

For the last ten years she'd heard the name Akharga bandied about among the humans, but not once had she considered it would be him. His name was always mentioned in relation to doctors, healers and apothecarists. Wherever there was a terrible outbreak of a disease, or a surge in the damp lung, a plague priest would show up to offer comfort and care for the sick and dying. And all of them wore his symbol around their necks. A triangle with an eye at its centre. Akosh suspected that none of them knew whose symbol they really carried and what it meant. Kai wasn't curing diseases or taking away pain and suffering. He was feasting on it.

The handsome human face he wore was completely at odds with what was lurking just beneath the skin. To a stranger he would appear to be a cultured and wealthy man in his thirties, judging by his fashionable clothes and long coat. His smile was warm and friendly, but her flesh crawled as she'd seen what was underneath the mask. The shadow on the wall behind him seemed normal, but at times she was sure it flickered and parts of it began to writhe like the many arms of a giant squid.

"You've been a stupid girl," said Kai, picking up his glass of wine. He held it up to the lantern and swirled the liquid around, watching it slide about. The tavern, and the wine, were among the best in Herakion but it was not somewhere she'd visited before tonight. He had chosen the place even after her insistence that they meet in what she had thought of as her city. It made her wonder how many loyal people he had in the Zecorran capital and how many were in the building right now.

No one had ever called her a stupid girl before. In front of any human she would have bristled at the insult or simply killed them. But he was not human and since they were alone she kept her mouth shut and let it pass.

"Why is that?" she asked.

Kai's eyes briefly turned red before returning to normal. "The list is long, but let's start with some of your most recent mistakes." He sipped his wine, made an appreciative noise and put down his glass. "You had one follower who was a Guardian and you let her kill herself."

"Someone had been taken prisoner at Unity Hall. I needed him silenced."

"What a total waste," he said, ignoring her protest.

"He was telling them all about—"

"He knew nothing of worth," said Kai, cutting across her. "So what if the Guardians found out about Habreel? He's insignificant. They all are. They're like moths, here for a moment and then gone. In a hundred years every single one of them will be dead. Which brings me to the second thing on the list. And this is a big one. You used your own name." He seemed both disgusted and disappointed, as if he'd found out that she was inbred.

Akosh clenched her jaw and dug her nails into the padded arms of her chair. He was right and she hated it. Many years ago, when her power had started to wane, she'd been desperate to find a way to reinvent herself. Survival was the only thing that had mattered. Creating the first orphanage had seemed like a brilliant solution.

Many of those she'd befriended had also started to wither away as the mortal races grew and their needs changed. After only a few years most of her friends were gone. For a time their chairs remained at the table before they too simply disappeared. Other new faces took their place, but by then she was committed to her new path with the orphans.

At the time she hadn't been focused on a long-term plan. Her goal had been her continued existence. It was only many years later that she considered how she might put her children to better use by nudging them closer to those in power.

By using her own name it had made it that much easier for Vargus and the others to know who was responsible. All it had taken was for one mouthpiece to say it out loud. That one utterance created a ripple and she was still feeling the repercussions now. She was an outcast from her brethren and her orphanages in Yerskania were gone.

"You've been this for too long," said Kai, gesturing at her body. "You've spent so much time around humans you think you are one. I had one of my people, Pavel, show you that caring for them had made you weak, but it seems as if it was too little too late."

"I'm dealing with it," said Akosh.

"Hmm, I wonder," he said, sounding unconvinced. "If I look beneath your skin, what will I see? The real you, or just human meat and bone?"

Akosh's tolerance was starting to wear thin. She was used to dodging those more powerful than her, working covertly and feigning respect when necessary, but no one had ever spoken to her like this before.

Reaching out with her senses she wondered how powerful he really was in comparison to her. She'd heard all the stories and once caught a glimpse of his real form, but perhaps it was all just a show designed to intimidate. Only ten years ago he'd been on the cusp of extinction, whereas she'd been gradually building her power for decades.

Kai sensed what she was doing and grinned, his eyes turning red again. All of the shadows in the room coalesced behind him on the wall, merging together into one massive shape. She tried to use her power against him, to hurt or control him, but quickly realised she had underestimated him. The scale and depth of his power dwarfed her significantly.

Akosh felt his presence fill the room as all light drained away and absolute darkness filled the space. With her eyes open or closed it was the same. An endless void of night. She sensed he hadn't moved from his chair and yet an immense weight began to press down on her, shoving her deeper into her chair which creaked under the pressure. Two malevolent red eyes appeared, glowing in the darkness, then four, then eight more, and soon a hundred eyes were watching her, all blinking in unison. A scream started to build up in her throat but she couldn't breathe and clawed at her neck. A tight band of pain was squeezing her chest, her heart, her head. This was the end.

Akosh stumbled out of her chair onto the floor, gasping for air. Slowly the darkness receded and the pain faded away. When she felt strong enough she looked around the room and everything was as it had been before. Kai was human once more, delicately sipping his wine and savouring the taste. With heavy limbs she wobbled to her feet and then fell back into her chair. After a few minutes she'd regained her breath but still felt light-headed.

"Would you like to try that again?" asked Kai, raising an eyebrow. Akosh shook her head then drained her glass of wine to wet her throat. "The only reason you're still here is because of me. They gave Vargus the job of finding you and he's very good at it." Kai shook his head and an unreadable expression passed over his face. She couldn't tell if it was fear, admiration, or both.

"Then why am I here?" she asked.

"Because I dealt with it. Six of your little friends saw you strolling around this city as if it belonged to you. Did you even notice them spying on you?" She hadn't and it made her wonder what else she had missed. "Each of them went running to tell good old Vargus all about it and earn themselves a pat on the head for their obedient behaviour."

Akosh had always assumed that many of the other younger gods had faded away over time when their power had waned. Now, staring at Kai with his insincere smile, she began to wonder about their fate.

"You killed them." It was a statement not a question.

"Oh no," he said, showing teeth. "I intercepted them, before they had a chance to speak with Vargus."

"They're not dead?"

He slowly shook his head. "The death of their bodies would mean they'd go back into the Void. And if their source of power remained then eventually they'd be reborn. No, they're all safe, here with me."

Kai opened one side of his long coat, revealing a tailored silk lining and fine stitching. As she started to ask the material faded away and she found herself staring deep into an endless void full of stars she didn't recognise. Somewhere in the dark she heard voices whimpering, begging for mercy and crying out in pain. As if they were caught in an ocean, faces swam towards her in the darkness, reaching out with beseeching hands, screaming desperately for help. As they drew close to the surface she recognised the faces of all her brethren that she thought had died.

Snaking around all of their naked limbs, snaring them like flies in a spider's web, was a tangled knot of deep purple tentacles. A thick red vine was embedded in each of their stomachs, standing out proud against their bare skin. As Akosh watched a pulse of bright white energy ran down the vine from their convulsing bodies before disappearing into the dark. A second later there was another pulse and their bodies seemed to contract slightly before recovering.

She stared in disbelief at her friends who saw her and were given a glimpse of hope. Someone finally knew of their horrific plight and had come to help. Then the tentacles flexed and dragged them away into the darkness again to be fed upon by the thing that lurked in the shadows.

Kai closed his coat and poured them both another glass of wine. "So, do we understand each other a little better?" he asked, clearly wanting an answer.

"Yes," she said, feeling as if she might vomit all over his expensive clothes. Her mind was reeling. What she'd seen was a nightmare worse than any she'd considered. For years she'd simply assumed their stars had waned, their power vanished and they'd passed beyond the Veil. But theirs was a fate far worse than non-existence. "What do you want me to do?" she asked.

Kai's smile, genuine or not this time, was still unsettling. "I want you to continue with your plan. Destabilise Yerskania and create a nation of your own here in the north, with one religion. Isn't that your big dream?"

"Yes."

"Good. Keep playing your little games and I'll make sure Vargus and the others stay away."

"Why?" asked Akosh. There was nothing she could do if he chose to consume her. But she still needed to know. "Why are you helping me?"

Kai shrugged. "Perhaps it's because it amuses me, watching you all scurry around, fighting over scraps of land. Or perhaps it's because scared prey tastes so much better." He licked his lips with a long purple tongue and she couldn't repress a shudder of revulsion. "If you need to contact me, send word via Bissel."

With that he drained his glass of wine, made another appreciative sound and walked out of the room.

Akosh stared at the closed door, listening to the sound of his receding footsteps. She only relaxed when she heard the front door of the tavern close behind him.

And with that everything she had been building for decades was gone. Her people and plans were still in motion, but only because he allowed it. Tomorrow he could change his mind and tell her to tear it all down, and she'd do it, without hesitation. Because it seemed there were worse fates than dying or disappearing into the Void.

CHAPTER 29

Tammy rubbed the skin just above her right eye in an attempt to stop the headache that was forming. For the last few days she'd been working all hours, hadn't seen any sunlight and had barely slept. The four walls of her office had become a prison of her own making. It was a vain attempt to try and keep her mind away from what she'd done.

The Old Man had provided her with a name and an address. It led her to an ordinary tailor's shop where she left a note. That evening at a tavern she met with a jolly, chubby man called Griss who told jokes that made her smile, if not laugh out loud.

If she hadn't known what he did Tammy's first impression would've been that he was a baker or a merchant. Griss had an easy-going manner that suggested he dealt with people all day. He tried his best to make her feel comfortable in his presence. It would probably have worked if she'd just met him.

Originally from Seveldrom, he'd been living in Perizzi long enough to be recognised and considered a local. After ordering drinks at the bar, which he insisted on paying for, they found a quiet table to talk. A few people in the tavern recognised him and stopped by their table to briefly shake his hand and thank him for their tasty meal. As it happened Griss was a renowned chef at the Queen's Rest, an expensive tavern situated close to the palace. She'd only been inside once, and that had been to speak in private with Kovac before he'd left the city.

Griss was adept at changing his manner depending on who he was speaking to. With her Griss was polite and his jokes were witty, but when a group of sailors stopped by their table he exchanged coarse banter as if he'd been at sea for years. It made her wonder what he was like when there was no one around. Tammy also wondered what people would think of Griss if they knew what he liked to do as a hobby.

When they were alone again Tammy quietly explained what she needed. When she started to give details of what it was for Griss held up a meaty hand.

"I don't need to know why. Only what needs doing," he said. "It's safer."

Given his hobby Tammy was surprised that she didn't sense anything untoward about him and that worried her. He was affable, relaxed and when he smiled, which was often, it was genuine. She'd worked with violent men and women in the past who liked inflicting pain. In each one of them there was a void. Something inside them was lacking and they attempted to fill the space with the screams of others. When they were silent, when they were still and she looked in their eyes, she could see the empty space within. They were broken people. Griss worried her more because he seemed whole and so normal.

As she explained what needed doing he listened intently, but his eyes roamed around the room, following the crowd, pausing on the trio of musicians trying to enthuse the weary crowd. It gave her an opportunity to study him but everything, including her instincts, told Tammy that he was just a chef.

"You won't find it," he said, turning back to face her.

"It?"

His wide smile showed off his white teeth. "Whatever you're looking for. The dark splinter. The sorrow lurking within that shaped me. It's not there."

Even now, two days later, as she went over a report about a series of thefts, his words came back to haunt her. A timid knock on the door provided a welcome distraction as Rummpoe stuck her head around the edge.

"Sorry to disturb you, ma'am, but that document has arrived." Tammy gestured for her assistant to come into the room which she did with some reluctance. Their relationship had been difficult at the beginning, but Rummpoe was proving to be a useful resource that Tammy had come to value. Despite mentioning this to her, Rummpoe frequently seemed intimidated, although on reflection Tammy realised some of that may have come from her recent brooding. The situation with Griss still weighed heavily on her mind and it had put her in a bleak mood.

She forced a smile and tried to make it genuine. "Thank you. Just leave it on my desk."

Rummpoe scuttled into the room, dropped off the envelope and left without another word, quickly closing the door behind her.

For a while Tammy didn't pick up the envelope and just stared at it. There was nothing inherently malicious about it, but once she read the names on that list she knew it would change her because of the means by which they'd been obtained.

Several of her best Guardians had questioned the bookkeeper, Bertran, and he'd not revealed a single name. A few hours alone in a cell with Griss, his tools and his intimate knowledge of causing pain, and the bookkeeper had given them everything.

The Old Man had told her there would be moments like this. When the only choices available were bad or worse. It all came down to what she could live with and what she was willing to do in order to serve the greater good.

Realising there was little point in delaying it, she opened the envelope and scanned the list of names. A low whistle of surprise escaped her lips. Many of them were familiar but she recognised two that normally would have been obscure if not for recent cases. Pulling down a volume of her journal from the shelves, Tammy scanned the list of crimes to confirm her suspicion. With a deep sinking feeling she sat back and carefully considered her next move.

"Rummpoe!" she bellowed and her secretary came running.

"Ma'am?"

Tammy scribbled down two names on a sheet of paper and passed it across the desk. "Have Guardian Faulk carry out a discreet check into the history of these two people. Place of birth, family, their faith, known associates. The usual. I need it done as soon as possible."

"Yes, ma'am."

"And Rummpoe?" she said, as her secretary turned to leave.

"Ma'am?"

"This stays between the three of us," said Tammy, holding her secretary's gaze to impart the seriousness. "Is that clear?"

"Yes ma'am."

Tammy was so familiar with the route through the palace to the Queen's office she'd stopped looking at the plush surroundings. Her mind remained elsewhere, trying to imagine the patience required by Akosh. The latest information about the names on the list indicated that there was a lot more to the woman and her cult than Tammy had realised. Despite that, she wasn't quite ready to accept Balfruss's suggestion that Akosh might be more than human. There was definitely a cult of personality around a central figure, but so far she'd found no evidence of anything magical or unexplainable. However, after all that she'd seen in the last dozen years Tammy remained open-minded. It also wouldn't hurt to take necessary precautions, just in case. Not for the first time she wished the sword on her hip was *Maligne* and not the plain weapon she carried instead. She'd always felt just a little bit safer with it close by. It might be necessary to retrieve it in the coming days.

When she entered the Queen's outer office her assistant, Dorn, was vainly trying to sort through a stack of old books. One slipped from his grip and a cloud of dust erupted from its yellowing pages making him choke and gasp for air. Nevertheless, he waved Tammy to go ahead before he'd regained the power of speech.

As usual Queen Morganse was seated behind her desk but at the sound of Dorn's wheezing she went to investigate before returning to her seat with a faint smile. "Did you lose a bet?" asked Tammy, jerking a thumb towards the secretary who she could still hear coughing through the door.

"He came highly recommended, but sometimes I wonder if they just wanted to get rid of him." Morganse pushed her papers aside and briefly studied Tammy. "You look tired," she noted.

"I've been dealing with some troubling issues," conceded Tammy.

"So your note indicated. Tell me," said the Queen, sitting back and giving Tammy her undivided attention.

"In an attempt to find out more about Akosh's cult, I recently acquired a list of names from one of her people. Many of them are familiar figures in the city, but two less well-known names stood out from the others. As I'm sure you're aware, Dockmaster Lohag recently died."

"I thought that old goat would outlive me," said Morganse. "He must have been at least seventy."

"Seventy-eight, according to his granddaughter. His death didn't seem suspicious, until I noticed who was to succeed him. It's a woman called Rohane. She's well known on the docks. The captains of several ships have told my people that she's firm but fair."

"What makes you think foul play was involved?"

Tammy took out the list of names, running down it again even though she'd memorised all of them. "Rohane's name was on the list I obtained from Akosh's bookkeeper. I had one of my people make subtle enquiries and he found out she was an orphan and doesn't visit any of the main churches. A discreet search of her home revealed an idol identical to this one, which we found in Guardian Brook's home," she said, holding it up. As ever Guardian Faulk had been very thorough in his work, but he'd left no trace that he'd been in Rohane's home.

Morganse took the crude idol and studied it briefly before setting it down on the desk. "That doesn't prove she was involved in Lohag's death."

"No, it doesn't. She may have no knowledge of what happened."

"There's more, isn't there?" she asked and Tammy nodded.

"The Minister of Trade recently passed away. He had a new young wife and overexerted himself. The family are contesting the inheritance. What's more interesting is that his successor is Tovin."

"I know Tovin," said the Queen. "He's been a loyal right hand and faithfully served in the Ministry for years. He deserves the position."

Tammy wished she had better news. "He's also an acolyte of Akosh. His name is on my list. One such death in a month might be coincidental but two . . . " She trailed off and shrugged her shoulders.

"Show me the list," said Morganse. Tammy noticed the Queen's hand shook slightly as she held it out. She passed the list across and watched the colour drain from Morganse's face as she scanned the names.

The Queen moved to the window and stared out at the city. When Tammy had read the list she'd also needed time to come to terms with what it meant. All the names the accountant had given her were those of orphans. All of them contributed a portion of their wealth to local orphanages dedicated to Akosh.

Both Rohane and Tovin had lived in the city for many years and each had worked hard in their respective roles. Despite the circumstances surrounding the deaths of their superiors, Tammy could find no proof that either of them had been involved. However, that didn't mean that someone else, who also followed Akosh, hadn't arranged it so that they could be promoted. Most troubling was that two deaths had occurred in less than a month. It could have been a coincidence of timing but she didn't think so. A plan was in motion.

Neither of those awaiting promotion had ever visited the cells or been in any serious trouble, and yet they were followers of Akosh. Their loyalty was to her above all others. Beyond their Queen and beyond the law.

So far neither had done anything untoward, but with so many people focused on Akosh and her network, Tammy wondered how long it would be before that changed. Guardian Brook had never shown any signs of disloyalty right up to the moment when she'd killed a witness and tried to blame his murder on Munroe. Rather than be questioned, she'd taken her own life and her last words had been about her Mother.

Any visitor's faith had never been an issue before. Yerskania was renowned for being an open nation that welcomed people from all around the world. As long as they didn't try to hurt anyone their religion was a private issue. Perizzi had churches and temples devoted to mainstream faiths like the Maker and the Blessed Mother, but also the uncommon in the west, such as Elwei. Tammy didn't believe in any of them and didn't care about what others believed. But being a follower of Akosh was now a matter of public concern and safety.

If they chose to be obstructive in their new roles, then individually Tovin and Rohane could disrupt trade in the city. Working together they could control what goods flowed into the port and a lot of money would flow their way to clear any obstacles. No one wanted their goods to rot because they were being held in a warehouse or in the hold of a ship, tying up the docks and the merchant captains.

The other names in the city were not all in such significant positions, but each of them was poised to inherit a more senior job. Two of Akosh's acolytes from the list had already been promoted and had been in control for some time.

If they, and everyone else on the list, were to work together it would change the heart of the city. It would change how Yerskania dealt with other countries in the west and beyond.

"This list of names. How certain are you that they're all genuine?" asked Morganse, without turning around.

"I'm certain," said Tammy. Griss had been recommended by the Old Man himself and she trusted him completely.

"I will have some of my agents look into them and keep a close eye on their activity," said Morganse. Tammy didn't know how many agents the Queen had in the city, but the Old Man had indicated that the number had increased since the war. All of the west had been unprepared for the Warlock and no one wanted that to happen again. "I need more information before making a decision. I need time."

In the blink of an eye Morganse seemed to age beyond her

years. With a slight stumble she sat down heavily in her chair. Sometimes Tammy forgot that Morganse was a grandmother who had been on the throne for a long time. Most of the time the Queen was as vivacious as a woman twenty years her junior, but not today.

Time. They both knew they didn't have enough of it. At any moment Akosh could give her people in Perizzi an order and they would leap to it, no matter the cost. They would willingly sacrifice their own lives to serve their god. Tammy knew the Queen and other monarchs employed agents who lived abroad, blending in with their communities, but this was something far beyond that. Sleeper agents that might be called on to serve, or perhaps not. They might live their entire lives without receiving a direct order from Akosh.

It also made her wonder if any of them had ever refused. Had anyone ever rejected an order from their Holy Mother? If so she doubted the others had left them alive. It was an interesting theory to investigate but very soon the Queen would have to make a decision about what to do with those names on the list.

"I'll send for you. Soon," promised Morganse as if she'd read Tammy's mind.

They would have to move quickly and whatever she decided Tammy knew the repercussions would be severe.

It was a little after midnight and with another busy day ahead Morganse should have been in bed. Instead she found herself thinking about her daughters and their family. About what she was willing to do to protect them.

When the Mad King had threatened her during the war she'd been certain he would come after her directly, but instead her son had suffered. All his life she'd been preparing him to inherit the throne, but because of her inaction he'd been castrated and had left Yerskania, never to return. That had put her in the unenviable position of remaining on the throne when she should have stepped down several years ago.

Back then it had been an insane monarch who had convinced himself he was a prophet mentioned in holy texts. He had planned to convert all of the western nations into one country, with him on the throne as both its god and king. Today it was a widespread cult devoted to a woman they believed was a god and for whom they would do anything. Break any vow, any law, any sacred oath.

The door to her private sitting room opened and a lean, middle-aged man with grey hair slipped into the room unannounced. Without making a sound he padded across the room and waited for her gesture before sitting down. Impeccably dressed as ever in black and grey, Ben cut a striking figure despite his years. Other than his name, which was fake, she knew very little about him. It had only been about twenty years, so perhaps he was getting close to trusting her.

Ben was a member of the Silent Order, a league of assassins who had been operating in Yerskania for a long time. With a code of their own that no one really understood a person could attempt to hire them. Sometimes they accepted the contract and at other times they would reject it without ever giving a reason. They could not be blackmailed, persuaded or threatened. They were anonymous and a force of nature.

The Silent Order had been instrumental in changing the course of several countries, but what only a handful of people knew was that they had a connection to the throne.

As well as being a retired assassin, Ben was a member of the inner circle, and his voice carried considerable weight.

"I believe all of the individuals on the list are being followed by your agents," he said, and she inclined her head. "Then, may I ask, why are my people also watching them?"

"Because I may need you to take decisive action. Because watching may not be enough."

"You have suspicions?" said Ben, raising an eyebrow. "Which of them do you believe to be disloyal?"

Morganse declined to answer. So far none of them had acted in a way that could be considered even slightly disloyal. All of them were dedicated to their respective roles, as well as active and well-liked members of their communities. Most of them had families and, apart from their unusual religious belief, they were no different from anyone else. She had no reason to doubt them. Not yet anyway.

Yerskania was an open country and Morganse took great pride that her capital city welcomed people from every corner of the world. It was a glorious melting pot with food, faces and languages from all nations. It was a home away from home for everyone who came here as they could always find something familiar.

She'd never thought of that as a weakness. Until now.

"Keep a close eye on them," was all she said. Ben bowed and left quietly without another word.

At this hour the hearth was nothing but cold ashes. Feeling a sudden chill, Morganse pulled her shawl tightly around her shoulders as she struggled with her decision and the repercussions that she knew would follow.

CHAPTER 30

Munroe had to work hard to keep an interested expression on her face as she was shown around the ground floor of the orphanage. After only a short time the muscles in her face ached from suppressing a yawn as her guide, Sianne, showed her the wonders of the washroom. The woman seemed to take great pleasure in explaining how the children's sheets were washed and then fed through the mangle. The last part of the riveting process was hanging them out to dry in the gardens at the rear of the house.

It was a relief finally to leave the dingy room and set foot outside, even if she did have to help with the laundry. As they hung and pegged the sheets on the line, Munroe stared in surprise at the vast overgrown gardens. Once, they must have been impressive, with a hedge maze at the heart and four quadrants of flowerbeds on all sides. Now the maze was a monstrous overgrown tangle of green. The flowerbeds had been reduced to broken soil or were awash with waist-high weeds.

"Impressive, isn't it," said Sianne. "I'm told the owner used to host parties here every year on the summer solstice. Two or three hundred people would gather for a day of feasting and music."

"It must have been something," mused Munroe. "I'd be happy to work on the garden. It would be so nice to give the children somewhere safe to play outside," she said, forcing a smile until it hurt.

"That's a wonderful idea. I'll suggest it to Gorell."

"Wonderful," echoed Munroe, thinking it would be far easier to work alone outside than directly with children. Being near them was difficult. They bore no resemblance to Samuel, but they were a constant reminder of what she had lost. One of her hands shook and she took a few deep breaths until she felt calm again. She reminded herself that all of this was a means to an end. That thought alone allowed her to stay in control.

"Are you ready for the exciting part?" asked Sianne, when they had finished hanging the sheets.

Munroe dreaded to think what that might be but forced another smile. "Oh yes."

"Wonderful, let's go and meet the new arrivals."

Much like the garden, the house itself was an impressive ruin that had seen better days. Once it had been a palatial home that now showed considerable signs of rot. Holes in the walls had been patched with straw, clay and bricks. The roof repairs also included a multitude of materials and daylight showed through in a few places. Sianne had told her it only leaked in a few spots, which was a vast improvement on how it had been when they first arrived. Each room in the house had been recently painted with whatever was going cheap, creating a rainbow effect as she walked through the building. The cobwebs and dust had been swept away but that didn't stop the house from feeling abandoned. It also smelled a little of mildew but Sianne had reassured her that it would fade in the coming weeks. Munroe hoped she wouldn't be here long enough to find out if that was true.

"We've only been in the building a few weeks," said Sianne, reading something in Munroe's expression. "We'll make it into a home."

She was saved from having to force another smile as a gaggle of children came hurtling down the huge winding staircase. One of the screeching brood, a young girl with red hair, was riding down the wooden handrail, while the others cheered and followed in her wake. Munroe was expecting tears and a painful end to the ride, but someone had assembled a collection of cushions at the bottom of the stairs. The girl flew off the end of the rail, grinning ear to ear as she hit her soft landing. With a dramatic wave of her hand she took a bow but her audience's applause began to fade as they spotted the adults.

"Children," said Sianne. Their mirth drained away and was replaced with guilty expressions and a sudden lack of eye contact. "What has Gorell said about sliding down the bannister?" The children offered half-hearted apologies and immediately started collecting up the cushions. A few of the children looked at Munroe curiously but she did her best to ignore them. She didn't want to know their names or anything about them. Sianne was talking, filling her in on some of the details about the children's difficult lives so far. Munroe listened just enough to nod in the right places, but she didn't absorb any of the details.

"The new arrivals are in here," said Sianne, leading her down a corridor.

In a room that had been set up as a classroom, half a dozen slightly older orphans were sitting at battered desks. Half of them were locals, with dark eyes and pale skin, but two were from Yerskania and one was a tall Seve boy about ten years old. A severe Zecorran man with grey hair and crooked teeth was going over some items on a chalkboard at the front. A quick glance revealed a list of basic rules about being at the orphanage.

Sianne knocked on the doorframe, as there wasn't a door, interrupting the induction. "Sorry to interrupt, Gorell."

"That's quite all right," he said. "We were just about finished. Is this the new member of staff?"

"This is Munroe," said Sianne, holding her by the shoulders and marching her forward as if she was a prize cow. Determined to make a good first impression with the man in charge, Munroe smiled and shook hands. She answered all his questions with a story that closely resembled the truth and even went so far as to laugh at a mildly amusing joke. It was difficult to swallow her natural sarcasm and pay attention, but she managed it as he seemed satisfied.

"Well, I'm sure we'll become better acquainted over the next few months," he said.

"I'm sure," she agreed. With luck her stay would be short, but she was willing to do whatever was necessary.

"Munroe had a wonderful idea about the garden as well," said Sianne.

"Ah, the old maze. Do you think you can tame it?"

"I'd certainly like to try," she said.

There was a frantic knocking on the doorframe and then another flustered member of staff arrived. "Tommi has had an accident." It was clear the woman was panicking but was trying her best not to scare the children. Seeing it as an opportunity Munroe spoke up before anyone else had a chance.

"I'll stay here and supervise the children until you return," she said. The members of staff hurried away, leaving her alone with the six children. Munroe lingered by the door, waiting for news while the children amused themselves with a deck of cards.

After a while she heard one of the children approach. The skinny Yerskani girl leaned against the doorway, facing into the room. She seemed to be watching the game and didn't make eye contact. Munroe pretended she hadn't noticed she was there.

"Do you have any idea how boring this is?" asked Dox, through gritted teeth.

"You're an orphan, aren't you?" asked Munroe, barely waiting for the girl to nod. "Then you should feel right at home. Or would you rather be back in Rojenne, working for Cannok."

"He's dead."

"I know. I killed him," said Munroe, making the girl squeak. She took a moment to regain her composure, looking back into the room to see if anyone had noticed. The card game continued without interruption and Munroe tried a different approach.

"Were you happy working for him?" she asked. Munroe had learned from Tok that Dox used to sit through all of Cannok's meetings in Rojenne, just to make sure his people weren't lying to him. "Wasn't that boring?"

"Most of the time," Dox reluctantly conceded.

"Has anyone said anything yet about the faith here?"

"Just a few vague hints. I think they want to ease us into it. Get used to having regular meals and a bed, then tell us."

"Did you ask them about it?" asked Munroe.

"Yes," said Dox, giving her that withering look that teenage girls seemed to master effortlessly. Munroe remembered giving her mother the same kind of glare more than once.

"And?"

"I asked if they were Eaters, or part of some sex cult." Dox snorted and swallowed a laugh. "The panic on Sianne's face was hilarious. She started babbling about her faith. She promised they weren't Eaters, or into anything weird, and they're going to tell us all about it soon."

"Is that it?"

"No, she started droning on about compassion and helping others. Something like that. She sounded like a priest."

"Did they name her?" pressed Munroe, grabbing Dox's arm and squeezing hard. The girl's face crumpled up in pain but then her eyes widened in fear as she saw Munroe's expression.

"Yes. It was Akosh. She called her Akosh."

Munroe released Dox and kept watch for other members of staff in the corridor.

"Most of the other children have no idea," said Dox, rubbing at the red marks on her arm. "All they know is the woman in charge of the orphanage has a lot of money. A few are still suspicious. They've seen things like this before, where orphans are loaned out to rich clients."

"There's none of that here," said Munroe. She didn't need to add any more details to reassure her. Dox would know she was telling the truth.

Munroe had told Dox only a little about why they had come north to Herakion, but almost nothing about Akosh and her followers. She didn't need to know and it was probably safer as well. That way her surprise would be genuine when they finally introduced her, and the other new orphans, to the faith and what it involved. Munroe had no way of knowing which members of staff were loyal to Akosh and which simply worked here. It was safer to assume all of them and trust no one besides the girl.

"Keep your head down and your ears open," said Munroe.

"How did you kill him?" asked Dox.

Despite everything, Munroe smiled to herself. She shouldn't have been surprised. When she'd been the same age as Dox she'd asked adults inappropriate questions.

"You know how," said Munroe, waggling the fingers on her right hand.

"Can you teach me?"

Since Dox had spoken so plainly Munroe thought brutal honesty was the best response. "If you want to kill someone, use a dagger. They're easy to find and you already know how it works. Just stab someone with the pointy end."

"Aren't you going to tell me killing is wrong?" asked Dox.

"I know you think I'm ancient, but I was once your age. So I know you'll do whatever you want, no matter what I say. If you want to kill someone, then go ahead. Besides, I'm not your mother." Munroe knew her voice was harsh but she couldn't help it. The pain and anger were constantly seeping out of her no matter how much she pushed them down. "But if you're serious about learning how to control your magic, then, yes, I'll teach you about that."

Dox was silent for a while as she mulled it over. "Where do I start?" she asked.

"The sea. Listen for the sea," said Munroe. Sianne was hurrying towards her down the corridor with another woman she'd not seen before. Rather than looking worried they were both grinning with excitement about something. "It's always there, at the edges of your perception."

"What is it?"

"The Source," whispered Munroe. She made a shooing gesture with one hand and Dox took the hint.

"Is everything all right?" asked Sianne, coming into the classroom. Perhaps she'd been expecting a bloodbath as she seemed oddly disappointed at finding a quiet game of cards.

"No problems. How is Tommi?" asked Munroe.

"It looked far worse than it was. Thank the Maker," said Sianne, which caught Munroe by surprise. The other woman, a fortysomething redhead, didn't react. Either she hadn't noticed because she was so giddy about something, or she was a far better actor than Munroe gave her credit for. With a final squeeze of

Sianne's arm the other woman practically skipped away down the corridor.

"Did something else happen?" asked Munroe, lowering her voice to a whisper. "You both seem very excited about something."

"I'm not supposed to say," said Sianne, biting her bottom lip.

"I understand. I don't want you to break a promise," said Munroe, going against every instinct in her body. Part of her just wanted to shake Sianne until all her secrets came tumbling out of her head, along with a portion of her brains.

"It's not that," said Sianne, struggling with something. She came to a decision and pulled Munroe a short distance away down the corridor. "Promise me, you won't tell anyone."

"I swear," said Munroe, putting her right hand over her heart.

Even though there was no one in sight Sianne lowered her voice. "Do you remember I mentioned our patron?"

"Yes."

"Well, I've been told that she likes to visit all of the orphanages, especially the new ones like ours."

"Is she coming here?" asked Munroe, holding her breath.

"There was a rumour that we would be seeing her in the next few days. Gorell just confirmed it. Isn't that exciting?" asked Sianne.

Munroe was stunned but eventually managed to speak. "Oh yes. That sounds like an unforgettable day!"

Sianne was so wrapped up in her excitement she was oblivious to the emotions that flickered across Munroe's face. Her vengeance was almost at hand and Akosh wouldn't see it coming until it was too late.

CHAPTER 31

A few hours after Wren and the others left Gillen's Jaw the raiders set off for their camp. Wren had no way of knowing what Boros and the others had done to the villagers, or their children, but as Danoph kept reminding her she was not responsible.

She and Danoph hid a fair distance away from the main road in a dense copse to conceal the horses from view. By augmenting her eyesight with magic Wren was able to watch the raiders leaving from her concealed position. She couldn't hear what they were saying but it was clear how the others deferred to Boros. At her previous encounter with the raiders in Sour Crown, fear of their leader had been apparent. Now she witnessed first-hand how they acted with deference and a peculiar sensitivity, as if she were brittle. Wren had seen such behaviour before.

As a small girl she used to play with the children on her street. They spent so much time in each other's houses she came to know everything about their lives and families. She knew whose parents were generous with treats, whose wouldn't tolerate running or noise in the house and whose parents were terrifying. There was no noise, no running and little fun to be had in Yortem's house. Everyone treated his father as if he were a bear in hibernation, afraid of what might happen if he fully awoke. A year later the village found out when he flew into a rage, killing seven people, including Yortem and his mother before he was finally stopped.

She wondered what Boros had done to create such fear among her peers. Raiders were not known for being kind and polite, but all of them rushed around Boros, all but bowing and scraping like she was royalty. Wren had witnessed the casual way she'd threatened the children in Gillen's Jaw. Whatever Boros had done in the past, such a savage act must have seemed tame by comparison.

Wren waited until the raiders were almost out of sight before they followed at a sedate pace. The dozen men and women rode with confidence and no fear of reprisal for their actions. Such an attitude made them arrogant, something Wren hoped to use against them.

For the next few hours they trailed after the raiders who stopped off at two other villages to collect a tithe. Part of her wanted to rush in and help them, despite knowing the villagers wouldn't thank her for getting involved once they witnessed her magic. The colder, more logical part of her knew that such an heroic act would serve little purpose in the long run and so she did nothing. Even if she somehow managed to overwhelm Boros and the dozen raiders with her, Wren wasn't sure she could kill them. Besides, there were more raiders back at their camp. Killing a dozen and their leader might slow them down but it wouldn't stop them.

Danoph had tried to prepare her for such a moment, and he believed she could bear such a burden, but Wren wasn't as confident. One violent act against Brunwal, even in defence of her life, had left her isolated from the other students. She worried how the others in the community would treat her if she killed again. Even worse, Wren was terrified how such an act would change her. Master Yettle's advice about not lying to herself was difficult to maintain. It often left her feeling fragile, but she persisted by trying to understand the repercussions.

One thought kept rattling around inside her head. It refused to give her a moment's peace and sometimes woke her in the middle of the night. What if she discovered that she enjoyed killing?

It sounded ludicrous and yet it was not unprecedented, even in Drassia. Some men who wore the mask refused to give it up, even when their bodies were too old and slow to fight. They often died on their feet with a weapon in hand and thought it a life well spent and a worthy death. Over time they had come to love the sound of steel cutting through flesh, the misting spray of blood, the anguished screams of the dying.

She could imagine it becoming addictive. To remove people from the world and carve your own path through history. To be, as a god, deciding the fate of others.

Others were addicted to seeing death reflected in the eyes of their victims. She'd even heard wild stories of a secret group of Drassi warriors that worshipped death, dedicating every kill in her name as if she were a black-hearted goddess.

All of it sounded like madness, and yet Wren found herself at a crossroads. When the moment came her head might take her in one direction but her heart could lead her down a darker path.

Magic gave her abilities far beyond that of most people. It allowed her to do wonderful and terrifying things purely on a whim. She was beginning to believe that such power should not be randomly given to any person as a chance of birth. Magic carried a heavy responsibility that, only now, was she beginning to understand.

If she were more like Boros and cared only about herself, Wren could live as a queen. She could kill and maim with abandon until people were terrified to speak her name. But she had walked away from the path of violence, away from Garvey and his rage, and yet now she found herself struggling with an impossible decision.

"I can hear you brooding," said Danoph, startling Wren from her reverie. They were still trailing after the raiders at a distance. Light was beginning to fade from the sky overhead as dusk approached. They must be getting close to the raiders' base.

"It seems as if the only choices left to me end in murder. It's either me or her," said Wren, gesturing at the distant figure of Boros.

"Perhaps," mused Danoph.

"Do you know something?" asked Wren. "Have you had a vision about her?"

"No, but perhaps you should gather more facts about her and the raiders before making a decision."

A short time later Wren saw the raiders turn their horses away from the main road and head east. By the time they reached the same spot night had fallen and they were forced to dismount and walk. The countryside was pitch-black and she didn't want to injure their horses. She was tempted to summon a mage lantern, which she'd finally mastered after weeks of practice, but decided not to take the risk in case they were discovered. Instead she relied on the Source to enhance her vision, peeling back the deepest shadows.

After fumbling ahead at a slow walk, noise and then light from up ahead made them pause. They tied up their horses and then crept closer to the raiders' camp. After checking for scouts, she and Danoph crawled into a dense thicket where they could observe the raiders' camp without the risk of being discovered.

In some ways that she found unsettling, Wren noticed a number of similarities between her new community and the raiders' base. On one side of a secluded valley the trees had been reduced to a sea of sawn trunks. Stacks of firewood were haphazardly piled up alongside their dwellings, which were a mishmash of crudely fashioned lean-tos, tents, rough log cabins, mud huts and hovels that went underground. There was no order to their layout in the camp. In one area she saw a shantytown with several homes clustered together, but a sea of space between them and the largest log cabin towards the back of the camp. She guessed it belonged to Boros but was surprised to see several raiders leading their horses inside. It made sense. They travelled all across the western region and relied heavily on their horses to cover so much ground.

A large well sat at the heart of the camp where several people were drawing up buckets of water. Three people were cutting up vegetables and throwing them into a large pot while others stoked the fire. All of it seemed incredibly mundane and normal, except that everything the raiders touched was tainted with blood.

Not far from the stable door Boros was distributing the tithe they'd taken from the villagers. Food was taken to a sturdy-looking log cabin while the other items were laid out on a sheet and a bidding process began between the gathered crowd.

"I need to know more about her," muttered Wren, but Danoph overheard.

"They're scared of her," he said. "As vicious as they are, as cruel and without compassion, she is worse."

"I thought as much," said Wren, having seen how they deferred to her. "Can you tell me anything else? Can you sense anything?"

It seemed as if Danoph was about to say he couldn't help, or that his Talent didn't work that way, when his expression changed. Perhaps he was beginning to embrace his gift, or perhaps he simply understood the personal stakes for her, in addition to the survival of their community.

"I will try," he promised, focusing on Boros. As far as she knew he had never tried to use his Talent on purpose. Wren really wasn't sure what she had been expecting. An echo through the Source as he embraced his power. A disturbance in the air around him, or perhaps something more extreme given his violent nightmares.

Danoph lifted his right hand towards Boros and she thought light blossomed on his palm, although it was difficult to be sure.

There was no rush of energy and Danoph didn't move a muscle. In fact, it was as if he had suddenly been frozen solid. Despite being close enough to reach out and touch him, she felt he had suddenly become part of their surroundings. He was beside her and yet she had the impression his mind was elsewhere, travelling to places unseen. Wren wasn't even sure if he was breathing and almost reached out to touch him but stopped herself in case she broke his trance.

When Danoph spoke she let out a squeak of surprise, but he didn't notice. "She's hollow," he said in a voice that sounded different as well. If she hadn't seen his lips moving Wren wouldn't have said that it was Danoph speaking. The voice was older and more cultured. "Her future is murky but all of it is violent."

"What about her past? What can you tell me about that?" asked Wren.

"It's very clear. There's only one road." Danoph's sudden smile was unnerving. He was staring at something far away and Wren felt goosebumps cover her skin. "It is drenched in blood."

"Tell me," said Wren, going against her better judgement.

"She was a child growing up in Seveldrom when the war began. Her village wasn't famous and held nothing of worth. But it was remote and found itself on the front line of the invading western army." Danoph spoke clearly and with such an icy detachment she heard neither compassion nor grief in his voice. "Some of her earliest memories are of moving house. Her parents arguing about which belongings to leave behind and which to take with them. All the children rode out of the village on the back of an old wagon pulled by a pair of donkeys. She thought everyone was going on a trip together, except they never went home again."

It was a common story in the western region of Seveldrom as many villages had been abandoned. The people fled east to the safety of the capital and beyond into the countryside. When the army arrived it passed through the empty settlements and, like a swarm of locusts, stripped the land clean, leaving nothing behind. After the war many of those who'd fled had nothing to go back home to and were forced to make new lives elsewhere.

"After that there were a lot of strange faces and shouting. She remembers weeks spent living in a tent, exploring fields with other children during the day and cooking food over fires outdoor at night. She remembers the smell of many people living close together and always wearing muddy clothes. Sometimes people argued over food and that was when she saw her first dead body." Danoph's smile was out of place and Wren wondered what he was seeing.

"Who died? Was it one of her parents?" asked Wren, but either he didn't hear or chose not to answer.

"There was an argument. She doesn't know what it was about, but she saw one man hit the other on the head. He fell down and didn't get up again. Boros found him lying in the field, his body hidden from view amid the long grass. At first she was afraid to go near him because he kept staring at her. Eventually she approached and touched his face."

To see a dead body at such a young age was one thing, but witnessing a murder would leave a permanent scar. Wren watched as Boros moved around the camp and the way the other raiders always kept one eye on her. It was difficult to bring together the two images of the innocent young girl and the ruthless leader.

"Is that what changed her?"

"Oh no," said Danoph with a half-smile, and this time she saw he was looking at her. Wren gasped in surprise when she saw his eyes, glowing from within with an intense white light.

"What happened?"

"A pattern began to form, one which she eventually changed. Her family travelled south in Seveldrom and started a new life. But violence found them again as the village was attacked by a group of thieves. No one there put up a fight. They gave the thieves what they wanted and they left. This went on for months until her parents decided to move on and start again. Violence and bad luck seemed to follow them wherever they went. And each time her father refused to get angry, refused to fight back and said faith would provide. Boros killed her first man when she was eleven."

Around the same age that Wren was discovering boys and daydreaming about the future, Boros had already taken a life.

"It was a chance encounter," said Danoph. "Boros recognised him as one of the thieves who had come to her village a few years before. He was older now, overweight and slow. She tempted him into a dark alley with a promise and stabbed him to death with his own dagger. Afterwards she expected to feel something. Joy. Satisfaction. Relief perhaps. But there was nothing. Just an emptiness and a hunger inside. She took his money, his dagger, and began to hunt the others. Moving from place to place she cut purses and throats. At fifteen she met a group of thieves and killers who laughed at her until she killed two of them. She was leading them by the time she was eighteen. The Queen of Seveldrom stamped down on raiders and they were hunted down by soldiers and a man called the Gath. Boros fled and came west with the survivors. Ever since then she's moved from group to group, butchering anyone who challenges her authority."

"Why does she do it?" asked Wren, hoping to understand what continued to drive Boros to commit such acts of brutal violence.

"She came to believe something." Danoph's eyes were still glowing in the dark. Wren felt more than a little unsettled by his impenetrable stare when it formed on her. "That people are fundamentally weak. That if you threaten them, they'll fall in line. All it takes is someone whose will is stronger, and she is merciless."

"Is it greed?" asked Wren. "What is driving her to do all of this? The murders and intimidating the villages in this area. What does she want?"

For the first time since he'd embraced his power, Wren saw an emotion briefly flicker across Danoph's face but couldn't name it. She didn't know if it was disgust or sympathy. "She desperately wants to feel something. Because no matter how much pain and suffering she causes, no matter how many people she kills or how much money they make, all of it means nothing to her. She simply doesn't feel anything."

The glow faded from behind Danoph's eyes as he lowered his right hand, coming back to the present. They stared at one another in silence for a long time, shocked at what he'd revealed about Boros, but also at his latent power. It went far beyond dreams and nightmares about the future. It was something they would have to deal with, but tonight there were more pressing matters.

Wren gestured for him to follow her away from the raiders' camp. They walked back to their horses and she came to a decision. "I need you to do me a small favour," she said. "Take both horses a little way down the road and wait for me there."

Danoph was still slightly dazed but he was present enough to look worried. "What are you going to do?"

"Show her that I'm not afraid."

His tendency to say little had never bothered her before, but now she wondered what Danoph was seeing when he looked at her. "Be careful," was all he said before slowly riding away.

Reaching out towards the endless sea at the periphery of her senses, Wren drew power from the Source into herself. Delving deeper than she had in a long time, perhaps since she'd faced Brunwal, she embraced the energy, letting it fill her with its light and glory. Her skin tingled, her senses sharpened acutely, and as the raiders' camp came into sight up ahead she released part of the energy into the air.

Bright flares of white light rushed into the sky, burning away the darkness and illuminating every corner of the raiders' camp. With cries of alarm they scrambled around for weapons thinking they were under attack. Boros emerged from a tent and began searching for the source of the light while others around her panicked. Eventually someone looked in Wren's direction and bows were drawn and pointed at her. To make it easier she summoned a mage lantern in one hand and raised it above her head, revealing her position to everyone.

A crowd had gathered at the edge of the settlement but none of the raiders seemed willing to step forward. Boros pushed her way to the front and boldly walked ahead of the others who still held back. A peculiar hush had fallen over the crowd until a dense silence filled the air.

Wren stared into Boros's cold blue eyes and tried not to show her fear. More important, she had found their camp and had apparently come alone, sending a clear message of its own. It wasn't over between them.

CHAPTER 32

Regent Choilan took his time settling himself into the chair before accepting the proffered glass of wine. His first wife, Selina, waved the servant away and waited until she'd left the room before speaking. Choilan had no concern about anyone overhearing their conversation as a Royal Guard was posted outside the door, but Selina was not taking any chances. She'd always been careful but more recently her behaviour was bordering on paranoid. He blamed it on indulging her interest in espionage. It was to be expected that after spending so much time with professional agents she would absorb some of their habits.

Selina's new passion had produced some remarkable results in the last few months, outdoing his own agents from time to time. After all, it was her new group that had found and imprisoned the person responsible for the murder of their predecessors.

"Are you even listening?" said Selina.

Choilan forced himself to focus on her face rather than the intriguing curve of her calves. "Yes, you were telling me about my cadre of young mages. So, they're all behaving? No signs of disloyalty?"

As expected it was proving difficult to convince the people

that any mages, no matter whose colours and what kind of uniform they wore, was a good thing. It would happen eventually, but it might take a few years. At the same time he wasn't naïve and made sure all the mages were closely watched. So far they seemed to be true believers in the cause, but after the initial rush of power he needed to ensure they remained loyal and didn't abuse their magic. As a secondary precaution a number of Royal Guards had taken to carrying a concealed poisoned dagger that was reserved for the mages. The snake venom wasn't deadly but even the smallest cut on bare skin would paralyse a large man in seconds.

Selina eyed him with suspicion but eventually continued. "No. So far all ten of the young mages are behaving. But you should be careful not to trust them too quickly."

Choilan raised an eyebrow. "I don't trust them at all. Give it ten years of loyal service and then we can have this conversation again."

The corners of Selina's mouth lifted briefly which he took as a small victory. "I must say, I've have been impressed with Tianne," he conceded. "So far we've rooted out almost every fraud and charlatan in the city. She has a real fire in her belly for them."

Selina was less impressed. "I take it you're aware that she's attracted to you?"

"Of course. I've played on that several times."

"Then isn't there a risk she's merely doing all of this to impress you?"

"It's possible, but I doubt it," he said with a shrug. "She came a long way to help, based on my amnesty. But surely wanting to impress me is a good thing?"

"Hmmm," said Selina, sounding unconvinced. "Then may I suggest you make a point of visiting her. My agents tell me her enthusiasm seems to be waning. I suspect she's having doubts."

"Doubts?"

"She was the first. Now, she's merely one of many. Give her something symbolic to make her feel special."

Choilan considered it and thought it an excellent idea. "Anything else?"

"I'd also suggest bringing in the parents, hers and others. Get them to talk about how proud they are of what their children are doing with their magic. Using it to help people. All of that nonsense."

That would be more of a challenge. Almost all of the parents had either disowned or tried to drown their children once they discovered their child had magic. It wouldn't be easy to make them sit down in a room and talk to their child, let alone make their praise convincing. However, he was confident once he explained how important this was, and the lethal consequences of refusing, the parents would be happy to comply.

"All of that should win her over," said Selina, offering a smile that made him nervous. "Failing that, if Tianne doesn't come around, then she'll end up like the others."

Those with tenuous magic, and anyone unwilling to serve, initially spent some time in the cells to convince them. If that failed they were beheaded and the bodies burned, just to make sure. He knew magic couldn't be eradicated, but Choilan intended to control those who were born with it in Zecorria. Murder was a crude and rather final tool, but he understood that sometimes it was necessary. The way Selina spoke about it so easily, and smiled at the idea, served as another reminder why he'd not invited her to his bed for several years. It was a lot safer to spend time with his other wives. Her smile widened as their eyes met. It was as if she knew what he was thinking.

"Do you have any more news for me?" he asked, covering up his discomfort. "Any news of foreign agents?"

Selina's smile faded. "No, not at this time."

He sensed she was withholding something. "Is there something I should know?" Choilan folded his arms and leaned back in his chair, waiting for an answer.

"They're unconfirmed rumours. It could be nothing."

"But?" he persisted.

Selina realised he wasn't going to budge but was equally stubborn. "I'll bring it to your attention at the appropriate time." She folded her arms and a staring match ensued, neither willing to concede. Choilan suspected it would have continued if not for a frantic knocking at the door.

A Royal Guard burst into the room looking uncharacteristically flustered, which made his heart race. "What is it? What's happened?"

"My apologies, Regent, but a group of soldiers has returned from the border with a prisoner." The guard's fear was making him increasingly nervous.

"A prisoner? What kind of prisoner?" he asked, but the guard was rendered speechless. Something had scared him badly.

"Spit it out. Who is it?" asked Selina.

The Royal Guard finally found his voice. "I think it's Garvey," he whispered.

The ground seemed to drop away from Choilan even though he was sitting still. He felt his stomach moving up into his throat and he struggled to breathe. Looking across at Selina he saw she was equally stunned.

"Are you sure?"

"I think you should see him." The guard seemed unwilling to answer him directly.

Choilan's mind started whirling as he tried to find something to hold on to but there were only questions. Why had Garvey surrendered? Surely there was no cell in the world that could hold him. So why was he here? Was it a trap? Had he allowed himself to be captured merely to unleash the full force of his magic in the capital? Where were his followers? A dozen more questions ran through his mind.

"The mages," he said suddenly, clutching at straws. They weren't ready. They were crudely trained, not battle-ready mages able to defend him against such a dangerous and powerful threat. But the children were also the only thing Choilan had standing between him and oblivion. What had he been thinking? He should have been looking for someone to train the children at the same time as cultivating their loyalty.

"Show me," said Choilan, gesturing at the Royal Guard. He felt something tugging on his sleeve and looked around to see Selina holding onto his jacket. He'd never seen her afraid before today. It made him think back to all that he'd done to reach this moment and be here. The sacrifices, the political games, the marriages to build alliances and the countless years focused on a single goal. Choilan would not be cowed. If this was a trap, and this was to be his final moment, then he would face it head-on like every other obstacle in life.

He patted Selina's hand and followed the nervous Royal Guard through the familiar corridors of the palace. They descended countless flights of stairs going deep underground past corridors echoing with the cries of prisoners rotting in their own filth. Down and down, away from any natural light, soon they were surrounded only by thick stone walls.

The temperature continued to fall as they went deeper into the earth, his breath frosting in the air, until finally they arrived at the lowest level. Historically this was where the Mad King had kept the most dangerous prisoners. Those he'd deemed the biggest threat to his power. In reality they'd probably been people he'd simply disliked because of how they spoke or dressed.

When Choilan had gained the throne he'd found the cells full of bones and rotting bodies. They'd been cleared out and remained empty until he'd ordered Tianne to be dropped into one of the water cells. His dramatic rescue of her had been carefully orchestrated and yet unfortunately her loyalty was still wavering. Selina was right. He'd make her feel special and if that failed she'd find herself visiting her old cell again.

A dozen Royal Guards, all heavily armed with swords and shields, waited for him at the main door to the cells. They weren't as anxious as his guide but he could see the tension in their faces and posture.

"Tell me what happened," he said to the Captain.

The burly man stepped forward and gave a short bow. "Regent, as per your instructions, patrols were regularly visiting all towns and villages close to the southern border. There had not been any sightings of Garvey and his rogue mages for some time. When they arrived at Ore Birch they found blood on the street and one building had collapsed. Garvey and his people had been holding the villagers hostage until they were rescued."

"By whom?"

"They don't know, but someone started killing Garvey's people. They heard a terrible fight and saw lightning fall from the sky. Then there was a long silence. When they emerged they found several dead mages and also Garvey. The patrol arrested him and brought him here to stand trial for his crimes."

"How did they arrest him?"

"He's injured," was all the Captain would say. Even so he was clearly nervous of Garvey and rightly so after everything that he'd done. Choilan considered that perhaps this wasn't to be his final moment after all.

"Show me," he said, gesturing at the door.

The three huge locks clanged open and a thick metal bar was removed before the heavy iron door could be pushed open. Flickering torches provided erratic light and strange shadows danced on the stone walls. This far down they were roughly hewn, damp in places with green moss and glittering with shards of crystal. It also stank. Of decay, sweat and stale piss. No amount of sluicing out the cells had got rid of the smells left over from the Mad King's paranoia.

Only the Captain came with him into the cell block. The others remained at the door, weapons at the ready, just in case. The further he went into the cell block the worse the stench became. Despite covering his nose with a sleeve and breathing through his mouth, Choilan gagged a few times before his stomach settled. The Captain led him to the last enclosure on the left.

The torchlight didn't reach the back of the dingy cell but he could make out most of what it contained. A stone shelf for a bed, a bucket in one corner and a scraggly old blanket. There was also a man chained to the walls by his wrists and ankles. The restraints were enormous with huge steel links, as thick as Choilan's wrist.

The prisoner's origins were difficult to pinpoint as he had no discerning features and any bare skin was tanned from being outdoors. Part of his face was hidden in shadow but Choilan could just make out a red beard and wide jaw. He was dressed in stained clothing that was marked with dried blood and dirt. At first glance Choilan noted the bruises on his arms and the blood on his chin, but couldn't see any crippling injuries that might explain his capture. It was only when he coughed at the smell that the prisoner shuffled forward into the light, revealing all of his face.

Someone had gouged out both of his eyes.

"I can hear you breathing out there," said Garvey, turning his face towards Choilan with an eerie smile.

The Captain gasped in spite of himself and reached for his sword. Garvey faced the Captain and lurched towards him, chains clanking. With a cry the Captain fell back against the far wall, tripping over his own feet in a panic. Garvey was brought up short, his arms and hands stretched out in front of him, but they were still some distance from the bars. He began to laugh at the Captain who scrambled back to his feet, untangling himself from his sword.

Garvey turned back to face Choilan and despite his blindness he knew the Sorcerer was studying him. "You must be someone important to have Captain Nervous accompany him. The body oils you're wearing are rich, much like your silk clothing. Regent Choilan, I presume."

Despite being dressed in rags, recently blinded, defeated and imprisoned, he remained defiant and arrogant. It was Garvey. Choilan had no doubts. Without saying a word, he walked from the cell block already planning what he would do next.

The greatest threat to his country and the west had been eliminated on Zecorran soil. It wouldn't take much to turn this to his advantage. Whoever was responsible for Garvey's defeat had not hung around to claim the glory. So, who was to say his new cadre of mages had not been responsible?

Such a victory would certainly help to convince the people that the new recruits could be trusted and were loyal patriots. But first they would parade Garvey through the streets so that everyone could see that their Regent had brought him to justice. It would be good for them to see the focus of their anger in the flesh. Then there would be a short trial and an execution. The people's faith in him would be restored. This would ensure that those lurking in the shadows, waiting for him to fall so they might claim the throne for themselves, would have to wait a bit longer. Such a grand spectacle might also encourage more young people to come forward and join his growing cadre of mages.

It didn't matter how it had happened, he would turn this opportunity to his favour and strengthen his position on the throne. His first task was to send messages to all of the leaders in the west, informing them about Garvey's capture. He'd also need to make a speech in the capital to let the people know that the danger had passed. Merchants and travellers would carry the news from there to the rest of the country.

The future of Zecorria had never seemed brighter and he would be remembered throughout history as the man responsible. Choilan didn't notice the smell or care about the cold any more as he climbed the stairs towards the sunlight, his mind whirling with possibilities.

CHAPTER 33

Tammy stared at the letter from the palace in disbelief. She had been staring at it for some time, considering the immediate repercussions and long-term effects. There were so many possibilities she was having difficulty making a prediction. All she could do was prepare for the worst in the city.

Garvey had been captured in Zecorria.

Regent Choilan had boldly made a proclamation and was taking full credit. He claimed that it was only because of his vision of creating a loyal cadre of mages. She had serious doubts that his newly recruited children could have defeated Garvey, a mage with decades of experience. As far as she was aware, his skill and power was on par with that of Balfruss. He, too, had used the title of Sorcerer which she understood was more than just a name. It meant that his understanding of magic had reached a deeper level that few ever achieved. All of which raised an even more worrying question. Who had defeated Garvey? She hoped it was Balfruss but at the moment there was no way to know as he'd disappeared.

Tammy had picked up a letter from the palace a few hours ago but on her walk back to her office she'd heard people gossiping in the streets. The news was already everywhere. On the surface Garvey's apprehension sounded like good news, and people were treating it as such, but she wasn't so sure. Without their leader his followers were faceless and nameless. She knew they were young, but beyond that no one really knew anything about them.

There was a possibility some of them would attempt to rescue their leader. Or worse, if the Regent rushed through a trial and then an execution that could make Garvey a martyr. In some ways that would be worse. If Choilan thought they had been dangerous before he would learn how destructive magic could be if Garvey's followers focused all their power on his capital city. That would certainly put his new cadre to the test.

Tammy also had to consider another possibility. That his followers would simply scatter into many smaller groups. Some could be on their way here. Others might go into hiding and never emerge, and some would go on a vicious killing spree, worse than ever before. There had been no dramatic escalation while Garvey had been in charge. The attacks on villagers, in both countries, had been oddly spaced apart but she couldn't explain why. It seemed ludicrous to suggest their restraint was because of him. And yet.

In the six hours since picking up the letter from the palace she'd heard about four magical attacks on communities in the north. She suspected it would also be the same in Zecorria.

Birds had been flying in and out of the aviary all afternoon. The news hadn't reached the population here yet, but when it did their brief surge of hope would fade. The xenophobia that had come with the revelation of Seekers living among them would return. Only now it would be directed towards any young person who was a stranger. Then the cycle of violence towards children with magic would continue.

The ban on Seekers had been a mistake, but she still wasn't

sure what would've been a better solution. Queen Morganse had been backed into a corner but at least the national ban had forced all Seekers to bury their masks. It would keep them safe for the time being until a child with magic in their community started to manifest.

"Ma'am," said Rummpoe, startling Tammy from her reverie. Her secretary was standing in her open doorway, looking at her with some concern.

"What is it?"

"I knocked twice," she apologised. "Are you all right?"

"I'm fine. What's happened?"

Rummpoe slowly came further into the room, still reluctant to spend more time in here than was absolutely necessary. "I've received a message about another attack on a town to the north."

"How far away?" asked Tammy, plotting the positions of the previous attacks on a map in her mind.

"About a day's ride."

It was as she suspected. Some of them were gradually heading south. The wise thing to do would be to avoid the capital city and continue south. To stay in the countryside where it would take a day or two before soldiers could be sent to investigate. Tammy's instincts told her they wouldn't go around. They'd come here and hope to go unnoticed in a crowd.

She would need to call on Guardian Fray a lot more in the coming months. His magic allowed him to see other mages which would be critical in finding the rogues hiding in plain sight. Only a handful knew about his magic and it would be better to keep it that way for now. She'd have to come up with a plausible story to explain his absence from normal duties.

"Tell the Watch Captains to be on alert, and increase the number of patrols down at the docks."

"Yes, ma'am."

The sound of pounding feet alerted them both to danger before they saw a novice Guardian racing down the corridor shouting, "Sir! Sir!"

"Report."

"There's a fight. Mages in the city," gasped the young woman between gulps of air. "It's chaos. Buildings are collapsing."

Tammy pulled on her jacket and belted on her sword. "Stay here," she said to Rummpoe.

"Yes, ma'am."

"Show me where," said Tammy to the novice. The young woman was out of breath, holding one hand to her right side, but she turned and began to jog back down the corridor with Tammy at her heels.

At this time of night the street should have been filled with noise from the many crowded bars and taverns. Instead as Tammy approached an eerie silence gripped the area. A small group of people had gathered at one end of the street but they were also oddly silent as they scanned the nearest buildings for danger. There were a few drinkers and one or two tavern owners, but mostly they were people who had been turfed from their beds, half-dressed or wearing only a blanket and boots. A few were anxiously staring at the figure lying in the middle of the street. They seemed to be waiting for the person to start moving, but she thought they were dead or unconscious.

The other peculiarity on the street was the shattered building halfway down on the right. Once it had been just another tavern but now it was a ruin. The front had been caved in, as if a huge force had struck it. Its roof had been torn open to the sky and shattered beams stuck out like the ribs of a huge beast. As Tammy watched another section of an outer wall tumbled inwards, raising a huge pile of dust.

When it had settled and the silence returned she found herself straining to hear any noise on the street or beyond. The whole city seemed to be holding its breath.

"Who is that?" she asked, gesturing at the body on the street.

"One of them evil mages," whispered a short woman beside her. She was dressed in a pair of trousers and her shirt was inside out. Her feet were bare but she didn't seem to care.

"Did you see what happened?" asked Tammy.

"Course I did," said the woman with a snort. "One of them came right into my bedroom, straight through the wall. Almost pissed myself."

"One of who?"

"He's one of Garvey's lot. Had to be. The young one in my room went back into the street to help his friend, but it was no good. The other one, the man in the hood, he threw them around and smashed one of them into the ground. We all heard his neck snap." She gestured at the body lying in the middle of the road.

"Did you see where the others went?"

The woman looked at Tammy as if she were mad. "Don't know and don't care. As long as they're not here."

Tired of standing around, she walked towards the body in the street. It turned out to be a young man from Yerskania. He was probably in his late teens and was most definitely dead. His neck was bent at an unnatural angle and his eyes were wide open. Blood had trickled from one corner of his mouth onto the street but there wasn't much, suggesting he'd died quickly. The stones around him on the road were cracked from the impact and he lay in a small depression. A huge force had slammed him into the road.

A flash of blue lit up the night sky and Tammy spun around to find the source. It was coming from a few streets away. She was already sprinting towards it when she heard a loud cracking sound. There was screaming and a crowd of people started running towards her, fleeing whatever was happening. Tammy was forced to slow down as she dodged around people wide-eyed with panic. She grabbed one man by the shoulder, pulling him to a stop.

"Let me go!" he said, trying to shake her off but she tightened her grip.

"What's happening?"

"Two mages are tearing up the street. They'll kill anyone who gets near them." Tammy let go and he sprinted away. She pressed on, going against the tide of people flowing in the opposite direction. As she approached a small market square a few stragglers ran for cover and then she was alone again in the heart of the city.

Elsewhere she could hear the march of heavy feet as squads of the Watch formed a perimeter around the area. She'd coordinated with the Watch Captains before coming into the dead zone. They couldn't do much to stop the mages, and could make it worse if they tried to shoot them. For now their job was to stay out of the way and wait for her signal.

The square was empty of people but there were signs of a recent struggle. One of the stone water fountains had been shattered, the statue of an old King leaning towards the ground at a jaunty angle. Water trickled out of the broken basin, slowly creating a new stream as it wound its way between the stones. She spotted a few frightened faces peering into the square from first-floor windows. They were probably people caught in the middle of the fight who had been too slow or unwilling to flee their homes.

"Show yourself!" someone shouted boldly, walking into the square. Kneeling, Tammy removed the bundle from her back slowly and unwrapped her sword. It had been a gift from an old friend many years ago. It was one of a kind and priceless as well as being incredibly unusual, which was why she'd given it to an old friend for safekeeping. As Khevassar she couldn't afford to stand out in any way and the sword was remarkable. Tammy drew *Maligne* from its scabbard, noting how even in weak moonlight the surface of the blade shimmered blue, purple and green.

In the square the young man from Zecorria was now standing beside the water fountain, his eyes moving from window to window.

"Are you afraid to face me?" he shouted, taunting his unseen opponent. If Tammy had believed in the gods she would have muttered a prayer to one of them to protect her. She would only get one chance at this and it was a slim one if he saw her coming. Just as she was getting herself ready to charge the air shimmered like a heat haze, and a hooded man materialised out of thin air. Tammy would have been amazed if she hadn't seen him do it before. The young rogue mage spun around in surprise, gawping as Balfruss lowered his hood.

"You cannot win. Stop this before you hurt someone, or force me to stop you, like your friend," said the Sorcerer.

The former student sneered at his teacher. "You're a slave. You bow and scrape to them, when we should be ruling! My power makes me a god."

Balfruss shook his head wearily. "No, it doesn't. This is your last chance."

The young mage didn't hesitate. Tammy saw something red streak through the air towards Balfruss from his outstretched hand. A second later a ball of fire seemed to engulf her friend from head to toe. She heard the crackle of the flames and thought it was over, but almost immediately the fire began to dwindle. Balfruss was standing in exactly the same spot. A white cocoon enveloped him and the remnants of the fire burned away. He remained untouched and his expression was one of disappointment rather than anger.

"Is that it? After four years of study. Did you learn nothing?" he asked.

With a snarl of rage the student began hurling what looked like balls of light at Balfruss but he shrugged them off. With a casual flick of one hand he redirected one of the missiles so that it looped around the square and flew back towards the student. With a startled cry he threw himself to the ground, narrowly missing it. The ball of light struck the statue behind him, blowing it into dozens of pieces which rained down across the square.

Trying a different tactic, the young mage lifted several large chunks of stone from the broken fountain into the air. Tammy could see the strain on his face as he sent them hurtling towards Balfruss. The Sorcerer continued to walk calmly towards the student, ignoring the stones which shattered as they came into contact with his shield. He simply sidestepped the largest stone which was the size of a grown man. With a wave of his hand he gently set it down before it struck the building behind him and caused more damage.

"Garvey lied and manipulated you. Even so, your magic doesn't give you the right to do whatever you want."

Balfruss's calmness seemed only to anger the student. "We trusted you. We believed your lies. You said we were going to help people." The student's mocking laughter echoed around the empty square and she thought it was aimed at himself. "They hate us, because we're better than them, because we're special and they're not."

Balfruss was still moving towards the student whose thoughts seemed to have turned inwards. "You need to stop," he said, but the young man didn't seem to hear.

"They're jealous. We can create wonders while they toil away in the dirt. We dream but they can only destroy."

"It's time to rest," said Balfruss, moving closer. "This isn't the way."

Tammy entered the square behind the student. If he turned his head even slightly he would see her creeping up behind. Doing her best to avoid the rubble, she slowly moved towards him as Balfruss approached from the front.

The student looked up suddenly and Tammy froze, willing him not to turn around. "What will we become?" he asked, suddenly alert. "Now that the Red Tower is gone, who will teach the children?"

"I don't know," admitted Balfruss.

"They can't kill us all, can they?" There was a hint of desperation in his voice, as if he thought it might be possible.

"No, they can't," said Balfruss, finally reaching the student's side. He laid a hand on the boy's shoulder, connecting him to the present. "They tried in the past, but it never works. They're scared because they don't understand. Garvey was right about that."

That caught the student's attention, and Tammy's. Focusing more on where she was placing her feet Tammy started to tiptoe forward again. She didn't know if Balfruss was aware of her presence but it didn't really matter. Stopping the rogue mage from destroying more of her city, by whatever means necessary, was her first priority.

"He was?" asked the boy.

Balfruss's smile was sad. "We've held ourselves apart for too long. To us the Red Tower was just a school, but to everyone else it was a dangerous mystery."

"We just wanted to learn," said the boy. Tammy could see his shoulders were shaking as he wiped at his face. "We didn't ask to be born this way."

Tammy was almost within arm's reach of the mage when he finally noticed her coming up behind. He spun about and at the sight of her sword and uniform energy began to gather in the palms of his hands. It dwindled and then vanished as Balfruss clubbed him across the back of the head. The Sorcerer lowered his axe and gently eased the boy to the ground.

They stared at one another in silence noting the changes until Balfruss gestured towards her sword. "I've not seen that in a while." He lowered his axe and raised an eyebrow. Taking the hint, she sheathed her sword, looking around at the damage. Apart from the fountain it was minimal. The building on the other street seemed to have sustained the worst damage.

"There was just the two of them," said Balfruss. "Unfortunately, I had to kill one. Now that we have this one, I'm not really sure what to do with him," he said, gesturing at the unconscious figure at their feet.

"We need to talk in private," said Tammy, noting the faces watching them from the surrounding buildings. "And I have an idea about that."

Balfruss stared at the walls of the eight-sided cell with a mix of wonder and surprise. She'd brought him to the secret cells beneath Unity Hall. It was where she'd previously brought Fray to summon the spirit of Guardian Brook.

"These are ancient," he muttered, tracing a hidden symbol with his fingers. To her it was just a blank wall, like every other part of the cell, but to those with magic it was a rich tapestry.

They put the rogue mage inside and she locked the door. Balfruss was still staring.

"What is it?" he finally asked. "And why is it here, beneath Unity Hall?"

"I have a theory, but there's no one alive to confirm it."

Tammy gestured for him to follow her back to her office. She would see that the prisoner's basic needs were met until they worked out what to do with him. Unfortunately, it would mean trusting someone else with the secret of the special cells. Tammy considered who she could trust as they retraced their path through the building.

"I must be brief. I have to speak to the Watch Captains and then report to the Queen about what's happened," she told him, gesturing at one of the seats in front of her desk. Normally she would have moved to sit behind it, but instead she sat down beside him. It was a small thing but Balfruss noted the difference and smiled at the gesture.

"It was you, wasn't it?" she asked. "You defeated Garvey."

Balfruss's smile faded. "Yes, and now I must hunt down those who followed him. They're too dangerous to be allowed to roam free."

"Will the cell hold him?" asked Tammy. Fray had tried to use his magic while inside but he wasn't as powerful as others.

"It will, but he cannot live in there for ever. I have an idea for something long term—"

"They'll need to stand trial first," she said.

"Would Queen Morganse really order their deaths?"

Tammy shook her head. The idea of sentencing any children to death was one more decision that she didn't envy the Queen having to make. "I don't know. Perhaps, given their crimes. But he's not going anywhere for a while."

"Then I'll trust he'll be safe in your care until I return," said Balfruss, moving to stand up. He stopped when she touched him on the hand. "What is it?"

"What happened with Garvey?" she asked.

"He was my friend," said Balfruss, his voice thick with emotion. "And I crippled him."

"He had to be stopped," said Tammy.

"He did, but, like the boy said, what happens now?" asked Balfruss. "What will those with magic become in the years ahead?"

Tammy had no answers but like Balfruss she was worried about the future. The tide continued to move only in one direction. Even this latest incident would be used as another example of the dangers posed by magic. How everyone was better off without it and that they should kill or shun those born with it. Nothing would be said of how the rogue mages had been stopped or who was responsible.

Time weighed heavily on them both and the future for mages and children with magic seemed bleak.

CHAPTER 34

Tianne stared at her new uniform in the mirror. What had once made her feel so proud no longer filled her with the same joy. A second blue star had been added to her uniform, denoting her as first among the Regent's cadre of mages.

There had been a small ceremony in the palace with the Regent, two of his wives, plus all of the mages in attendance. The room had also been lined with Royal Guards, their multi-coloured uniforms creating a strangely bright background to what was an otherwise sombre event. It should have been a wonderful day. One that she would remember with great joy. Tianne didn't expect a parade or weeping crowds chanting her name, but she had come back to Zecorria based on a promise. That if she served the Regent faithfully then by working together they could change the country and change how people viewed mages.

So far little had changed.

The Regent had explained that it wasn't safe to give her the accolade in public, which spoke volumes about the progress that had been made. This was in spite of their efforts to rid the city, and now beyond into the surrounding areas, of charlatans who exploited desperate people.

She had been the first to take the risk of coming home and

her reception had been the worst. A cynical part of her wondered if that was why the Regent had given her this honour. Out of a sense of guilt about what had happened. Kalina had briefly been put in a cell, but the others who came after had not suffered at all. They'd been treated as honoured guests. Moved directly into comfortable quarters and had received fitted uniforms. They'd been put to work after only a few days. And now there were ten mages in the cadre.

Tianne didn't want to leave her room. She didn't want to see the smug faces of the Royal Guards waiting in the corridor who were her constant shadows. They were only there for her protection, of course, not because she was a prisoner. Despite not being able to go anywhere by herself outside the palace walls.

People were slowly getting used to seeing mages in uniform walking through the city. They wouldn't risk offending the Regent and, even if they tried, any of the mages could take care of themselves. Crudely trained as they were, even the weakest of the cadre could push back an angry mob long enough to run. The patronising smiles and constant reassurances that it was all for her safety were starting to wear a little thin.

There was a rapid knocking on the door and a moment later Kalina bustled into the room, not waiting for permission to enter. Tianne was about to ask her what she was doing when she was struck by Kalina's expression. A second later she saw the tattoo.

"What have you done?" asked Tianne, pointing at her face.

Tattooed above Kalina's right eye and just below was an intricate design comprised of overlapping black sickle shapes. The one above her eyebrow had been made to resemble Tianne's scar.

"Do you like it?" asked Kalina with a big smile. Tianne bit her tongue to stop herself from saying the first thing that came to mind.

"What is it? Why have you—"

"It's to show our loyalty," said Kalina. "To the Regent and to our country. This way, even out of uniform, people will know us and who we serve. They wouldn't dare risk causing offence to the throne. I thought you'd be pleased."

"I'm just so surprised," said Tianne, forcing a laugh. She noticed that the skin was still inflamed on that side of Kalina's face. "Did it hurt?"

"Only a little, but it will be healed up in a few days." Kalina shrugged as if what she'd done wasn't significant. "You gave us the idea for this."

"Me?" said Tianne, putting a hand over her mouth in shock.

"It was just after you rescued me from the cells."

"You did that by yourself," said Tianne.

"You told me about the warrior monks in the desert." It was true. She'd told Kalina about the Jhanidi who tattooed their faces. This was so that any person who met them immediately knew who they served. To offend them was to offend the Desert King and no one would dare in the far east. "The Regent was very impressed by our dedication."

Tianne was only half listening. She was still in shock by what she'd inspired. She'd told Kalina that story to show her that mages were treated better in other parts of the world. In time she'd hoped the people of Zecorria would see magic as a good thing. But they weren't ready yet and now the tattooed children would only inspire fear.

"Wait, did you say our dedication?" asked Tianne, glancing at Kalina.

"We've all had it done," she said with another broad smile. Tianne was horrified but found herself copying the other girl's expression as she teetered on the edge of hysteria. "I'm proud to be a mage," said Kalina. "I shouldn't have to hide or feel ashamed of my power. That's what you talked about."

"Yes. It is," said Tianne, a wild laugh bubbling up from inside. She couldn't believe Kalina and the others had been so stupid. They had permanently branded themselves and tied their fate to the Regent's. Right now, he was on the throne and in favour of mages, but only a few months ago he had banned all Seekers. Rumours had indicated he was about to ban all mages until Garvey's rampage. It would take many years before the people would trust mages and by then Choilan could have been replaced. Or he could have changed his mind to protect his position and keep the people happy.

"So, do you like it?" asked Kalina.

"It's amazing," lied Tianne and the girl hugged her, laughing as well.

"I nearly forgot," said Kalina. "That's not why I rushed in here."

Tianne felt her stomach begin to churn. "What's happened?"

"Garvey is here. He's being held prisoner below the palace."

"Are you sure?" It was hard to believe. Impossible, in fact. He was the most ruthless man she'd ever met and one of the most powerful Sorcerers in the world. Their cadre was a crudely trained group of infants in comparison. They couldn't have stopped him.

"I was spending time with one of the guards," said Kalina with a wink. For once Tianne was glad not to know all the details and didn't ask. "A patrol found Garvey near the southern border and they brought him back here."

"How did they restrain him?"

"He was injured when they found him. He'd been in some huge battle. Half of a village had been destroyed."

"What about his students?" Tianne was suddenly aware that they could be on their way right now to set him free. She wasn't ready. None of them were. Those who had fled with Garvey

were older students who'd been studying at the Red Tower
for years. They had more experience than her and were more
familiar with wielding magic. They'd also spent the last few
months on a rampage, killing or maiming anyone who got in
their way. She didn't think they'd have any compunction about
murdering a few more people, especially if they were holding
Garvey prisoner.

"They vanished. Whoever beat Garvey sent them running.
They probably fled south rather than face us."

Kalina's opinion of herself and the other Zecorran mages was
vastly inflated. They'd never fought another mage, never even
sparred against one in the dormitories. This cadre of mages
was doomed to fail unless they were trained by someone with
experience. Tianne had been doing her best to show the others
some of the basics, but her own skills were still developing.
She'd taught all of them how to sense magic in others and it
was this skill that the Regent was putting to use. It was what
happened after all the charlatans had been revealed or chased
away that worried her. What would the Regent ask them to
do next?

"Don't look so worried," said Kalina, misinterpreting her
frown. "He can't hurt you any more."

"Why not?"

Kalina's smile made her skin crawl. "He's blind." Tianne
swayed on her feet and Kalina grabbed her arm to hold her
steady. "What's wrong? Are you all right?"

"You don't know what he's like. The things he did to us at
the school." They sat down on the edge of the bed and Tianne
put her head in her hands. Kalina put a protective arm around
her shoulders. "He pushed all of us so hard. At least one student
collapsed in all of his lessons."

"He sounds like a bastard."

Tianne didn't disagree but a small part of her wondered if Garvey had been right. Not his methods, of course, but the reasoning behind it. In his own brutal way he'd been preparing them for a time like this, when the whole world was turned against magic, and they weren't ready. She had walked into the palace and been soundly defeated by two unarmed thugs. That's all it had taken.

In the Red Tower they'd been living comfortable lives in seclusion, far away from the real world and its problems. Only Garvey and other teachers had been leaving the school to tackle them head-on.

"He's the most dangerous mage I've ever met," said Tianne, giving Kalina's hand a squeeze. "I'm not sure blinding him will make much of a difference."

"My friend told me some stories about what they've done to him." The way she said it made Tianne feel sick. She knew that Kalina expected her to ask what had been done but she couldn't.

"What will happen to him?" she asked instead.

"There's going to be a short trial, but the Regent also wants him to make a public confession."

"He won't do that," said Tianne, shaking her head. "Ever."

"He will, once they break him," insisted Kalina. "They tried beating him, but that didn't work. So they dropped him into a water cell, but he just froze the water and climbed out. They tried burning him, but the flames and brands couldn't touch his skin. At one point they hung him from his neck, but it didn't seem to have any effect. Why didn't he choke?"

Tianne shrugged, even though she could guess at some of the reasons why their torture was proving ineffective. Even without his eyesight Garvey could still freeze water and create a shield to protect himself from the fire. It made her wonder what else he could do and why he'd allowed himself to be taken prisoner.

"I want to go and see him," said Kalina. "I think I can persuade my friend to let me down there."

Tianne grabbed her hands. "Don't. Don't do it. He'll hurt you."

"He's chained to a wall. What's he going to do?" scoffed Kalina, proving what Tianne had suspected. She was incredibly naïve. "I'm not afraid of him."

"You should be," said Tianne. "He's incredibly dangerous."

"I'm so sorry," said Kalina, but her sympathy burned Tianne. "I didn't realise what they'd done to you at the Red Tower. I'm so glad I wasn't made to go there."

She didn't understand. In spite of all the problems Tianne had experienced with other students, the school had been a refuge. Garvey was only one out of many teachers, and while his presence loomed large there were so many bright spots in her memory. The most recent was time spent dozing on the grass beside Danoph and Wren, daydreaming about what they'd do once they became Battlemages in the real world.

"We'll make sure he suffers," promised Kalina with a smirk. Tianne tried to say something before she left but her throat closed up. The ease with which Kalina spoke about torturing someone scared Tianne. Garvey was a bastard and she knew he'd murdered people since the fall of the Red Tower. He deserved to be punished for his crimes, but torturing him for pleasure made her feel sick.

A few weeks ago she would have wondered how the Regent could allow it. Since then she'd made a number of disturbing discoveries from people working inside the palace. As long as she didn't leave the building Tianne could visit parts of the palace without her escorts.

In the last few weeks she'd been frequenting the servants' part of the palace. At first they'd been wary and her presence had made them uncomfortable. Once they realised she wasn't there to spy on them some had started to relax. Over time she'd become friendly with a handful of the kitchen staff, although many still viewed her with suspicion. Tianne was also still adept at getting people to talk. Several members of staff had told her about the meals being sent down to prisoners in the cells.

After that it didn't take her long to notice a pattern. Soon after one of the cadre apprehended someone with a minor Talent, they spent some time in a cell under the palace. Tianne had believed they were being offered a choice. To use their magic in service of the Regent or they had to leave the country. She'd even risked asking the Regent about those who were arrested and he'd given her the same story.

At first she didn't want to believe it, but after a while she couldn't ignore the truth. Faith in the Regent, for all that he'd done for her, made her think the best of him. Now she knew different. None of the people arrested were ever released.

It wasn't just the servants in the kitchen she spent time with. The wagon drivers loved to chat and were happy when she offered to help them unload. Without her uniform they didn't know who she was and assumed she was just another servant. It was when they refused to let her load the wagons that she knew. A quick look when one of the drivers was distracted confirmed it. Frohake's corpse had been covered with bruises and other injuries. It also looked as if someone had sliced open his chest then sewn it up again.

Since then she'd mostly kept to herself and stayed in her rooms except when she had to leave as part of her duties. Seeing his body made her wonder about many things. She thought about how easily Kalina and the others spoke about using their magic to hurt people. She thought about all of the mages with minor Talents rotting in cells beneath the palace and if they had even been given a choice. She wondered about the future of the cadre and her place in it. But mostly she wondered what would happen to her now that she knew coming back to Zecorria had been a huge mistake.

CHAPTER 35

Wren kept staring straight ahead as she walked towards the raiders' camp. The last time she'd been here, five days ago, it had been to send a clear message to Boros. This time she was here to bring the fight to all of the raiders.

As Wren had anticipated attacks on settlements and the merchant trains had stopped. Boros couldn't risk sending people out in small groups to collect a tithe. She knew Wren had at least six mages, but not precise numbers. A small group of raiders working by themselves would pose no threat to one mage, never mind two or more. A bold move would have been to empty the entire camp of all raiders and risk everything in one huge fight. But Boros had no way of knowing what traps Wren had set up before showing herself so brazenly. It would also be an incredibly stupid decision. After their last encounter at Gillen's Jaw, Wren knew better than to underestimate her enemy.

And so Boros had been watching and waiting for her next move. If this was a game of Stones, Wren would have been doing the same. Playing it safe until the other player's strategy revealed itself. Now, after five days of careful planning, Wren was ready to make her next move.

The last time she had been here the camp had been a jumbled

mess of structures with no fortification. Boros had not been idle since her last visit. A waist-high drystone wall now surrounded the front of the settlement in a wide semicircle. In addition, there were also two elevated watchtowers at the corners of the camp where raiders armed with bows watched her approach. Their weapons were strung but none of them had nocked an arrow. Not yet at least. A dozen more armed men and women knelt behind the wall, showing only the top half of their heads. Standing brazenly in the middle of the wall was Boros, watching as Wren walked closer. After five days of stewing Boros was struggling to hide her annoyance.

"What do you want?" asked Boros.

"I've come for your surrender," said Wren. A few of the raiders glanced around for other mages but she seemed to be alone.

"You want all of us to surrender to you?" said Boros with a laugh. Some of the other raiders chuckled along with her. One or two smiled at the notion, but Wren could see they were nervous. No one would be stupid enough to walk into their camp by themselves and start making demands. Hands were gripping weapons tightly, bows were being strung and they were all waiting for something more.

Somewhere nearby Wren felt a slow build-up of energy and couldn't help smiling at Boros.

"Lay down your weapons and surrender," said Wren. "In return I'm sure the Queen will give a fair trial to those who come peacefully. If you don't then—"

"Then what?" said Boros. "What will you do? Do you think I'm impressed by this?" she said, gesturing at Wren, before scanning the trees. "I know you didn't come here alone. Even you're not that stupid, girl. So, where are your friends?"

"Oh, they're not far away," said Wren, rubbing her forearms as her skin began to tingle.

"Neither are mine," said Boros, putting a hand to her mouth and whistling.

A dozen raiders appeared from the trees on either side of Wren. All of them were armed and focused on her. More raiders poured out of the camp until sixty or seventy of them were standing behind the wall. All of them were grim, weathered and seasoned warriors. These men and women, from across the world, had chosen this path and this life. They brutalised, stole and murdered other people and they liked it. Wren reminded herself of that as the pressure on her skin became worse. She could see there were a few raiders moving around inside the camp, but that could not be helped.

Boros was asking questions and making demands but Wren wasn't listening. It was just a dull buzzing sound, like the irritating drone of a fly. Instead she reached out towards what sounded like the rushing tide, drawing power from the Source into her body.

The energy coursed through her flesh, amplifying her senses until she could smell the fear sweat coming off the dozen raiders that surrounded her. They'd drawn the short straw. Boros must have told them she was a mage and they would have heard from the others about what she could do. Ironically, they would be the lucky ones.

The build-up of energy continued until it felt as if the air around her was writhing with insects, clawing at her skin. The air reeked with a sweet tang that made her nostrils twitch. Nevertheless, Wren took a deep breath and braced herself.

When Boros realised Wren wasn't listening she fell silent but kept searching for the source of the danger. Her instincts must have been screaming that something was about to happen, but she had no idea what it was.

"Now," said a voice. It was whispered in Wren's ear as if they were standing right beside her, but she was alone on the road. With that she knelt down and started weaving a dense shield about herself, adding layer upon layer as fast as she could make them. Thinking it was the beginning of an attack the raiders on either side rushed towards her with their weapons drawn. Arrows were nocked and Boros started shouting orders at her people on the wall, scanning the trees for the enemy.

The first fireball streaked out of the sky with a roar, trailing a line of black smoke like a burning comet. It was as big as two or three horses and even Wren marvelled at its size. With a huge crash that shook the ground it landed in the middle of the raiders' camp, knocking people down and setting buildings alight. The shockwave from the impact travelled outwards in all directions like ripples on a pond. Screaming raiders fell out of the lookout posts to the ground below. Those closest to Wren were knocked off their feet before they had a chance to attack. It wouldn't have made a difference. Her shield was too dense and the shockwave of the fireball rolled over and beyond, stirring the trees around her.

As Boros scrambled to her feet Wren saw her mouth widen in surprise. A dozen more fireballs, not as large as the first, were falling towards her camp. She started shouting orders but it was too little, too late. Tents and lean-tos were already on fire with men and women trying to smother the flames. The whole settlement was so focused on putting out the fire at the centre that they didn't hear the other fireballs racing towards them.

One landed in the middle of a group of raiders, scattering them like twigs while the unnaturally sticky flames set their clothes and hair alight. A few raiders started rolling around, while others tried to smother the flames, but some ran in a blind panic, spreading the blaze wherever they went. More fireballs hammered into the camp, burning flesh and scorching shelters until more than half the camp was on fire. And still more fireballs were falling.

A loud crack echoed through the air as the front door of the log cabin blew outwards. Smoke was filling the camp, making it difficult to see more than a few steps in every direction. Some raiders were trying to draw up water from the well but were having some difficulty as the rope had been severed.

In among the coughing and shouting, people began to scream as the horses charged out of the stables. The herd ran through the camp knocking down tents, stampeding over bodies and spreading the chaos until they burst out of the front. Those raiders who had been lingering beside the wall were too slow to move and many were ridden down. Horses jumped the wall until one stumbled in the smoke and knocked down a section of the wall. The rest took advantage and poured through the gap.

Raiders began running from the camp as well in the wake of the animals as a final volley of fireballs fell from the sky.

Wren stayed exactly where she was, totally focused on her shield, as the horses came thundering straight down the road towards her. All but one of them went around, avoiding her despite their panic. The hooves of the final horse clipped her shield, but the blow wasn't severe and she was able to maintain control. When the last of them was gone she stood up and reinforced her shield again.

A massive grey and black cloud had formed above the settlement, wreathing the surrounding trees in shadow. Their swaying limbs became the spectral arms of huge beasts dancing around the bonfire of the raiders' camp. The fire could not be stopped and it continued to spread. Soon everything would be consumed by the flames.

Seeing that it was a lost cause, bodies began to stream out

of the settlement. Some crawled, others dragged or carried friends away from the fire and smoke. Everyone was coughing, desperate to breathe clean air. Their weapons and conflict with Wren were forgotten, but as they moved away from the blaze a few noticed her standing in the middle of the road. With a feral scream a burly woman raced towards her drawing a mace from her belt. With a sweeping gesture Wren flung her off the road. She heard the woman collide with a tree and tried not to wince at the dull crack upon impact. It could have been a tree branch or the woman's spine.

A few arrows rained down out of the smoke, peppering the ground all around Wren. A few impacted on her shield but they snapped, blunting the heads and turning the shafts into kindling. Boros came next with her bow and six more archers behind her on either side. All the raiders were stained with ash, bloody from injuries and on the verge of collapse. But, even now, they were more afraid of Boros than her, and quickly followed their leader's commands. Another volley of arrows flew towards Wren and she ignored them as she had the first.

"Surrender now," said Wren, amplifying her voice to be heard over the crackling flames and the collapse of timbers.

The raiders were watching her but one by one they all looked towards Boros for a decision. "Scatter," said Boros with a snarl. That was all it took. One word. She must have planned for such an eventuality as they separated into distinct groups and ran in several directions. Those on the ground unable to run were left behind despite their cries and reaching hands. Their former friends shook them off and ran, vanishing into the trees.

Boros was the last to go, stubborn to the bitter end. It must have been so galling for her. To be driven out of a country by a King was one thing. But to be burned out of her own home by a teenage girl was something else entirely. The hatred burning in her eyes was intense. For a moment Wren thought Boros would charge and try to kill her. Part of Wren wanted her to try, if only to beat her today and end the conflict between them, but that wasn't the plan. Instead Boros spat on the ground and strode away into the smoke.

A short time later half a dozen people walked up the road behind Wren and she breathed a huge sigh of relief. It hadn't been her idea to stand alone against the raiders, but she understood the symbolic reason for it. Despite that, it hadn't made it any less terrifying. Boros still had no idea how many people were in her community and how many of them were mages. The less information Wren gave her the better.

"You did very well," said Master Yettle.

"Very convincing," said Leonie, patting her on the shoulder. It was the smith who had summoned the huge fireball from the sky. Her knack with fire bordered on a Talent, but she claimed anyone could learn it and that her knowledge only came from working in a forge.

"We can't let the fire spread beyond the camp," said Wren, worrying about the forest going up in flames.

"We'll take care of it," said Leonie, walking towards the camp with Yettle and three other adults beside her. The flames began to shrink even before the smith set foot in the camp and Wren knew all fires would soon be extinguished. Master Yettle moved from body to body on the ground, tending to the wounded. There were perhaps a dozen lying in the road and she suspected there would be others inside the camp.

"It all went to plan," said Danoph, coming up beside her.

"The horses?" asked Wren.

"We managed to grab most of them down the road. I'm sure we can find the others before night."

"I still wonder if we should have tried to end it today," said Wren. "Maybe we could have grabbed all of them."

"Perhaps, if we'd brought everyone here, but you saw how quickly they scattered. She'd planned for this."

Ever since Danoph had told her about Boros being chased out of Seveldrom by the King, Wren had been turning it over in her mind. Wren didn't think she was the kind of person to make the same mistake twice. Somewhere in the back of Boros's mind she must have been wondering about Queen Olivia of Shael. She would only tolerate the presence of the raids for so long, even with her limited resources. Eventually she would muster some soldiers to wipe out the raiders and Boros would be forced to run again. But this time she hadn't intended to leave empty-handed. There was a second camp and a stash.

Wren didn't believe the money stolen from merchants and the local communities was in the burning ruins. Not one raider had tried to run back into the fire to retrieve the gold.

It was possible Boros would decide it wasn't worth the effort of staying in western Shael and just move on to another area or country. Part of Wren hoped that would happen, even though the raiders would then become someone else's problem. She still wasn't sure that when the time came she'd be able to kill.

Her instincts told her that Boros wouldn't leave. The raider hated her with a passion and she was not about to run. The west of Shael was as perfect a hunting ground for them as they were ever likely to find. She would regroup and then come after Wren and the others.

"Well, it's all set out. You're ready for what comes next," said Danoph.

"Maybe." He had more faith in her than she did in herself.

"It's time for me to leave," he said.

She'd been dreading this moment and couldn't stop herself asking the inevitable question. "Do you have to go?"

"You don't need me. You know what you have to do and you have people around you who can actually help. I just get in the way," said Danoph with a wry smile. Everyone appreciated his efforts in the community on a day-to-day basis, but his magic was so unique and limited it didn't help with their most pressing issue.

"I need you," said Wren. She'd already lost Tianne and didn't want him to go.

"This isn't goodbye. You'll see me again." He sounded so certain it was more than a little unnerving. She hugged Danoph tightly, not wanting to let go but eventually released him, wiping at her face.

"Are you going home?"

Danoph turned towards the east and took a deep breath. "Yes. I need to know why my mother sent me to the Red Tower."

"I hope you find some answers."

"Me too. I need to know more about my Talent," said Danoph.

"It's not just a Talent. Your magic is something else. Something I've never heard of before," said Wren, thinking back to when he'd summoned his power and given her insight into Boros's history. She'd told Master Yettle about it as well but he'd been equally baffled.

"Then it's time I found out what I'm truly capable of," said Danoph, sounding more decisive than ever before in his life.

CHAPTER 36

Tammy glanced at the sign above the tavern door to make sure this was the right place. The Thirsty Ferret wasn't the nicest place in the city, far from it in fact, and as soon as she pushed open the front door a cloud of smells assaulted her nostrils.

Dried vomit, stale beer and suspicious meat that could even be ferret. The faces of the customers were surly and suspicious, as if they expected her to steal the clothing off their backs or the beer from their mugs. The sour owner was no better. With a face riddled with warts and a mouth stained blue from venthe she didn't make Tammy feel welcome. She merely grunted and jerked her head towards a door at the rear. It felt unusual to be out of uniform, but it had been a request she couldn't refuse.

With one hand resting on the plain short sword at her waist Tammy pushed open the door and followed the narrow corridor. She went past the grimy kitchen and approached the last room on the left. Before she had a chance to knock it opened to reveal the Captain of the Queen's Royal Guards, out of uniform, of course, but she still recognised him. He inclined his head and stepped aside before taking up his post outside the door.

The room was small to begin with but was overly cramped

with just her and the Queen. In addition, there was a stack of beer barrels, boxes of old vegetables and sacks of rice. The Queen sat behind a rickety old table with her back pressed against the wall. Like the rest of the tavern the room was covered with dust and grime. Apart from the Queen the only thing that seemed out of place was the delicate green tea set on the table in front of her. Even in a plain grey dress there wasn't a person in the city who wouldn't recognise her.

"Majesty," said Tammy.

The Queen gestured at the battered chair opposite. "Keep your voice down. The walls are thin."

As she sat down the chair creaked alarmingly. Tammy felt it tilt to one side and thought it might buckle under her weight. "Captain Gardner didn't look too happy at this arrangement."

Morganse rolled her eyes and drained the last of her tea. "He thinks I'm taking too great a risk. I can't walk five steps down any street in the city before I'm stopped by a dozen people. If I talk to a stranger they only tell me what they think I want to hear. They're too afraid to speak the truth. This way I can find out what the people really think."

It made sense but given the current threat of rogue mages coming to the city Tammy agreed with the Captain. She'd spotted three Royal Guards dressed in plain clothes watching the street and guessed there were several inside the tavern, but, even so, it seemed risky.

"So, tell me about Balfruss," said Morganse, keeping her voice low.

"He was here, briefly, but he left again this morning. There was a sighting of another of Garvey's pupils in Zecorria."

"How many has he captured now?"

"Five. One died, and four are being held in prison awaiting trial."

Morganse poured herself another glass of tea. "Are you sure they're secure?"

"Yes. For the time being, although it's only a temporary solution." She'd not shared the arrangements of where or how the mages were held and so far Morganse had not asked. But she would, because they both knew this arrangement could not continue indefinitely. Balfruss was an effective manhunter, but he was not an executioner. The weight of what to do with them rested with the Queen. If they had been ordinary criminals they would be put on trial for the murders they'd committed and sentenced to many years in a labour camp or hanged from the neck until they were dead. But all of them were mages and, more importantly, children. Dangerous, cruel and violent individuals, but also children who had been misled and perhaps manipulated by a powerful and charismatic mage.

These pupils could not be put on trial in the normal fashion and even if convicted they couldn't be punished in the traditional manner. A swift death was perhaps all that awaited them. There seemed no other alternative beyond holding them in the special cell for the rest of their lives. It was cramped with four of them and there were others still out there.

"I haven't made a decision. Yet." It was clear that the decision was weighing heavily on her shoulders and Tammy didn't envy her.

"I have a suggestion." It was something that had been rattling around in her head for a while now. "But it's unprecedented here in Yerskania."

"Please," said Morganse, gesturing for her to speak. "At this point we're entering new territory."

"I think you should recruit Balfruss to work for you in a formal capacity."

The Queen chuckled but quickly stopped when she saw

Tammy was serious. "Do you want me to offer him a role as the royal mage to the court?" she asked sarcastically.

"No, I had something else in mind."

"I can see you've been thinking about this for a while. All right, I'm curious. Tell me."

"Magic isn't going to go away. People blamed the Seekers and the Red Tower, and now they're gone, perhaps for good. I'm angry and horrified at how it was done, but I can't change the past. So, looking ahead, I think we need something new. Something different."

"Are you suggesting a magic school here, in Yerskania?" asked the Queen.

"No. That was one of the problems with the Red Tower. It was wrapped in secrecy. No one knew what happened inside and it created more of a division between mages and everyone else. We need to include them, not push them to the fringes."

"Then what are you suggesting?"

Tammy chose her next words carefully. She didn't want to reveal Fray's secret. "Treat them like everyone else. Make them sign up to the Watch and, if they excel, they can become a Guardian. I know what you're going to say, but it's not unprecedented."

Morganse sat forward in her chair. "What did you just say?"

"I've been reading some of the Old Man's journals, and based on a hunch I went further back and read those of his predecessor." Some of that was true but the Queen didn't need to know the whole story just yet. "There are several veiled mentions of special Guardians using unique abilities on unusual cases. Baffling mysteries or bizarre deaths that were swiftly resolved. I also have some physical proof that I can show you, if necessary."

"That's quite a claim." The Queen sipped her tea thoughtfully.

"I need to speak to the Old Man to confirm my hunch."

"It's an interesting idea, but there's still the problem of the children. How would you teach them?"

"Not to be indelicate, but Balfruss isn't a young man any more. He was already a teacher at the Red Tower. I'm confident he could persuade others to come here if it was safe."

"It sounds idyllic, but public opinion towards magic is the worst I've ever seen. Bringing the rogues to justice will help a little," conceded the Queen, "but it could be years before the hatred begins to ebb."

"I admit it's not a perfect solution, but I thought I would suggest it."

"You're right, we need to plan for the future. I will consider it carefully. For the time being I've informed all my agents to send any sightings of rogue mages directly to your office."

"Thank you, Majesty."

"I hope Balfruss can catch them all."

Tammy was confident he could stop them all, but the problem of what to do next loomed large in both their minds.

Tammy followed the Old Man through his house into the small garden at the rear. Much to her surprise she found a tidy patch of recently turned soil and small green shoots growing in uniform rows. A plum tree at the back provided some shade in the yard and a glass-fronted shed was overflowing with tools and clay pots. The Old Man pulled on a thick pair of gardening gloves and started yanking weeds out of the less tidy half of the garden.

When he saw Tammy's expression he grunted. "I can't sit around all day doing nothing during my retirement."

"No, Sir. Of course not." She couldn't think of anything more tedious than gardening. Then again, at least he had some hobbies.

"You wanted to ask me something?" he said, reading her expression.

"I had an interesting conversation with the Queen today," said Tammy, slowly lowering herself into one of his wooden garden chairs. Much to her surprise it didn't creak and showed no signs of stress. At this point showing care for furniture was a lifetime habit for someone of her size.

"Don't keep me in suspense." The Old Man pulled up another weed and slung it onto the pile. When she didn't reply he paused and glanced over his shoulder. "This is something about being Khevassar, isn't it?"

"I need an honest answer."

He pulled off his gloves and sat down beside her with a sigh as his joints creaked. "Ask your question."

"Before Fray, and before his father, were there other mages who worked as Guardians of the Peace?"

His sly smile was answer enough. "Of course, although it's never officially stated in the records. Like you, I was a few weeks into the role when I found a few peculiarities in the journals of my predecessor."

"What kind of things?"

"Oh, certain cases where a specialist Guardian was called in. They always had a codename, like the Shadow Fox, or the Red Kite, to protect their identity but it was obvious to me who they were. When I asked him about mages he told me the truth and showed me the special octagonal cell."

"I showed it to Balfruss. It was necessary," said Tammy, holding up a hand before he could protest. "He's hunting down the rogue mages and we needed somewhere to hold them. He'd never seen anything like it before."

"Do you want to hear my best guess?"

"Please," said Tammy, gesturing for him to speak.

"I think it was built by the Red Tower. Maybe it was done as a favour, or perhaps because the Guardians of old worked more closely with them in the past. So much has been lost to history, I guess we'll never know the truth," said the Old Man.

Tammy knew he was talking about magic but it also made her wonder about who he used to be. His identity and past had been erased on purpose. But at least there was a record of his deeds that covered a large portion of his life. It would stand as a testament and proof that he had lived.

"What will you do with the rogue mages?" he asked.

"I don't know. The normal way of doing things is impossible. The Queen has some difficult decisions ahead."

The Old Man grunted in agreement. A comfortable silence settled on them and for a time they listened to the muted sounds of the city. In the secluded garden they shared a brief moment of peace before the storm that was to come. He had done more than enough in service of the city and the country. The burden was now hers to bear.

"I should get back," said Tammy, wishing she could stay longer.

"It never stops," he said with a wry smile.

"Are there other secrets you're not telling me?" she asked. "About the Guardians and the city?"

He chuckled and slapped his knee. "Of course, but you don't need me to tell you. You've proven that you're more than capable on your own. You're ready to be the Khevassar without me looking over your shoulder." It wasn't the answer she'd been expecting, but at least it was an honest answer. "Even so, I'd still like it if you came by for a visit from time to time. I don't tend to get many visitors."

Being the Khevassar meant you had to pay a steep price but only now, as she stared at him in his little garden, did she realise how lonely the future promised to be. The whole city knew his name and his deeds but there wouldn't be many still alive he could call a friend. It was all there, waiting for her, in the future.

"I may still need your help with some difficult cases," she said, although from his smile they both knew that wasn't true. "It's always good to get a second opinion."

"Yes, it is," he said, fondly patting her hand. "I'd be happy to offer my expert advice whenever you need it."

They shared another smile and she quickly left the house before she started crying for him, but also for herself and what lay ahead, many years from now.

CHAPTER 37

Tianne kept her smile fixed in place by gritting her teeth as she listened to her mother extol her virtues.

It was an awkward and staged meeting that the Regent had arranged for her as a special surprise. As the senior member of the Regent's cadre of mages she'd been asked to meet him to discuss their progress. Tianne had been under no illusions about it being a request as two surly Royal Guards had shown up at her door. She was fairly confident that if she'd refused they would have dragged her there by her hair.

Upon entering the room she'd found the Regent waiting, but also her parents. Their rictus grins were almost identical to hers and her father couldn't stop sweating. The collar of his new and probably borrowed shirt was turning dark yellow as perspiration continued to trickle down the sides of his neck. Her mother, always fussy about her clothes, had been shoved into a green monstrosity that showed off her ankles. No doubt once this farce was done she would go home and flagellate herself for such gross indecency.

The only person in the room who seemed relaxed was the Regent. He lounged in a corner sipping wine from a crystal glass. But then again, he'd staged this whole drama for her benefit, he probably thought it was a good thing he was doing for her. Trying her best to convince him that it was a wonderful surprise, Tianne relaxed her shoulders and unclenched her jaw, but her face still ached from keeping her fake smile in place.

Her mother's words sounded terribly rehearsed but no one else seemed to have noticed. As well as apparently being proud of her for becoming a mage, her mother had missed her since she'd left home. It was amazing that the Regent had been able to persuade her to say the words out loud. Tianne knew how much it must be physically hurting her to lie so much.

Her father had not said a single word since she'd entered the room. He was clearly afraid for his life if he refused to play along with this charade, but Tianne didn't know if he was petrified of the Regent or what she might do to him.

Every time she left the palace people stared. They were beginning to understand what the uniform with a blue star meant but despite her efforts Tianne was always met with suspicion and hostility. Even those people who had been tricked by charlatans were angry at her when the truth was exposed. Somehow it became her fault that they had been played for fools. The charlatan had given them false hope but perhaps that was better than none at all.

Tianne knew that in the right hands magic was a gift but part of her was beginning to wonder if the people would ever view magic as a good thing. If she helped them, healed them and kept them safe, would it make a difference? How long would it be before they trusted her? How long before she could leave the palace by herself?

To make matters worse the rest of the cadre had gone to the other extreme. They proudly wore their facial tattoos and expected to be treated with respect because of who they served and what they could do. They wanted the people of Herakion to show them respect without first earning it. Tianne knew a storm was brewing. Much like her time at the Red Tower when Garvey entered a room, she was constantly walking on eggshells around the other mages.

Her mother's litany of false praise came to a sudden conclusion and the awkward atmosphere in the room became unbearable in the silence that followed. Everyone was clearly waiting for something and Tianne realised from the way her father's eyelid was twitching that she was supposed to respond.

"I'm very touched by this," said Tianne, focusing on the Regent as she couldn't bear to look at her parents. "I'm so surprised I think I'm still a little in shock."

Her laughter wasn't faked and it eased some of the tension in her chest. The Regent's grip on his glass eased and a real smile returned to his handsome face. Tianne couldn't believe she'd been so naïve. Buried beneath the charm and kind words she could see he was a vicious rat, biding his time. He'd kill and eat his own mother if it kept him on the throne a little longer. She was merely a means to an end for him.

"You do seem stunned," conceded the Regent and Tianne laughed again. She moved across the room and took her mother by the hand. For a second she felt her mother start to pull away but then Tianne tightened her grip until it must have been painful. Not a single muscle twitched on her mother's face to show her discomfort.

"Thank you for coming to see me. It's so good to see you both." She included her sweaty father in her too-wide smile. He flinched but to his credit managed not to run screaming from the room. "I hope you'll visit again soon, but the Regent is very busy and I have my duties as well."

Her mother took the hint and squeezed her hands before

letting go and turning to face the Regent. "My deepest apologies, Regent. We didn't mean to keep you from important business."

"Nonsense. I'm delighted to oversee such a happy family reunion." Tianne could see him watching her closely for signs of discomfort. Tianne almost jumped out of her skin when her father rested a hand on her shoulder but she forced herself to relax.

"Well, I'll leave you three to catch up. You must have so much to talk about," said the Regent, moving towards the door.

The three of them stayed in exactly the same positions until the sound of his footsteps had receded down the corridor. When they were sure he was gone Tianne shook off her father's hand and moved across the room to put some distance between them. The fake smiles slipped and the fear that had been just under the surface became more apparent.

"They threatened us," gasped her father, speaking for the first time. Tianne thought he looked much older than the last time she'd seen him a few years ago. There was now a peppering of white in his hair and he was thinner than she remembered. It made him look frail. Growing up she'd not thought of her parents like other people. In her mind they never aged and would live for ever. Now she understood they were just as human and just as flawed as everyone else. "If we didn't come to the palace they suggested our house might burn down in a freak accident. We could have ended up as beggars living on the streets!"

"It's true. They've done that to others," lied Tianne. She had no desire to comfort him or quash his fears. Her father stared at Tianne with horror while her mother just sneered.

Once again all of this was somehow her fault.

Many times in the past Wren had told her that no matter what she did it was never good enough for her mother. It was an impossible standard to meet. Tianne would have preferred that instead of being ignored. At times it felt as if she'd been an accident, although they'd never said that to her face. She believed her parents resented her for being born. For intruding on their life and as such they had refused to change their ways to accommodate her. It was why from an early age she'd sought out others for companionship and guidance since there was none to be found at home. She'd placed too much trust in the wrong people and they had led her astray, filling her head with lies.

Tianne hadn't been sure how she'd feel about seeing her parents again. She hadn't expected a tearful reunion with apologies, but their continued blame was another reminder of why she'd been glad to leave. Just being in the same room with them again made her angry.

"Where are you going?" asked her mother as she opened the door.

"Stay here for an hour and then leave."

"But what if—"

"Stay here," said Tianne. Blue flames erupted on the palms of her hands as she vented some of her anger. Her father whimpered and hid behind a chair while her mother just stared at her with distaste. Unable to even look at their faces any more she left the room in a hurry.

Whatever the Regent had intended the reunion to achieve it had failed. More than ever before she resented her parents and now hated them on sight. Any illusions in her mind about the Regent being a benevolent saviour were also being eroded. As she mulled over the future Tianne didn't notice where her feet were taking her until she began to descend several flights of stairs. Pausing on the first level of cells she wondered if this was a good idea. The worst that could happen was that they put her back in a cell. Only this time if they tried she was determined not to be such an easy target.

It took a bit of dodging patrols, fast talking and at one point a threat to use her magic before she was finally admitted to the deepest cells beneath the palace. Tianne knew she'd have to deal with more of the same on the way back up, but right now it didn't matter.

Emotions were churning through her, making her reckless and angry. Normally she would never have lashed out with her magic but the guard had been in her way and she'd just snapped.

Part of her also needed someone to blame for all of this. For all of her problems but also the growing hatred towards mages. She needed to see him for herself. Part of her still didn't believe it was true.

The smell has been growing worse for a while and as she set foot in the lowest cell block Tianne couldn't help gagging. It was a horrific mix of rot, stale, sweaty bodies and rank piss that made her nose twitch. There were no lanterns outside the cells and only one pathetic torch beside the bottom step. It gave off enough light for her to see the winding staircase and little else. The cells were in absolute darkness but she could hear someone breathing in the heavy silence.

Tianne shivered and her breath frosted on the air. Her anger began to ebb away as she found herself alone, deep beneath the earth, surrounded by a dense blackness.

Even without looking in the cells she knew he was there. She could feel him. The loud echo of his magic pressed against her senses. It was just as strong as she remembered, making her question again why he'd let himself be taken prisoner.

"You've come all this way," said a harsh whisper in the darkness. "May as well take a look."

Taking a deep breath to steady her nerves Tianne summoned a small globe of light. The shadows reluctantly peeled back but not enough to see right to the back of the cells. She could only hear one person breathing so she purposefully avoided looking into the other cells. Out of the corner of her eyes she saw ugly, twisted shapes and heard the buzzing of flies. The further she went the worse the smell became until it was so ripe it made her eyes water.

In the last cell on the left she stopped and peered into the shadows. Apart from a moth-eaten blanket and a bucket the cell was empty of furniture. A thick coil of chain, with links as wide as her wrist, ran from the wall to one of his skinny ankles. His skin was pale and bruised, much like the rest of him, where it wasn't covered in filth or dried blood. He was sitting against the back wall and most of his face was hidden in shadow, for which she was grateful. Tianne had no desire to see his face again.

Part of her wanted to just turn around and run back up the stairs. She didn't have to prove anything to him. He wasn't her teacher and she wasn't a student any more.

"Come to gloat?" asked Garvey, his breath rattling in his chest. He'd lost a lot of weight since she'd last seen him. They were probably starving him until he agreed to make a public confession.

"I wanted to see if the stories were true. I was told they've been torturing you to try and get a confession."

Garvey's harsh laugh was just as she remembered. "They were very creative for a while but seem to have run out of ideas. I don't think they know what to do with me now."

Tianne wanted to hate him. To laugh at him for finally being caught and humbled. To hurt him with harsh words or even her magic, but instead she felt hollow. A part of her was also still afraid of Garvey despite him being such a pathetic creature now. Tianne couldn't help laughing at herself for that. The heavy drumbeat of his connection to the Source was almost as unbearable at this distance as the stench.

"Have we met before?" he asked.

"I'm Tianne."

"Ah," he said and smiled. "I hear you're first among the Regent's mages. You must be very special."

Tianne laughed. "I'm a prisoner, just like you, only my cell has a soft bed and a window."

"A window wouldn't be much use to me," said Garvey, leaning forward. Tianne gagged at the sight of his face and put a hand over her mouth to stop herself from screaming. Both of his eyes were gone. It looked as if they'd been burned out. The empty sockets were surrounded by pink and red scar tissue.

She turned her face away but it didn't matter. The image remained etched into her mind. "Why did you come here?" asked Garvey.

"I told you," she said.

"No, not my cell. To Zecorria. Why come back? Weren't you happy in your new life with Wren?"

"The Regent declared an amnesty. He wanted loyal magic users to protect him and the people from rogue mages. I came because of you!"

"That's a lie," said Garvey, settling back against the wall. Mercifully the top half of his face was in shadow again. "Don't blame me for your decision."

"You murdered people. You betrayed the Red Tower. Everything you told us was a lie." Tianne's voice echoed around the cells, over and over until it disappeared into the dark. "How could you do it?"

"The school was doomed. Something new needed to rise from the ashes." After everything that had happened to him and the school, he seemed without remorse. "But you didn't answer my question. Why did you come back?"

Another angry reply was on the tip of her tongue when Tianne stopped herself. What she'd told him was a lie. A small part of the reason for coming back had been about helping people, but the other reasons were selfish. She could have stayed in Shael and helped others there, but somehow she'd convinced herself coming home was more important. That if she was seen doing good work in Zecorria the people would see her as a patriot. She would be a hero. Then her old friends, and perhaps even her parents, would be full of regret and guilt about how they'd treated her.

"I wanted to prove them wrong. To show them I was special."

"You are special," said Garvey. "From the moment you felt the majesty of the Source. It set you apart from others."

"Magic doesn't make me better than anyone else." Tianne didn't know why she was telling him. Perhaps it was because she had to lie to everyone else about her true feelings.

"No, it doesn't. Magic is a tool, and like any other, it can be a dangerous weapon in the wrong hands." Tianne watched as a cherry-red mote of fire danced across his knuckles like a coin, moving from one hand to the other and then back again.

"I'm just as selfish and arrogant as you," she said. "I thought the Regent was creating a cadre that would help people, but so far all we've done is brutalise those with minor abilities. We're just a bunch of thugs."

The other young mages were nothing more than blunt instruments. They had no formal training, beyond what Tianne could show them, and once they'd learned control they stopped coming to her for help. To them magic was nothing more than the physical manifestation of will. She'd tried to explain that they could do so much more with magic. That with training a mage could heal people and that Talents gave them unique and wonderful abilities. They didn't care. With their magic under control they couldn't be brutalised, and with the Regent standing behind them they had been transformed from victims into bullies.

"You've had better training than them. So why don't you leave?"

"And go where?" said Tianne. He made it sound so simple.

"I heard about Wren's community. It sounded like she was helping people."

Tianne shook her head. "I can't abandon the others. They're not evil, they're just drunk on power."

"Are you their keeper? Their mother?" he asked. She wasn't either but Tianne still felt responsible for them.

"You made a mistake. Stop punishing yourself," said Garvey. "You don't need to pay penance for the rest of your life by staying here. You can just walk away."

"Why?" said Tianne. In all the time she'd been at the Red Tower he'd never spoken to her this way before. He'd endured much in the last few weeks but it seemed like a dramatic and sudden change. It was as if she were talking to a completely different person. "Why are you here?"

"I was captured."

"Now who's lying?" said Tianne, surprising herself. She would never have dared speak to him like this in the past. "I can feel your connection to the Source. It's just as strong. Why would you let yourself be subdued and locked in a cell? Why would you let someone blind you? Is this all part of some bigger plan?"

Garvey's smile showed too many teeth and even now he still had the power to unnerve her. "Those are the right questions." He turned his face away and coughed up something that he spat on the floor of his stinking cell. "Forgive yourself and leave Zecorria. Go back to Wren and help her create something new. She will welcome you back with open arms. You made a mistake, but you can choose something new. It's not too late."

"Is this your penance?" she asked, gesturing at the cell. "Are you punishing yourself for what you did?"

"Yes, but I never imagined what it would reveal."

"I don't understand."

"Neither did I," admitted Garvey. "Not until now."

In spite of everything she saw him grin. Tianne felt as confused as ever about him. She wanted to hate Garvey for what he'd done, murdering innocent people and his treatment towards all of the students at the school. But part of her was beginning to realise she'd never really known him at all.

Feeling overwhelmed, she hurried away from the cells and made the slow ascent back to her room. Just as she was rounding a corner Tianne ran into someone coming the other way.

"Are you all right?" asked Kalina.

Tianne didn't know how to explain what she was feeling. The guilt. The self-loathing and anger churning inside about her parents and the Regent. She tried to put some of it into words, but failed and found herself crying.

Kalina pulled her close. "What happened?"

"I went to see Garvey," she managed to say between sobs. Kalina swore under her breath, blaming him for her current state of mind. Tianne said nothing as it was far easier than telling her the truth. She couldn't trust what Garvey had said to her. He was an expert at lying and deception, but one fact remained. It had been a grave mistake coming back to Zecorria. She had to escape as soon as possible.

CHAPTER 38

As Wren had expected, Boros's hatred for her meant she couldn't move on without getting revenge. Her pride wouldn't allow it. But after their previous encounters, Wren didn't presume that rage had made her enemy reckless or stupid.

After the destruction of her camp, Boros and the surviving raiders had fled, but Wren was confident they wouldn't have gone far. Once she and her friends had gathered up the horses they set off for home, taking the most direct route. Laila had noticed the wide trail they were leaving and had commented about it being easy to follow.

"That's the idea," said Wren.

At least fifty raiders were now standing in line waiting for the order to attack. Boros was at the centre of the line with a bow in one hand and a grim expression on her face. Wren wasn't sure how Boros expected this to be any different from their last battle, but she was ready for the unexpected.

Beside Wren were half a dozen young mages and Leonie the blacksmith.

As she'd expected the raiders had followed their tracks all the way back to their community. And now they were trapped at the mouth of their valley with no way out, except to retreat or to go through the raiders. Or so it seemed.

One raider struck flint and tinder, setting fire to a rag before moving down the line, lighting arrows. Even from where she stood Wren could feel the waves of hatred rolling off Boros. She was going to throw everything into this fight. There would be no retreat and no mercy.

"Ready," shouted Boros, raising her own bow with its flaming arrow. Half of the raiders followed her lead while the others drew their weapons. "Loose then shoot at will!" she shouted. Drawing back her bow, Boros sent her arrow high and more followed, arcing up into the sky. Wren and the others tracked their movement and when they reached their peak she tapped Kimme on the shoulder. She raised both hands and tightened her fists, instantly extinguishing the flames. Making a twisting motion with one hand Kimme shattered all the arrows as they began their descent. Laila wove a shield above their heads while around them bits of wood and metal began to rain down like a freak storm.

While Kimme was doing that half of the raiders began to charge with spears and swords held ready. The archers stayed back and sent more volleys as fast as they could. Boros had dropped her bow and now ran forward with the others. No doubt she wanted the pleasure of being the one to kill Wren herself.

"Can you manage the arrows?" said Wren.

"We'll be fine," said Kimme, smiling at Laila who was still nervous about using her magic. "You take care of the others."

"Toree, watch for anyone trying to throw something," Wren warned him. It was possible one of the raiders running towards them might throw a dagger, a spear or even have a crossbow. As the raiders approached Wren noticed they were all carrying a water pouch. Normally it wouldn't have been something that stood out in her mind but it was a strange thing to have when going into battle. And for every single raider to have one was even stranger.

She expected Boros and the others to charge until they were able to use their weapons. To prevent that Wren nudged the other young mages beside her to do as they had practised. Working together they wove a wide shield six feet in front that extended across the mouth of the valley. To the naked eye there was nothing to see. No disturbance in the air to show its presence, but if the raiders kept running they would rebound off it as if they had run straight into a wall. As predicted the first raider smashed into it face first, spraying blood and teeth across the invisible barrier. The others slowed and then stopped, feeling along the shield to find the edge. When they realised the shield extended to both sides of the valley entrance she thought they would retreat.

"Time for a drink," said Boros with a feral grin. All of the raiders beside her uncorked their waterskins and splashed the contents all over the shield. The thick viscous fluid made it difficult to see what they were doing and soon there was a solid black wall. They could drop the shield, rendering the sticky liquid useless but it would also mean they were open to attack.

"What's she doing?" asked Kimme.

A horrible thought started to creep into the back of Wren's mind. "Get ready to run," she yelled at those beside her.

A few more arrows rained down from overhead but Laila's shield kept them at bay. When flaming arrows fell they too were instantly destroyed upon impact, extinguishing the flames. Then one of the arrows struck the sticky black wall.

With a roar and a surge of bright yellow fire the combined shield burst into flames. The three mages beside Wren screamed as they felt part of the heat through their connection to the Source. Normally fire would rebound from a shield, but this was in permanent contact with an extension of their senses. The smoke and heat were also a problem, making everyone cough and splutter.

"It burns," said one of the young mages, rubbing the skin on her arms, looking for blisters.

"Drop the shield and run. All of you, go now," she ordered everyone.

The combined shield vanished instantly and the others ran. Without the shield to hold it upright the flames died down a little but not completely. Some of the black substance had been consumed but the rest fell to the ground in a flaming line. Wren summoned a gentle wind and sent the smoke back towards the raiders, aiding their retreat.

Boros had won the first round.

Boros sneered as the girl and her friends ran from the fire.

So far she'd only seen six mages and it was beginning to make her wonder how many there really were. Ten or twelve at most was her best guess. Despite the wind at her back the smoke blew into Boros's face, but she told her people to hold their position.

Caution. Especially now when it seemed as if victory was so close. She'd celebrate as hard as everyone else when the girl's head was mounted on a pike. Then she'd wave up at her lifeless eyes and raise a mug of ale.

The smoke continued to drift towards her and the others but eventually the fire burned itself out. The unnatural wind stopped and she signalled for her raiders to form up. Holding shields in front and weapons at the ready, they slowly walked down the path into the valley. Two groups of six went ahead. The rest stayed back with Boros in case it was a trap.

Before showing herself Boros had studied the valley. There was only one way in and one way out. If this next assault went badly she would pull back and starve out the girl and her friends. Mages or not, they still needed to eat. It wasn't the most heroic of victories but she didn't care and neither did her people. Once the girl and her friends were dead they could go back to collecting a tithe from every town and village in the west of Shael. Word was already beginning to spread about what she'd achieved. The law was tougher in other countries and Shael was looking more appealing all the time for bandits. With enough bodies she could expand her territory and push further east. But all of that was for tomorrow.

The first twelve went into the valley and didn't return. There were no cries of alarm or sounds of battle. After waiting a while Boros realised they weren't coming out. They were simply gone. It was a trap. The girl probably had all her people waiting in the valley below.

In the distance behind her a horn began to blare, over and over again. The ground started to shake and turning around she saw at least fifty riders coming towards her. Boros didn't recognise any of them but there were many young faces. She didn't believe all of them could be mages and intended to test her theory. If the girl expected her to run at their numbers she was going to be very disappointed.

"Archers, form up," she shouted, shoving those who moved too slowly. "Ready." She nocked an arrow and looked to her left and right, checking the line. They were scared but were still following her orders.

As the riders drew closer she judged the distance and then waited, her bow held ready. Just before they were in range the riders slowed and then stopped. At the centre of the line was a big woman with short blonde hair who seemed to be their leader. Oddly she wasn't carrying a weapon and neither were those beside her. Leaving the horses behind, the line of strangers started to walk towards her. They were making this too easy.

"Loose," shouted Boros, drawing and then releasing in one smooth motion. She nocked a second arrow and loosed again before stopping to see the impact. The big woman raised her arms and all the arrows in flight crumbled to dust. All along the line the enemy raised their hands and made strange twisting motions with their fists. Boros cried out in surprise as her bow snapped in three places. Beside her the others were all suffering the same fate as every bow was destroyed.

The mages continued to march forward and now Boros could see the expressions on their faces. Most of them were scared. They were just children playing at war. They knew nothing about suffering but she was happy to teach them.

"Prepare to charge," said Boros, drawing her sword and a dagger. With a great clattering of metal she heard others readying themselves.

"Fire!" someone shouted. Boros searched for the blaze but couldn't see anything. Then a six-foot wall of fire rose from the ground in front of the big woman at the front. The flames were bright blue but seemed like a normal fire as she could see it scorching the earth. Those beside her were waving their hands about as well and more fire appeared, creating a wall that began to stretch the full length of the line.

The collective heat from the flames reached Boros and she winced. The smell of burned grass and hot soil flooded her nostrils. Grey smoke rose up from the wall of fire as it burned the earth. The man beside her began to cough and splutter. Boros knew others would start to falter as well if she couldn't end the fight quickly. She needed to test the strength of the flames.

"Barker, break through the wall," she said to one of her men. He was big and strong and dumb as a rock. With a feral grin he hefted his axe and charged at the mages. The other raiders cheered and bashed their weapons together, creating a huge din.

Barker bellowed as he reached the fire and jumped. He passed through the fire and disappeared. Boros and the others fell silent and waited. Less than two heartbeats later he reappeared wreathed in flames. Screaming like a wounded pig he raced back towards them trailing black smoke. His weapon was forgotten as he tried to put out the flames with his hands before he burned to death.

Boros noted Barker was coming straight towards her and swung at him with her sword. She caught him on the temple with the flat of her blade and he dropped to the ground like a stone. She and several others tried to smother the flames with their coats but then something worse started to happen. The blue fire spread. It was far too sticky for normal fire and seemed to jump from one piece of clothing to another as if it had a mind of its own. Boros dropped her coat and tried her waterskin instead but the fire just hissed and continued to rage as if she'd poured lantern oil instead.

"Leave him," she told the others who stepped back from Barker. He'd stopped screaming now but his body continued to burn like a candle.

"Forward," shouted the big woman and the mages all moved six paces towards them. And with them came the wall of fire. It crawled across the ground, bending in places and occasionally showing gaps that were quickly plugged.

Creating the wall seemed a challenge in itself. Moving it was something else entirely. Those gaps suggested there were weak links among them and that was something she could use.

"Take three men and go right," she said, tapping one of her

raiders. "Take three and go left," she said to someone else. "And make plenty of noise."

As her people split up Boros felt something slap her across the shoulders which sent her tumbling to her knees. Behind her, coming out of the valley, were the girl and the other five mages. All of them were using their magic as people all along her line started falling over for no apparent reason.

Those trying to get around the wall of fire were lifted off the ground by invisible hands and thrown backwards towards the rest of the group. In front the fire continued to creep forward. Behind Boros the girl and her friends were keeping her people off balance. Time was running out.

Boros reached under her shirt and passed a necklace to the man beside her. "Jarke, this necklace will protect you from the fire. I want you to charge through and kill the big woman in the middle. We'll be right behind you."

As she'd expected Jarke was dubious. It was a plain silver chain with a simple oval-shaped bronze locket. "Why? What's special about it?"

Boros leaned in closer and whispered. "It's magic. The locket itself is normal, but what's inside is special. Remember last year, when you asked me what I spent all my money on? This is it."

Some of his suspicion began to fade. "All of it? On that?"

"I swear by the Maker." Boros passed it across to him but held onto the chain. "I want it back after. You're not keeping it." His greedy little eyes focused on the locket and he licked his lips.

She waited until he agreed to return it before letting go. They were still losing the fight. Her people were being thrown off balance and knocked over like drunkards. No sooner had they regained their footing they were sent stumbling again.

Jarke slipped the chain over his head, took a deep breath and drew his sword. "I'm right behind you," said Boros, pulling two raiders close to her. "We all are." Jarke charged at the wall of flame screaming like a maniac. She waited a few seconds before following behind. As she'd expected the moment he touched the fire he began to scream and tried to move backwards. Boros hamstrung him from behind and he fell forward, temporarily blocking the fire and creating an opening. She jumped through and several others followed in her wake.

The mages were surprised and scared. This wasn't something they had anticipated. Some of them began to scream as she raced towards them with weapons drawn. Something struck Boros on her right shoulder, numbing her arm, but she held onto her dagger. With her left she hacked at the nearest person, cutting down a teenage boy, her blade biting into his neck. As blood spurted across her face the screaming intensified all around as her people went to work.

Something gripped Boros around the neck and she was lifted into the air. It felt like a rope but there was nothing to see. Behind her the fire continued to rage. Black spots danced in front of her eyes and she looked around to see who was doing this to her. One girl was staring at her with a fierce expression. Boros focused on her and threw her dagger. Her arm was still numb and her throw wide but the girl panicked and the pressure vanished.

Boros landed badly, twisting one ankle, but quickly scrambled to her feet. She was almost out of time and out of luck. A fist slammed into her jaw, spinning her head around. Before she could recover another struck her in the stomach, knocking the air from her body. The force was so strong she fell to her knees and began to retch, spitting bile and blood onto the ground. She wouldn't give up. This couldn't be the end. She tried to get up but her arms and legs wouldn't support her weight and she flopped down onto her face.

The heat from the fire dwindled and then faded. The screaming and sounds of battle had stopped. By the time Boros could breathe again she realised it was all over. Lying beside her on the ground were at least a dozen of her people. All of them were dead and she couldn't see any wounds. But there were also a few faces she didn't recognise which made her smile. They were bloody and gouged from steel, as they should be.

"You think this is funny," said a voice right before someone's fist hammered into the side of her head and the world turned black.

Wren stared down at the six dead people from her community and the bloody wounds they bore. Even Master Yettle had his limits and couldn't raise people from the dead. Six lives for sixty. That was how many raiders they had now captured.

The plan had been carefully put together and she'd been prepared for the need to adapt. It had all been going so well until Boros's final attack, which wasn't something she'd ever considered. For the raider to sacrifice one of her own people in such a merciless way was unimaginable. If not for the quick thinking of Leonie, who ordered everyone to drop the firewall, more lives would have been lost.

Boros and the others were being chained together and loaded into wagons that had been converted into prison carts. Many people from the community wanted to kill Boros and the others, to bring about a final end, but Wren knew it wasn't their place. Part of her wanted to do it as well to balance the scales. The urge quickly faded when she thought about the Red Tower and those who had died so that she and the others could escape. There had been enough killing.

Wren also realised that if she and the others in the community were going to have a future in Shael they could not put themselves above the law. Their magic did not make them better than anyone else. The raiders would be taken to the capital city and judged for their crimes.

"Are you ready?" asked Laila, once the prisoners were secure.

"Not really. I've never met a Queen before," said Wren. "But I'm looking forward to it."

CHAPTER 39

Queen Morganse had just finished her evening meal when there was a knock at the door of her private dining room. She frowned and waited, expecting one of her Royal Guards to open it but nothing happened. There were two of them stationed at the end of the corridor and several more throughout the palace.

"Come in," she said.

Ben, her main contact in the Silent Order, entered the room. As ever, he was dressed in plain grey and black clothing and his shoes made no sound as he crossed the tiled floor.

"Majesty," he said with a deep bow which showed her that his grey hair was starting to go thin on top. Time seemed to be catching up with them both. "Given my news I thought it best if no one saw me."

Morganse thought she knew all of the hidden passageways in and out of the palace but he continued to surprise her. The thought of being alone with him in the room, when no one knew he was even there, was more than a little unsettling. If he was so inclined he could kill her and slip away without anyone knowing he'd been there. Thankfully that didn't seem to be her fate this evening.

"Please sit," she said, gesturing at the chair furthest away from her at the table. A little bit of prudence never hurt. "What's happened?"

Ben settled into his chair and rubbed his mouth as if trying to dislodge something sour. "It's not good news. The head of the Mining Guild was found dead this morning."

Morganse had met with the man on a couple of occasions and thought him as dense as the iron his miners dug out of the ground. But to his people he was a fair and effective leader. He didn't work for her but he was an important figure within the community. Yerskani steel might not be up to the standard of Seveldrom but it was an important commodity that was shipped around the world. "Was he murdered?"

"That's unclear at this time. However, I thought it prudent to investigate the man being considered to replace him. All of the miners seemed to be leaning towards one name in particular. Cal Hemsey. My people searched his home and found this."

Ben took something from his pocket and placed it on the table before sliding it towards her. Morganse caught the cloth pouch and tipped out its contents. A familiar and crudely made stone idol, of a benevolent mother holding a child, rolled onto the table. Akosh.

For almost two weeks Morganse had been wrestling with her decision. She'd asked the Silent Order to keep an eye on some of the people named in the list that Tammy had acquired. Her own agents were following the other less senior figures and were sending her regular reports of their activity. So far none of them had done anything untoward and were going about their daily lives as normal. The only anomaly, and the one trait all of Akosh's agents shared, was their ambition.

Until now she had thought the list acquired by the Guardians included all of Akosh's people in the city, but the death of the

Mining Guild's leader seemed to prove otherwise. It made her wonder how many other followers Akosh had seeded around the city in positions adjacent to those in power. How many more agents should she be monitoring?

Ben's normally grave expression seemed distracted. "Is there something else?" she asked.

"I don't believe in coincidences," he said.

"Neither do I." Experience had taught her that even if she couldn't see the person pulling the strings it didn't mean they weren't there.

"This is the third death that struck me as unusual in two weeks. The first was an influential blacksmith and the second an important merchant. At first glance both deaths were not suspicious."

Morganse didn't like the sound of where this was going. "And now?"

"I made some thorough enquiries. It was difficult work," he said, rubbing his hands together. Morganse noted the dried blood under his nails and the swelling around his knuckles. She liked details but on this occasion was happy not to know what methods he'd used. "The thief who robbed the smith was quite skilled. It wasn't a random attack, although he didn't know who paid him. A very rare poison was used on the merchant, but once again the apothecarist who supplied it didn't have a name."

"And the people set to replace them? I take it you visited their homes as well?"

Ben reached into his pocket and placed two more identical idols on the table in front of him. Three murders in two weeks. Akosh was making a move on her city. Perhaps it was payback for the rededication of all her orphanages in Perizzi. Or perhaps that was merely a coincidence and her plan remained unchanged. Either way three murders in such a short space of

time, in addition to the two previous ones Tammy had brought
to her attention, indicated something was about to happen. If
Morganse did nothing then the slow trickle effect of Akosh's
people spreading across the city would continue.

Working alone they couldn't inflict significant harm, but
if Akosh sent an order to even half a dozen of her people they
could prove disruptive. Trade was the lifeblood of the city and
if it was interrupted the knock-on effects would be far-reaching.

It was yet another problem she had to manage. This was in
addition to the Regent and his continued demands that she ban
all mages in Yerskania. The gall of the man was astonishing.
Especially when everyone in the west knew about his amnesty
for Zecorran mages. Her agents in the north also reported that
his cadre was still small in number, and consisted of young
people, which was both a blessing and a curse. While it meant
they lacked significant training and experience it also suggested
they were impressionable and naïve. Whatever else he was she
knew Regent Choilan was a charismatic man who could be very
persuasive. Either he or one of his three wives would find a way
to bind the young mages to ensure their loyalty.

For the time being they had shown no signs of moving beyond
the capital city but it was only a matter of time. Once all of
Zecorria was secure his gaze would inevitably turn outwards.
Before that could happen he, too, would have to contend with the
will of the people who still loathed anything to do with magic.

In the meantime, she had to deal with the rogue mages who
had fled south after the capture of their leader. Morganse still
had no idea how that had happened or what to do with the few
that Balfruss had already imprisoned. The idea of putting them
on trial and then executing them for their crimes did not appeal.
It would be right in the eyes of the law but she wasn't in the
habit of murdering misguided children.

She also had yet to properly consider Tammy's proposal to set up magical schools in the country. The looming magical threat in the north made her consider it again, but her people's hatred of magic was still so raw she wondered at the wisdom of the idea. Yerskania would need some level of magical defence in the future, but the matter was not as pressing as Akosh and her agents. They could undermine everything she had worked so hard to build. Her life was dedicated to the safety of her people and she was not about to let a new cult destroy her legacy.

"Majesty?" asked Ben, interrupting her reverie.

"I was just considering my choices," she admitted. They were few and none were particularly appealing, but a decision was needed. So be it. She would make it and face the consequences of her actions. "This cannot continue."

Tomorrow more people could turn up dead and quickly be replaced by those loyal to Akosh.

"I agree, Majesty."

"The people you're watching, have you investigated those around them?"

"Yes, Majesty. We needed to know which were loyal and which are part of her network."

"How difficult would it be to find suitable replacements for all of those being watched on the list?" she asked.

"It would be relatively simple," said Ben. "There are several people vying for each role."

"That's good."

"What are you asking me to do, your Majesty?"

Morganse stared down at the idol and took a deep breath. When she felt calm she met Ben's gaze. "Eliminate them. Tonight. And make sure people know the Silent Order was responsible for a few. I want to send a clear message."

She'd given him orders before to take out certain targets but her decision made him pause. This was not one or two people. All of them had the potential to be dangerous targets, but so far none of them had done anything untoward. When Tammy had given her the list she'd hesitated. When the Dockmaster and Minister of Trade had died she'd hesitated.

She couldn't wait around any more to see what they did. It was too late to save those who had already been killed, but if she did nothing others could soon die in suspicious circumstances. Then her regret and compassion would mean nothing to those who suffered. Decisive action was needed.

"Are you certain?" asked Ben.

"Kill them all," said the Queen.

CHAPTER 40

Tianne stared around at her room trying to find anything that she would truly miss. Her pack, containing all of her belongings, sat on the bed. It had been a lot easier and faster to gather everything up than when she'd left the Red Tower. Then she'd agonised over every item of clothing. This time she was only taking what was truly hers and would leave the rest behind. The only concessions were a new pair of boots and some warmer clothing for the journey south. Her experiences on the road last time had taught her to be ready for anything.

After shoving the bag under her bed she went for her last meal at the palace and then returned to her rooms to wait for midnight. When the building was silent and still she took a deep breath, wrapped her head and face in a long black scarf and retrieved her pack.

The sensible part of her mind was telling her to leave immediately. To find the shortest route outside, use her magic to climb over a wall and disappear into the streets. From there she had enough money to buy a horse, although sadly not the one on which she'd arrived. As part of his pretence of caring about her the Regent had attempted to find it, but unfortunately had not been successful. Tianne doubted he'd actually tried. It was yet another lie intended to make him seem like a compassionate man.

By bribing one of the stable boys she'd paid a different horse trader for a new mount, but had only given him half. The rest she would deliver in person tonight. If nothing else her recent experiences had made her a lot more cautious in all things.

Ignoring the sensible part of herself, Tianne followed her instincts. They were telling her to do something else. It was the part of herself that she wanted to ignore but it guided her feet down into the earth again. This time she had no need to argue or threaten any of the guards. Most of them were asleep at this hour and those who weren't she rendered unconscious from a distance with her magic. They never saw her face and would be unable to tell anyone which of the cadre had done it. For once not being the only mage in the city had its advantages.

This time when Tianne entered Garvey's cell block she was prepared for the stench. Even so the smell was so overpowering it still made her eyes water. The sputtering torch at the end of the cell block provided only meagre light, keeping the worst horrors in the shadows. A low hum filled several of the other cells as moving blankets of flies feasted on the rotting flesh of their dead occupants. She moved down to the last cell on the end and was grateful he remained wreathed in shadows. Only his feet were visible and she didn't summon a mage light to reveal more.

Garvey's breathing seemed incredibly loud in the dense silence this deep underground. Tianne's breath frosted on the air and she wondered how long he would make himself endure such horrors.

"Back again so soon," he whispered.

"I'm leaving. I came to say . . . " Tianne trailed off, not really sure why she'd come. Her instincts had told her she needed to see him one last time. To say something, but now she was here the words wouldn't come.

"Say what?"

"What did you mean the last time I was here?" It wasn't what she'd wanted to ask him, but it had been on her mind. "You said something had been revealed to you."

The echo of her words faded and the cloying silence returned. At first she thought that he wouldn't respond, but then he shuffled closer, the chains clinking with every move. Tianne braced herself for the grisly sight of his ruined face. Thankfully he'd wrapped a piece of cloth around his head, covering his eyes.

"Do you know how many Sorcerers there are in the world?" he asked. Tianne shook her head then realised he couldn't see her. "Four," he said, before she could respond. "And you met three of them at the Red Tower. Sorcerers are regarded as the most experienced and the learned mages in the world." Garvey's mocking laughter surprised her as it was so loud and bitter, echoing over and over again off the walls. It felt very out of place in this miserable hole deep underground.

"I don't understand."

"I can see so much now," he said, smiling ruefully at his choice of words. "As a Sorcerer I thought I understood the Source on a deeper level. In my arrogance I believed I knew the full potential of magic. I was so wrong."

"Is that why you're still here?" she said, gesturing at the filth around them.

"It's so quiet and there are no distractions. The peace has allowed me to clear my mind. Here I can focus on what is being revealed. Up there it's teeming with people. I can feel them all," he said, glancing at the ceiling. "Hundreds and thousands of them, scrabbling around in the city. They're like ants crawling across my skin. Don't you feel them?"

"I don't feel anything. We're too deep underground."

"Embrace the Source," he said, standing up and moving towards the bars of his cell. The chain on his ankle stopped him short and he glanced at it with irritation. Tianne felt a brief rush of power and then he simply touched the chain with two fingers. The metal chain dissolved and struck the floor as a liquid, splashing her on the face. Tianne wiped it away in disgust but then realised it had been transformed into water. That was impossible. In all the time she'd been a student at the Red Tower she'd never read or heard of such a Talent. Changing one thing into another was a fanciful myth that the ignorant used when talking about magic, like lead into gold.

"What do I do?" she asked.

"Open yourself to the Source," said Garvey, who was now standing at the bars of his cell. "Let it flow through you. Let it fill every corner of your body and mind."

Tianne focused and reached out towards the tide that always waited on the edge of her perception. Drawing power into her body from the Source was still a feeling that she couldn't put into words. Her senses became more acute, the shadows peeled back and the stench in the cells became even stronger, filling her nose with its putrid filth. Now she could hear the steady drip of water, see the pale green moss growing in the corner of Garvey's cell and the rodent-chewed corpse in the next cell. But all of it was insignificant compared to the warmth inside. It made her feel stronger, more confident, and with it she believed anything was possible.

"Reach out with your mind," said Garvey, his voice hypnotic in the gloom. "Let it drift up through the stone and beyond. Far above the city there's a hawk wheeling in slow circles. A murder of crows is watching, nervous about their chicks. Can you see them?"

Tianne tried to follow his instructions but all she could feel was the dense, immovable weight of all the stone above their heads. The earth around it was damp from a downpour and she sensed tiny specks of life as insects crawled and burrowed. Without channelling any power it felt as if she was trying to stretch a piece of string beyond its limit.

"I can't reach beyond the earth."

"Ah," said Garvey, but she didn't think he was speaking to her any more. His face was tilted towards the ceiling but she had the impression his mind was far away. A frown creased his forehead and Tianne felt a peculiar wave of nausea pass through her which made her stagger.

"What was that?"

"There's something here, in Herakion. A person. A being of immense power. It's old. So old and monstrous." Garvey gripped the bars of his cell with both hands and would have fallen as something invisible seemed to wrench him sideways. His knees buckled but he recovered and held himself upright. Garvey's smile was a mix of surprise and wonder. "I think it's aware of me. I can feel it searching."

The hairs on the back of Tianne's neck began to stand up and a primal urge to run started to build up in her chest. She released her connection to the Source but the awful feeling remained and there was a strange pressure in the air.

"Stop," she said, trying to swallow the lump in her throat. "Stop, stop, stop."

She was babbling but couldn't help it. Garvey had attracted the attention of something primal and dangerous. It was a predator and she was its prey. Her instincts were telling her to run far away if she wanted to live.

"What is it?" said Garvey.

"Stop!" shouted Tianne.

Garvey finally heard her and she felt him sever his connection to the Source. She was breathing heavily and sweat had soaked into her clothing. For a time neither of them spoke and merely listened to the silence. There was a strange itch between her shoulders and a strong feeling of being watched. The hairs on her arms were still standing upright and her heart thumped loudly in her chest. Slowly, so slowly, her sense of the other began to ebb away. Tianne fell to her knees, her whole body awash with relief.

They'd both come very close to attracting the attention of something powerful, malicious and far beyond their understanding. She should have ignored her instincts and listened to the sensible part of her mind. It seemed as if she hadn't learned. Garvey's expression was a reminder of everything she'd forgotten. While she was terrified by what had just happened he seemed elated at the discovery.

Garvey was dangerous. He didn't know when to stop and eventually it would be the death of him. She didn't belong here and had no intention of being caught up in his schemes.

Without saying another word Tianne ran from the cells, leaving him alone in the darkness. She never wanted to see him again in her life.

Tianne made it back to the ground floor without any problem and took a moment to catch her breath. The sooner she put some distance between her and this city the better off she would be. Now all she had to do was get out of the palace without being seen.

Just as she was creeping down a corridor a voice called out from the shadows sending her heart racing again.

"I knew something was wrong," said Kalina, moving into the light. She was fully dressed in her mage's uniform but so far hadn't embraced the Source. "Ever since you went to visit Garvey you've been different."

"It started long before that." There seemed no reason to lie at this point. "I don't want to fight you but I'm leaving Zecorria tonight," said Tianne.

"Tell me why? I need to understand."

Tianne sighed and leaned against the wall. She was just so damn tired. All she wanted to do was lie down and go to sleep. "The Regent doesn't care about us. The only reason he created the amnesty was to protect himself against Garvey and the other rogue mages. He said it was for the people, but he only cares about himself."

"What about the charlatans and the con men?" said Kalina. "They were hurting people."

"You're right, they were, but what do you think happened to them?" asked Tianne. "Do you think he let them go with a warning or a beating? I saw Frohake's beaten and bloody corpse. There's someone else rotting in the cell next to Garvey if you want to take a look."

A crack showed in Kalina's brave façade. "Why would he do that?"

Tianne shrugged. "Because he can, and who can stop him?"

"I can't believe the Regent would do that."

"He did." Tianne knew in her heart the Regent was a far worse con man than any of those they'd caught in the city. "There's already been too much violence against magic users. It needs to stop."

"You're running away."

"I'm surviving. He banned all Seekers and then, when it suited him, created the amnesty. If the wind blows south tomorrow he could change his mind again and ban all mages. You need to be careful."

"Stay. Help us build something different. Teach us how to fight. He can't stand up to all of us if we work together."

It was a noble idea and the sentiment appealed to her, but even Tianne could see it was naïve. If they stood up to the Regent he would wear them down or have them murdered in their sleep. The cadre was fumbling along with its magic and with only a couple of years' experience she wasn't the right person to teach them. They would lose if they ever came across a trained Battlemage or worse, a Sorcerer. Tianne knew that if Garvey really wanted to he could destroy the entire cadre by himself. There was also the real possibility he might bring doom to himself, and anyone nearby inside the palace, with his meddling. It was much safer to be far away from him.

"The Regent is cold and ruthless. They threw me into a water cell when I first arrived."

"I know, but that was just a mistake," said Kalina, making excuses for him. Her faith in him was admirable but misplaced.

"Was it?" asked Tianne. She'd thought about this a great deal since the Regent had apparently saved her. The more she went over it in her mind the more she believed it had been staged for her benefit.

"Come with me," said Tianne.

"What?"

"Tonight. Right now. We can leave together and build a new life somewhere else."

"Where would we go? How would we live?"

"I have a friend who can help us," said Tianne. She wanted to trust Kalina, and would tell her more about Wren and her community once they were on the road, but right now she couldn't tell if this was another of the Regent's ploys. "She's building a different kind of community."

Kalina considered it but eventually shook her head. "I can't. My father is here and this is my home. You should stay. We can find a way together to make it better."

"I'm sorry, I can't," said Tianne. "I should never have come back. I don't belong here."

"The Regent will be disappointed."

"Are you going to try and stop me?" asked Tianne, bracing herself in case she had to form a shield.

"No. You were right about one thing. There's been too much violence against mages. I'm not going to stop you."

"That's a relief," said Tianne with a smile. Kalina was perhaps the only thing she would miss about Zecorria. "Be careful. The Regent is not as kind as he seems. It would be safer if you pretended that you hadn't seen me."

Kalina nodded and turned away, heading back towards her room.

Tianne embraced the Source and crept through the corridors of the palace, listening for other people with her enhanced hearing, but she saw no one. She emerged into a courtyard and found the night was cool and crisp with faint grey clouds scudding by overhead. Taking a deep breath she tasted the air and wondered if she would ever return to Zecorria again.

Moving with purpose she crafted a crude set of stairs by freezing the air into blocks of ice. The surface of each was incredibly slippery but she took her time and eventually reached the top. By the time the sun came up the ice would have melted and she would be riding south. She glanced at the palace one final time and then turned her back on it and everyone inside.

CHAPTER 41

A kosh gestured for Doggett to continue with his report but she wasn't really paying attention. She heard enough to pick up the main points but her mind was focused on a larger issue.

Doggett continued to tell her about the Regent. He'd now secured the capital city and all potential mages had been rounded up and either indoctrinated into his cadre or eliminated. Any charlatans had been beaten and were in hiding or they'd been murdered. Now he was setting his sights on expanding into nearby towns and cities. With twelve, previously thirteen, mages he'd begun to change the mood towards magic in Herakion. It was years away from a significant shift, but Zecorria was on the right path.

The thirteenth young mage had apparently run away, much to the Regent's annoyance. Attempts were being made to find her but Doggett said they weren't actually spending much time on it. He and Selina's other agents had more important matters to focus on, such as continuing to earn the Regent's trust and the respect of those closest to him. He and his first wife, Selina, were regularly relying on Doggett and the others which she would be able to use to her advantage in the future.

Akosh's mind kept drifting back to her meeting with Kai. She wondered if he knew about Selina's agents and that they were all loyal to her. Perhaps they could do some investigating to find out how many people he had in the city. Beyond the doctors and apothecarists she was willing to bet there were people hiding in plain sight just like some of hers. If she was going to make a move against him she would first need to secure the capital city.

"Mother?" asked Doggett, sensing her distraction.

"I'm listening," she said, gesturing for him to continue.

Kai had been so strong. Beyond anything she'd imagined. The only comparable experience she'd had was her first encounter with Nethun. The weight of his presence and vastness of his power had been humbling. One of her brethren had been driven to his knees. Part of her wondered how she could oppose someone almost as timeless and equally dangerous. Kai was worse in some ways as he was more devious.

He'd grown so powerful without the others noticing. But then they were always distracted by the mortals. They tended to focus on the larger issues of wars, the continual death of magic and political scheming between nations. And all the while Kai had been establishing a new following to grow his foundation, while gobbling up smaller gods and absorbing their power.

The image of her friends trapped inside Kai while he continually feasted on them still made her squirm. That was why she had to proceed with caution bordering on extreme paranoia. If he sensed what she was doing Akosh knew he wouldn't give her any kind of warning. She would go to sleep one night and wake up inside that abyss as he slowly drained the life from her. It would be a long, painful and very slow death. She would beg for the emptiness of the Void long before it found her.

Perhaps an alliance was her only chance of survival. Perhaps she should turn to her brethren for protection. He would never expect her to do that. Akosh couldn't believe she was even contemplating it, but in her desperation she was willing to try anything.

Despite the pretence of being a peculiar family, her kind rarely aided one another and many were in direct competition. Each was busy pursuing their own goals and it didn't profit them to help someone else become more powerful.

Every year there were more distractions for the mortals that took them away from religion. New pursuits created traditions of their own and sometimes this meant prayer was such a low priority it disappeared from their daily life. The mortals were always so busy chasing their ambitions, obtaining wealth or land, that faith became unnecessary.

It was why she continually saw new faces appearing at the banqueting table while others were forced to transform themselves in order to survive. She'd done it and had thought it made her powerful in comparison to her peers.

"Mother?" said Doggett. She realised he'd stopped talking a while ago. "Are you well? Can I help?"

"No. You can't. Be silent." As obedient as a trained hound he closed his mouth.

If she told Vargus the truth, or at least part of the truth, and begged for his protection then perhaps she could survive. She would not be a slave to Kai. He'd not given her any direct orders but had told her to continue as normal for now. Akosh knew it wouldn't last. Very soon he would send one of his people to her and ask for a favour. It would be something small and apparently insignificant but Akosh wouldn't be able to refuse. And if she said yes to him once then it would be increasingly difficult to say no after that. It would be the beginning of the end.

Would Vargus protect her? Or would he throw her to the wolves?

Despite her orders the sound of rapid footsteps in the corridor brought Doggett to his feet. His first instinct was still to protect her. He stood next to the door with a dagger held low as the runner approached. Someone frantically knocked on the door and Akosh could hear them breathing heavily.

"Yes?"

"Mother, I have urgent news," said a muffled voice.

"Come in," she said.

A red-faced woman she vaguely recognised stumbled into the room, wheezing and holding her sides while she tried to get her breathing under control. "A bird just came into the aviary. Bad news from Perizzi," she said.

Akosh had been expecting the opposite. Three more of her people were due to ascend to key positions of power in the city. It should have moved her one step closer to destabilising Yerskania and unseating Queen Morganse from the throne. "Take a moment, then tell me exactly what's happened."

Doggett had sheathed his dagger and handed the woman a glass of water. She sat down in the chair opposite and Akosh gave her a moment to compose herself.

"Something awful has happened, Mother," said the woman. Akosh was listening but couldn't help staring at the birdshit on the shoulders and one sleeve of the woman's jacket. That would be why she didn't recognise her. She'd never been in the aviary as it stank and she had no desire to be crapped on by a messenger bird.

"Did someone die? Was it one of my people?" she asked, refusing to call them children. It was a term she was starting to despise, much like when they called her Mother.

The woman began to cry and one of Akosh's hands twitched.

She wanted to slap the woman hard across the face but that would only prolong the conversation. Instead she gripped her hand and gave it a squeeze she would no doubt interpret as comforting. "What has happened?" Akosh asked again, through gritted teeth.

"Everyone is gone in Perizzi, Mother. At least thirty-seven of your children are dead. They were all killed in one night."

"Who? Give me some names?"

The woman listed a dozen and Akosh held up a hand to silence her. Rohane had been her replacement for the Dockmaster and Tovin the new Minister of Trade. The others were all key figures spread out across the city, either in a position of power or due to inherit very soon.

"How did they die?" asked Akosh.

"Some had what seemed like accidents. They choked on their food. Three drowned and seven died in their sleep. It wouldn't have been unusual, except they all died on the same night."

It was possible Kai had done this but it seemed unlikely. It made no sense for him to tell her one thing only to do the exact opposite. He had an agenda of his own and for now it suited him to let her continue with her plans. That meant it was one of the human groups working against her. The Guardians wouldn't kill that many people. They would want them arrested and put on trial. Perhaps the mages from the Red Tower were moving against her and seeking revenge.

"Was there anything unusual about any of the murders?" said Akosh.

"At least eight were eliminated by the Silent Order. Their symbol was found beside the bodies."

The woman shuddered as she mentioned their name. The Silent Order. It was an ancient league of assassins that possessed a fierce reputation. Most humans were afraid of them as they seemed as elusive and difficult to catch as a shadow on the wall. It was rumoured they were responsible for the deaths of kings and queens and had shaped the course of history down through the centuries.

The reality behind the organisation was a lot more mundane. Akosh only knew the truth as, during her first incarnation as the deity of killers, she'd learned their secret. Despite the appearance of being an independent group who made their own decisions, the Silent Order had connections to Queen Morganse.

The group often carried out dirty work that left the hands of the Yerskani ruler clean. Their symbol was left beside a body when a clear message needed to be sent. At other times the murders were so carefully staged they were made to resemble accidents. Akosh wasn't fooled. The Silent Order had killed all thirty-seven of them.

"Why would they do it?" asked the woman.

"Why indeed?" said Akosh.

A few weeks ago she would have been distraught at the loss of so many of her children. She would have been crippled with grief, and raging. She would have gone on a drunken binge for days. Now, thanks to Kai putting the mortals and her true nature into perspective, she only felt irritated at their deaths. It was another serious setback to her plans in Yerskania but no more than that. She had other less prominent children in Perizzi and it would take her years to manoeuvre them into position of power, but she was not about to give up.

Her plans in Zecorria were continuing apace as her people made themselves indispensable to the Regent and his wife. Choilan would be the fulcrum she used to create a nation of her own, but this attack on her could not go unpunished. Especially when it was only a mere mortal she was dealing with.

"This was all Queen Morganse," said Akosh, thinking aloud. "She orchestrated it."

"Are you sure?" asked the woman.

Akosh ignored her question and gestured at Doggett to get rid of her. The sight of her was beginning to be a distraction. He escorted her from the room and returned alone a short time later. It had been a bold move by the Queen. It was one thing to find out someone was attempting to undermine your city from within every organisation with influence. It was something else entirely to cut them all out like gangrenous flesh. Sever the limb and with luck the infection wouldn't spread.

If those had been her only people in the city it might have worked. Akosh scribbled down a note and held it out.

"What do you want me to do, Mother?" asked Doggett, taking the message.

"Send this to Perizzi as soon as possible. A clear message needs to be sent to those who would interfere in my plans."

Until now she had worked hard to keep her name and identity a secret. It was starting to seem as if that no longer mattered. Both her brethren and the mortals were increasingly aware of her name and activities.

The Silent Order had left their mark beside some of the bodies. Now it was her turn.

CHAPTER 42

Morganse was supposed to be reading the stack of reports waiting on her desk, but instead she was staring out of the window at the city below. It was still early in the evening but she had a half-empty glass of wine in her hand and it wasn't her first. Overhead the grey sky was turning black and spots of lights were appearing in the buildings as candles and lanterns were lit. The sea of glowing embers began to spread and snatches of music drifted through the air.

Despite the hour she was already tired. For once she just wanted to spend an evening sitting in the back of a tavern, drinking and singing along with the crowd. As a young woman, and not yet old enough to be recognised in public, she and some friends had sneaked out and done just that. Even though none of them had come to any harm the King, her father, had been furious. That night of revelry seemed like a long time ago.

She swirled the red liquid around the glass and drained the rest, not really savouring the flavour. It tasted too bitter and metallic, like blood. Perhaps she should have chosen a bottle of white instead.

The city seemed so quiet from up here. Everyone down there just wanted to live in peace. If only they knew the price of their freedom. She was contemplating another glass of wine when the sound of approaching footsteps drew her attention. There was only one person who walked like that who had access to her office. Morganse poured herself another glass and went back to the window.

As she'd expected Tammy came stomping into the room without being announced. "Do you know your assistant is asleep at his desk?" she asked.

Morganse glanced over her shoulder. "Let him sleep. He's been working late for several nights."

The Queen was expecting explosive anger from her new Khevassar but instead Tammy seemed deflated. "Are you not going to shout at me?"

"I'm working up to it," said Tammy with a wry smile.

"Drink?" said Morganse, lifting her glass.

"Never acquired a taste for wine." Tammy sat down with a long sigh that seemed to come from her boots. "I'm surprised to see you drinking."

"Isn't there something in the book of the Maker about raising a glass to the dead?"

Tammy shook her head. "I wouldn't know. I never had much time for religion."

"I used to visit the Maker's church every week with my children when they were young." That also seemed like a long time ago. She was a grandmother now, four times over and a fifth was on the way. Her eldest granddaughter was almost a teenager and already Morganse was looking towards her to take over the throne. But that was still several years away and the problems of today would not go away because she ignored them.

"Why?" said Tammy. "Why not imprison them?"

"I could not hold that many prominent figures in the city indefinitely without just cause."

"There could be others in the city. The names on the list might not be all of her agents," said Tammy.

"I'm sure you're right, but I'm safe here," said Morganse, gesturing at the building around her. She had several Royal Guards just down the corridor and more around the palace. After the events of the war additional precautions had been taken to ensure her safety. A clear message had been sent to Akosh. She knew there would be repercussions for such a bold attack but for now the city was back in the hands of people she could trust. A thorough search had been conducted into all the individuals who suddenly found themselves in line for a promotion. None of them were loyal to Akosh.

"We suspect Akosh has a few loyal mages as well," said Tammy. "What if she sends someone after you here? I'm not sure the Royal Guards would be able to defend you against a mage."

It was something she'd considered but right now didn't have an answer for. "We'll cross that bridge if we come to it."

"Have you considered my suggestion about asking Balfruss for protection and setting up a school?" asked Tammy.

"I have, but I don't think the people are ready. If we were to adopt such an approach it would have to be done in secret."

"Majesty, I would advise against that. Keeping it a secret was one of the problems with the Red Tower."

"It doesn't matter. It's a problem for another day. Has Balfruss returned?" asked Morganse.

"No, not yet."

Morganse had doubts that even if Balfruss was in the city he would be willing to protect her. She had once been instrumental in the introduction of monthly tests by the Seekers but had also banned them, putting more children at risk and heightening people's fear of magic.

"We will have to muddle on without Balfruss unless you

know of another mage who's willing to help." Morganse said it as a joke but from Tammy's expression she could see the Khevassar was struggling with something. "Is there something you want to tell me?"

"Yes, your Majesty. Only that I would like one of my Guardians to patrol the palace. Just in case the Royal Guards miss something." They were the toughest and most skilled soldiers in the country, but she was aware that even they had their limits. A crudely trained mage could best the strongest and most skilled of warriors.

"I see. And did you have a particular Guardian in mind?"

Tammy winced. "Yes, your Majesty."

The Old Man had always given Morganse the impression that he knew more than she told him during their regular meetings. It seemed as if his replacement was equally adept at keeping secrets.

"Are you sure they're loyal?" she asked.

"I have no doubt, given his history."

"Very well," said the Queen. "Have him report to the palace from tomorrow."

"Thank you, Majesty. I think both of us will sleep a little better knowing that he's here."

"Do you think I made the right decision?"

Tammy took a long time before answering. "I don't know. Were I in your position, with the same pressures and responsibilities, then perhaps. A wise friend once told me that sometimes the only choices available are bad and worse."

"I see the Old Man has been sharing his wisdom," said Morganse. He'd said the same thing to her more than twenty-five years ago and had repeated it on occasion through the years. They shared a brief smile at the memory before Tammy departed, no doubt to return to her own duties.

Morganse stared out of the window again noting the sky was now completely dark. A few stars showed overhead, pinpricks of white in the endless black. Spread out below her, hundreds of yellow and amber lights carpeted the ground.

The door to her office opened again and Dorn shuffled in. He yawned and shook his head, trying to wake himself up. "Do I have another visitor?" she asked.

"No, Majesty, I wanted to speak to you about something. It's rather personal."

It was highly unusual but she gestured at one of the seats in front of her desk. Dorn was an able and highly organised secretary, if not a particularly thrilling conversationalist. She'd hoped for someone with initiative who would make suggestions, but he seemed content with doing exactly what he was told and nothing more. His loyalty and efficiency gave him some leeway if nothing else.

"What did you want to talk about?" she asked.

Dorn took a cloth from his pocket and mopped at his sweating brow. His thinning hair was getting long and she had the feeling he was trying to cover up the bald spot with volume.

"I'm struggling with your recent decision, your Majesty," he said, unable to meet her eye.

Morganse raised an eyebrow but said nothing at first. She was used to discussing her decisions with senior figures in her government, as well as the Khevassar, but never her secretary. Her patience was starting to wear thin. "Which one?" she asked, curious to know how much he'd been eavesdropping.

Dorn shook his head sadly. "You ordered the murders of almost forty innocent people."

The only other person in the room when she had given that order had been Ben, from the Silent Order. She was confident he hadn't told anyone and neither would other members of his group. Only a handful of the murders had been openly attributed to the Silent Order. The rest had been made to resemble accidents.

"If you are unable to carry out your duties any more, I will see that you're given a similar position elsewhere," said Morganse.

"How could you do it?" he asked, looking up at her. The rage simmering behind his eyes was so alien it surprised her. Until this point he'd never shown a hint of passion for anything besides his food.

"Leave now, or you'll make it worse for yourself."

Dorn remained in his seat and didn't seem intimidated by her threat. "They were loyal," he insisted.

"Get out!" said Morganse, but he continued to ignore her.

"Why did you do it?"

"I don't have to justify my decisions to you. This is your final warning."

"Tell me," he shouted, slamming a fist on the desk.

"This has gone on long enough." Her patience had run out. As she stood up to call for a Royal Guard Dorn drew a dagger from his sleeve.

Morganse froze. Dorn was still the slovenly, overweight man she'd seen every day for months but now there was an unfamiliar coldness to his face.

"You're right," said Dorn, standing up and kicking away his chair. They faced one another with the desk between them. "This has gone on long enough. You're not fit to be the Queen. You killed loyal servants."

"Their loyalty wasn't to me, or this country." Morganse looked around her office for a weapon while she kept him talking. The nearest item that might be of use was her glass of wine. She could reach it before he came around the desk. His arms weren't long enough to stab her from where he was standing. "They would've done whatever they were told by Akosh, even if it meant betraying this country."

Dorn twitched slightly and Morganse cursed herself for a fool. Her previous secretary had been ancient and had died of old age. He should have retired years ago but had stubbornly held on. When it happened she'd been upset but it hadn't come as a surprise. No one had suggested an investigation into his death, including her, but now she began to wonder if his demise had been natural. Dorn had been recommended to her by a number of trusted advisers who were probably unaware of his true loyalty.

"How old were you when Akosh found you?"

"Three," he said with an unsettling smile. "Mother saved me from a life of crime, begging or prostitution. I owe her everything."

"Ah, Captain," said Morganse, looking over his shoulder. "I want this man arrested."

As Dorn turned around Morganse leaned across her desk and smashed her glass across the side of his head. Wine splashed all over his face and clothes while the glass shattered, shards embedding themselves in his face and neck. Screeching in pain he reeled back, clawing at his face as Morganse ran towards the door.

Something caught one of her feet and she tripped, landing face down on the tiled floor. Blood ran from her nose but she scrambled to her hands and knees in time to see Dorn coming towards her. One of his eyes was a bloody mess and shards of glass stuck out of his face like a pin cushion. Despite his wounds he still clutched a dagger in one hand which he raised high above his head.

Morganse scrambled to one side, but felt the edge of the

knife on her forearm, drawing a thin line of blood. Kicking out, she caught Dorn on the leg. He cried out in pain and fell over backwards, clipping the back of his head on the desk. Not waiting to see if he was stunned she kicked off her shoes and yanked open the door to her office.

The next set of doors was closed and when she tried to push them open she found they were locked. Dorn had broken the key in the lock sealing her in with him. She could hear him groaning and moving about. Pounding on the door, she shouted for the guards and then put her ear against the wood.

"Majesty?" said a muffled voice.

"He's trying to kill me. Break down the door!" she shouted and then stepped back.

Something heavy slammed into the door and Morganse heaved a sigh of relief. It wouldn't take them long to break it down.

"Murderer!" shrieked Dorn.

Morganse turned around in time to see the dagger coming down. She didn't feel it pierce her flesh and only noticed when she saw the patch of red spreading across the front of her dress.

Behind her the banging grew louder and she heard wood splintering, but she wasn't sure why. Dorn was shouting something and she saw him raise the blood-smeared dagger again. With a scream of her own she shoved a hand into his ruined face, driving the shards of glass deeper. Keening like a maimed animal he tripped and fell backwards. Morganse grabbed a heavy book from the nearest shelf and smashed Dorn over the head with it. With his face covered in blood he glared at her so she hit him again and again.

"Your Majesty!" shouted one of the Royal Guards from somewhere nearby.

Finally, he dropped the dagger but she brought the book

down one more time on his face, smearing the cover with blood and glass.

A terrible weight settled on Morganse and she fell back suddenly feeling tired and cold. Part of her realised that closing her eyes was a mistake but as the cool surface of the tiled floor touched her face it was so difficult to stay awake. Her eyelids fluttered and then she fell into the black.

CHAPTER 43

The tavern was busy when Akosh entered and for once she didn't mind the crowd. By expending a small amount of her power she was able to disguise herself as a plain-faced woman that no one really noticed. When she sat down at her contact's table he looked up from his ale in surprise.

"You've got the wrong table," he said. Akosh let her illusion slip momentarily and his expression transformed. "Apologies, Mother."

She replaced the illusion but his grovelling tone remained. "Sit up straight or people will get suspicious," she told him. He did as ordered and adopted a bored expression that was only partially successful. When the serving girl passed their table Akosh ordered herself a drink and waited until it had arrived before leaning forward.

"You have news from Yerskania?"

"Yes, Mother," he murmured, keeping his voice low but he need not have bothered. The table on her left was occupied by a raucous group of revellers telling jokes and laughing at regular intervals. On her other side a clutch of women were gossiping and beyond them two merchants were haggling loudly about a deal. The noise of the crowd around them almost swallowed his words but she was close enough to hear. She'd chosen this tavern on purpose because it was not one that she'd frequented before. Even her contact was not one she'd met in person until today.

Before her meeting with Kai she'd become a creature of habit, living a comfortable life as she believed herself safe in Herakion. Eating and drinking at the same bars. Sleeping in the same taverns and always taking the same route to bed through the city. Now she watched every face in the crowd for signs that they were serving another master. Her path here had been strangled and she was confident no one could have followed her. It paid to be cautious. He could have spies anywhere.

"What's your name?" she asked.

"Koyle, Mother." He bobbed his head and she gritted her teeth. So far no one had noticed his subservience, but it wouldn't last. She gestured at him to get on with it. "A bird came in this morning. Queen Morganse was attacked in the palace last night," he said.

Akosh sat back and took a long gulp of ale to cover her smile. It might take a few days for the news to trickle through to the north, but it would reach here eventually. She'd intended to destabilise Yerskania using her people on the inside, but it could work just as easily by removing the head of the snake. Chaos bred conflict and from that came murder and more orphans in need of a benevolent mother and teacher.

"Were there any more details?" she asked.

"Only that the Queen was injured, but no one knows how badly or if she will survive."

She might be dying. She might already be dead for that matter. Either option was acceptable.

The Queen had several daughters who had renounced their claims to the throne, which was why Morganse had been grooming her son for the position. That was until an unfortunate incident that left him castrated. With no clear successor what followed would be a mad scramble for power with lots of back-stabbing and chaos. It was an assassin's dream come true. For the time being it would serve her purpose while she continued to strengthen her hold in the north.

In some ways Kai had done her a favour. She had become complacent and soft. Thinking of her followers as individuals and herself as human. Kai still terrified her and, if he really wanted to could snuff her out with little effort, but she would not live in fear. Until the time came when she had to face him Akosh would do as she'd always done. If he held up his part of the bargain then she would avoid the clutches of Vargus and the others. If not, there might be a deal to be made to ensure her continued survival. There were always possibilities.

"That's wonderful news," said Akosh, raising her mug to Koyle.

After finishing her drink she left the tavern with a big smile and decided to attend her next meeting. Part of her was tempted to spend the rest of the day drinking and celebrating. It would be a fun way to pass the time but it was an indulgence and she'd had too many of those lately. For the time being she would focus on her duties, even though she expected the next few hours to be an exercise in tedium.

As Bollgar had promised he had expanded her network of orphanages in the city. It was customary for her to visit each new orphanage within the first few months. The children would have been told a little about her by now but nothing solidified their belief more than a visit in person from their benevolent and loving god.

Fixing a caring smile on her face, Akosh pushed open the door of the first orphanage. The matron in charge was delighted to see her and made a point of introducing her to all members of staff before they went on a tour. The building was still in desperate need of repair but there were signs that the money was being put to good use. She could smell fresh paint and see that the floors had recently been scrubbed. A pair of builders were repairing a crumbling wall in one of the bedrooms and elsewhere she saw a carpenter building sets of bunk beds for the children.

As expected, when she first met the children they attempted to swarm all over her like locusts. Akosh braced herself for an assault of tiny, grabbing hands and screeching voices. She was almost knocked off her feet by the tide and forced herself to endure it for a while, answering an endless barrage of questions. Sooner than the children would have liked she signalled to the matron that she was ready for an extraction. The children were disappointed to see her leave but she made them all promise to be true to her for all their lives. As they solemnly swore Akosh felt a tingle of energy run across her skin and her smile stretched wider.

By the time Akosh walked into the third orphanage the tedious chore had become a valuable reminder of their importance. Without the orphanages and the children she would have disappeared years ago. While being close to so many children tested the limits of her endurance, Akosh bore all of it with a smile. Even so a headache was starting to form. There was a dull throb at the back of her head and it seemed to be growing worse. If she hurried through this last visit it might not be too bad.

The man in charge of the orphanage was more organised and efficient than the previous two. The building was already in a much better state with all repairs completed. The classrooms were busy with children and he went on to boast about the wonderful work they'd done in the garden.

"One of our members of staff has been spending a lot of time on it," he said with a hint of pride. "It's amazing."

As they passed down a corridor Akosh saw several children staring through doorways at her in open-mouthed wonder. A flurry of whispers followed in her wake and she graced the children with a brief smile and wave. The pain in her head was starting to get worse. She gritted her teeth and hoped that it would pass but, if anything, it seemed to be spreading.

"We've been telling the children for weeks that you might visit us," he said. "They're so excited to meet you. We're all so excited!" he admitted with a laugh.

Akosh chuckled at the startled look on his face. "Didn't you think I was real?"

"No, I mean, yes. Of course, but whenever I've asked people to describe you they're unable to tell me very much." He was looking directly at Akosh but she knew in a couple of hours he would struggle to tell others about her face, her build or her height. The only things he'd be able to remember clearly were the emotions she projected and the echo they created within.

Nothing strengthened a child's first impression of their god more than a strong memory of love, compassion and kindness. It rarely converted any of the adults to follow her path, but it did make them more open to her visits in the future. It required she expend a small portion of her power but it was something she always did on a first visit.

"Well, I'm here now," said Akosh. "When will I meet the children?"

"Soon. Their lessons are almost over. Would you like to meet the other members of staff?" he asked hopefully.

Akosh swallowed a sarcastic reply and inclined her head. She needed to leave but could endure this a little longer.

He led her into a sparsely furnished room where three women and one man were sitting talking and drinking tea. They rose to their feet and seemed almost as excited as the children to see her. Akosh extended her aura of euphoria as the administrator introduced her to all of them. She pretended to make a note of each one and mouthed their names, but made no real attempt to try and remember them.

"We have one more member of staff," he said. Just then a petite woman with dark, wavy hair came into the room brushing dirt off her hands. "Ah, here she is. I was just telling Akosh about the wonders you've been doing with the garden."

The woman stopped and stared at Akosh as if suddenly unable to move. She seemed utterly dumbstruck and barely seemed to be breathing. This happened from time to time and Akosh smiled indulgently at the woman.

"Akosh, this is Munroe," said the administrator.

"I've been waiting for this moment, for a long time," said Munroe. "I've been dreaming about it."

"I'm sure." It was probably the highlight of her boring little life. That was when Akosh noticed something unusual about the newcomer. The other members of staff were still staring at her with wide-eyed adoration but Munroe hadn't even smiled. In fact, Akosh could see rage building up behind her eyes. The air in the room suddenly felt close and the hairs on the back of Akosh's hands began to stand up. The others remained blissfully unaware and continued to stare with reverence.

Something made Akosh extend her senses and Munroe twitched as if she'd been pinched. She gasped in surprise as she realised the reason for her headache. The woman in front of her was a mage whose connection to the Source was so strong it set her teeth on edge. As Munroe started to draw power into her body Akosh felt the pressure of her will beginning to build.

"Gorell," said Munroe to the administrator. "Get everyone out of the building."

He looked at Munroe as if she was mad but something

slapped him across the face and he came out of his trance. "What's happening?"

"You need to run," said Munroe, still drawing power into herself. It was impossible. She'd never seen any mortal that was so powerful. Akosh could see her skin beginning to glow with the build-up of energy. "Now!" hissed Munroe.

Gorell looked between her and Akosh and finally noticed something was terribly wrong. He didn't understand what was happening, only that it would be dangerous to remain. Shoving the others ahead of him, they hurried out of the room. Akosh could hear him shouting at others in the rest of the building but Munroe didn't wait.

With a feral scream Munroe lashed out with her magic. Something slammed into Akosh and she was thrown against the stone wall, which shattered upon impact.

CHAPTER 44

Regent Choilan wanted to slap the girl for being so stupid, but instead he maintained a disappointed expression.

"And you had no idea that Tianne was thinking about leaving?" he asked Kalina.

"No. I didn't."

"Do you know where Tianne might go?" Kalina took a moment to think about it but then shook her head. "And you didn't see her leave the palace in the night?"

The girl shook her head again. Her face was the picture of innocence but even so he wondered. Selina's people all reported that the girl was loyal and that getting the tattoos had been her idea. To permanently mark her flesh and dedicate herself to his service was noble and patriotic, but it was also naïve, reminding him they were only children. At times he could see them as lost little lambs looking for their flock. But when he saw them practising their magic in the walled courtyard, a shiver of fear ran down his spine. The primal forces they commanded made him wonder if they were really wolves in disguise. A wolf wasn't a faithful hound that could be trained to obey commands. It was a wild beast and eventually it would revert to its true nature.

"Do you want to leave my service as well? Maybe go back home to your father's tavern?" he asked.

A hint of steel crept into Kalina's expression. "No." The way she said it told him many things about her past. Someone who'd been told always to be polite to the customer, no matter what they said or did. An only child with dreams that were bigger than serving drinks for the rest of her life. The fire in her belly made her ambitious but it also fuelled her anger. It was all in tune with what he'd read from his agents. "I belong here," she insisted.

"I'm glad to hear that. You are now first in my cadre," he said, holding up a second blue star for the front of her uniform. "Can I count on you?"

"Yes. Of course." She was on the verge of tears.

"Get some rest. You have a big day tomorrow." He dismissed her with a wave and she hurried out of the room, practically skipping.

"Deftly handled," said Selina, coming into the room from a side door. He suspected she'd been eavesdropping.

"Do you believe her?" he asked.

"Maybe," said Selina. "But it doesn't matter. The tattoos are hideous, but now there's nowhere she, or any of the others, can go without someone recognising them." Selina helped herself to a glass of watered-down wine and picked at the grapes beside him.

"True. That's why I'm sending them out to find other children."

Now that the capital city had been swept clean of all charlatans, and any youngsters with magic had been recruited, it was time to widen the net. Six mages from his cadre would soon begin a two-week journey to several of the larger towns and two cities to find more recruits. He wanted at least a hundred mages in his cadre by the end of the year, if not more. Then Zecorria would be secure against any invasion, whether or not they had magic of their own.

"I've been thinking, it's time we went to church," said Choilan. Selina raised an eyebrow, baffled by his suggestion. Choilan felt an extra thrill as he'd managed to surprise Selina. She was so rarely caught off balance.

"Why?" she asked with suspicion.

"We need to be seen as loyal followers of the Lady of Light, the true faith."

She still couldn't see where he was going with it. "And?"

"And, I think it would help the people if they saw the mages at prayer. Being a patriot and servant of Zecorria might not be enough for some. If they are seen as being dedicated to the faith, then it might ease some of the remaining tension."

"Perhaps, but you'll need a gesture," said Selina. "Something to make it stand out and generate gossip."

"I thought the High Priest Robella might personally bless them," said Choilan. "If she announced in public that they were noble and faithful, it would be remembered."

"She might object to that."

"I'm sure she can be persuaded," he mused. Bettina and the others had detailed personal information on almost everyone in key positions in the city and their vices. This included areas where pressure could be applied to make them more compliant.

He needed to shift public opinion. Children with magic were seen as dirty, dangerous and something to be hidden. Choilan imagined a future where parents would be proud to have such a child and would bring them forward to his people. A place where mages were seen to be as dedicated and loyal as his Royal Guards. It was going to take time, and a lot of patience, but a few large gestures would put them on the path. He was going to create a strong nation. One that could never be manipulated or controlled as it had been in the past.

"The High Priest will have to be very convincing for it to be effective," said Selina.

"I'm sure Bettina can find a way to motivate her," he said and they briefly shared a smile.

After Selina had left Choilan was alone for a short time before his next meeting. His mind drifted as he considered the possibilities of having his own army of mages. Seven mages had changed the course of the war and one had brought about its end. He wondered what fifty or a hundred mages who were loyal to him could accomplish. It was a remarkable and slightly terrifying idea.

They would have to be rigorously assessed to ensure they were true patriots. He didn't want any more of them running away. The earlier they could be recruited the better. Then they could be indoctrinated and made to feel important. Few people would find it easy to walk away from power, privilege and a form of authority.

A crisp knock on the door told him Bettina had arrived. She swept into the room in a pale yellow dress with a high neck and a trailing hem. Even the sleeves were uncommonly long. Her choice of clothing that showed as little bare flesh as possible had been noted and investigated. He was very aware of her secret and the marks on her flesh the dress was hiding. Everyone had their vices.

"I bring good news, my Regent," she said with a formal bow. It was exactly the right depth to show the appropriate level of respect. If only everyone who worked for him was so precise. "The parade seemed to work. People were pleased at seeing Garvey in chains."

Telling everyone in the city that they had captured the most notorious rogue mage was not enough. They needed to see it. And to believe that his cadre of mages were responsible. Another grand gesture to help tip the scales in their favour.

"Excellent. Has the inquisitor managed to extract a confession from him yet?"

Bettina's expression soured. "Not yet. He's exhausted all of his usual techniques and is now trying other methods." She didn't elaborate and he didn't really care. He just needed Garvey to admit what he'd done in public and beg forgiveness. It didn't matter if he really cared about his victims or not. He just had to say the words and make them sound convincing.

"Have they tried starving him?" he asked. Mages had to eat. For all their power they were still flesh and blood. As he'd seen in the last few months they could die like everyone else. The inquisitor had tested his theory on a number of those brought in with minor powers who wouldn't serve the throne. He'd assured the Regent that magic didn't change the inside of the body in any way.

"He's not been fed for six days now." When other people spoke about Garvey he could see they were angry. After all, hundreds of innocent people had died because of him and his group of rogue mages. Bettina's voice remained cold and dispassionate. "They've given him a little water to keep him alive, but nothing else. It shouldn't be long."

"I hope so. Failing that we'll just have to execute him with a gag. It won't be as powerful a message to the people, but it may be all he gives us." If only Garvey would do as he was told this would be much easier for everyone. Once he'd confessed they'd cut off his head and his suffering would end. It was really that simple. He was just prolonging his misery. Maybe he wanted to be punished for some reason. It seemed odd that he would suddenly develop a conscience, but it could happen. Either that or sometimes they went mad and were sent to an asylum like that poor fool Habreel. It seemed as if the pressure had proven too much and he'd cracked under the strain.

"Start making arrangements for Garvey's public execution," said Choilan. "The people have seen him in chains. Now they need to know he's paid the ultimate price."

"Yes, my Regent."

"We'll give the inquisitor another week. And make sure Garvey knows there's a deadline if he doesn't comply." Choilan thought it might motivate Garvey to confess if he knew his days were numbered.

The sound of heavy footsteps in the corridor made them both look up in surprise. The door flew open without announcement and a dozen Royal Guards burst into the room bearing their weapons.

"What is the meaning of this?" asked Choilan. For a moment he thought there'd been a coup and they'd come for him. But then the Guards formed a protective ring around the edge of the room, facing outwards.

Beyond them a wall of four more Royal Guards took up their positions outside the door to block the corridor. In addition, he could see more Guards posted at intervals in the corridor. The Captain of the Guards entered the room and bowed. Beside him a scraggly man with remarkably clean hands also bowed deeply. The stranger had lank greasy hair and a rather plain face, but when he straightened up Choilan saw his eyes were two different colours. One was a deep brown and the other bright blue.

"Apologies, my Regent, but Inquisitor Marsh has urgent news."

Choilan had never seen the inquisitor before but this weak-chinned man was not what he'd been expecting. "What has happened?"

The Captain nudged Marsh who bobbed his head and cleared

his throat. "I went to check on the prisoner, to see if he was ready to confess, and found his cell was empty."

Choilan's mouth fell open. "Empty?"

"His chains were gone, the door was open and no one had seen him leave. He just disappeared."

"We're having the entire palace searched," said the Captain. "If he's still here we'll find him."

Marsh shook his head but said nothing. "You have something to say?" asked the Regent.

"No, my Regent."

"Spit it out. Tell me!" said Choilan in a shrill voice. Fear was tightening his stomach and making him sweat.

"You won't find him here," said Marsh. "He's gone."

"Where? Where is Garvey?" asked Choilan, but no one had an answer.

CHAPTER 45

Munroe heard a loud crack as Akosh struck the wall hard enough to punch a hole in it, knocking her into the next room. With a snarl she slammed her will into the stones, gouging an opening large enough for her to step through. Akosh seemed a little stunned as she was still lying on the ground amid the rubble of a classroom. The room was empty except for the broken remains of desks and chairs which had shattered upon impact.

Akosh was still moving so it wasn't over yet.

This might be her one chance to kill Akosh for what she'd done. Munroe only intended to stop when she'd ripped Akosh's head clean away from her body. Drawing more energy into herself from the Source she forged a spear of molten fire. The cherry-red flames licked around her arms but didn't burn her skin while the tip started to glow white hot like the heart of the sun. As Akosh stumbled to her feet Munroe charged, stabbing her in the chest.

As the spear came into contact with Akosh's body there was a peculiar form of resistance. It wasn't magic like any she'd felt before, but there was definitely a barrier of sorts. She could feel something trying to divert the power from her weapon and redirect it around Akosh. Channelling more energy into the spear, she held it steady and drove it forward with both arms.

Akosh screamed in agony as the spear pierced her right side just under her ribs. Pressure against Munroe stopped her limbs abruptly, preventing her from driving the spear right through Akosh's body. She intended to pin Akosh to the wall then tear her apart, piece by piece. Munroe focused her will and pushed back against the barrier which was slick and flexible. She could feel it bending under pressure and the spear was driven a little further into Akosh's torso.

It became a battle of will as Munroe tried to impale her and Akosh's strange magic kept her at bay. She would not be denied. She would have revenge for her family, for every Seeker and all those murdered when the Red Tower had fallen.

Reaching out towards the Source, the heart of creation, Munroe drew more energy into herself, feeling it soaking into her entire body, infusing her being with its power. Her already sharpened senses became more acute, revealing a few peculiarities about Akosh. The way she smelled, like old blood and rot. The empty space behind her eyes where a soul should live. And the fear starting to creep in around the edges of her fierce expression.

Munroe grinned and thrust her arms forward with a scream of unbridled fury. The flaming spear burned a hole straight through Akosh's body and she howled in agony.

Something caught Munroe on the side of her head, breaking her concentration and then she was flying through the air. Working instinctively, she wove a shield around herself to cushion the impact. A second later she collided with a solid wall. Even through her shield the force was hard enough to rattle her teeth. Scrambling to her feet she was surprised to see that Akosh hadn't fled. She was holding a hand against her side but no blood was flowing from the cauterised wound. The skin around the edges was burned and blackened; however, there was a little blood on her hands.

"So you can bleed," said Munroe. Akosh tried to say something but the time for talking was over. There was nothing she could say that meant anything. Munroe forged a hammer of pure will in either hand and went to work, raining blows down on Akosh.

Akosh dodged the first few blows and the hammers struck the wall behind, tearing chunks from the stone fireplace. Cracks ran up the wall from the impact and the ceiling beams groaned and creaked.

Every time one of her weapons struck Akosh's raised forearm, or caught her on the side, there was some resistance. She was using her own form of magic, or life-force, to reduce the impact of Munroe's blows. Despite that she could see the damage being done as Akosh was bleeding. A normal human would have been crippled with shattered bones after taking one or two such attacks on their arms or torso. But Akosh wasn't normal. She was still standing as they struggled around the room. Ducking one blow aimed at her head, Akosh retaliated with an open palm to the shoulder, spinning Munroe around.

As she fell to one knee a huge weight fell on Munroe's back and something tight snaked around her neck, choking her. Grabbing a handful of Akosh's hair to keep her in place Munroe stood up and then fell backwards heavily, landing on top of her enemy. There was a loud crack and Akosh's arm loosened around her neck. The dancing black spots receded and she elbowed Akosh in the throat, making her choke.

A section of the stone wall had collapsed from where they'd punched through. Munroe lifted it with her magic and sent it hurtling at the prone figure of Akosh. Some of the impact was absorbed by her power but she still took the brunt of the collision on her head and shoulders. She should have been dead but was merely stunned.

"You can't kill me!" snarled Akosh, getting to her feet. "You are beneath me!"

Munroe thought about her husband and her son. She thought about her mother. She thought about the fact that she'd never see them again and that Akosh was responsible. Using those emotions to fuel her magic she lashed out with vicious abandon.

A brutal attack threw Akosh through the stone wall into the next room. Munroe scrambled through the gap and found they were now inside a huge kitchen.

Before Akosh could recover she lifted a section of wall and slammed it into her with so much force it broke apart on impact. Blood was trickling from Akosh's nose and ears but she still wasn't done. She wouldn't fall so Munroe drove her into the ground, hitting her again and again with her will, fuelling it with her boundless rage. With all of the anger she'd been holding in for so long. For all of the special moments she'd never have with her son. For the many years she'd been looking forward to sharing with her husband as they grew old together. For just one more day with her mother. Channelling all her fury into a scream, her voice was transformed into a weapon, tearing into Akosh's flesh, shredding her clothing and ripping chunks of meat from her bones.

Part of the ceiling fell into the room and a few stones struck Munroe on the shoulder. She wove a shield to keep the worst at bay but her assault didn't relent. Like a hammer striking the anvil she kept up the pressure on Akosh, throwing her one way and then the other. Gathering up a handful of knives she hurled them at her enemy. A few rebounded but the rest stabbed her in the torso, turning her into a pin cushion. It wasn't enough. It was too remote. She needed to feel the bones break.

Wreathing her fists in blue elemental fire Munroe clubbed Akosh across the face, scorching her flesh and driving her into the far wall which cracked. Splinters ran up the wall from the point of impact like a broken pane of glass and a section rained down into the room.

Someone was shouting but Munroe paid them no attention. It didn't matter. Nothing else did. She wouldn't let Akosh out of her sight. Not even for a second in case she tried to escape. When Akosh looked up at her Munroe noticed the burned skin on her face was already recovering as the blistered flesh repaired itself. The skin had not completely healed but it wouldn't be long.

As more stones fell from the ceiling Munroe inhaled some dust and started to cough, which made her eyes water. A tight band wrapped itself around her chest and began to squeeze. Akosh drew a pair of daggers and charged while the restraint around Munroe's chest tightened, driving all the air from her body. Instead of running or worrying about her chest she reached out towards Akosh, gripping her by the wrists.

As she struggled to breathe, and they fought over control of the daggers, Munroe knew she only had a few seconds before she lost consciousness. Reaching deep inside herself she instinctively used her Talent. Her oldest power, to manipulate the odds, and the first magic she'd ever wielded.

A section of the ceiling cracked and a huge chunk of stone and wood fell into the room landing exactly on top of Akosh, catching her on the shoulder. It ripped Akosh out of Munroe's grip as she was pinned to the floor by the weight of the furniture and wooden ceiling beams.

The pain in Munroe's chest vanished and she gulped in fresh air as a cloud of dust and debris began to fill the room making it difficult to see. Whirling both hands she summoned a strong wind to blow all of the dust away so she didn't lose sight of her enemy.

In the quietness that followed Munroe heard someone shouting for help. Looking up she saw half a dozen children clinging to the sloping floor of the room above. Other children were trying to reach them but they were too far away. "Help us!" screamed one of the children but she couldn't be distracted. They didn't matter. The only thing that mattered was killing her enemy.

With a groan Akosh made it to her hands and knees, shrugging off the massive weight of stone and wood across her back. She was bruised, bloody and burned, but far from done. The missing chunks of flesh on her face and neck had started to regrow, leaving fresh pink skin it its wake. It wouldn't be long before she was fully restored.

Shrieking with fury Munroe charged at Akosh. Grabbing her around the neck with both hands she lifted her off the ground and hammered her into the wall. Drawing deeper from the Source she fed power into her arms and out into her hands. Bright yellow and white light erupted from the pores of her skin, wreathing Akosh in swirling motes of energy that seemed alive. They moved in the air, dancing to an erratic beat, before digging into her skin with razor-sharp hooks.

Akosh screamed as they burrowed into her flesh, trailing wires of pure white light that was so bright they were difficult to look at. More and more tendrils flowed from Munroe's hands into Akosh, digging into her face and neck. With Akosh grabbing Munroe around the neck, the pair began to batter each other into the walls, breaking bones and bruising skin. Inside Akosh another war was raging as Munroe sought to destroy her core as power from the Source started to unravel her.

They struck another support beam and part of the floor above came tumbling down. The children had escaped that room but Munroe didn't notice. Her hands tightened around Akosh's neck and she smiled with delight as her enemy's face began to turn red and then purple.

Stones began to pelt them both, then larger chunks of stone and one caught Munroe a glancing blow on the temple. One of her hands loosened and Akosh gulped in fresh air. As a shadow fell over them, blotting out the light, Munroe looked up in time to see part of the building sliding towards her. With a hiss of frustration she dived aside and quickly wove a dense wedge-shaped shield above her head. Akosh tried to run but a section broke off landing across her legs and lower back, pinning her to the ground. More pieces of the building and furniture rained down all around Munroe. Objects struck her shield and fell to either side leaving her in a debris-free oasis amid the chaos.

"Help!" someone screamed but Munroe ignored them again. The voice was vaguely familiar but they would have to wait. The building was starting to settle and once it stopped she would finish this. Akosh's head was still attached to her body.

"Munroe, help me!"

The voice seemed to be coming from somewhere above her head and, turning in a circle, she saw Dox. The girl was two floors up and two rooms across. The only reason Munroe could see her was because huge sections of the floor and even the ceiling had fallen through. Dox was cradling one of the younger girls in her arms who appeared unconscious. Huddled beside her were half a dozen more children. All of them had cuts and bruises and were covered in dust.

"Get out of here. Run!" shouted Munroe.

"We're trapped," said Dox, gesturing at the doorway beside her. Through it should have been the stairs but Munroe could see it was blocked with broken beams and tiles from the roof that had collapsed. The section of floor they were huddled on creaked alarmingly and started to tip forward. The children screamed and all scrambled further up towards the blocked doorway. A fall from such a height might be lethal or they could just injure themselves.

"Climb down!" said Munroe.

"We can't," shouted Dox. "There are people trapped in the rubble." She gestured to where part of the building had collapsed. Munroe could see someone's arm poking out of the wreckage and she wondered if there were more buried underneath.

Behind her she heard the sound of rocks grating together as Akosh slowly began to pull herself free. A loud groaning began as more cracks ran through the remaining shell of the building and it started to come apart. The whole structure creaked and shook.

For the first time she and Akosh noticed the level of destruction they'd caused. It wouldn't take much for the rest of the building to fall apart. Munroe could see at least one dead body and knew there would be others buried beneath the ruins. These were Akosh's people, her orphans, and yet she showed no regard for them at all.

They both seemed to know what the other was thinking as a grin slowly spread across Akosh's face. As her bones popped back into place and her flesh slowly began to rebuild itself, she rested a hand against an outer wall. Munroe felt a strange distortion in the air. It was as if the weight of everything had suddenly increased as moving her limbs became difficult. Akosh was bringing her own power to bear on the building's skeleton. The grinding sound began again and stones started to rattle down from above. There was only a handful to begin with but more were falling all the time. If she kept up the pressure the whole structure would come tumbling down. And while she and Akosh might survive none of the others would stand a chance.

"It's time to choose," said Akosh, spitting out a wad of blood.

Dox and the others were screaming for help as the two of them faced off against one another.

"One day, I will find you again," Munroe promised her. "And I will finish what I started. I will tear your head from your body and piss on your corpse."

"We'll see," said Akosh.

With a heavy heart Munroe turned her back on Akosh, letting her escape, while she went to help the orphans.

CHAPTER 46

As Danoph stared around at Balov, the village of his birth, he was surprised he didn't feel happier to see it again after so long.

Some parts of it had changed, with more houses than he remembered and different shops on the main street, but overall it was much the same. A tiny, nowhere village, surrounded by farmland, huddled up to the base of rolling hills that were covered with a forest of green.

As he stood at the end of the main street a few of the children running around at play gave him curious glances, but no more than that. Even in this remote place visitors were not uncommon. Three horse-drawn wagons laden with timber passed by, driven by surly merchants and guarded by masked Drassi. The rare wood in the hills would be taken to the capital where the finest carpenters would craft it into furniture for the Queen and others with money.

To the west he could see farmers busy at work in the fields and in the distance hear the faint sound of saws in the dense forest. It was almost midday and bright sunlight shone down from a crisp blue sky. Most people were busy at work so the main street was empty. There were a few small children but the older ones would be at school or at work themselves.

Danoph drifted down the street, pausing from time to time to peer into shop windows, a ghost in a place where he no longer belonged. No one seemed to recognise him as he walked about, which made him wonder. How much had he changed since his last visit? How long had it been?

He remembered learning his letters at school as a young boy. He remembered the kind face of the teacher, a handsome woman with curly golden hair. He vaguely remembered the names and faces of some former classmates. It made Danoph wonder where they were now. Working in the fields? Chopping down trees in the forest? Had any of them left the village and sought their fortune elsewhere?

At the centre of the village was the main crossroads. Danoph was pleased to see the Fat Goose hadn't changed much. It had been repainted and the sign straightened, but it was still the same old tavern with frosted windows. Sometimes at night in the summer, when it was hot and sticky, the owner would throw open the windows and doors in a vain attempt to keep the customers cool. On those nights music would drift to all corners of the village and Danoph would lie in bed and listen.

The jaunty tunes were amusing, but it was the more sombre tales that he remembered most clearly. Those that spoke of faraway places. They conjured images in his mind that were so clear it was as if he'd actually been there. Such was the power of the memory Danoph didn't realise how much he'd missed hearing music until now. Few students at the Red Tower had played an instrument and there hadn't been an opportunity to visit the nearby tavern. Perhaps he'd stop by the Fat Goose tonight and there would be some musicians.

Taking a path he'd walked countless times, Danoph wandered through the village towards his mother's house. It was a small cottage wedged between a number of larger homes, but it had been perfect for the two of them. From the outside it looked exactly the same. Herbs were drying in the rafters of the small porch at the front. The roof still sagged on the right side and the climbing vine had crept further up the west wall. A wealth of tiny yellow flowers was in bloom. They were so bright and cheery it more than made up for the peculiar smell they produced in the summer. But it kept the insects away and beneath the vine his mother was still growing fruit and sunflowers in clay pots.

As he approached the cottage Danoph was surprised to see the front door open and his mother emerge. He'd expected to find her at work in her shop. She seemed in a hurry to be somewhere and with the sun in her eyes didn't see him at first. When she passed into shade she paused and her mouth fell open.

They stared at each other in silence for a time, Danoph noting the slight changes. She seemed smaller than he remembered, or perhaps it was that he had grown that much taller. There was a touch of premature grey hair over her ears but he thought it made her look wiser. It was very much in keeping with her role as the local herbalist as people often expected her to have all of the answers to their problems.

"You've grown," said his mother. She made no move to embrace him and Danoph felt strangely shy about taking the initiative. "And put on weight. It suits you," she added quickly in case he misunderstood.

"They fed us very well," he said, trying to hide his anger about what had happened. The Red Tower was gone. Burned down by a rampaging, ignorant mob who had murdered those who'd chosen to stay behind. He owed his life to them.

Trying to hide anything from his mother was pointless. She could read him so easily. "I heard about what happened. I'm sorry about the school."

"They destroyed everything."

"Is that why you're here?" she asked, moving a little closer. "Have you come back to live here?"

"No. I came because I need some answers," he said. At first she seemed relieved by his reply but then fresh concerns surfaced.

"About what?"

"About why you sent me away. About my magic and also my father."

His mother grimaced as if she'd swallowed something bitter but then nodded, accepting the awkward questions. She must have known that one day he would ask.

"I need to get back to the shop. I'd run out of fresh mint so just came back for more." She hefted the basket and he caught a whiff. "Come back tonight and we'll talk."

"All right."

She came a bit closer and then stood just within arm's reach. Again he felt awkward and wasn't sure why. She was his mother. She was his blood. He'd not been home for years and yet this wasn't the tearful, happy reunion he'd imagined. Thankfully she took the initiative, carefully putting her arms around him and he held her as well. He'd barely closed his eyes when she pulled away and he was forced to let go. She hurried away towards her shop leaving him feeling puzzled and oddly bereft.

Danoph drifted around the village for the rest of the afternoon visiting all of his old haunts. In the woods not far from his mother's cottage the remnants of his treehouse were slowly being reclaimed by nature. Overgrown with weeds and flowering shrubs it was now home to a nest of birds that were making better use of it than he had. Growing up he'd sometimes come here to dream about the future. He'd imagined himself travelling all over the world as a soldier in the Queen's army. He'd wanted to be a hero whose brave deeds the bards sung about in taverns up and down the land.

After the war he never again imagined himself as a soldier. He had no desire to carry a weapon or go to war. He'd seen more than enough bloodshed and torture to last a lifetime. The treehouse then became his refuge where he'd spend hours by himself. The camps had been crowded and filthy, full of noise and other people. Here it was so quiet and peaceful. He was occasionally lonely after that but never felt uncomfortable in his own company.

By the time the afternoon had drained away Danoph realised why he'd hesitated coming home for so long. His early memories of glorious days full of wonder and imagination had been replaced with darker thoughts that lingered on what he'd endured during the war. The more time he spent exploring the streets and surrounding areas the more he realised why leaving had, in many ways, been a relief.

The Red Tower had been a chance to start afresh. The emergence of his magic had been unexpected, but it had presented him with an opportunity to build a new life. All of which brought Danoph back to thoughts of his mother and why she had sent him away. Something must have triggered it and he needed to know what had happened.

With sore feet and a slightly heavy heart he knocked on his mother's front door. Danoph realised he didn't even think about it as his home any more. It was her house. He had no home.

His mother answered and gestured for him to sit on the porch in the rocking chair while she brought out another seat. Danoph knew it was strange that she'd not invited him into her home, but part of him had been expecting it. It also made him wonder if she was trying to hide something or someone she didn't want him to see.

They sat together in silence for a while, listening to the distant drone of insects and the rustling of the trees in the wind. After a time she found the courage to turn towards him and speak.

"Ask your questions."

"Why did you send me away? Was it because of my visions?" he asked in a rush. The questions had been bottled up inside him for a long time. "Did I hurt someone?"

"Around here people have been afraid of magic for a long time. They still are today. But yours was something different," said his mother. "At first I thought they were just stories you'd made up. But the details were always so vivid."

"But they weren't stories," said Danoph.

"No, and they weren't just visions. They were glimpses of other places and other times. It was as if you'd been spying on people through their windows. Sometimes they were things in the past. Secrets from other families that I thought you'd overheard. Then you started telling me about things that hadn't happened, that later came true. That's when I knew you were different."

"Different?"

His mother sighed and ran a hand through her hair. "You weren't the first child born in our village with magic. Years ago there was a boy who could light fires without flint and tinder. Another could talk to dogs. He'd just stare and they obeyed him. They were both strange but, up to a point, people could understand their magic. Your visions were worrying, often predicting tragedies or crimes. Some I couldn't prove were real because you talked about places in other countries. I tried to hide your visions but other people in the village started to notice. If I hadn't sent you away I think you would've been lynched."

There was a hint of regret in her voice and hearing her reasons didn't sting as much as he'd expected.

Rather selfishly he'd not realised how difficult it must have been for her as well. To be the only woman in the village raising a child without a husband. Tragedies had been uncommon in their small community but when it happened widows were not shunned. Danoph had no memories of his father but he remembered the way other villagers stared at him and his mother. If she hadn't been the herbalist, and an important figure in the community, she might have been driven out. Danoph wondered if she'd found someone in the years since he'd left.

"Who was my father?" he asked.

His mother shook her head, not yet ready to answer the question. He'd thought the reason for sending him away would've been the difficult question to answer. As a small boy he'd daydreamed that his father had been a hero killed in battle. Or a member of the royal family who loved his mother but had been forced to leave by his wicked father and marry someone else. Now he suspected the truth was a lot more sinister. Even so, he needed to know.

"Did you know Talle and I were betrothed?" said his mother, breaking the tense silence.

"No."

"We grew up together. Did everything together. None of the other girls even tried to catch his eye. He only wanted me." She smiled wistfully but all too quickly it drained away. "We were married young and it lasted for three years. We visited the village Wise and several herbalists, but the answer was always the same. We couldn't have children."

"They were wrong," said Danoph.

"The local priest agreed to our unbinding and later he married Jodine. Now he's running a farm and they have four children."

"But they were all wrong," he said again, staring at his mother. "You can have children."

She stubbornly shook her head. "No. It's not what you think."

A cold prickle of fear ran across the back of his scalp. "Who was my father?"

"No one."

"You didn't know his name? Were you attacked?" he asked. It was far worse than he'd anticipated. Perhaps it would have been better not to know the truth.

"You don't understand. After Talle, I was alone. One day I wasn't pregnant and the next I was. Everyone assumed it was a passing merchant, and I never said otherwise. It was a lot easier to accept than the truth."

"I don't understand."

"Neither do I. I still don't, but I didn't care. You were my miracle."

It was impossible. It was ridiculous. She was lying to cover up something. "Was he already married? I'm not going to cause any trouble. I just want a name."

His mother took him by the hand and stared straight into his eyes. "You have no father."

Danoph didn't think she was lying and yet he had no other explanation. He didn't notice the man approaching the cottage until his shadow fell over them both. Danoph and his mother looked up in surprise at the tall, grizzled Seve with a sword on his back. At first Danoph thought this was his father. The man his mother claimed didn't exist until he saw the lack of recognition on her face.

"Danoph, my name is Vargus. I know you have many questions and I can help."

"Who are you?"

The old warrior smiled. "A friend."

The world shifted around him and Danoph found himself standing inside a huge banqueting hall. A massive wooden table ran down the centre of the room and arranged around it were dozens of chairs. Each looked identical and yet he instinctively knew they were unique. At the head of the table was a massive seat that dwarfed the others and without asking he knew who it belonged to and that its owner was still absent.

Images and pieces of memory swam to the surface but he couldn't focus on them. He'd never been to this place before and yet somehow he knew so much about it. Danoph should have felt scared to find himself in another place but for some reason he wasn't alarmed. It felt safe and so familiar.

Vargus stood beside one of the chairs towards the far end of the table. Danoph's instincts told him it belonged to Vargus. The longer he stared at the warrior the more familiar he seemed, although he didn't know why.

"For all things there is a season," said Vargus. "Over the years our star wanes, or the body breaks, and we pass into the Void. At other times we evolve, becoming something new in order to survive. Once, long ago, I had a different name and a different power. Now I am a Brother to all who carry a weapon into battle. Years ago my old mantle was reborn. And with it came the power to see the future and all of the possibilities it contains. To dream of tomorrow and see the choices that lay ahead for us all. To travel through the skein of time and know what's to come. This is the Weaver."

Vargus approached Danoph and put a hand on his shoulder. "Welcome home, brother."

The story continues in book three of the Age of Dread.

ACKNOWLEDGEMENTS

Many thanks to Juliet Mushens, my agent from CaskieMushens, for reading all the words. Thanks to Nathalie, for sorting out all the paperwork and making it all so easy for me.

I'm very grateful to everyone at Orbit for all of their hard work on my behalf to beat this book into shape, in particular Jenni, Brit and Joanna. Thanks also to Nazia for all the work she does organising events for me and all Orbit authors. Special thanks to Gemma and Tom for our regular "Two Authors and Tom" lunches out.

Finally, thanks to my family and friends for their continual support and enthusiasm.

extras

www.orbitbooks.net

about the author

Stephen Aryan was born in 1977 and was raised and educated in Whitley Bay, Tyne and Wear. After graduating from Loughborough University he started working in marketing, and for some reason he hasn't stopped. A keen podcaster, lapsed gamer and budding archer, when not extolling the virtues of *Babylon 5*, he can be found drinking real ale and reading comics.

He lives in the West Midlands with his partner and two cats. You can find him on Twitter at @SteveAryan or visit his website at www.stephen-aryan.com.

Find out more about Stephen Aryan and other Orbit authors by registering for the free monthly newsletter at www.orbitbooks.net.

if you enjoyed

MAGEFALL

look out for

YOU DIE WHEN YOU DIE
West of West: Book One

by

Angus Watson

YOU DIE WHEN YOU DIE . . .

You can't change your fate — so throw yourself into battle, because you'll either end the day a hero or drinking mead in the halls of the gods. That's what Finn's people believe.

But Finn wants to live. When his settlement is massacred by a hostile nation, Finn plus several friends and rivals must make their escape across a brutal, unfamiliar landscape, and to survive, Finn will fight harder than he's ever fought before.

Chapter 1

Finnbogi Is in Love

Two weeks before everyone died and the world changed for ever, Finnbogi the Boggy was fantasising about Thyri Treelegs.

He was picking his way between water-stripped logs with a tree stump on one shoulder, heading home along the shore of Olaf's Fresh Sea. No doubt, he reasoned, Thyri would fall in love with him the moment he presented her with the wonderful artwork he was going to carve from the tree stump. But what would he make? Maybe a racoon. But how would you go about . . .

His planning was interrupted by a wasp the size of a chipmunk launching from the shingle and making a beeline for his face.

The young Hardworker yelped, ducked, dropped the stump and spun to face his foe. Man and insect circled each other crabwise. The hefty wasp bobbed impossibly in the air. Finnbogi fumbled his sax from its sheath. He flailed with the short sword, but the wasp danced clear of every inept swipe, floating closer and louder. Finnbogi threw his blade aside and squatted, flapping his hands above his head. Through his terror he realised that this manoeuvre was exactly the same as his rabbit-in-a-tornado impression that could make his young adoptive siblings giggle so much they fell over. Then he noticed he could no longer hear the wasp.

He stood. The great lake of Olaf's Fresh Sea glimmered calmly and expansively to the east. To the west a stand of trees whispered like gossips who'd witnessed his cowardice in the face of an insect. Behind them, great clouds floated indifferently above lands he'd never seen. The beast itself – surely "wasp" was insufficient a word for such a creature – was flying southwards like a hurled wooden toy that had forgotten to land, along the beach towards Hardwork.

He watched until he could see it no longer, then followed.

Finnbogi had overheard Thyri Treelegs say she'd be training in the woods to the north of Hardwork that morning, so he'd donned his best blue tunic and stripy trousers and headed there in order to accidentally bump into her. All he'd found was the tree stump that he would carve into something wonderful for her, and, of course, the sort of wasp that Tor would have battled in a saga. He'd never seen its like before, and guessed it had been blown north by the warm winds from the south which were the latest and most pleasant phenomenon in the recent extraordinary weather.

If any of the others – Wulf the Fat, Garth Anvilchin or, worst of all, Thyri herself – had seen him throw away his sax and cower like Loakie before Oaden's wrath, they'd have mocked him mercilessly.

Maybe, he thought, he could tell Thyri that he'd killed the wasp? But she'd never believe how big it had been. What he needed to do was kill an animal known for its size and violence . . . That was it! That's how he'd win her love! He would break the Scraylings' confinement, venture west and track down one of the ferocious dagger-tooth cats that the Scraylings banged on about. It would be like Tor and Loakie's quest into the land of the giants, except that Finnbogi would be brawny Tor and brainy Loakie all rolled into one unstoppable hero.

The Scraylings were basically their captors, not that any Hardworker apart from Finnbogi would ever admit that.

Olaf the Worldfinder and the Hardworkers' other ancestors had arrived from the old world five generations before at the beginning of winter. Within a week the lake had frozen and the unrelenting snow was drifted higher than a longboat's mast. The Hardworkers had been unable to find food, walk anywhere or sail on the frozen lake, so they'd dug into the snow drifts and waited to die.

The local tribe of Scraylings, the Goachica, had come to their rescue, but only on two big conditions. One, that the Hardworkers learn to speak the universal Scrayling tongue and forsake their own language, and, two, that no Hardworker, nor their descendants, would ever stray further than ten miles in any direction from their landing spot.

It had been meant as a temporary fix, but some Scrayling god had decreed that Goachica continue to venerate and feed the Hardworkers, and the Hardworkers were happy to avoid foraging and farming and devote their days to sport, fighting practice, fishing, dancing, art or whatever else took their fancy.

Five generations later, still the Goachica gave them everything they needed, and still no Hardworker strayed more than ten miles from Olaf's landing spot. Why would they? Ten miles up and down the coast and inland from Olaf's Fresh Sea gave them more than enough space to do whatever they wanted to do. Few ever went more than a mile from the town.

But Finnbogi was a hero and an adventurer, and he was going to travel. If he were to break the confinement and track down a dagger-tooth cat . . . He'd be the first Hardworker to see one, let alone kill one, so if he dragged the monster home and made Thyri a necklace from its oversized fangs surely she'd see that he was the man for her? Actually, she'd prefer a knife to a necklace. And it would be easier to make.

A few minutes later Finnbogi started to feel as though he was being followed. He slowed and turned. There was nothing on the beach, but there was a dark cloud far to the north. For an alarming moment he thought there was another great storm on the way – there'd been a few groundshakers recently that had washed away the fishing nets and had people talking about Ragnarok ending the world – but then realised the cloud was a flock of crowd pigeons. One of the insanely huge flocks had flown over Hardwork before, millions upon millions of birds that had taken days to pass and left everything coated with pigeon shit. Finnbogi quickened his pace – he did not want to return to Hardwork covered in bird crap – and resumed his musings on Thyri.

He climbed over a bark-stripped log obstructing a narrow, sandy headland and heard voices and laughter ahead. Finnbogi knew who it was before he trudged up the rise in the beach and saw them. It was the gang of friends a few years older than he was.

Wulf the Fat ran into the sea, naked, waving his arms and yelling, and dived with a mighty splash. Sassa Lipchewer smiled at her husband's antics and Bodil Gooseface screeched. Bjarni Chickenhead laughed. Garth Anvilchin splashed Bodil and she screeched all the more.

Keef the Berserker stood further out in Olaf's Fresh Sea, his wet, waist-length blond hair and beard covering his torso like a sleeveless shirt. He swung his long axe, Arse Splitter, from side to side above the waves, blocking imaginary blows and felling imaginary foes.

Finnbogi twisted his face into a friendly smile in case they caught him looking. Up ahead their clothes and weapons were laid out on the shingle. Bodil and Sassa's neatly embroidered dresses were hanging on poles. Both garments would have been Sassa Lipchewer creations; she spent painstaking hours sewing, knitting and weaving the most stylish clothes in Hardwork. She'd made the blue tunic and stripy trousers that Finnbogi was wearing, for example, and very nice they were too.

The four men's clothes, tossed with manly abandon on the shingle, were leathers, plus Garth Anvilchin's oiled chainmail. Garth's metal shirt weighed as much as a fat child, yet Garth wore it all day, every day. He said that it would rust if the rings didn't move against each other regularly so he had to wear it, and also he wanted to be totally comfortable when he was in battle.

In battle! Ha! The Hird's only battles were play fights with each other. The likelihood of them seeing real action was about the same as Finnbogi travelling west and taking on a dagger-tooth cat. He knew the real reason Garth wore the mail shirt all the time. It was because he was a prick.

Despite the pointlessness of it, many of the hundred or so Hardworkers spent much time learning to fight with the weapons brought over from the old world. All four of the bathing men were in the Hird, the elite fighting group comprising Hardwork's ten best fighters.

Finnbogi *had* expected to be asked to join the Hird last summer when someone had become too old and left, but Jarl Brodir had chosen Thyri Treelegs. That had smarted somewhat, given that she was a girl and only sixteen at the time – two years younger than him. It was true that she had been making weapons, practising moves and generally training to be a warrior every waking hour since she was about two, so she probably wouldn't be a terrible Hird member. And he supposed it was good to see a woman included.

All Hardwork's children learnt the reasons that Olaf the Worldfinder and Hardwork's other founders had left the east, sailed a salty sea more vast than anyone of Finnbogi's generation could supposedly imagine, then travelled up rivers and across great lakes to establish the settlement of Hardwork. Unfair treatment of women was one of those reasons. So it was good that they were finally putting a woman in the Hird, but it was a shame that it had robbed Finnbogi of what he felt was his rightful place. Not that he wanted to be in the stupid Hird anyway, leaping about and waving weapons around all day. He had better things to do.

Out to sea, Wulf the Fat dived under – he could stay down for an age – and Garth Anvilchin caught sight of Finnbogi on the beach. "Hey, Boggy!" he shouted. "Don't even think about touching our weapons or I'll get one of the girls to beat you up!"

Finnbogi felt himself flush and he looked down at the weapons – Garth's over-elaborately inlaid hand axes the Biter Twins, Bjarni's beautiful sword Lion Slayer, Wulf's thuggish hammer Thunderbolt and Sassa's bow which wasn't an old world weapon so it didn't have a name.

"And nice outfit!" yelled Garth. "How lovely that you dress up when you go wanking in the woods. You have to treat your hand well when it's your only sexual partner, don't you, you curly-haired cocksucker?"

Finnbogi tried to think of a clever comeback based on the idea that if he sucked cocks then he clearly had more sexual partners than just his hand, but he didn't want to accept and develop the him-sucking-cocks theme.

"Fuck off then, Boggy, you're spoiling the view," Garth added before any pithy reply came to Finnbogi, curse him to Hel. Garth might be stupid but he had all the smart lines.

"Leave him alone," said Sassa Lipchewer. Finnbogi reddened further. Sassa was lovely.

"Yes, Garth," Bodil piped up. "Come for a wash, Finnbogi!"

"Yes, Boggy boy! Clean yourself off after all that wanking!" Garth laughed.

Wulf surfaced and smiled warmly at Finnbogi, the sun glinting off his huge round shoulders. "Come on in, Finn!" he called. Finally, somebody was calling him by the name he liked.

"Come in, Finn!" Bodil called. "Come in, Finn! Come in, Finn!" she chanted.

Sassa beckoned and smiled, which made Finnbogi gibber a little.

Behind them, Keef, who hadn't acknowledged Finnbogi's presence, continued to split the arses of imaginary enemies with his axe Arse Splitter.

"I can't swim now, I've got to . . . um . . . " Finnbogi nodded at the stump on his shoulder.

"Sure thing, man, do what you've got to do, see you later!" Wulf leapt like a salmon and disappeared underwater.

"Bye, Finn!" shouted Bodil. Sassa and Bjarni waved. Garth, towering out of the water, muscular chest shining, smiled and looked Finnbogi up and down as if he knew all about the wasp, why he was wearing his best clothes and what he had planned for the stump.

"I don't know why you give that guy any time . . . " he heard Garth say as he walked away.

He didn't know why the others gave any time to Garth Anvilchin. He was *such* a dick. They were okay, the rest of them. Wulf the Fat had never said a mean word to anyone. Bjarni Chickenhead was friendly and happy, Sassa Lipchewer was lovely. And Bodil Gooseface ... Bodil was Bodil, called Gooseface not because she looked like a goose, but because Finnbogi had once announced that she had the same facial expressions as a clever goose, which she did, and the name had stuck. Finnbogi felt a bit bad about that, but it wasn't his fault that he was so incisively observant.

He walked on, composing cutting replies to Garth's cock-sucking comments. The best two were "Why don't you swim out to sea and keep on swimming?" and "Spoiling the view am I? You're the only person here with a good view because you're not in it!"

He wished he'd thought of them at the time.